A BOND WITH THE WRATH OF DEMONS

THE BEAUTIFULLY BROKEN SAGA:
BOOK THREE

INARA GAGE

For the girls with quiet souls, who find pieces of themselves inside of books.

For the ones who crave chaos and catharsis—

Thank you for letting me take up space on your shelves—and in your hearts.

This journey hasn't been easy, but it's been extraordinary. And you, dear reader, are the reason I kept writing through the dark. I wrote these books for you—for the ones who crave emotion, danger, longing, power, and just a little bit of ruin.

🖤 *With love and literary madness,*
Inara

TRIGGER WARNINGS

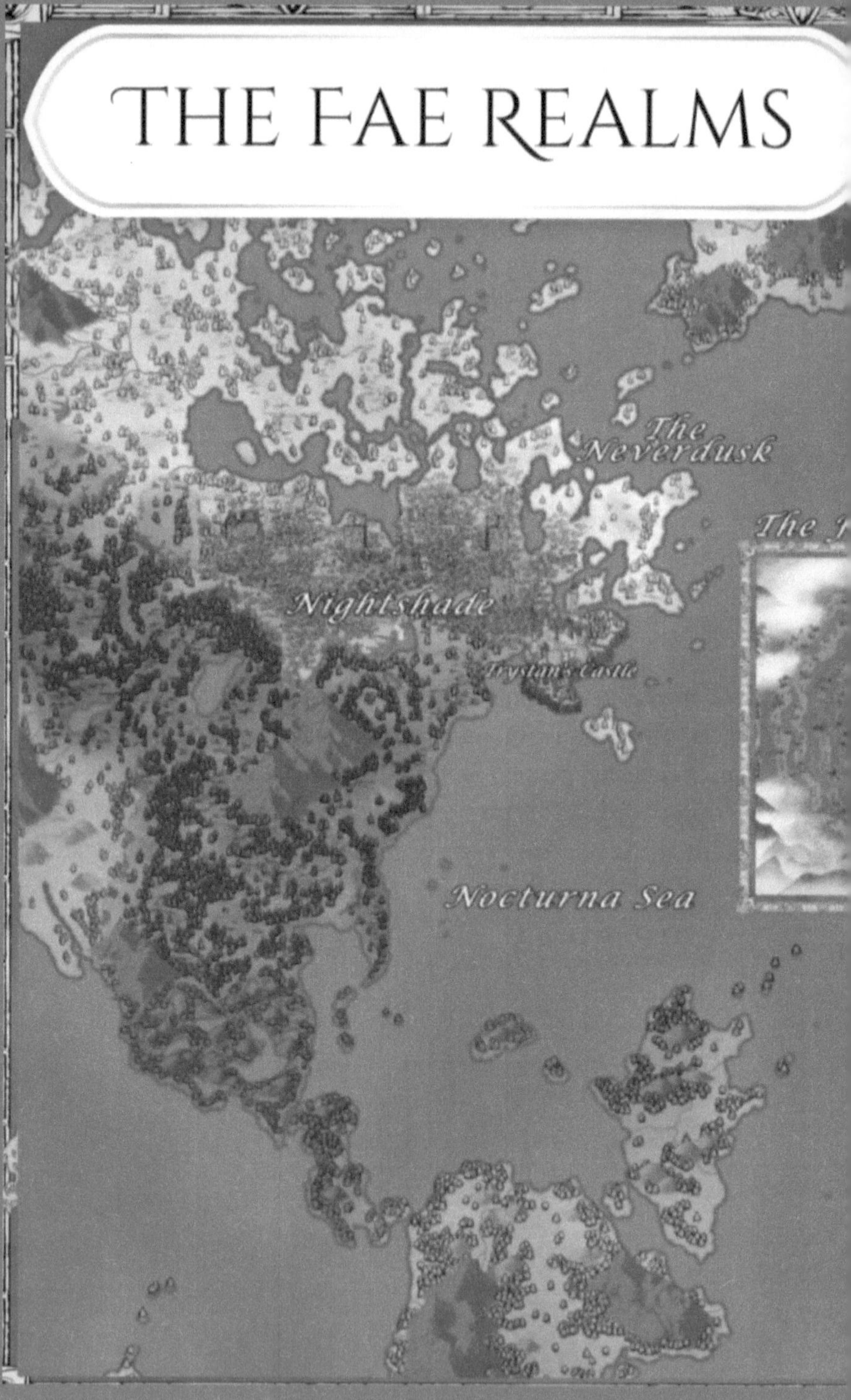

THE FAE REALMS
The Neverdusk
The
Nightshade
Trystan's Castle
Nocturna Sea

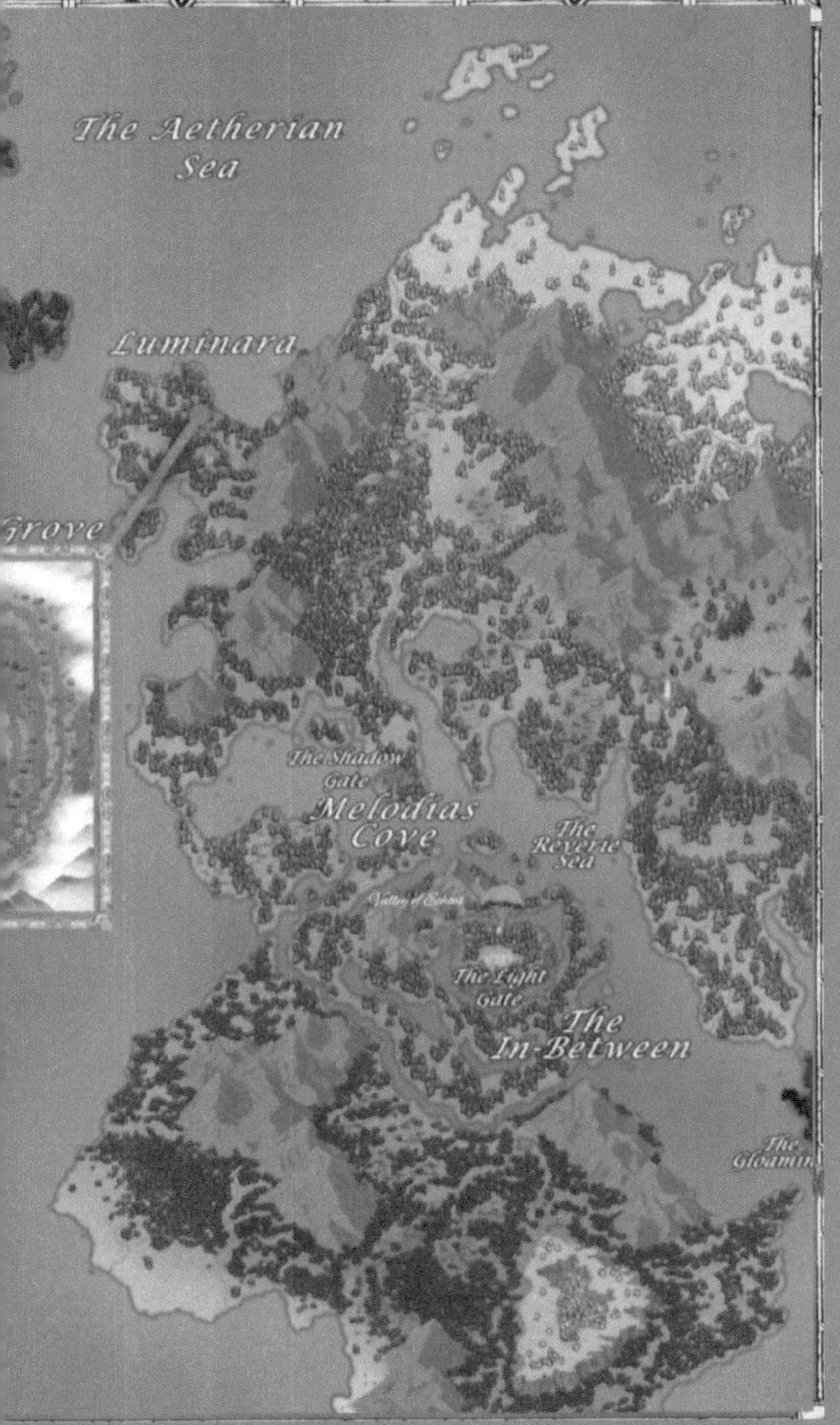

The Aetherian
Sea
Luminara
Grove
The Shadow
Gate
Melodias
Cove
The
Reverie
Sea
Valley of Echoes
The Light
Gate
The
In-Between
The Aetherian
Sea
The
Gloamin

THREE MONTHS IN THE FUTURE

We all begin in darkness.

The sleepy town of Honolulu stirs as night surrenders to the creeping embrace of dawn, the sky painted in the bruised hues of its final battle. People emerge from their homes, bleary-eyed, and unsuspecting, as they go to shuffle through the rituals of a new day—morning jogs along sunlit beaches, the hiss of coffee machines in bustling cafés, and the low hum of cars queuing at gas stations. It's an ordinary day until the fabric of reality itself tears apart.

A fiery seam unzips the heart of downtown Honolulu, spilling an infernal glow that spreads like wildfire. From the gaping Shadow Gate, monstrosities of unimaginable horror crawl forth. Towering beasts—larger than dinosaurs—lurch into the city. Their decaying flesh dangles in grotesque strips, revealing glistening bones beneath. Milky, lifeless eyes scan the terrified masses, unseeing yet aware. They leave devastation in their wake.

Screams rip through the streets. Humans flee in chaotic waves, but escape is futile. Wyverns pour out of the portal, their leathery wings blotting out the rising sun. They spew streams of green fire, inciner-

ating buildings, melting steel, and reducing palm-lined avenues to charred skeletons. The air fills with the acrid stench of burning flesh and molten concrete.

A swarm of dark fae surges from the portal, their sharp, serrated teeth glinting in the eerie glow. Like a storm of ravenous locusts, they descend on the fleeing population, tearing through flesh. The Earth itself quakes beneath the force of the portal's seismic eruption. Lava gushes from awakened volcanoes across the island chain, vomiting columns of fire and ash into the sky. The ground cracks open, swallowing cars, and splintering buildings like fragile toys.

Tsunamis, conjured by the chaos, crash against the shore, sweeping debris and bodies into the ocean. In mere minutes, the vibrant city of Honolulu is reduced to smoldering ash and fractured rubble.

But the destruction doesn't end there. Across the globe, new portals yawn open, unleashing the same cataclysmic terror. One tears into the bustling heart of Madrid, casting shadows over its ancient streets. Another splits the neon-lit skyline of Tokyo. In the United States, Shadow Gates erupt in New Orleans, New York, California, and Florida, their infernal legions spilling into the chaos of urban life. Rifts riddle through Mexico and South America, while Canada faces five of its own. Russia becomes a breeding ground for the abyss, with twenty portals scattering their hellish legions across the frozen tundra. Europe burns under the weight of countless invasions while Africa's skies darken with winged horrors.

Flame and fury engulf the world. Every continent evolves into a battlefield of destruction. Abyssal Sprites, demons from unspeakable dimensions, and a swelling army of Neverdusk fae rampage through the streets. Their ranks grow as they convert humans into dark fae and vampires, spreading their monstrous influence like a plague.

With Earth's defenses crumbling, the veil between Desoloth and this world collapses entirely. Freed from the chains of separation, Trystan unleashes the full might of the fae realm, tearing down the remaining barriers. The darkness of Desoloth spills unbridled into the mortal world, heralding the dawn of a new, monstrous age.

CANVAS OF NIGHTMARES

PRESENT TIME

—BASH—

"**S**hut. The. Fuck. Up."

I'm lying on this gods-forsaken cot in a cold fucking basement or dungeon or whatever-the-fuck it is, and I've been here for gods know how long. The only sounds that chop up the deafening silence are the incessant dripping that is driving me fucking mad and then . . . well, there are the voices.

The voices keep me company even though they tell me to do murderous things. Which, I mean, well, I'm Bash, and that's what I do, but these voices want me to kill Sayah, and that's just not fucking happening.

I swing to my side and punch the wall as hard as possible. "To fucking hell with your demands!" I yell to the nothing—the nothing that's the only accompaniment to the ear-piercing silence and life-swallowing loneliness down here.

I remember mostly everything leading up to this moment, but it's still hazy, like I lived it through a bout of binge drinking bourbon. I remember Sayah being there with me, and her face suddenly morphing into Sadie's, and that fucking confused the shit outta me, but I went with it because who the fuck knows these days.

The memory of flashing away and running into a brick wall of a person, looking up and seeing a face similar to Dom's . . . His eyes were blackened to coal, absent and far away. He grabbed me by the collar and dragged me back to that room, and then Tallyn locked me away down here.

I keep seeing Tallyn, or some shadowy being resembling Tallyn, repeatedly through the bars of my cage, thinking she's spying on me. But then she runs away laughing.

It's fucking odd.

If it's even real.

I don't fucking know.

I didn't even figure out I was hallucinating until I saw a kid from my childhood—Henry.

Henry was the shit!

We still lived in Italy then, and Henry was our nearest neighbor. He and I were best buds. It was awful when he died of consumption.

Well, so yeah, he visits me a lot down here.

There are no windows where I am; my only light source are these purple floating spirit lanterns ensconced in the dark stone walls. I've dubbed them spirit lanterns because they're little orbs of light floating in their little alcoves. They flicker like flame but glow like lanterns. When I asked one of the voices what they're called, they just laughed at me, so spirit lanterns are what they're called.

There is no way to measure the passage of time. I have no fucking clue how long I've been down here. I've been trying to sleep as much as possible, but the hunger rumbling in my stomach tells me I haven't eaten in some time.

I don't remember Tallyn bringing me anything to eat, blood bags or people—everything is a big, hazy blur.

Usually, after we feed, the hunger doesn't come back this fierce for a week if we drain someone to death. If we only feed enough to sustain ourselves without killing our prey, we have a few days where hunger is not a problem.

My hunger roils in my stomach, echoing in the dark dungeon, causing me to cramp, and I put pressure on my side to stop the ache.

This must be what desiccation feels like.

How long does it take for a vampire to desiccate?

You should just kill her when you see her again, says Henry's voice from the wall.

He is one of the voices encouraging me to kill Sayah.

I clamp my hands over my ears and pray the voices will end.

No matter how crazy I become down here, I am certain something is wrong more than I am certain of anything else. I know whatever concoction Tallyn gave me saved me from dying from a formweaver bite. Before we arrived here in Feylight Grove, not only was I going mad seeing people like Sadie and other people I've killed, but I also felt like utter hell. The worst I've ever felt in my entire life—and I've died before.

That sickness was unlike anything I'd ever felt before.

It was more than feeling sick; it was as though my very being was trying to crawl out of my skin, like my stomach was trying to lurch itself up and out of my existence, like my bones were made of lead, my hair made of fire, my blood made of razor blades, and my teeth were pushing into my skull. They were all at war to see which would end me first. I wanted to die and be released from the pain.

At least I don't feel like that anymore.

Inhaling a heavy breath, I close my eyes, and within a second, warmth fills me up. I open my eyes, and all around me is a sunny, grassy knoll. I sit up all the way, startled, looking for anything familiar.

I'm still in Feylight Grove. Purple consumes the sky. Two moons rest with the stars twinkling in the velvety sky. Unicorns and pegasuses roam the land, bending their necks to graze.

Meanwhile, little ones run through a stream that cuts through the scenery. The rolling green hills paint the horizon in elegant dips and swells.

I stand, looking around for anyone I know.

Am I dreaming?

Or am I really just losing it?

I suddenly feel watchful eyes on me, halting my steps. It cuts me to my bone, and I turn to see someone standing on a hill. She's gorgeous, even from afar. Her long brown hair billows in the breeze, and her voluptuous body sends heat down to my toes and makes the darkness in me shiver in delight. She is tall and willowy, a painting of perfection in a canvas of nightmares.

As she saunters toward me, I'm filled with overwhelming feelings of love, lust, and desire. Her aura is familiar, and when she nears, I know who it is in a moment.

Her soul is the only one of its kind and speaks to me in the only language my soul understands.

Sayah.

I want to run to her, but my feet won't move that fast. While I feel as light as a feather, my feet feel as though there's cement in the soles of my shoes.

"Sayah!" I call to her.

She does not quicken her steps; they are careful and strategic.

Her face comes into focus as the distance between us is closed.

Everything in me sags with relief at the sight of her.

Why is she here, though?

"Why are we outside?" I ask once she draws closer.

Her midnight crystal-blue eyes move up my body, carefully drinking in each feature of my face. She does not speak; she ceases movement altogether.

"Why are you being weird?" I ask her.

She smiles, and the sharp ivory of her fangs pierces her lips.

Crimson runs down her chin, dripping blood onto her white nightgown.

"Sayah?" I question. I know she has fangs, but those are not her phoenix fangs.

Those are the fangs of vampires.

"Shh," she coaxes. She reaches me then, and I want nothing more than for her to bite me and drain me dry.

"Oh, Sayah, my love," I say to her, grasping her around her waist. I want to kiss her, to pick her up, and whisk her away from all this madness.

I bend to kiss her lips, but she grabs my chin and forces me to look to the side, and before I know it, she is sinking those fangs into my carotid artery. The feeling of someone drinking my blood from my neck is new, but I like it. It makes me hard.

Then there's the fire.

It begins at my toes before spreading to my legs, my thighs lighting up the night. As it engulfs my middle, she pulls my face back toward her and she says, "You burn, I burn."

I nod, wrapping her against my chest as the fire consumes us both.

I wake up to the sound of rattling metal.

Opening my eyes, I think I see Tallyn, but I don't know for sure if she's there.

"Tallyn?" I ask, my voice echoing in the dark as I sit up.

Kill. Her, says the whisperer in the wall. This one is Monica —a woman I ate back in the '60s.

"Yes, Bash, it's me." That's Tallyn's voice.

"Stop!" I shout at the wall.

"What?" Tallyn asks.

"Nothing."

My heavy boots are still on, and the clothes I was wearing from the night by the fire when the bitch Laureya bit me are still on me, stinking and ripped and bloody and crunchy. "Why have you left me down here so long?"

Her face crumbles in confusion. "I've been bringing you blood every eight hours or so; do you not remember?"

"No," I say timidly. "But I'm talking to walls so . . . Who the fuck knows what's real anymore."

She smiles sympathetically, passing me a bag of blood through the bars. "This will do you some good. How are you feeling today?"

"How long have I been down here?" I ask, taking the blood bag, and biting the top off.

"Five days," she states, and I nearly spit out the contents.

"Five fuc—Tallyn! What the fuck?"

"Bash, shut up and drink. I didn't choose to shove you down here and keep you against your will. You were trying to kill anyone who got close. We had to. We had no choice."

I slurp back the blood bag like it's my last meal, squeezing every last drop into my mouth.

My trying to kill people comes as no surprise to me.

"Bash." Tallyn's voice is sharp. Something terrible is following my name, and I don't want to know what it is.

Unless it involves Sayah.

"Sayah?"

"My brother has her," she says, no emotion behind her words.

"What?" I ask, throwing the empty blood bag over to the corner where I now realize a small pile of them resides. She really has been coming to feed me every eight hours.

Kill. Her. This time, it is Dominic's voice, and that somewhat confuses me.

So far, they have only been voices of the dead.

Tallyn's face withers by the torchlight beyond the bars. "He figured out a way to teleport. He came into my realm without tripping any of my detection spells off. Also, he got through the boundary spell I had to deny portal magick, which included teleportation. He managed to slip in undetected and—"

"And?" I ask.

"He killed Dominic. He's dead. And Sayah's gone. He stole her away to hi—"

"Wa-wa-wa-wait a minute, back the fuck up there, sparkles. What did you say about my brother?"

Her orange eyes remain steady on me. "Trystan pierced his heart with a stake made of thorns. Dominic's dead. I'm sorry."

All the blood drains from my face.

I am trying to figure out what to do with this information. So many emotions hit me at once, and I feel lost.

My brother?

My little brother is gone?

No.

This can't be.

"What?" I say again. I'm going mad, so I probably didn't hear her right.

"Dom is dead. Sayah is gone."

The floor bites my knees as they hit it with a force that the world could've broken in half. It's been so long since I've cried; I've forgotten what it feels like, but tears fall from my eyes, and I can't stop them. My chest tightens with a swell of emotion I can't place. Grief maybe? The strangest sensation that something existed there—fragile, real, and irreplaceable.

My brother?

Don't cry for me, brother. I'm not gone, Dom's voice.

"What?" I ask the wall.

"I didn't say anything," Tallyn answers.

"Where is he?" I ask, sitting on the backs of my legs.

"He's in my tomb chambers. Your mom is preparing the

burial, or whatever you vampires do to mourn and lie your dead to rest."

Words are lost on me. I am alone in the vast universe, where echoes of centuries of battles and love, alliances and ailments, oaths and betrayals float around me like stars. I have no idea how to lasso them. I've no idea how to lasso the thunder rippling through me at the thought that I'll never be able to mend the brother's bond we once had.

He can't be gone.

He just can't.

I'm not gone, says the wall again.

I gather my strength to speak. "And what of Sayah?" I ask, still fearing the answer. "Why did he take her? And where?"

Tallyn shifts her weight and slides her fingernails along the bars, making them clink. "He took her to the Neverdusk Dominion, to his castle, in the Nightshade sector. He wants to —" She looks at me, and her fathomless orange eyes stake me to my soul, searing something deep within me. It's like I can suddenly read her emotions, the heat in her body, the speed of her heart.

"He wants to?" I press, standing up to face her.

Her lip curls up as though she likes torturing me. She grasps the bars with both hands, her long, spindly fingers with glittering nails coming at me like monsters. She puts her face close to mine through the bars and whispers, "Make her his queen."

My stomach hollows out.

DREAM SWITCH

—SAYAH—

A drafty gust makes my eyes shoot open. The dream I'd just had sits lovey and strange on my soul. I grasp at it, but it slips away like a fog giving way to the morning summer sun.

I was in a valley on a hill, looking down at Bash. Even though I couldn't move or speak at first, those wonderful feelings of warmth, love, and longing wrapped me up. But I couldn't say anything; I could only watch as someone controlled me.

I could feel my feet gliding up to Bash, him saying I was being weird, and I wanted to say, "Yes, I know. I know I'm being weird; I can't help it." But the words were stuck in my throat, and all I could do was tell him to hush and bite him.

I knew I had to bite him like one knows to take their next breath—but I didn't know I was going to burn him.

How fucking weird.

My neck is stiff from the cot I've been unconscious on for gods know how long. I don't remember much of anything other than Dom being staked with those thorns and Trystan blowing that shit in my face.

I woke up down here, wherever *down here* is—if it's even down, I have no idea—but it's dark and smelly and damp. I'm chained, but not to anything in particular. There's a golden shackle at my ankle and one at my wrist with a chain connecting the two. They're made of a heavy metal I don't recognize—it looks like gold, but it's sparkly and metallic, matte and glossy, all at once. I feel like they are more to keep me from doing magick, not so much to keep in place, as there are no bars, just boundaries I cannot pass.

With my magick gone, I have nothing but dreams connecting me to the people I love. The cot I sleep on rests in the corner, then there is a pot to do my business in when I have to, and empty food trays in another corner.

I haven't seen Trystan in—well, I don't know because it's dark down here, and I have no concept of time. I have no idea what he wants from me or why I am here. The only indication of the passage of time is the hair growth on my legs, and let's say I'm in my winter era.

I remember him saying something about me being his queen, but it's blurry.

I remember Dom.

Dom being stabbed and turning gray and bleeding, falling to the ground.

I hope someone was able to get to him after I was kidnapped and that he's okay.

I'm worried about my son.

Gods, Gauge is probably so worried about me.

How will I ever talk my way out of this one?

Maybe when I see Trystan again, I can convince him to at least let me tell my son I'm alive and okay. I don't know how well that will go down, though. If I'm being held prisoner, there's a fat chance in hell he'd let me get word to my son.

"Ahem," comes his voice and suddenly he's here with me, on my cot.

I sit up in a gasp of air, pulling my knees up to my chest.

I swear he wasn't there before.

His eyes are peerless, a cerulean blue like still water in a mountain spring, but depthless—as though he's looking at me and seeing into my soul. He still doesn't have a shirt on; the thorns coming out of his sternum wrap around his shoulders, connecting to swirl down his arms. His pecs jump as he flexes them one at a time. There is an inhuman sharpness to him, making me think I'd slice my hand open were I to graze any feature of his face accidentally.

"You look surprised to see me," he says, casually crossing his legs. He acts like we're about to exchange recipes. "Don't worry, I haven't been here long. I just appeared. As is one of my many, many talents."

Ah. He's a cocky fuck. "What do you want with me?" I ask him, shrugging away his gesture when he tries to grab my hand.

His lips curl into an evil smile, displaying his ungodsly white teeth. "Sayah. I've had this conversation with you three times. I want to strip you of your humanity, get those filthy blood-suckers out of your mind, and make you my queen. Not too much to ask." His voice is malevolent, even when speaking calmly, but with a hint of magick. The sort of voice I would obey, even if my life didn't depend on it. It isn't kind, but it's powerful and as sharp as the tip of a sword.

"I will never marry you, you prick!" I shout, and he shrinks back slightly. I damaged his ego a bit. "I want to go back home to my kid. Please. Just let me send word to my son that I'm okay. I'll do anything to speak to him."

"Tell you what." He stands and walks away from me, his back muscles flexing beneath his gorgeous blue wings. "You give me something I want, and I will let you message your son."

I blink, thrown. That was relatively easy.

But wait . . . The fae are never to be trusted. There's always something deeper behind their meaning.

I cross my legs and lean my elbow on one. "What do you want from me—the one thing?"

He turns to face me, his wavy locks swaying while his pointy ears stick out of the locks. "I want you to let me do one spell on you that lets me tap into just a small bit of your power." He shows the measurement of how much he means by signifying a pinch with his fingers.

Chills scurry down my arms.

"Nuh-uh," I say, folding my legs under me and clasping my hands in my lap. "No way. I know what that little tweak of words will do. If I let you in to get my power, there's no telling what you'll do with it. I have no desire to help you in any form or capacity. Nope."

He leans against the stone wall, eyes displaying a power I don't understand. "That's a shame, Sayah. Just one little thing, and you can send a message to your son."

The breath I inhale is sharp and cool—it feels tangled. "How can I trust you'll only take a little bit? *And* how can I fully trust you won't use it against your sister to conquer Feylight?"

He crosses the distance and kneels before me. "You don't."

I hold his stare. "Then no. I cannot let you do that."

"You realize that if you don't give me what I want, I can just take it from you, right?"

"If you could, you would have already. It can't be that simple."

"What if I wanted to earn your love and respect the decent way first?" He entangles his finger into a bit of my hair resting on the side of my face. "I just want you to love me. To be my queen. To be the queen of the Nightshades."

"Why me?" I ask, shrugging my hair out of his hand. "You can have any woman you want. What could you possibly want with me?"

The look in his eyes resembles something like hurt. "Sayah, you are the most powerful being on Earth. Why would I not want you?"

"Oh, it's all about power with you." I turn my head away with a frown.

"Well, yes, but I also think you are stunningly beautiful," he says, turning my head back to him with the tip of his finger. "It just helps that the most powerful being is gorgeous, too. If you were a swamp witch, well. I don't know what I'd do in that situation."

I bite back a scoff. "I don't know what to do with that information, Trystan. I'm in love with someone else. I love Bash. I want to be with him."

At this, he gets up and stalks off, but not too far. "I'm going to change that."

"I don't know that you can," I say honestly. "Bash and I have something that defies any semblance of normal. We're connected in ways even I struggle to comprehend. There's not a person on this plane, or any others, who could ever compare or replace him."

Again, he turns to face me, his enchanting stare hypnotic. "There are things I can give you that he wouldn't even be able to dream of. You will see. "

Now I do scoff. "He is all I will ever need."

Like magick, he wisps across the room and kneels in my face again, his lips dangerously close to mine. He swoops my hair off my neck and whispers into the shell of my ear, "You will fall for me. Of that, I am certain. And when you do, I will also give you your world and all the others. You will be queen of Earth, Nightshade, Feylight, Neverdusk, and Luminara. In my realms, your child will no longer have diabetes, and not only will he be able to walk, but he will also be able to fly. You are a woman who will stop at nothing to give her child the world. And I am here to give you three of them to give to him."

Against my will, his words meld to me, bending me like silk to steel, and I don't want to feel the rush of excitement he is enticing me with. He makes it sound nice and pretty, all packaged with a beautiful bow, but what does that mean?

"At the destruction of what? What is the cost of this, Trystan?"

He lets out a tut. "Now, now, my pet, no need to get into specifics now. Just dream of that life for your child. I'll let you dwell on it some." He gets up and walks away. "Oh, and one more thing."

I flick my chin at him, intrigued.

"Your beloved Dom is dead." He bows his head like he actually feels something other than selfishness. "I'm so sorry for your loss."

And he disappears.

AGARES

—BASH—

My chest tightens with a swell of emotions I can't place, though it feels like a faint reminder of a human life I lived long ago. The memories are aged with sepia tones and withered on the edges, as the warp and weft of time and aging and an immortal existence have muddled them. The sensation is strange; it feels like something existed there once, and I had forgotten it long ago but didn't want to relinquish it. Once I let this engulf me, it will forever be gone.

At this point, it's hard to tell which is worse: my grief over losing my brother or my anger toward Trystan taking what's mine.

How dare that fairy fuck think he can take my girl and make her his queen!

The anger bubbling inside me is so much worse than anything I can describe. The demon within my bones threatens to rip my skin apart and come forth, ready to unleash a fury fit for Poseidon, churning hurricanes after losing Medusa. The anger is like a savage storm, whipping winds of fury so loud in my skull that even the voices in the wall quiet to listen.

My grief weighs me down to the cold stone of this dungeon floor. The darkness in my soul feels right at home with this grief. The dark feelings of sadness are coming home to me. Even though I hate the way it feels, it also makes me realize the grief I feel is because I loved him so much. The love that was always there in the shallows, in the sharp edges and bitter words, hiding in the darkness we harbored for each other outweighs our centuries of fighting and making up and fighting again.

You never loved him; you were always jealous of him. You envied him. This voice belongs to Sadie. She's been quick to remind me of the hatred I always felt for Dom.

"*Shut up!*" I yell toward the wall.

The cold steel of the poor excuse for a bed I'm lying on bites into me. Tallyn was pleasant enough to provide me with a pillow—if you can even call it that—despite this hard-ass cot being more comfortable without it.

The sickness from the addiction hasn't been plaguing me as severely as I would have imagined.

Maybe there's something in that blood she's been feeding me.

The side effects of the formweaver venom have been fucking with me the most, and right now, I see a shadow out of the corner of my eye, like a living, breathing being beyond the bars lurking, watching me.

Thinking it's just the madness, I turn to face the wall, and grip my stomach. The pain I feel is neither from the addiction nor the side effects—no, this pain is all grief.

Sebastian, says the voice in the wall.

I don't recognize this voice.

"Go away!" I yell, covering one ear with the pillow and the other with my hand. "Leave me be."

"Sebastian."

Holy shit, that's a real voice.

I sit up.

Even my intensified sight can't make out a face; it's still just an obscurity in the shadows, but it's definitely a person.

A woman.

"Who's there?" I ask, swinging my legs to the side of the cot. I really need to take my boots off and let my feet breathe. I need a shower.

"Bash!" the voice shouts.

I stand this time, and then vamp-flash to the bars to see who this mystery person is creeping in the shadows. My fangs protrude and my eyes go laser-focused, which only means they're turning white.

"Who. The fuck. Is there?" I say with purpose.

The shadowy figure glides toward me, carefully avoiding places where the spirit lanterns cast golden pools of light along the ground, staying in the dark crevices between where the lanterns cast their shadows. Yet, the darkness seems to follow her, as if she is made of it—absorbing the shadows with every move.

"Hello, Sebastian," she says, coming as close to me as she can without being within arm's reach.

"Who are you?" I ask again, the anger in my bones simmering to a boil. It's not only the madness that's scathing; the addiction, the grief, the side effects—this unfortunate person who's been put in my path—grates against every molecule of my fabric.

I'll rip her to shreds.

As she steps closer, the shadows fall off her like a dark veil. Her beauty comes into view. She's short, and her dark red hair cascades to her knees. Her eyes are a glowing green; she wears a corset of black thorns. The shadows turn into a cloak of black velvet. She taps her long fingernail onto the bar, and the shadows from within her skin meld to the bars, bending them to her will.

"Now tell me again, Sebastian." Her voice resembles that of rocks skipping across a still lake. "Who will you rip to shreds?"

What the fuck?

Her words freeze me.

The shadows coming from every corner snake up under the bars and wrap around my ankles, not only holding me to the floor, but they also make me numb. I can't feel my power, my connection to the Earth. Shit, even if I tried to veilweave her, I don't think my voice would come out the same.

"What do you want?" I force myself to say, but my tongue barely cooperates. It's like I have a mouthful of peanut butter.

The evil smile that pulls at the corners of her mouth is devious enough to make even me wince in wicked delight. She's a villain like me. Her teeth are so white that they're quite the juxtaposition to the darkness of this dungeon.

I think I love her.

I want to have wickedly evil babies with her.

No, that can't be right. I love Sayah.

"What's happening to me?" I mouth through the peanut butter of magick.

"Oh, Sebastian." She tuts like scolding a kid in trouble. "Have you never met a ShadowMaiden before?"

This word is confusing.

"Uh, no," I admit. The shadows have climbed all the way up my body now, tickling my ears. I use all the strength I have to fight whatever magick this fairy bitch is trying to trick me with. "Listen here, Cruella." The demon in me rears up and fights back the darkness, finding where the shadows are penetrating my skin and pushing back. "You better tell me what the fuck you want. You got about five seconds before this demon in me cracks through the fissures in my soul and kills you."

The laugh she lets go of is malicious and bitter, yet something about it still sings to my demon, making him purr.

I don't fucking like it.

I fight the shadows even more, and they recede to at least my legs.

"Oh, Sebastian, ever the villain. I love that."

She taps her fingernail, and the shadows purge forth, shooting up my whole body, lunging me forward, and slamming me into the bars of the cell. They wrap around my wrists and tie them outside the bars in front of me.

"I was just trying to have a little fun," she hedges, pulling a long golden weapon from her hair.

"The fuck is that for?" I ask, still fighting the fucking shadows.

Come on, demon, where the fuck are you when I need you the most? I plea to him.

I should name him. Maybe that's why he doesn't listen to me.

Every demon needs a name. That's Dom's voice.

"Brother, not now."

"What?" Shadow lady asks.

"Nothing."

Drake?

No. That's awful, says Dom.

Clint?

Really, Bash? Clint?

Jorge?

Odin's ghost. Something demon-y.

Shadow lady takes the golden pin-looking thing and starts to drag it along my skin.

My skin splits open, the sting of the slice biting. "Ow, what the fuck are you doing?" I grouse, yanking my arm back as far as I can, which only makes the slice longer.

"Shhhh," she says, tapping her finger again, and the shadows around my arms pull tighter. Taking a jar from her cloak pocket, she collects my blood.

Oh, shit.

This can't be good.

Name him! Dom commands, but I don't know why it's so important now.

The jar is filling fast—a third of the way full already.

Bash! Dom's voice yells at me. *This cannot be good. Fucking name your demon, and he'll take over your body.*

"*Agares!*" I scream, not knowing where I got the name from, but the minute it leaves my lips, blackness tunnels my vision, and I almost pass out. I fight the feeling.

The transition into Agares is foreign; nothing like transitioning into a vampire. My senses heighten and numb simultaneously. Liquid fire courses through my veins and my muscles scream as they elongate, ripping through her shadows, binding my wrists like they're made of twine. Shadow lady's green eyes widen with stunned realization, like she's watching her worst nightmare unfold before her. Abandoning my blood, she backs away, her shadows receding from me and seeping back into her.

The bars bend easily in my hands—hands that are now red with thick black talons. The rods burst like icicles coming off a roof. She stows the blood in her cloak and runs. I shoot after her in a breathless rage. We fly down the winding dark tunnels, and she tries to thwart me by melding with pockets of shadows, but I can see her any which way she turns. In this new form, I can see heat clearly in the dark, as though I'm a ghost hunting and have infrared goggles on.

There is nothing more I want than to taste her death on my lips.

Sebastian! shouts the wall—an unknown female voice—but I will not stop until I get that shadow bitch.

It seems like the chase will never end around dark corners, twisting, turning, and going on forever, but I continue following her scent, watching her try to play in the shadows, but she cannot play me.

I own the dark.

Another fairy who has purple wings pops out right in front of where Shadow Bitch faded into the dark, and with a flick of her wrist, all the lights within the castle teleport to her finger, lighting up the darkness in a way that's blinding.

"Gotcha!" the purple fairy says.

But Shadow Bitch takes her cloak, swoops it over her head, and she is gone.

"Fuck!" the purple fairy shouts, slamming her hand against the stone wall.

Tallyn is running up behind us, the blinding light fading back into the darkness.

"Who the fuck was that?" I ask, feeling the demon settling back into my bones.

Tallyn's orange eyes search my new form as it fades, drinking up each foot of Agares's height. "Ember," she finally says, a little breathless.

Where the fuck did Tallyn come from? Was it her voice in the wall? Maybe I just thought it was the wall, and it was her all along.

Agares grumbles low in my soul before retreating to the dark corners of my being.

"And that would be?" I ask, rolling the crick out of my neck the demon overtaking me caused.

"She's the ShadowMaiden of Neverdusk," Tallyn explains, her heels clicking on the stone as she approaches us. "She's the High Councilor to the Neverdusk Dominion. Trystan's most trusted adviser."

"Well, that can't be good."

"Why? What did she want?" asks the purple fairy.

"Who are you?" I question her.

"Aurora. At your service." She curtsies to me like I'm a fucking king.

"That means nothing to me," I say to her, looking back at Tallyn.

"Aurora is our resident lumokinesis fairy. She can control and manipulate light."

"Ah." I nod. It still means nothing to me.

"But what did Ember want from you?" Tallyn asks. We walk back the way we came.

"She took some of my blood."

Tallyn stops walking. "Shit."

"My question is"—I stop walking—"how the fuck did she get in?"

"She controls shadows," Tallyn tells me, like that will clear everything up. "Ember is a ShadowMaiden. She can seamlessly meld with the shadows, becoming one with the darkness. She can become invisible in them. She can also navigate them, teleporting from one shadowy area to another. It lets her get in and out without being detected."

"Don't you have some sort of boundary spell voodoo shit you can do to prevent that sort of thing?" I ask.

"I did. But whatever way Trystan used to get to Sayah... that's how she got in too."

"Okay, well, you need to really do something about that, don't you think?"

She glares at me like she wants to eat me.

Eat her, says the wall. This time, I think it was Joe's voice—Jasantha's man I killed a few months ago.

I almost balk at the wall, but Tallyn already looks at me like I'm crazy. I'm out of that cell, and I don't want to go back in.

"I'm working on it. Right now, we need to prepare for war 'cause whatever Trystan is going to do with your blood can't be good."

She turns to walk away again, and I follow her, not wanting to draw attention to the fact I'm outside the cell and not wanting to go back into it.

"Well, she didn't get that much. He can make, what, one or two dark fairies with a third of a cup of crazy vamp blood?"

"That's enough for him to do some awful shit with," she remarks as we walk by my old cell without stopping at it. Thank the gods she isn't putting me back in there. "I needed bags of Dominic's blood to make one darkling fae. But only one drop of yours turned them into something awful." The look she gives me is one of terror; dread knits her black eyebrows together.

"What the fuck was it?"

"We called in an abyssal sprite. It was just awful. I didn't make another one; I put your blood in a very secure place for safekeeping. In case something like this happened and he got a hold of your blood. He must have found out about the abyssal sprite."

We've begun to climb the stairs out of the dungeon, and the darkness we're leaving behind seems to be following us up.

"And, what, pray tell, is an abyssal sprite?" I have a feeling I really don't want to know.

"They're essentially like grimspawns—"

"Oh, those ain't bad—"

"Grimspawn with eight to ten rows of razor-sharp teeth that can drain your soul, have a corrosive touch, and insatiable blood lust—among other things."

I scoff. "Pfft. Nothing to bat an eyelash at."

Tallyn's glare collides with mine, and we have an unspoken terror that slithers between us.

4

CELESTIAL PHOENIX

—SAYAH—

The guilt is like a heavy monster sitting on my chest, constricting my lungs, and making it hard to breathe. Agony, relentless and wild, rips at parts of me that never existed before this moment. The moment I found out a man I loved was dead. His death is a ceaselessly cold whisper on my neck, needling its way down to my bones. The cold metal of the cot digs into my spine—through the pathetic thing called a mattress—and feels like blades against my skin, as though I make one wrong move and I'll be cut in two.

It's my fault he's dead.

If he had never met me, I wouldn't have gotten him marked, which was what led to all this. I meddled in things I didn't understand and stumbled upon my destiny.

But was this his?

What was his death for?

I release a labored gasp and cry out into the darkened cell. My sobs cradle me in my sorrow.

The pitiful blob of down feathers wrapped in scratchy fabric suffices as a pillow, rescuing my head from the blades below, threatening to rip me apart. I've been sobbing into it for so long. The outer layer is soaked, but its coolness is a balm to my cheeks, which are raw and achy from crying for so long.

I've drained my well of sorrow, and my tears have all dried up. My breath is coming in hitches now, my lungs burning.

The grief I feel is different from Mama's. It's woven different and tangled, chaffing against the fabric of me. It's raw and new, quiet and loud, calm and feral. The conflicting emotions scratch my soul, drilling into my mind, and depleting my ability to form rational thought.

Is it because I didn't truly get to mend things between us before he died? Is this what unfinished reckoning feels like?

Maybe the fact he knew I'm in love with his brother also salts the wound—knowing how badly I must have hurt him.

His own sins, the deaths of the innocent people he murdered, weighed on his soul, dragging him to the dark place he dreaded.

But it's also the lighter things. It's the memories we made together, the laughter we shared, how easy it was to be near him, how his smile calmed me.

I don't know whether I made the right decision to choose Bash.

Am I the reason he's dead?

The racing thoughts become living, breathing parasites, gnawing at my being, cutting me to the bone.

How can Dom be dead?

How can the last words that left his lips toward me truly be the last words he'll ever say? How the fuck will I ever go on with life—back to the world without him? The whole world continues to move forward as though reality and life didn't entirely upend.

It doesn't help that I'm stuck in this fucking cell with my grief crushing me like the dark surrounding me.

Dom.

Oh, Dom.

What the fuck do I do now? How will I ever get over this?

He can't really be gone, can he?

I want my mom.

I want my son.

I just want to get the fuck out of this place and go home.

Small, flickering orbs cast dim light against the walls closest to me, lining the space, and trailing off into the tunnels that lead to the exit—an exit I can't reach because of the magickal barrier. The room is circular, like a cul-de-sac at the end of a foreboding tunnel.

When I first awoke, I explored the area and found I could only make it as far as the tunnel's mouth, which spills into my cell. There's plenty of space to move, yet it feels restrictive, the freedom an illusion. Beyond the entrance, the dingy orange orbs barely illuminate anything.

After Trystan delivered his devastating blow with the news of Dom's death, I've been weeping alone in this place for what feels like hours. The loneliness and quiet make his death that much louder.

I want Bash.

Gods, I would do anything to see him. I wonder how he's doing with the news or if he even knows. I wonder if he's still hallucinating or going through awful shit because of the formweaver venom.

When I feel the sadness ebb enough to take a complete breath, I refocus my thoughts.

There has to be a sliver of power left inside me.

These stupid bracelets shouldn't have the power to contain the wild power that lives inside me. I search myself, closing my eyes, and feeling for anything—buzzing, tingling, searing—but nothing remains.

It feels empty, hollow. Though new, my powers still belong to me; they are fierce and fiery, yet tender and comforting. I've grown used to how my magick moves inside me. Even when I wasn't using it, it was always there, like stars in daylight.

I wish I had a way to dreamwalk to Bash awake, to talk to him, and to know he's okay.

He and Dom were never close, but I know Bash loved Dom as much as he loved the moon. Dom was part of him, a section of Bash he closed off and buried, but it existed just the same.

Gods, why can't I have the power to wish things true?

I'd send a wish to Gauge to let him know I'm okay and one to Bash to remind him I'm still there. Even though they can't see me, I'm wrapping them up with love and warmth.

But fuck, if I'm wishing shit true, I'd wish myself the fuck out of here.

It is useless.

I feel nothing. Where there used to be a slight buzzing, there is nothing but darkness and cold.

Trystan's words have also been echoing in the breeze of my grief. What he said about Gauge not having diabetes anymore and having the ability to use his legs . . . In a heartbeat, I'd give him my legs, my pancreas—any part of me necessary to keep him alive and well.

Is my love for Bash worth giving up that dream for Gauge?

You can never trust the fae.

Would that mean Gauge and I would have to live here forever, and he would never see his dad again?

There's no way he would go for that. Both Gauge and his dad.

And Neverdusk is in perpetual nighttime. What would I do without the sun?

Dom.

I think of him and him meeting the sun for the first time in two hundred years, and again, my soul cracks open and bleeds all over any other thought I'd just been having.

Poor Dom.

He never wanted this. He never wanted this life, let alone being swept up in the realms of the fae. Regardless of what he was saying to me on that balcony, I knew he had been under some sort of spell; it wasn't him saying those things. He was not in love with Tallyn. That was her and her dirty fairy magick.

I gulp as another bout of tears rips me in half. Air bending makes my ears perk up. Tingles on the back of my knees announce Trystan's presence, and it makes me uncomfortable.

He's watching me.

I sniffle and rub my hand across my nose, trying to act like I don't know he's here.

The way he controls his breaths is impressive. He inhales short intakes to render me oblivious to him being in here with me, staying hidden.

How many times has he done this? Does he know that I know he's here?

I decide to see how long he stays hidden before he announces his presence.

Maybe being able to hear the bending of the barrier spell is a sliver of my magick remaining or proof it still flits inside me like wild fireflies caged.

Laying on the cot, seconds fade into minutes, waiting for Trystan to show himself.

I can hear him getting closer. The pressure of his weight on the stone floor still makes a sound, even if it's just for supernatural ears.

It's when I feel his breath on my face that I startle, nearly kneeing him in the groin.

A wicked shiver runs over me as he materializes, horizontally hovering above me, his wings and magick holding him aloft.

"Hello, my darling," he says, his lips against my neck. The orb lights in the room flicker to bright yellow, casting long shadows of him over me.

It's like they get brighter with his presence and pulsate at his beating heart.

I cringe, moving away from him.

He is still shirtless.

"Do you own a shirt?" I snipe at him.

The laugh that escapes him is a touch dark, hinting at malice with a dust of intrigue, almost as though he likes how I jab at him.

"Oh, my pet, you are *feisty*!" he says, trying to tickle me, but I'm in no fucking mood to be tickled, so I don't give him the satisfaction of squirming for him, even though the place he's touching is very ticklish.

"What do you want, Trystan?"

His face falls. He almost seems wounded at my nonchalance. "I came down here to see if you would like a better room?" His blonde brow quirks up. "One with a view, perhaps?"

"What's the catch?" I ask him, trying to get out from under his weight. He's practically lying on me.

"You wound me," he says, hovering up two inches. "I am merely trying to give you everything I said I would. I don't want my future wife all alone down here. I want to give you everything. So, for starters, a room with an ocean view."

"Isn't it always nighttime here?"

His glass eyes shatter. "Do you not like the night?"

"I do when it comes and goes."

He exhales softly. "We are not all creatures of light and sundust. Daylight is a death knell."

My insides want to crawl to the outside and burst into flames at having him so close to me, hovering over me. "How can I have a room with a view you're offering if I can't see anything?"

His face softens. "We are all tied to the night in one way or another. Just wait. The room at the top of the tower can be seen across the Nocturna Sea. And both moons are out, preparing for the Dread Harvest Eclipse in a few days. They are just glorious; you have to see."

It does sound beautiful. And anywhere would be better than down here. "Okay," I say, wondering at what else I'm making promises to.

His eyes light up. For such an evil being, he is very beautiful. His wings pick him all the way off me, and he lands on his feet, shattering the boundary between air and sky in one sultry pirouette. "Okay. Okay, c'mon on. Follow me."

I stand from the awful bed and follow him through the cell. When we get to the boundary spell, he grabs my hand and pulls me through.

It feels like walking through a waterfall without getting wet. It is thick and viscous, almost like slime, but it doesn't leave a residue.

He pulls me through the long tunnels, and when we get to the end, he stops and faces me.

"All right. This may hurt a little."

"What! What's gonna hurt?"

"I'm going to bloodport with you to the top tower. It's much faster that way. But since your body isn't used to bloodporting, it may hurt some."

"Bloodporting?"

"Think teleportation, but different," he offers cryptically.

"Meaning?"

His eyes narrow. "I can only bloodport to places I've bled before. Since you're supernatural, you are able to bloodport with me—but the first time will hurt if you're traveling some-where you haven't bled with someone who has. It's like you earn your right to return to the spot that caused someone pain."

So, that's how he's gotten into my dungeon cell without noise.

"How much is some?"

"Oh, Sayah," he says, stroking my face. "You lived through much worse than this; this will be nothing more than a pinch." And before I know it, he pulls my hand out and slices it open with a blade I didn't see.

"Ow!" I try to pull my hand back. Before I can, he pulls it forth and drips it onto the dirt floor beneath my feet. "What are you doing?"

"So when we return, it won't hurt again." There's vinegar in his tone, even though it seems he's doing something sweet.

Causing me pain now so I won't hurt later.

He pulls me into him like we're about to dance, and the world whooshes upward, similar to going up in an elevator.

Up and up we go until I feel like I'm going to be sick from the movement, and when we finally arrive, I fall to my knees, gasping for air.

"Oh, yeah, sorry, I forgot to tell you to breathe in before we did that."

"Yeah. Thanks," I breathe out, desperately grasping for my calm to return. I feel faint. The world is hot and tunneled, and my brain feels mushy.

When I finally gain my composure, I stand, taking in my surroundings.

As he said, the room is at the top of a tower. The entire room is spacious, with a cold floor of flagstones covered in vibrant rugs, ensconced with floor-to-ceiling windows cut right out of the stone, and no curtains, glass, or bars. A large bed in one corner is draped in soft blue velvet. A decent-sized armoire and beautiful purple orb lights paint the room in a weird, romantic ambiance. The room is circular with a panoramic view of the ocean, which, in the perpetual nighttime, appears inky black.

Gilded mirrors of all shapes and sizes adorn the walls, nearly covering every bit of space.

"Why so many mirrors?" I ask, feathering my finger over one as I pass it, trying not to look at my horrid reflection in it.

Oops, I looked.

I need a shower. Badly.

"Because vampires," he says, looking up at the mirrors like a proud father looking at his children. "Nothing will tame a wild vampire faster than making them the age they really are."

Maybe he doesn't know my vampires are spelled, so even regular mirrors wouldn't faze them. I don't risk saying it aloud.

I approach the double French doors on the far side, and he catches my hand. "Just so you know. There is a magickal barrier in this room, too. So, if you got any bright ideas to . . . I don't know . . . jump. You couldn't."

I don't even know why he says this to me. "Thanks, but I'm not suicidal."

His face softens in an expression that withers to sympathy. "Not yet. But you may be at some point while being here."

Weird. Why would he say that if he is trying to win me over?

He walks to the balcony, and I follow, not knowing what else to say about the comment.

He's a strange fellow.

When we walk out into the moonlight, the air is warm and feathery, with a briny scent that reminds me of back east in New Jersey. The vast Nocturna Sea expands beyond the horizon, and two glorious moons shatter the heavens with their beauty. The stars are brighter here, and there are planets within eyesight in the sky, which is a brilliant cerulean, reminiscent of Trystan's eyes.

"Beautiful, isn't it?" he asks, laying his long, elegant fingers on the thorns making up the balcony railing. "Dark creatures are best left to the darker nights."

Thorns seems to be his theme.

"What are they called?"

His eyes catch mine curiously. "The moons?"

"Yes. Do they have names?"

"Yes. That one right there"—he points to the one on the right—"Darkmyst. And that one"—he points to the one on the left—"we call Umbralune. Umbra is a little pinker than Darkmyst."

The moons are nearly full, almost touching each other; one is a dusty pink, and the other is a soft pale purple. They look like they are murmuring secrets of ancient stories, weaving hidden wisdom into the air.

How he looks lovingly at the moons makes me realize he may have a soft side. His love for his land and realm, sky, moons, and ocean may be the key to getting him to trust me. If I can get him to trust me, maybe even play along with this little game of being his queen, then maybe he will remove my shackles, and I can use my magick to get away from him and back to Bash.

"Tell me about this place," I say, staring out toward the sea.

It is beautiful. No matter what ocean it is, it speaks to my soul. All oceans do.

It's wild I'm still on Earth. Or am I?

"What would you like to know?" he asks, turning toward me.

"Well, I know it's always night here. Don't you miss the light and the sun?"

He looks up at the moons, his face bereft of human presence. "No. The light never did me any good. I was always better in the dark. Tallyn was always better with light. And the magick I have is just better in darkness. So when I started taking parts of the realm for myself, the night sky, moon, and darkness cried for me and devoured the light so that I may thrive. It was the darkness's way of welcoming home her king."

Interesting. "What is your magick?"

He glares at me like that was not part of the deal of me coming up here.

When he turns to walk away, I grab a hold of his arm. When he looks down at my hand, I let go, not wanting to piss him off. "I'm sorry. I don't need to know. I was just curious about this place. It's so beautiful." I turn again and lean on the balcony, looking down. The tower we're in is on a cliff's edge, the craggy rocks almost a mile below.

He doesn't walk away; he comes back and joins me.

"Do you have seasons here? I mean, since it's always night?"

"We do have seasons, but not like winter, spring, summer, or fall. We have the Eternal Nocturne, which is the perpetual night. The skies are adorned with stars, the moon, and celestial phenomena like aurora borealis, et cetera. We have the umbral veil, which is a period where darkness deepens, and the mysterious umbral veil descends upon us. It is a time when shadows become more animated, and the magick in the dominion intensifies. We have Lunar Embrace, which is the phase when the moon's influence waxes, making a more pronounced glow upon us. It's also a period of intense magickal activity. Then there are Shrouded Dreams, which is the season in which dreams and nightmares take on a tangible presence within the dominion. The boundaries between the dream realm and reality blur, leading to unpredictable and surreal experiences for us. This is the season we're in now. Lastly, there is the Eclipsed Silence, which is a rare event that happens when a celestial alignment causes an eclipse in the Neverdusk Dominion. During this time, the night becomes even darker, and the magickal energies may surge or wane, affecting the environment and the beings within it. That will happen during the Dread Harvest Eclipse."

"Wait, didn't that happen already?" I ask.

"In the mortal realm, yes. Here, we're a few days behind. Time is different here."

"And this Dread Harvest Eclipse is when you are doing the Wild Hunt, right?"

His face slackens from the adoration for his realm he just

had and turns frigid. It's so cold I shiver, and it's not cold here at all. "Where did you learn that term?"

"Oh, that . . . that's just what the people of Earth call the—"

He smiles, and it surprises me. "I know. I'm fucking with you. It's okay to call it that. Sort of what it is, but much, much more intricate."

"Can you tell me about it?"

He tuts and pulls my chin to look at him. "Sayah. I won't tell you everything you want to know right now. It's late in your world, and you're probably starving. Do you want some food?"

I've heard somewhere that you should refrain from eating the food or drinking wine from fae.

Lucky for me, I don't drink.

"No, I'm okay." I walk back inside and toward the settee at the foot of the bed.

"Well, I'll send some food up for you anyway. You may change your mind. There's a bathroom through there if you want to wash up. Clothes in the armoire. You will love what I put in there for you."

He moves toward the door.

"I would love to know one thing," I say as he tarries on the threshold.

He turns back to me, pressing his shoulder into the door's wooden frame. "I would love to maybe answer it for you."

"Before you brought me here, you called me the Celestial Phoenix. What does that mean?"

His look shades his smile—a vicious grin. This being who created the warlocks that spell the grimspawn to do atrocious shit to people is standing before me, looking at me like I'm his shiny new toy. "Oh, my darling. What doesn't it mean?" His eyes turn hungry and greedy, craving something he means to acquire in me. "It means you are the most powerful being on this plane and any others you enter. You have the power to destroy my warlocks—a feat that has not been accomplished since I first made Mederio and Matrasia, and you and your sister killed them like they were nothing. She was a seemingly indestructible being, yet you destroyed her in seconds. You have a rare convergence of angelic, formweaving, witch, and demonic blood. Now think to yourself, if you can obliterate a being like her, who is that powerful? What kind of beings would your blood create?"

Chills run to my bone at his smile. He then turns on his haunches and disappears.

5

HENRY

—BASH—

Tallyn ushers me into a vast chamber that rivals the grandeur of the queen's sitting room at Buckingham Palace—I would know since I once vexed the queen's sister, Princess Margaret, with my charms.

A tale for another time.

The expansive room we walk into is awe-inspiring, boasting sky-high ceilings crafted from imposing stone seemingly stretched into the heavens. Above us, an open roof reveals a canvas of night sky, reveling a Michelangelo painting with a magick twist. This ceiling is alive with darkness, the twinkling stars promising enchantment while the moons lend their silvery light, touching every regal piece of furnishing with a lunar kiss. Red velvet covers much of the furniture, and a fireplace fit for giants roars on the right, bathing everything in a warm glow.

Spirit lanterns climb up towering bookshelves on all the other walls, hovering in front of them like ghostly balls of light. Staircases and balconies—intricately carved and adorned with leaves and vines—crawl up the shelves' walls.

Tallyn sashays straight for the bar at the other end of the

chamber, flicking her long hair off her shoulders. "Welcome to my lunar room," she says, flicking her wrists. The purple lights turn yellow. "Want a drink?"

"Love one," I answer, stringing my neck in admiration at the expanse of the room.

More like lunar grand ballroom

A small, childlike person jumps out from behind one of the pillars and lands directly on my path. I startle, my skin leaving my body for a fraction of a second. "Fuck!" I yell, and Tallyn turns.

Henry doesn't move; he is small, like the child he was in the 1700s, wearing a spectral waistcoat, once a deep shade of indigo that now bears the faded patina of the time. The delicate stitching along the edges of a bygone era hints at the attention to detail that adorned even children's clothing in the eighteenth century. His breeches, reaching just below the knee, were likely once a contrasting color, perhaps a muted brown or an earthy tone. The fabric, now ethereal and translucent, maintains the structure of the original garments, plucking the image and memory of him right from my memory.

My eyes widen as I look through Henry to Tallyn, who's frozen and staring at me like I've lost my mind. "Are you okay?" she asks, seemingly oblivious to the ghostly presence hovering between her and I.

I really don't want to go back to that cell.

"Uh, yeah . . . fine. Just—well, it's so magnificent in here. Look at that sky!" I flick my gaze back up to the ceiling and walk through Henry, cringing at the frigid air that passes over my body.

He evaporates like mist as Tallyn turns and finishes walking to the bar.

I must still be hallucinating. Otherwise, I would have screamed like a girl.

Child ghosts scare the shit out of me.

"Yes, I do love Feylight in the nighttime," Tallyn says, pouring silver, thick, sparkly shit into two goblets.

I take a seat on a barstool, then glance over my shoulder to see if Henry re-materialized after I walked through him, and sure as shit, he did.

He's staring right at me.

I shiver and turn back around. Tallyn hands me the drink, and I jump again.

Her bows knit together. "You sure you're okay?"

Grabbing the goblet from her, I swirl it around, and smell it. "Perfect. So, you have normal nights and days here in Feylight, unlike Neverdusk?"

Leaning back on the comfy bar chair, relishing in the squishy fluff pillows should have, I take a drink. I know I'm not supposed to eat or drink anything in fae land but, I'm already going crazy, so what the hell?

It. Tastes. Wonderful. Like coconut and pineapple and some other fruity flavors I cannot name.

"Yes, we have night and day here," she resumes after she sips the liquid. "But they're quite longer than yours, each day and night lasting an equivalence of three mortal days and nights. There are different seasons here as well."

The chill on the back of my neck tells me Henry is right behind me now. Slowly, I turn my head to look.

Fuck.

The sight of him makes me jump, spilling a bit of the silver shit.

"Bash?" Tallyn inquires, her orange eyes sparkling in the dim light of the library. "Are you quite all right?"

"Yep, just still seeing shit." I situate myself away from Henry. "I'm good, though, promise. I don't want to murder anyone."

Yes, you do, encourage the voices. They are no longer in the wall but all around me.

This is fun.

"It is to be expected," she says, walking around the bar we're sitting at to grab a towel. "I have no idea how long the side effects of the venom will last, but I imagine it won't be too much longer."

Fucking hope not.

Child ghosts are for the birds.

My stomach, echoing throughout the vast chamber, reminds me I need a real meal.

I imagine that eating from blood bags would be the equivalent of someone eating a bag of popcorn for lunch. The vitality of the blood has waned, and it doesn't have the same effect. It staves off starvation, but it isn't sustaining.

I look up at Tallyn hungrily, noting how the vein in her neck pops from her mopping efforts. Her blood's woodland and spice scent wafts in the air; it is different from the coppery metallic scent of humans. Fae blood is wild and feral, like nature.

"I need to eat soon, too. Real blood from a real person. Have any of those lying around?"

Her orange eyes catch me looking at her neck. "You can drink from me. I'll let you."

Eyeing her with a speculative seduction, I stand, pushing the barstool into Henry. "That would be most appreciated. Thank you."

I flinch as I walk by Henry, trying to make him back the fuck up, but he stands firm, arms crossed, height reaching my navel.

Tallyn swoops her long hair off her shoulders and tilts her head, awaiting my vampiric kiss of pain. I'm right behind her in a blink, the scent of her intoxicating and inviting.

Salivating drops of hunger fill my mouth, and my incisors elongate. I'm ready to feel the satisfying crunch of skin when the sound of a heavy door closing has me halt millimeters away from her skin.

A woman walks toward us with a fiery confidence in her gait that proclaims her presence to be of importance in this realm.

She is tall and willowy like Tallyn, with sable locks that bound around her face in waves before cascading down her front, nearly reaching her waistline. Her bright blue eyes pierce into mine as she closes the distance between us. The familiarity in her nature stuns me. She's gorgeous in a sisterly way, the same way Scarlet is deadly beautiful to me but not, like, hot.

I back up from Tallyn and put my fangs away.

"Mom," she says, stopping on the other side of the bar, next to Henry.

His ghostly eyes track over to her, then back to me.

You should kill her, Henry says, and I shake my head at him.

This must be Sariana.

My long-lost little sister.

Tallyn's shoulders tense. "Yes, darling?" She moves away from me, grabbing the bottle, and filling my glass back up.

The angles of her face are sharp and inhuman, yet the features are more vampire than fae. "There's a problem with the portal. We've been trying to get the others here like you said to once this one was better." She indicates to me by shoving her chin in my direction. "But it's glitching or something."

Tallyn scrunches her nose. "Ah, yes. The boundary spell to stop portal magick within the boundary of the castle. Seems to work for us, but not anyone else."

"Hi, you must be Sariana," I say, though she is not warm and welcoming to my politeness. "I'm Sebastian. Or Bash. Your bro—"

"None of that now, Bash," Tallyn scolds me, holding up her hand to shut me up. "She knows who you are. She has no desire to put you in any familial category like that."

"Yes, Sebastian or Bash," she says in a dulcet tone, her accent unfamiliar. Having been raised in Feylight, I know it's a fae accent. Her blue eyes flicker to mine. "Not a pleasure to meet you. Please don't talk to me again."

Tallyn's gaze shoots back to Sariana. "Now, Sari, no need for hostility. He is our guest and will be helping to defeat your evil uncle. So, treat him with some respect, will you?"

Her eyes flash purple—like Jasantha. "Charmed, I'm sure."

The fuck?

"I'll be there in a minute, love. Just keep trying."

She nods and saunters off.

Henry watches her go and then looks back at me. *Shoulda killed her.*

I flip him off. "Thanks."

"For what?" Tallyn asks as I put my finger away.

"Nothing, I, uh . . . Your blood. Need it now."

She wisps her lengthy black hair over her shoulder and reveals her long, pale ivory neck. My skin tingles as my fangs protrude. I grab her neck, sinking my sharp canines into it. The decadent crunch of her skin being pierced sings to my soul. I begin to suck the life force from her, feeling the glorious nectar of blood enter me and feed my being.

"So, the seasons," she says as I drink from her. "We have eternal spring, which is like the default season, where the air is filled with the fragrance of blooming flowers. The temperature is also mild and pleasant."

As she says this, I swear I smell the flowers.

"There's Summer Radiance, where, periodically, we have the intensifications of magickal energies, leading to a season of heightened brightness and warmth. The daylight becomes more luscious during this time, and the magickal flora reaches its peak vibrancy. The magick of Feylight is intensified. Brings back dead things to life. Part of why Trystan wants it."

I'm starting to feel full, but her blood is so delicious I cannot stop. I know she'll stop me when I get close to killing her. I'm not high like with Sayah's blood, but gods-damn, it's delicious.

You shouldn't stop, Henry says, appearing next to me.

"Enchanting autumnal glow is similar to fall in the mortal realm," Tallyn continues. I've ignored Henry. "Magickal energies of the Luminara Domain ebb, and the leaves and trees trans-form into a breathtaking display of radiant colors. And then there's Winter's Luminescence." She removes her neck from my hold to take away my meal. "This is when a gentle luminescence pervades the landscape instead of darkness. Snowfall consists of delicate, glowing crystals illuminating the realm during the colder months. Winter's Luminescence represents a serene and magickal aspect of the domain's seasonal cycle."

I wipe away the excess blood dribbling down my chin, and my fangs retract back into my gums. Most vampires take on the traits of their subjugates after feeding on them. Some tend to take on their personalities, and sometimes even absorb some of their memories. With Tallyn, I feel nothing. It's like she's been around for so long that she's learned to keep every part of who she is bound to her bones.

"Lovely story, really nice," I say, slipping from behind the bar and grabbing my goblet. "So, what about this portal, and getting the rest of my family here?"

Tallyn takes the same towel and dabs at her neck. The holes I left evaporate. "The boundary spell I put up to prohibit teleportation and portal usage must be damaged. We'll help her in a bit. Right now, I want to bring you to the outer ring of Feylight. I have fairies I've captured from the realms of Never that will be great subjects to infuse with your blood."

Murder! yells Henry from behind me, causing me to jump, and spill more fucking silver shit.

Tallyn releases an exasperated breath, sliding me the towel to clean up my mess.

I smirk at her, taking the towel. "You said my blood turns them into abyssal sprites?"

Taking a drink of the silver liquid, she leans on her elbows, casting me an intense gaze. "I did, yes."

"What will we do with these murderous, soul-sucking, corrosive beings until you unleash them?"

The wicked grin that pulls at her face is intoxicating. "Oh, Bash. You're so naïve sometimes."

I chuckle self-consciously. "Meaning?"

"I'm unleashing them tonight. Before the eclipse. To hinder his Wild Hunt."

6

MOONSHADOW NECTAR

—SAYAH—

I feel like a brand-new woman after my shower. Although I'm still a captive in a realm stranded in perpetual night-time run by a crazy, sexy fairy, at least I feel better.

With a black onyx marbled tub giving 'tub of ancient Greek goddesses', more gilded mirrors everywhere, and floating orbs lights secreting amber tones, the bathroom is reminiscent of a spa at a gym.

The counters are flat, giving the impression that if you were to turn the faucet on, water would run everywhere—even all over the floor. But there must be a subtle dip in the marble and an invisible hole, for when I turn it on to wash my hands, the water slips down the marble and just . . . disappears.

An electric toothbrush appears on the countertop, freshly slathered with teal paste, so I take it and brush my teeth meticulously. I have no idea how long it's been since I've done this, and it feels so good.

When you're deprived of every day, mundane things, it makes you appreciate the small things once they return to your life.

Similar to when I was bathing, the eerie feeling of being

watched unsettles my nerves once again. I shrug and flip off the corners of the bathroom as though there are cameras there.

Let them watch me.

I wrap myself up in the fuzzy, warm white robe, and flip my hair up into a giant white towel. The floors here are heated, too.

I've never experienced something so luxurious. As ominous as being here is, at least I now have comfort.

As I pad into the bedroom from the bathroom, there is a knock on the large mahogany double doors. I walk over to them to open it.

A small sprite with pointy ears who stands about three feet tall and has dark skin, even darker eyes, and black wings strides in with a rolling cart filled with delicious-smelling food. Eyeing it closer, it doesn't look as delicious as it smells.

"Hello," I say to the scary-looking grumpy fairy over the sound of the squeaking wheels. "What do you have there?"

He rolls it to a stop at the table in the far corner—if you can call it a corner, since the room is round. The table is large enough for four—maybe six—people. Ignoring me, he flicks his wrist, and the shadows in the room slither up to the table, weaving together a dark cloth, and he begins to set the things on top of it.

When I approach him, I ask, "What is all this?" again, hoping he'll answer.

There is enough food on the cart to feed my neighborhood back home; some don't look like anything I'd typically eat: a salad filled with weird things, a pitcher with a mysterious glowing substance, a large white fish with more glowing matter scattered on top, and a brown squiggly pudding-looking thing topped with more glittering things.

"Moonshadow Nectar," he says, pointing to the pitcher. "That is harvest salad, veil-wrapped celestial fish, ember steak, ambrosia pudding, twilight tea."

"Oh." I look at everything he sweeps his hand by to show me. "And will you be joining me during this meal?"

He scoffs and begins to roll his cart away. "His Majesty will come by in a bit, I'm sure, to ensure you're eating."

To make sure I'm eating?

Not making me want to eat this weird shit any more than I already didn't.

"'Kay, thanks," I say, ignoring the food and walking over to the armoire

Fairy dude stops and looks at me. "You are going to eat, aren't you, miss?"

I shrug at him. "Um, no. I don't think so. Thanks for bringing it up, though. I appreciate it."

His face squints, each and every tooth in his mouth pointy. "What is it about the food you don't like?" His tone indicates he's offended, standing with his hands on his hips.

Maybe he's the chef of this meal. I don't want to offend anyone in this place. Especially those with scary black eyes.

"Oh, nothing. I'm just. I'm vegetarian."

I'm not, but I don't like fish, and I'm not keen on eating things that glow.

"His Majesty never told me such things."

My posture stiffens. "I'm not sure he'd know since he never asked me."

"He was certain you'd enjoy the meal I prepared." He takes a terrifying step toward me, leaving his cart behind.

I walk toward the table again, focusing on what's there. "It's quite all right. What's your name?"

"Dreadwynd." He puffs his chest out with pride. "Resident chef."

"Nice to meet you, Dreadwynd. I'm Sayah. It all looks wonderful, really. I'll try some, I promise. No need to worry."

His shoulders unclench, and the crease in his brow softens. "I can have His Majesty come join you for dinner if you'd like. It may make you feel better to see someone eat the food you're not used to in the mortal realm. I assure you, it's nothing like anything you've ever tasted."

"That'd be lovely, Dreadwynd, thank you."

With a bow of his head, he takes his squeaky cart, stops when he's over the threshold, and closes both doors.

I take one of the funky-looking utensils and poke at some of the glowing orbs that decorate the pudding. The steak does look somewhat edible, and the tea, which has floating unfamiliar fruit in it, looks interesting. The iridescent cups gleam in the twilight.

It wouldn't hurt to try the stuff.

If Trystan wanted me dead, I'd be dead already.

I pour myself some of the tea and take a sip.

Wow. Oh. My. Gods. It is like the nectar of them.

It's tangy and sweet with flavors I can't explain, and my mouth waters for more. I chug the glass all the way down and then fill it again to gulp another one.

Sitting down at the table, I spoon some of the harvest salad onto an empty plate Dreadwynd had set out and take the fork-like thing—it has two tines that are thick—and pierce some of the leafy greens. The flavors of different berries, nuts, and cheeses enter my mouth and the combination of whatever they are is a delicious and mysterious taste.

I decide to try some of the steak when I don't keel over and die from the whole-ass salad I just ate. The meat is so tender and juicy that it melts in my mouth and has a distant taste of smoke from an otherworldly fire. The steak is marinated in a secret blend of spices, and I devour the whole thing.

I'm surprised I'm not full yet. I've eaten way more than usual, and I keep going.

As I said, I don't usually eat fish, but I decide to try it since everything else is so amazing, and a symphony of flavors explodes in my mouth. It doesn't taste like fish but some essence of mystical water with flavors that can't be described in any modern tongue.

Once the fish is gone, all that's left is the pudding and the Moon Shadow stuff.

The pudding is a velvety concoction infused with magick itself. Each spoonful unfolds layers of celestial sweetness, leaving an enchanting aftertaste that will linger in my memory for the rest of my life.

Even when every single morsel of food is gone, I'm still not even remotely full. I could eat a whole other table full of the wonderful array of magickal food. I'm still hesitant to try the Moonshadow Nectar because I don't know what's in it and I don't drink alcohol. Three years of sobriety is not going down the drain for some fairy wine.

The air before me wavers, and a shape morphs into place. The air thickens, sounds seem to stop, and the very colors of the orb lights merge like brushstrokes on a canvas, painting a picture until Trystan is sitting in front of me, solid and commanding, making my heart stutter from the shock.

"Fuck!" I scream, pulling my robe more closed than it already is. "You gotta quit doing that," I scold him.

"My apologies, my pet." His blue eyes linger on mine. He finally has a shirt on. It's white and unbuttoned most of the way down, showing his immaculate chest with the thorns growing out of it. So. Still pretty much shirtless. "Did you enjoy your dinner?"

I nod, keeping my head down while allowing my eyes to wander to the entire table of food I ate. "It was very delicious."

"You upset Dreadwynd. Seems you told him that you don't eat meat and. Well"—his eyes scan the table, empty of any evidence there was ever food there at all—"looks like you lied."

"Now you gotta understand why I lied, though," I say, playing with the robe's tie. "I'm in a strange realm filled with food made from things I don't understand—that glows, mind you. You'd be skeptical, too."

He nods, pouring some of the glowing liquid into an equally glowing goblet. "Yet you didn't try the Moonshadow Nectar. It's exquisite, you have to try it."

"I would have, except I don't drink alcohol and had no idea if it has any in it."

He hands me the glass. "I'm aware you don't drink. There's no alcohol in here. It's Dreadwynd's specialty. It's infused with extracts from elusive midnight blossoms. The elixir offers a refreshing start to mornings or a wonderful end to nights, so it will either awaken your senses or dull them for a peaceful sleep."

Fuck it, I already tried everything else. I take a sip, and it sings to my senses with a wonderful blend of ethereal flavors. Sweet and nectary, I gulp it down to the last drop.

"That's my girl," he says, and now I'm suddenly worried about what was in the food and drink I just devoured.

I set the empty goblet down. "What's really in there?"

He smiles his wicked smile. "Nothing other than what I told you."

Something tells me he's not entirely telling me the truth.

My mind swims with exhaustion.

"Did you find everything to your liking in the bathing room?" he asks, standing, and stretching his glorious wings outward. I look at his pants, where his cock would be.

It would be interesting to fuck someone with wings. Like, I wonder if he can float us in the air while I ride him.

Fuck! Sayah, *no!*

Why the hell would that cross my mind?

I feel my cheeks flush from the lustful thoughts. I stand and walk over to the armoire. "Yeah, uh. Yeah. Great. Just. Um."

I have no idea what I'm saying.

Am I drunk?

The laugh he emits is equally menacing and comforting. I turn, but he's not there anymore.

Things are fuzzy and beginning to echo. "Trystan?"

"Yes, my pet?" He is standing next to the armoire now.

"Am I drunk?"

"No, love." He sooths a stray hair back into my towel. "Like I said, the nectar will dull your senses and make you sleepy, preparing you for bed."

I blink rapidly, looking in the armoire for something to wear to bed. All I see are dresses.

Very elegant dresses.

My mind is too fuzzy to determine why there are ballgowns in the closet, so I close the doors. "What do I wear to bed?"

The wicked smile picks up the corners of his mouth. "I sleep naked. I just assumed you did, too."

At home, I usually sleep naked unless Gauge is home. Otherwise, I'm in a tank top and boy shorts. "Sometimes," I admit, crossing to the settee at the foot of the bed. I'd like to not sleep naked here, though. "Do you have a tank top and shorts or something?"

He nods and holds his hands before the armoire. When he opens it, a whole new collection of clothing is in there, not a trace of the shimmering ballgowns I had just seen.

"Will these do?" He hands me a black pair of booty shorts and a gray tank top, identical to a pair I have at home.

"Yes. Thank you."

"Get some sleep," he says, moving to the doors.

"Trystan?"

"Yes?"

"Will you please let me contact my child or just send him some sort of assurance that I'm alive?"

He grants me a smile that doesn't quite reach his eyes. I meet them for a brief, unguarded moment. "I told you. You give me a bit of your power, and I will let you send word to Gauge."

Hearing my son's name on his lips does something wicked to my soul. But now, I would do anything to talk to my kid again. "Okay," I whisper, unsure what doom I just placed over Feylight.

He nods. "First thing tomorrow, then. We'll do the procedure, and I'll let you send word to Gauge."

He closes the doors, and the orb lights flicker in the wind.

What in Freya's name did I just do?

7

MURDER OF DRAGONS

—BASH—

Emerging from large iron doors, the cold, fresh air soothes my confined soul. I breathe it in, reveling in the freeing feeling of being outside. As I take in the vast expanse of Feylight Grove, the doors clang shut.

"Instead of wings, Feylight Castle has rings," Tallyn explains as we emerge onto an expansive front deck made of stone, leading to the longest walkway I've ever seen. "Each ring is made of an element. First one's air, with the second being fire, third is water, and lastly, Earth."

I walk to the edge of the balcony wall, relishing the jaw-dropping view from up here.

Feylight Castle is a sprawling estate, the castle's focal point in a series of rings. Stone and turrets entirely compose the inner part we stand on. The towers have spires, and there are notches for cannons.

The immediate rings aside from the castle are being blocked by fluffy, pink and white clouds. They sprawl out over the horizon, lit elegantly by the moons.

Nothing looks on fire.

"And we're going to the outer ring, you say?" I ask, measuring the distance the outer ring must be from here.

"Yes, that's the safest place to keep prisoners trying to break into the castle. Putting them in a dungeon within the castle would be madness."

"Yeah, madness is so unlike you," I jab at her, making her orange eyes alight with fire. "So, things will, what, burn the shit out of us and sweep us up in currents of death or ..."

"No." She laughs, brushing back the locks the wind blows into her face. "They're under barrier spells. The first four outer rings are dormant right now, so they're just dust and coals," Tallyn says, pointing to the landscape unfurling into eternity.

The view from this vantage point is incredible.

Her castle is so high in the sky that clouds float around it like a halo, and the walkway we're on dips down into them. Mountain tops, capped with white snow, peek out from the clouds.

She starts down the stone walkway.

"It'll take days if we move at this pace." Tallyn stops to survey the landscape. "Since they're still working on the portal, we'll have to hoof it."

"Hey, I can vamp-flash if you can keep up," I say, thrusting my body sideways down the narrow stairs nine yards.

The sound of her wings fluttering cuts through the air like a hummingbird. She catches up to me in a blink. "I can fly as fast as you can flash," she challenges, hovering ten feet in the air. "Let's go!"

Black streaks paint the sky when she shoots off.

I remove the weight I keep on the magick of movement and feel myself fly, racing down the tower walkway, zigzagging down at speeds maxing at a hundred miles an hour. The rush of the air and collaboration of speed beneath me is exhilarating, like it's removing layers of dirt the last five days have been.

When we finally reach solid ground, the first ring we pass

through is an empty valley, barren of everything except grass and trees with no branches and dirt. As I speed through it, chasing Tallyn's silhouette above, streaking the starry night sky in shadow, the dust kicks up behind me, leaving a trail of clouds.

This valley turns into a wall of wind, judging by how all the grass is bent to lie on its side.

Crossing over into the next ring, a section of blackened coals stretches on for miles. The fact that they aren't hot eases my mind a bit, but being in fae, the knowledge they could ignite at any second, sits wearily on my shoulders.

Tallyn's wings guide her to the ground; I slow my pace.

"This is the fire ring," she says, landing on the tips of her toes before walking beside me. "It ignites if there's a threat, throwing a mile-high and wide wall of fire with serpents and dragons made of flame within to keep anyone out."

As we approach, a ceiling of flame comes to life, blotting out the fully occupied night sky. "And when there's no threat, just someone visiting?" I ask, gazing up at the atmosphere that is now swirling three-dimensional fire above us—birds, dragons, and snakes flitting within it.

"Just a pretty fire show," she says, casting her orange eyes to the fire above us.

"It's nice. It's hot, but it's nice."

She smirks and then races off in front of me, her wings blasting me with a force of wind that kisses the sweat from my forehead.

I chase her shadow, the inferno above a blur of orange.

The next ring is a massive, churning river. The sounds of water scurrying over rock mix with the echoes of waterfalls in the distance, falling off the floating mountains.

"The water ring," she says. We've come to the edge of the impressive white rapids. She waves her hand, and two stone spires on each end rise out of the water, stretching toward the sky. As the top of the bridge reveals itself, it keeps moving up until a structure the size of the Brooklyn Bridge appears.

Tallyn smiles and steps on to it.

We fly across the bridge in a matter of seconds, the raging rapids beneath us churning recklessly, reminiscent of a watery grave should one fall.

The floating mountains are the Earth ring. A part majestically floats high above us, though some of the mountain ranges are also on the ground.

Tallyn, once again, graces the ground with her presence.

"This is the only remaining quadrant of Feylight that is inhabitable," she says. We climb up a hill leading to a valley between ground mountains and floating ones. "Because most of Luminara is in ruins or has been acquired by Neverdusk, most everyone lives in this outer ring."

As we continue our rushed journey to the outer edge of this ring, we pass several villages and houses, markets and farms, and spirit lanterns freckled throughout the mountainside. Everywhere is aflutter with life. Beings are all around us, fluttering in the sky, diving into the waterfalls, lakes, and rivers, and grazing on the grassy meadows we pass.

Most of the beings are fairies, but there are a lot of other creatures. So far, I've seen elves—which Tallyn told me are pretty much fairies, but without wings—gnomes, nymphs, sprites, and pixies.

What sets them apart, you ask?

Not a fucking clue.

I've deduced that the gnomes are beings around a foot tall who do most of the cooking and cleaning around the castle grounds.

Nymphs can be any sort of woodland creature without wings.

We passed by water nymphs in the water ring, which are crazy beings made of water. They had been splashing in the rapids, but they had no facial features. Men and women are distinguishable by their statures. Men are burly and muscular, while women are slender with curves. When they saw us, they melted into the water, either splashing into the pond or disappearing into the spray of the waterfalls.

The wood nymphs are tending to their tree houses when we walk underneath them. Giant willows—that put California Redwoods to shame—harbor an intricate city in the sky that mingles with the floating mountains, connecting massive buildings with smaller huts through suspension bridges made from twigs. The spirit lanterns gilding the entire branchways above us with a golden sparkle.

Pixies are just smaller fairies, about the size of a robin or blue jay.

A teal one has been fluttering around me for a while now, so when we stop for a breath, I hold out my hand to invite her to land. Her teal skirts pirouette in the breeze as she lands, her wings the color of bubbles. Her face is tiny, yet beautiful. She smiles at me right before she bares her sharp-as-fuck teeth and bites a chunk out of my finger.

"*Ouch!*" I scream, flinging her off.

Tallyn snickers and continues walking. "Be careful; they bite."

"Yeah, you don't say?" I say, licking the blood off my finger.

"We're almost there. Just a few more miles."

"Miles?" I shake my hand to relieve the tingling. "Just how big is this 'castle' of yours?"

"Feylight Grove is more of a sanctuary than a castle. It's all connected by these valleys, and we're all connected by these rings."

Once we pass under one rocky underpass of a mountain, we emerge on the other side to the brilliant night sky again. An enormous red dragon flies by overhead, followed by two green, and a gigantic blue dragon. Then, two tiny pink and purple dragons trail behind, screeching and biting at each other's necks. Another smaller teal one brings up the rear, blowing fire toward the little ones' butts to get them to catch up with the rest.

"Woah," I breathe, craning my neck to see the beauties high up in the sky.

"My babies," Tallyn says lovingly, having stopped to look up at them. "My murder of dragons. I've overseen each hatching since I've been queen. It's an amazing experience, and I've bonded with them all."

"Murder of dragons?" I still track the gorgeous beings gliding across the sky, ducking under mountain tops, and careening through the floating valleys.

The corners of her mouth pull up, and her orange eyes glitter. "Yes. I named it that. I wanted them to have a cool name for a flock like crows do. So, I call it a murder of dragons."

"Can you ride them?"

"Only the big ones. And only if they don't incinerate you first."

"Hmm," I say, thinking of burning to death.

"They may sense that you belong in the Neverdusk Dominion, being a vampire-demon hybrid."

"Yeah, I was just thinking that."

"Halcyon!" Tallyn calls over to a large man fairy with sky-blue skin and biceps the size of Texas who is chatting up a pink fairy over by a large mess hall cut right into the mountainside, looking like an entrance into a magickal fairy glen. He spots Tallyn and me walking toward—wherever the fuck we're walking toward—and comes fluttering over.

He bows his head in reverence. "Yes, my queen?"

"I need you to go help Sariana with the portals. Make sure whatever is making it glitch is resolved in thirty minutes. We're making abyssal, and we'll need to get out of there immediately after."

"Yes, my queen," he utters before flying off.

She heads toward the tunnel of trees. "C'mon, Bash, we should hurry."

"Who was that dude?" I ask, rushing to catch up with her.

"That was Halcyon. He's one of my lieutenants. He's a light fairy who specializes in vortexes and portal magick. I trust him to figure out what's making ours glitch."

"And that'll help to get the rest of my family here?"

"Yes, and to send these nightmares we're about to make into Never."

We are passing by the pink fairy with giant breasts, wearing nothing but skimpy petals covering them and a skirt made of flowers almost the same shade as her skin.

"My queen," she says and bows as we pass. She lowers her eyes to Tallyn but looks up at me, and a smile flirts with the corner of her lips.

"Elowen, go see what you can do to prepare for war. Ensure all the trenches are ready and the boundary spell is running. Also, see if Rowan can prepare the twilight weave, wind the enchantments into the boundary spell, and get Thistlewynd to prepare the dragons."

"Yes, my queen." She bounds into the air, making those boobs of hers bounce. She turns a glorious shade of blue before she takes flight.

"And who might that be?" I watch her fly off, getting a wonderful glimpse right up her skirt.

I may be with Sayah—at least I think I am—but I'm still a man.

You could still fuck her. Sayah would never know, says a voice. This voice is British, so another person I've killed in my life I'm sure.

"That was Elowen," Tallyn shares, seemingly not hearing the same shit I am—thank the gods. "She's a master at cerulean flight, meaning when she turns that shade of blue, she can travel faster than light. Rowan has mastery over twilight energy, allowing her to weave subtle enchantments, create illusions, and manipulate shadows—which will help in the boundaries. Thislewynd can also communicate with and influence the animals. She can telepathically speak to the dragons and tell them to be ready for anything."

"Damn, must be cool to be a fairy."

I race to catch up to her.

"We gotta step on it." Tallyn splits the air with a swoosh as she does her own form of cerulean flight. I also ramp up my supernatural speed, following her closely as we swerve around the mountain valley for miles.

By the time we get to the outskirts of the outer ring, I'm almost depleted of power.

The mountain valley gives way to a cliffside, overlooking the wide-open, purple meadow I think we traveled to by portal when I first came here.

I was a little delulu then, so it's hard to know for sure, but it looks familiar. Aside from the fact there are now deep trenches zigzagging across the scene, looking like someone took a paintbrush covered in brown paint and whipped it across a beautiful painting.

Two pole-looking spears are poking up from the side of the cliff. At our approach, I see two giant statues guarding an entrance directly below us.

"So, unless your powers involve levitation or hovering," Tallyn says, surveying her land. "I may have to fly you down."

"You'd like that, wouldn't you?" I ask her, sidling up to her flirtatiously.

"Or you can go ahead and see if your supernatural powers will soften your landing," she quips, fluttering up and into the air, hovering above the cliff.

I look down again.

It's a long fucking way down.

"I s'pose you can take me." I offer a subjective smile.

She rolls her eyes and approaches me.

"So, how do you wanna do this?" I ask her, holding up my arms. "You wanna piggyback it or cradle me like a granny or baby-side-hug style?"

"When I get above you, just hold on to my feet. I'm sure you're strong enough to keep hold, yes?"

I scoff. "Yeah, I definitely was just kidding about all that other stuff."

She gives me a speculative smile and hovers above me. I grab her black, thigh-high army boots, and she shoots into the air, then flutters us down the cliff's face.

The statues are fairies kneeling in sovereignty, helmets covering their heads, tunics made of nature lined with armor, spears in their hands, crossing their bent knees, and blocking the entrance with a magick shield. It's very intimidating. I know they're made of stone, but I feel that one flick of magick and they'll awaken and trample us.

Tallyn lands us before them.

"Valaethrin dor'an seilira, thyranith velas lirien!" she says in an old Luminarian language I recognize but don't understand.

The statues bow their heads, and the rumbling of stone makes the Earth quake as they stand to full attention, removing their spears, the glittering shield of magick following their movement.

I gape up at them, and the one on the right sets his eyes on me.

I'm pretty sure he wants to stomp me—which he very well could—but doesn't.

Bite their ankles! Henry says, standing beside a pillar directly inside.

It makes me jump again. "Stop that!"

He giggles and scampers ahead—if a ghost can scamper.

"What's that, Bash?" Tallyn says, glancing over her shoulder at me.

"Nothing. Just . . . nothing."

"Ah. More hallucinations?"

"I don't want to talk about it."

Tell her! Tell her I'm here and bound to you and destined to torture you until your last waking breath! Henry teases from a little ways ahead of Tallyn.

If I could snap a ghost's neck, I would start with Henry's.

"You know, Bash, if you are still seeing things, you might try to accept that this may just be your life now."

I quirk my eyebrow up at her. "What do you mean? I thought you said the side effects would pass?"

"No, I never said they'd pass. I said they may start to lessen. But I've been around a long time and have seen lots of things. I would imagine that if it isn't lessening, it may just be part of who you are now."

"Seeing ghosts is who I am now? Hearing the voices of people I've killed and other dead people is just who I am now?" My voice is laced with more annoyance than I intended.

She stops walking in the brown dirt tunnel we've been in since passing the statues. "Yes, Bash. It may just be part of your DNA now. Maybe you should try embracing it. See what happens."

I scoff and begin to walk ahead of her. Henry pops out from behind a dark curve in the tunnel again, and I jump. "*Fucking stop!*" I scream at him. He sticks his tongue out at me and pulls his ears. "You're telling me you can't see him?" I point to where Henry is standing, blowing raspberries at me.

"I don't see anything there, Sebastian."

"Fuck my life."

I move around Henry and continue down the tunnel.

"What do you see there, Bash?"

"I see this kid Henry that I used to play with as a kid. He died of consumption when he was six."

"Ah. Interesting. And whose other voices have you heard?"

"Joe, Monica, some voices I can't name . . . Dom."

"Dom?" She seems to perk up at this information. "You've heard Dom's voice?"

"Yes. He's the one who told me to name my demon in order for him to take over when Ember was stealing my blood."

Her smile flips upside down. With an approving nod, her eyebrows draw together as if she's deep in thought.

"What do you think that means?"

"I'm not sure, Bash. It may be that your dark power has now metastasized into something different. Something darker. Maybe you communicate with the dead now. Try talking to Henry when you're alone with him."

"I dunno. He seems only to want me to murder things and bite statues."

"Either way. When you're lying alone at night, talk to him. See what he says. Ask why he's here. Maybe you aren't hallucinating but seeing ghosts of the past."

I contemplate what she is saying as we descend a dark, damp-smelling tunnel.

As we arrive at the bottom, we smell wet dirt, melting wax, and body odor. Cells line the dirt walls, and inside each one is a different-colored fairy yelling and trying to grab through the bars. It seems Tallyn has some sort of soundproof boundary spell on the cells.

A teal fairy wearing a face of anger reaches for me through the bars. I duck out of her grasp, only to be grabbed from behind by another man fairy.

"What the fuck, Tallyn?"

"What?" she asks as we pass by at least thirty of these cells. "They're Nightshades. They're all bad, don't worry."

Like you're one to worry about someone being a monster, Henry says, walking alongside me.

"Shut up," I snap.

"I'll assume you're talking to your ghost, Bash, and not me," Tallyn says, a few feet ahead of me.

"Yeah. Where are we going exactly? And what do you intend to do?"

Tallyn takes a sharp left and another right to a set of very old wooden doors with a giant chain secured with a padlock. "Right here, Bash. And we're going to make an army."

8

ABYSSAL SPRITES

—BASH—

Tallyn opens the door to what could only be described as a war room. Carved into the mountainside, this room is far greater than the grand lunar room she had me in earlier. Weapons of every sort line the walls, a fireplace is chiseled out of stone, tables large enough to seat armies rest in the middle, and there are more bookshelves.

We cross the room to a far corner at the end, where she pulls a level. A statue turns on its axis, and another tunnel opens. Following her inside, spirit lanterns flicker on. We delve deeper into the mountainside, and we are met with long, winding pathways that would have anyone else lost. Darkness thickens, causing the lanterns to gleam brighter, making it seem we are gaining on the center of the earth.

Creepy innit? Henry asks. I glare at him, wishing he would just disappear altogether.

Tallyn's steps slow when we reach the end of the tunnel, a seemingly dead end. Her long sable locks whirl around her as she bends and moves her hand in a large circular movement. A glowing green line brightens the darkened chamber. The lines meld together with her completion of the circle, creating a bright neon portal undulating before us. With one sultry look back at me, she takes a step into it, disappearing altogether.

"Go on then," I tell Henry, motioning my arms for him to go first.

He shakes his head.

Tallyn pokes her head out, the sheen of the green veil wavering. "Bash. Move it!"

Before I can even think, she grabs my arm, and pulls me through.

Portal travel is always unpleasant. It feels like my insides are turning inside out, pressing against my skin, while the air shifts between hot and cold, leaving my body feverish. The disorienting sensation of tearing through time and space sends my stomach into a sharp ascent that leaves me on the verge of vomiting.

The vortex of black and blue crystals eats away at my vision as I warp through dimensions and barriers of existence, finally hurling me out of its exit. I fall to my knees, gasping for breath.

Swallowing down the contents of my stomach, I finally look up, and see we're back in the mirror village of Lake George.

"Why are we here?" I ask, arising from the ground, and taking in the crumbling scenery, dusting the sand from my already crusty and dirt-ridden pants.

"Because this is where I stored your blood," she answers shortly, like I should've known the answer.

"I don't understand why you couldn't have just come to get it and then brought it back with you instead of having me portal travel here. Also, how are we portal traveling if you said: a, that portal travel was banned, and b, you said it was broken?"

Ducking around a fallen tree, we go up into the little cabin I decimated her faes last time. "Sebastian." She sighs, seemingly tiring of my wonderful company. "Too many questions."

I look at Henry, who is walking beside me. "I think they're perfectly legitimate questions."

Henry bows his head in agreement.

"A, portal travel had a boundary on it, and we are outside that boundary. I did that for a reason in case of emergencies. B, I never said it was broken. I said it was glitching, and this one is always to here, so I knew it'd be fine. And c, because I want you here to get more of your blood and this place is already set up for it."

"Ah," I say, moving over to the chair in the corner I'd sat in.

The remnants of the fae I killed are still there—I mean, their bodies are gone, but there are deep brown and blue bloodstains on the walls and floor.

As Tallyn sits me down and rummages through the drawers for the supplies needed to gather the blood, there is a commotion of someone entering the domain we're in and the shuffling of feet, followed by commands.

Three fairies enter the room, one dressed in a uniform while two others are bound, gagged, and chained.

"Where do you want us to store the insurgents, my queen?" He is a strong, burly fellow with pointy ears and iridescent wings. Wearing brown-colored leaves that shape his tunic with tight brown pants, he dons a weapons belt with an array of different killing utensils and a machete strapped to his back. He is decorated with many medals, and multicolored stripes line his shirt cuffs.

There is a line of these soldiers out the door, with more and more insurgents tied up at their reign.

"Use some of that Luminis Bloom Pollen over there"—she points to another corner of the room—"and knock them out. You and Briar can set them up outside, chained to that wall where Gwynlyn and Thalira can get ready with the droplets. We'll go down the line one by one and feed them each one or two and then, when they all have had some, we'll prepare to leave, and close this portal for good."

"Of course, my queen," says the big soldier fairy dude,

pulling the other three fairies in chains with him. He then grabs a large jar filled with glowing blue powder.

"Thank you, Eirian."

I now see the other reason she wanted to come to this domain. It used to be part of Luminara, but since Trystan has taken over, it will soon be part of Neverdusk.

"How will you ensure they wreak havoc on Trystan and his Wild Hunt?" I ask, wincing when Tallyn stabs my vein to draw blood.

"Part of my Luminis Bloom Pollen has a spell in it that will guide them to any of Trystan's magick. They will be lured to it. We just want to ensure we're out of here before they break free because they also have orders to kill any fairy they come across."

"Oh. Lovely."

Kill! Kill! Kill! Henry shouts at the soldier, though he doesn't see Henry.

One of the tied-up fae looks exactly where Henry is standing, and I squint, about to ask her if she sees him.

Tallyn shoves a needle so far into my arm, and I swear I feel it hit my bone.

"*Freya's ass!*" I scream, while the corner of Tallyn's mouth quirks up.

"You all right there, Bash?"

Henry is doubling over with laughter.

I'm really starting to not like that ghost.

"Odin's ghost, Tallyn, I don't know if you got down far enough. You may want to—"

She shoves it in farther, and light blurs the corner of my eyes. "That far enough?"

"Fuck me. I need a drink. Anyone got any bourbon?"

A willowy fairy with short, bobbed black hair and blue wings, dressed in the same uniform as Eirian, smiles at me, yanking the chained Neverdusk fae to follow her. Her weapons glow, and she wears fingerless gloves, revealing pointy nails painted black. She pulls a flask from her back pocket and hands it to me.

"Yes! You are an angel." I twist the flask free and down four or five gulps of the stuff. It isn't bourbon, but the biting, peppermint flavor tells me it is hard liquor of the fae sort.

Dangerous for me to drink, but I really don't give any fucks right now.

"Easy there, Bash," Tallyn scolds. "I don't need your blood thinner."

Taking another swig, I hand the flask back to the fae girl. "Thank you . . ."

"Thalira. Nice to meet you . . . Bash, is it?" Her voice is like wind-chimes and musical flutes mixed with viper venom. Soft and sweet and potently stabby.

"Yep. The one and only."

Tallyn scoffs and squeezes my arm tighter. "Thalira, grab the bags out of the back room and then help Eirian line them up outside. This shouldn't be too much longer."

She bows her head. "My queen."

"You 'bout done there, *majesty?*" I ask once my mind feels hazy. "I need some left to continue living and gracing you with my glorious presence."

"Just . . . about . . . there." The last few drops drizzle into the bag she holds.

She pulls the needle free and lets my blood drip down my arm. I lick it up and stand, fighting the fainting feeling.

"You good there, Bashy-boo?" she asks me, the nickname making her grin.

"Yep. Right as rain. Let's go," I say, following her out the back door where the soldiers have tied the Neverdusk fairies up. "Hey, just a few minutes ago, that one there"—I point to the fae lady who saw Henry—"looked as though she saw my ghost boy. What do you think that's about?"

"That tells me that you are, in fact, seeing ghosts now, and not just hallucinating."

"Great."

She stands in line with her other soldiers, looking at the twelve fairies lined up on the wall, heads lulled with their chins touching their chests.

"No, it's good, Bash." She looks at me, and her orange eyes twinkle into mine. "You can use it to your advantage. Even summon them. I'd think of it as a gift."

I am a gift! Henry says. I go to kick at him, but he wavers.

"All right. Ready your droppers," Tallyn instructs her soldiers. They do what she says, each taking their droppers, and dipping them into the bags that both Tallyn and Eirian have. "When I say go, use a buddy system to open their mouths and drop no more than two drops into their mouths. Then we'll have approximately five minutes to return to the portal."

I cross my arms over my chest. "What happens after five minutes?"

Tallyn shoots a murderous glare my way. "They begin to rip you apart."

Oh. Just. Oh.

The fae soldiers each have a dropper, and two by two, they approach the twelve chained fairies. One of the soldiers takes the chin of the knocked out Nightshade fae, and the other readies the dropper.

"What can I do?" I ask, standing back with Tallyn.

"Just watch. Ready?" Tallyn asks. They nod. "Go!"

Each soldier carefully releases two drops of the blood into the fairies' mouths. Immediately, their skin begins to turn gray, their hair darkens, their pallor fades, and their wings turn corrosive to the point of resembling black tar. The sound of their morphing bodies is one of the oddest sounds I've ever heard, like squelching and squeaking mixed with a slither. Their heads tilt back, their faces elongate to the point of losing their features, and rows and rows of jagged teeth emerge.

A large fairy soldier at the end catches my eye. He hovers until everyone else has freed their drops before he even steps forward to do his. His buddy looks at him impatiently, and when the dude takes a step forward, his partner widens the mouth of the Never fae. Instead of being lithe and calculating, he squeezes the rubber tip, emptying the entire vial into the fae's mouth—at least ten to twenty drops.

"Veridian, what the fuck?" another soldier shouts.

The Nightshade fae that just swallowed the full contents of the dropper begins to morph at an alarming rate, not only blackening, but he starts to waver and shift, growing wider and taller. Eight black eyes pop out from the side of his head; his body turns round and hairy, and his arms and legs elongate and even grow new joints—where six more of them emerge from the sides of him, too—like a spider. The chains holding him burst with his height, and he shrieks, the rows and rows of teeth shimmering in the moonlight.

"Shit!" Tallyn says. "We gotta go! Now!"

I look back over my shoulder as the stupid-ass fairy dude that fed him too much blood is ripped to shreds, a limb of his landing in front of me. I'm forced to leap over it.

I use my vamp-flash to get the fuck out of there, soaring to the point where I know the portal lies. The soldiers are flying behind me, and when I am just about there, the fucking fairy-spider thing lands in front of me, having grown wings.

A flying fairy-spider with the torso and head of a man, while the rest of him is a giant fucking arachnid. Claw-like arms come out of his body and eight beady black eyes all blink their fathomless dead glare into me, close enough that I can see my reflection in them.

Yeah, no. I don't do spiders.

I shudder. I already feel a grotesque intensity inside me

when I see normal-sized spiders, but this is intensified a hundredfold. I try to ignore the whooshing of air that follows a very creepy skittering that can only be the flying spider. I spot Tallyn and the others across the distance and move toward them, only to be cut off once again by the spidey fuck.

I am not about to get bit again by yet another fucking supernatural thing.

Bash, over here! shouts Dominic's voice, within a cave caused by a toppled tower. I divert my flashing to where I heard his voice.

I dive under the tiny hole between the tower and the ground —it's just enough space to hide a person, and spidey slams into the stone of the column, trying to swipe at me with one of his legs. Luckily, I'm just out of reach, so he backs up a few inches, his hot breath and ugly twitching sound still too close for my comfort.

The abyssal sprites break free one by one, taking to the sky in an abysmal brush of black against the purple velvet sky, going after the Luminara fairies. I see one of the Feylight soldiers get mauled to death by those razor-sharp teeth—a singular smear of death to my broken eyes.

Tallyn flies over to the portal but she doesn't make it before spidey barrels into her, knocking her down. He tries to stab her a few times with his claws, but she blocks them with a skittering golden shield of sparks barely scathing the blow.

Are you going to go out there and fight that thing? Or stay in here like a scaredy-cat? Henry asks, his face and body glowing in the dark tunnel the column creates.

"Shut. Up. Bro. I don't see you doing anything to help them out there."

I can't. I am a ghost.

"You don't say."

I don't know, Bash. I don't think you can take him, Dom's voice says.

"Where are you, brother?" I ask the air.

One of the abyssal sprites must have sensed me or some shit because there is an opening between two toppled stone columns, and that fucker is getting in. I am pushed to the other side, the way I came in, and I have to move because that fucker is coming at me.

And fast.

Twisted gray limbs and fangs and claws are all I see before I fix my vision ahead of me and fly to the opening I came in.

Once I'm outside again, I find that all hell has broken loose. I have no weapons except for my powers, which won't do me much good right now.

I flash toward Tallyn, who just rolled under one of spidey's knife-claws. The sharp foot of the fairy-spider blows up dust, and the puffs of dark and glittering soil intensify the scene. As Tallyn rolls onto her back, another one of his legs is about to come down straight into her heart when I yell, *"No! Stop!"*

And the strangest fucking thing happens.

Every single abyssal fairy freezes in mid-air, mid-flight, mid-stab-the-fucking-fae-queen-in-her-heart.

The fuck?

I have no idea what just happened, but Tallyn rolls out from under him, and I race to her, worrying that, any second now, the damn fucking thing will come back to life.

The rest of her soldiers meet us—some bloodied and dirty, others seemingly unscathed.

"Caelum, use your shield, quick!"

The fairy dude who must be Caelum has a striking presence; his sharp facial features and high cheekbones define his jawline. His piercing blue eyes stand out against his fair complexion. His dark brown hair is slightly wavy in a tousled disarray, his pierced pointy ears sticking out from the tresses. When he throws his hands up, it reveals tattoos slithering down his arms. A shimmering bubble expands around us, knitting itself together with all the dew and condensation lingering in the air.

"Caelum has dewdrop resilience magick," Tallyn tells me, an odd expression twitching over her face, which she quickly discards in favor of a simple smile. Catching my face knit together in confusion, she explains, "Enhanced agility and resilience with the ability to summon protective barriers made of dewdrops, providing shields."

"Ah," I say. We are standing under the shimmering bubble now. The minute the shield completes itself, the movement of the abyssal resumes, and the gods-awful spider reactivates its menacing mission. The loud skittering and scraping chills me to my bones, and I just hope this shield thingy works until whatever-the-fuck Tallyn has planned to get us out of here happens.

"What the fuck was that?" I ask Tallyn. She is looking at Thalira, who has her fingers pressed to her temples and is seemingly whispering something to someone.

"It seems you have the power to control these things," the one who must be Caelum says, for he's standing spread eagle—his arms outstretched above his head. The sparks of light are leaving his palms and fueling the bubble we stand under.

"You mean they're bloodlinked to me?"

"Sure," he says, giving me a gaped-toothed grin, "whatever that means."

"It's when—nah, never mind. There isn't time. What's the plan?" I ask Tallyn.

"I just got word from Halcyon, who says the glitch in the portal around the castle is fixed," Thalira states, pressing her fingers to her temple. "He's going to move it from where it was on the other side of the lake to here. He's working on it now; should be any—"

She's cut off by the sound of crackling coming from the ground below us. It's as though an invisible hand unzips a zipper. Blue mass undulates beneath us, resembling a liquid puddle, yet offering no reflections.

Tallyn faces her soldiers. "Go!" she commands.

A small soldier—the size of a middle school child with features of an adult—moves toward it, crosses his arms, and jumps into the puddle, reminiscent of a skydiver jumping from a plane. He's followed by each one of his comrades until it's just me, Caelum, and Tallyn left in the bubble.

Caelum's shield starts to wane. One of the blade covered legs of the spider pierces through it and misses Tallyn by a hair. Caelum moves in the nick of time before the next one comes through.

"Bash, go!" she shouts over the fray, sounds of the wild creatures outside getting louder through the tear.

Sounds of scraping follow me as I jump into the portal. The awful upending of myself flipping through a vortex undoes me once again, and when I hit the ground of a room with cold stone floors, I land on my knees and retch.

Luckily, nothing comes out, as we're now in a room filled with people and that would be embarrassing.

I heave one more time, my stomach struggling to get a grip on reality. Tallyn's heels gracefully hit the stone floor behind me and I glare at her army boots with disdain.

If portal travel was an Olympic sport, this bitch would have just received a perfect ten for landing.

Caelum appears next, though he is not as graceful as Tallyn. He falls on his side, landing next to me.

Halcyon zips the portal shut and offers a hand to Caelum to help him up.

"Bash." My mom's voice comes from above me. How long she's been standing there, I have no idea. But I look up, heart swelling, to see my mother's face all the same.

I take her offered hand and stand; she pulls me into a hug.

"Mom," I say, enjoying her existence. I've never been so happy to see my mom.

I may be a big bad vampire villain, but fuck spiders. And that one was scary as fuck.

"Sebastian," she says, stroking the back of my neck. There's a splinter in her voice, something raw and watery, like it's taking everything she has not to fall apart. I don't even want to think about that right now. I let her go, and Ollie is right there, pulling me into the next hug.

"Hey, little brother," I say into the nape of his neck.

"I was so worried we were going to lose you, too." Ollie's voice comes out creaky, like wood on the verge of collapse.

His words bite into my soul, and again, I fight back the tears that threaten to swallow me alive. I cannot cry right now. I just cannot. "I'm good, brother. I'm good."

Clearing my throat, I let go of Ollie and scan the room.

"We lost Liora, Branthorn, Kairn, and Veridian," Tallyn says, brushing the dirt from her black leather and corset uniform.

"Veridian was a moron," Thilara states, cleaning off black blood from her long sword. "We had to kill three abyssal just 'cause he wanted to play scientist."

"Yeah, what the fuck was that . . . thing?" I say, shuddering at the thought of it.

I want to burn the image of it from my mind. It's going to make me have nightmares for months.

"Awe, Bashy-poo," Tallyn teases me. "Are you afraid of spiders?"

"Not afraid. I just don't like them."

"He's afraid," my mom chimes in, nudging me with her hip.

"Anyway." I turn the attention back to that gods-awful thing. "That . . . spider-fairy thing. Will that get to Neverdusk?"

"Yeah," Caelum says, holding his arm, and wincing. "That thing's lethal. It got me in the arm right before I jumped through."

Tallyn's face turns to worry. "What? Where?" she asks, pulling his injured arm toward her and rolling up his sleeve.

"Oh, fuck." Caelum gasps, and we all come closer to look.

The scratch is as black as coal, running from his wrist to elbow. Dark, spidery veins are creeping away from the scrape, as though each of his capillaries have gone to tar. The skin around the scrape is gray like old movies, looking like a deep fissure of tar running through the middle.

"Oh, no, Caelum," Tallyn breathes, pulling his sleeve back down.

Caelum's sharp features turn flummoxed. "What? What is it?"

"They have corrosive components in their venom. Not only does it desiccate you, it will slowly devour your soul."

Caelum's eyes widen. "What does that mean? Do you have an antidote?"

Tallyn looks at me. "Maybe." She turns back to Caelum. "But it may kill you."

9

BLOODLINKED

—BASH—

"**M**ind elaborating there, miss 'queen of intense cliff-hanging sentences?" I ask Tallyn. I try to force the exasperation back down, but I'm tired of these fae innuendos.

"Since your blood made the damn thing," Tallyn says, her bright eyes winking in the low light, "we may be able to use your blood to combat it. But it could backfire. He may combust with the venom of the abyssal spider or turn into something nefarious. Or it may kill him."

The possibilities are endless, Henry's voice says, though I don't see him anywhere.

Caelum's jaw tightens, his gaze unwavering. "Let's do what we must." He turns to me, squaring his shoulders, and rolling his neck, the way a boxer does before stepping into the ring. "If I turn into one of them, don't hesitate—take my head. I won't become one of those mindless things." Tallyn gives him a quelling look. "We will. Let's go down to the war room, just in case. Halcyon, did you get the other portal to work?"

"Yes, my queen. We just needed Rowan and Elowen to help

with the last part. We've repaired the barrier spell, but the glitch needs more. I can portal you to the war room, and by the time you're back, we shall have the rest of the Sangravellis and the like."

"Very good, Halcyon, thank you. Bash, you ready?"

Goodie, more portal travel.

"Yeah," I answer, then grab my mom's hand. I give her a smile that hopefully quiets her worry. "I'll be back soon."

Her eyes are puffy from crying, and I don't want to cause her any more pain.

I wonder what they've been up to since I've been . . . incapacitated.

Halcyon takes his hand and forms a blue orb, which he places in the air and stretches. This time, instead of a swirling blue vortex, it simply looks into the war room we were in before spidey fuck.

Holding his injured arm close to his chest, Caelum steps through. When he looks back at us, it's like he's in a painting.

"Fae's wild," I say as Tallyn steps through next. "All right. This has to be better than portal travel," I joke to Halcyon as I walk by him. He doesn't like my jokes.

Ollie sends me a smile before I step through the wormhole.

Once on the other side, the portal zips up, and the heavy doors shutting echoes in the vast room, Tallyn slams a large bolt home, sealing the doors shut, locking us inside.

She saunters up to a cabinet on the wall beside the fireplace, bringing out more glowing liquid and three goblets. Caelum takes his; she hands mine to me and keeps one for herself.

"I'm thinking," she says as she swirls the golden liquid around in her glass, "that because you could control the abyssal, you are somewhat of a sire to them. And because of that, I think your blood may suffice as an antigen to the venom."

Caelum takes a drink from his goblet. "Or?"

"Or it could have a negative effect," she says, setting her goblet down on the hutch.

"Either way. It has been an honor serving you, my queen." He bends to her in a low bow before straightening and slamming the rest of the liquid back. "Just promise me that if I turn into an abyssal . . . pierce me through the heart with this." He hands her the sword hanging from his back. The blade shimmers within the strange phantom light, a metal unlike any I've ever seen. It's as though it's forged from moonbeams. The hilt is adorned with intricate silver vines curling up and around emerald gemstones, pulsating like a living, breathing thing. The blade is impossibly thin and sharp, with a subtle radiance that shifts colors when it catches the fae light. It looks ancient and alive. "I am ready to die."

How fucking valiant.

"Okay, how do we do this?" I question, tipping back my goblet, and downing the liquid. It's sweet and tart and makes me feel lighter.

Tallyn brushes her hair back behind her shoulders. "I want you to bite him where the scratch is, but don't drink his blood. Pierce deep enough that your venom gets into his bloodstream."

Nodding, my silent conversation with my inner vampire breezes through me like a melody, taunting him to come out to play. The tingle in my gums welcomes my fangs, and I feel them elongate. It's wild, like feeling your hair grow. As the whites of my eyes seep into the blue, my focus zooms in, noticing the flecks of dust in the air, the perspiration beads on Caelum's head, and the growth of Tallyn's hair. Everything is hyper-sensitive in vamp mode.

Caelum squares his shoulders and prepares for my bite. I take his arm and hiss just before I bury the fangs deep within the scratch. The crunching sounds send chills to my marrow. Caelum tips his head back and takes a deep breath, embracing the coin toss of his fate as it unfolds.

I'm careful not to draw any of his blood into my mouth, though it is difficult to deny.

The sweet drug of crimson is one quick suction away, but I refrain.

When it feels deep enough, a strange tingle has me hasten to get my teeth out of him.

The two holes left by my fangs glow with blinding, brilliant gold. The light chases away the black veins and ashen tones of his skin, receding back to the original wound. When the golden light reaches the black fissure, it intensifies and dissolves it, then ricochets through the rest of his body. A radiant halo bursts from within him, mirroring the shield he once cast around us, expanding until it engulfs the entire room.

I look over at Tallyn, who's staring in wonder. Her blasé demeanor melts into enthrallment while Caelum's entire being rises off the ground, the fissures of light encapsulating his every molecule. The corrosive marks melt; his eyes go golden bright; the air in the room heats up. It looks as though he may explode.

I back away in case he does. I'm about to duck behind a chair when the light dies down, and he returns to his feet. His eyes close with the fading of the fissures, and when the room's temperature recedes to normal, he opens his eyes again, only to reveal they're still softly glowing.

"Caelum?" Tallyn asks.

He doesn't answer, only looks at her intently with a blank stare, eviscerating his stoic demeanor.

"Caelum?" I ask.

He looks directly at me. "Yes, Sebastian?"

That's weird.

Tallyn's dark brows draw together. "Caelum, do you feel all right?"

Henry appears and laughs. *He's in love with you!*

I mouth "Shut up" at him and glance back to Caelum.

"I feel fine, Tallyn, thank you."

She sets her eyes on me, and for a second, it seems she isn't pleased about him not addressing her as "my queen," but she lets it go for a minute. "All right. Well, good. It seems we have a cure for an abyssal scratch or bite."

"Yeah. That's . . . okay, then. Shall we?" I motion for us to leave this little circle we're in.

"I know where they are," Caelum says in a monotone, creepy, almost robotic voice.

Tallyn's heels clack as she steps closer to him. "What do you mean? Who?"

"The abyssal sprites. I can see them in my head. I can hear them communicating telepathically with each other. They're heading to the Nixia Portal, where Trystan will make the first stop of his Hunt."

"Interesting," I say, looking at Tallyn.

"Indeed," she concur. "That little gift will indeed come in handy, I'm sure."

"Shall we see if they could get the rest of my family here?" I ask, watching Henry as he draws closer to Caelum.

"Who might you be, little sir?" Caelum asks Henry.

Henry freezes. As do I.

"You can see him?" I question.

"That little guy right there?" He points, and Tallyn and I look at Henry.

I see him. The vacant and gaped-mouthed look Tallyn is displaying tells me she does not.

She looks back at Caelum. "You see Bash's ghost child?"

"I do," Caelum states, waving at Henry.

Henry merely stares at him.

Fucking weird.

"This is weird. It's all weird. Can we go?" I ask, feeling my mind breaking. "I need a fucking shower and to change my clothes."

Tallyn nods, and while she and I walk toward the doors, Caelum remains standing still. "Caelum, let's go."

He doesn't move.

She looks at me in exasperation.

"Caelum. Move," I demand.

Caelum twitches his head in a nod and moves his feet forward.

10

WILL-O-THE-WISP

—BASH—

Tallyn presses a glowing blue glyph on the wall, signaling Halcyon that we're ready for a portal home.

A wormhole unzips between us—silent and sudden. It stretches open like a wound in the air, warping light around its edges. I can see *through* it, see *around* it—see Tallyn standing across from me and Halcyon waiting on the other side.

It's like staring into a mirror that refuses to reflect.

Tallyn steps through first, crossing the threshold with the calm of someone who's done this a thousand times. She reappears beside me in the room with my family, as if she never left. I glance through the portal again—Caelum's still on the other side, watching me.

His gaze pins me—expectant, unreadable. Like he's waiting for me to move, to speak, to do *something*. But I don't know what.

And honestly? The whole *bloodlink* thing is messing with my head. I don't know how I'm supposed to feel about having a guy literally tied to my veins.

"Go on then," I tell him.

He smirks at me, nods, and steps through, his golden eyes fading into their blue.

With a shake of my head, I step through it next and find myself in the beautiful lunar room gilded by stars.

The rest of my family is finally here with us.

As the portal zips back up, I glance over at the fireplace where my dad and mom are holding Scarlet, who's fallen to her knees on the rug by the fire.

Ollie is kneeling before Hattie and Jasantha. They are sitting on the brown leather couches, also by the fire, while Claire sits on a table behind him, resting her hand on his back. The others with Laureya—Kaston, Draelle, Laith, and Ryan—are sitting around a table talking, seemingly undisturbed by the knowledge of my brother's death.

Two things happen when we enter this room.

The first is Caelum immediately loses track of life, storms, and the meaning of words the minute he sees Scarlet. I don't know if she notices or feels it, but I do.

And second, I spot Laureya.

I. See. Red.

I haven't seen her since the whole "she-bit-me-and-I-almost-died-from-a-formweaver-bite" incident.

White overtakes the red of my vision and tunnels it, sending stars where everyone else is concerned.

I pull the weight off my power to speed over to Laureya and break her fucking neck, but there's a bitter cold sensation wrapping up my legs. I glance down. My feet are literally frozen to the floor. Ice has formed around my legs and feet, cementing me in place.

Looking over my shoulder, I spot Tallyn's hand on Caelum's shoulder. The touch tells me she's forcing him to use his dew magick on me, freezing me to the ground.

Traitor, Henry jabs at Caelum.

"Sorry, little guy, I still answer to her," Caelum tells Henry, his arms outstretched, and palms wide. Magick sizzles between his fingertips.

Tallyn, still not seeing Henry, shakes her head. "Yes, and we don't need you killing any others who could be useful to me. We may need her and her faux phoenix power."

Turning back around, Laureya is smirking, flipping me off.

It doesn't help the murderous rage I feel toward her.

"Besides," Tallyn continues as I growl at Laureya, "your girl-friend may not like you murdering her sister."

I hold Laureya's stare. "Oh, on the contrary, I think Sayah will be fine with me ending Laureya for her."

"Regardless. Not now. Wait until after my war with Trystan, and then you can do whatever you want with her."

I nod. "I'll accept that."

"Good. Now—" She lets go of Caelum's shoulder. His blue eyes pierce mine as he shrugs, like he's sorry he had to vex me with his stupid dew power. He drops his hands, and the ice melts to nothing. "Maybe go see how your sisters are doing with news of Dom. And shower. You stink."

I wink at her and smirk.

My sisters and I have no relationship. They hate me; I hate them. Yet, something stalls my heart when I see the look on Scarlet's face. Her mascara is running down her face, Dom's death coloring her emotions.

I stroll up to her and my mom and dad and throw my arms around them, joining them in mourning and sadness and unadulterated grief.

I've seen men cry before—Ollie, Dom, my friends, cousins, uncles. I've watched grown men piss themselves, beg for their lives, and soldiers weep on battlefields. I've seen warriors brought to tears by their losses. But nothing—nothing—shatters me faster than seeing my dad cry.

I have never seen this man cry at any point in all my two hundred thirty-six years of life. Seeing him now, holding Scarlet and my mom while sobbing, rips my heart apart anew. Every morsel of pain, every molecule of sorrow I've shoved back down over the years, breaks open like a dam. A deluge with such force fractures my dam like paper, shredding me into tiny little bits. I can't help the sob that erupts out of me, weeping into my father's shoulder.

I cannot remember the last time—before this morning or whenever I found out about Dom—I did cry. If I could remember, I know it's never been in front of them.

Especially in front of my dad.

He already despises me, so crying in front of him would only confirm what he's always believed—that I'm weak.

I think the last time I cried where he could actually see me was when I was seven. Ollie had broken my favorite toy, and I got whipped for it.

It was a different time then.

No one has ever seen me and my father embrace. The fact he allowed me to wrap my arms around them and even leaned his head in my direction is something that would only happen in a circumstance such as this.

Dom's death.

The air feels different. It's heavy, like a storm pressing down on the world, ready to send updrafts back into the atmosphere in a vicious cyclone of loss. The room slants to this sad reunion, all the fairies quietly watching the vampires weep, and time itself sets down its sword to honor the life that was my brother.

Scarlet wriggles out of our embrace, and I step back, swiping my tears with my shirt.

"Can I see him?" Scarlet asks, wiping her dripping nose with the back of her hand.

"I'll take you to him." Caelum is here suddenly, stepping up from where he was bracing the wall.

"Who the fuck are you?" she bites out.

"Caelum Skysong, m'lady." He bows his head, and her face

winces even more. "Second lieutenant in Luminara's second infantry division."

Scarlet shrugs away from Caelum as Tallyn steps between them.

"I can also escort you there," Tallyn offers, sending Caelum a "What the fuck?" glare. "He's in my burial chambers. I've fixed the temperature down so that he may rest peacefully while you all prepare for burial or whatever it is you do for your dead."

"I'd like to go as well," my dad says, nonchalantly dabbing at his tears and squaring his shoulders.

"We all can," Mom adds, taking his hand. "Bash, would you like to—"

"No," I cut her off. I hadn't meant to. "No, thank you, Mom. I can't. I can't see him like that. I'm not ready."

My mom gives me an understanding gaze. My dad, on the other hand, looks at me contemptuously. I don't really give a fuck right now; I can't handle his distain at this moment. I need to keep my head clear and help Tallyn prepare for this battle of our lives, and I won't be able to do that if my thoughts are weighed down by the visions of my brother lying still, gray and desiccated, on a cold slab of marble.

"It's all right, Bash." My mom reaches for my hand. "We'll see you in a bit."

I take her hand, and she gently strokes the back of my palm with her thumb.

"Right this way," Tallyn encourages, her heel clack echoing as she saunters off.

My mom lets go of my hand and turns, grasping onto my dad's elbow and leaning her head on his shoulder. They follow Tallyn. Scarlet barely looks at me as she passes, but I swear there's a tiny smile on her face for me.

Progress.

I do fucking stink.

"I need to shower," I announce to the room.

"There's a washroom down the hall," Thalira says, pointing toward a long stone hallway. She grabs a drink and sits by the fire. "Just ask the wardrobe for clothes you want and your size, and they'll appear."

Nodding, I make my way to the washroom.

Once I find one of the enormous bathroom and shower, clothes my exact size appear in the wardrobe.

I change and return to the room.

Ollie and Claire remain, and so do Laureya and her fuck-tards. I really don't feel like being around her, so I grab a bottle of glowing amber shit and head out onto the balcony. Ollie and Claire join me.

The air is still warm from the day, the two moons are getting closer to each other, and bright stars blister the night with their ambiance.

"So," Ollie says, grabbing the bottle from me after I shoot some back. This time, it tastes like oranges, pineapples, and other fruit flavors I cannot name.

"So," I say.

"What's been going on with you since we saw you last?"

Ollie sits in a brown and thorny chair that resembles wicker before pulling Claire onto his lap.

"Oh fuck, where do I start?" I ask, sitting in the chair next to him. He hands the bottle back to me, and I take another drink. I pass it to Claire next. "I see dead people now, so there's that."

Ollie's face twists up in a weird, intriguing way. "What?"

"Yeah. Cool, right?"

"How the fuc—What do you mean?" he asks, leaning back. "What do you see?"

"Well, it started with just thinking I was going nuts from the formweaver venom. I heard voices in the walls. Even Dom's. But then Henry. Remember Henry?"

Ollie's blonde hair twists in a gust of wind. "The bloke that lived down the road from us when we were kids? That Henry?"

"Oh, yeah. That one. Five-foot-one of him and his old Victorian garb, too. All glowy and shit. He's fun."

Don't! Henry's voice is right behind me, making me jump five feet into the air. *Don't talk about me like I'm not here!*

"You all right, brother?" Ollie asks, his face strained to not burst out laughing.

I flip Ollie off and turn my head to see Henry's ghostly ass leaning against the balcony, glowing in the moon's light. "Fuck you, too," I say to Henry. I turn back to Ollie and Claire. "Yep. Just Henry. On cue."

"He's here, now?" Claire asks, hunkering her head down like Henry will sit on her.

I snigger. "Yep. Right behind me. You can't see him?"

"I don't see anything," Ollie states, trying to look over my shoulder.

Claire squints. "Yeah, me neither."

"Welp. He's there. Trust me. One of the Nevers saw him when we went to make the abyssal, and now Caelum can see him, too. So I know I'm not completely mad."

"Do you see any others? Like . . ." Ollie stops here because he doesn't want to say Dom's name.

"No, Henry's the only one I've seen. Dom's voice saved me from Ember earlier, though." I explain who Ember was and how Dom's voice helped me name my demon.

"So Dom saved you," Ollie concludes, his eyes a soft mixture of ominous and intrigue. His voice is tinged with disbelief when it comes to Dom being dead, but in a way, he is still with us, fighting for us and keeping us safe.

"He did," I mutter. I am just as hesitant to truly dive into what that means. Part of me is not ready to unpack that just yet.

"And what did you all just get back from doing when that Caelum dude got bit by that—"

"Giant flying spider?"

The corners of Ollie's lips pull up like he's fighting a grin again. "Yeah."

"Don't fucking laugh. You weren't there. You don't know."

Claire's smile steals her whole face. "Are you afraid of spiders, Bash?"

"Bro!" I grab the bottle from her as she and Ollie collide into giggles. "You have no idea how fucking big and ugly and hairy that thing was. And did I mention that it *flies*?"

They both collapse in on each other.

Think it's so fucking funny.

"Guys. I'm not playing. It was huge. And scary."

Claire grabs her abs like it's hurting her to breathe.

"I'm not . . . This ain't . . . Fuck you guys." I stand and take a pull of the golden shit. I start to walk back in.

"Bash, wait!" Ollie says, laughing still but grabbing my arm. "Don't leave. Tell us about your spider thing."

"I'm glad you think it's so funny."

I'm not mad. I sit back down. It's a moment of levity that we all need. I laugh with them for a bit.

But they really have no idea how dangerous and disgusting and terrifying that flying fucking spider is.

An hour or so later, after everyone has retired to their rooms, I'm sitting on the balcony alone, having a repartee with the moonlight. I gaze up at the two moons as they silently spill their heavenly secret to the night sky. I feel an intrinsic force pulling me to them more fiercely than the single moon back home.

Knowing Sayah is under these same moons fills me with

some comfort, but then I think of her face and miss her so much it steals my breath and pierces my lungs with turmoil.

Nothing makes sense right now without her.

I hope she's okay.

I wish she could send me a sign to let me know she's still alive.

A twinkle on the horizon catches my gaze. A layer of clouds sits above the rings of the castle, the moon turning them into a blanket of silver. Three or four break loose from the pack and float in my direction, dancing like jellyfish dance under the water.

At first, I think they're just new parts of Luminara I've yet to experience, but as they dance closer, the intrinsic force pulls at me again, telling me there's more to them than that.

They are a sign.

As they come closer and closer, they look like upside down dandelions—their hypnotic dance making their tentacles sway in the breeze. They get smaller with their approach; one breaks free of the other three and floats up to me.

I hold my palm out, and it hovers three inches above it.

The light it gives off is melodic, soothing, and warm, and I can feel the vibrations coming from it. It undulates, as though it's breathing the same air I am.

I don't know why, but it reminds me of Sayah.

The little thing feels like Sayah.

It's a will-o'-the-wisp, Henry says, suddenly by my side, staring at the gorgeous thing fluttering above my palm.

"Thanks, but I don't know what that is," I say, leaning closer to get a better look.

Before Henry can answer me, the dandelion-looking jellyfish thing turns into vapor and flies up my nose.

It smells like menthol and is soothing to my lungs. All my worries melt from my being, and I feel light and tired.

I put the bottle down, go into my room, and climb out of my boots.

Undressing to my boxers, I slide into the giant bed, the cool sheets greeting me. I close my eyes the moment my head hits the pillow.

Then, what feels like mere seconds later, I open my eyes to find the room has dissolved around me. Startled, I'm sitting in an endless expanse of darkness. A golden tether lies on the floor, trailing from beneath my bed. It winds into the infinite shadows, glimmering softly, tempting me to follow and discover where it leads.

When I stand, my bare feet hit the surface of what looks like a dark, black lake, chilling yet warm simultaneously. I walk beside it into the black void.

The only thing lighting up the dark is this golden tether.

Silence is warped; it unfolds around me, muffling the warbling of the world outside.

Dreams are wild.

I've been walking for hours when a boat on the horizon comes into view.

The familiar outline of it stalls me.

It's my houseboat back in California.

The boat's rustic black wooden exterior, though weathered by time and the elements, greets me like an old friend. The ramp up to the front door unspools before me, reflecting the golden tether wavering in the black surface I'm walking on.

Rhythmic waves, set to the beat of my heart, lull in the background. The metal of the ramp clangs as my bare feet incline toward my red front door, mixing with the sounds of the ocean. I turn the brass handle, a saltwater aroma entering my nostrils. The intimidating gargoyle knocker looms around the peephole, glaring at me as I enter.

I open the door and am welcomed by all my things.

The entire space opens up to the top floors above the deck,

with wooden rafters for ceilings and long windows overlooking the ocean—covered in the double-paned UV-protected windows I had installed before Sayah made me my necklace. A huge, plush brown sectional divides the rooms from the kitchen to the living room, where I have my favorite of all my things.

My collection of books.

The bookshelves cover the entire wall on the far side. A rolling ladder on casters is the only way to reach the books at the top and also to get to my loft bedroom.

The open loft where my California king sits overlooking the living room can also reach some of the books. It runs perpendicular to the bookshelves—so one end of my bedroom is covered in the same wall of books.

But that isn't what draws my eye.

What sets my whole world on fire and stops the breath in my chest is the love of my life, sitting on the couch, reading a book.

Sayah.

11

THIS IS HIS SHATTER

—SAYAH—

My head feels fuzzy as I pad my way into the bathroom to splash water on my face.

Trystan said that the elixir I drank didn't have alcohol, but gods-damn do I feel fucking drunk. I haven't had this feeling in my body in such a long time. The way everything inside me loosens, the tingly euphoric bubbles tickle up my arms, and the filter in my brain seems to weaken. I want to talk all night and tell stories of my life and watch people's reactions to the shit I've been through and still stand before them.

Catching a glimpse of myself in the mirror, the towel remains around my hair and I pull the tangled locks free. Glancing around the room for some sort of drawers or anything a brush would be kept in, I spot built-in shelving at the far end of the bathroom.

Tossing the towel into a pile on my way, the cold tile kisses my feet as I cross the room, drawn toward the shelves like they might answer all the questions I haven't dared to ask.

The built-in shelves contain an array of things I would likely have at home—brushes, combs, rubber bands, scarves, bobby pins, hair dryers, a straightener.

How long does he intend to keep me here?

I pick up the bamboo brush and stalk back to the mirror, brushing out my hair. Once it's all good and untangled, I slip out of the robe and into the boy shorts and tank he gave me.

The magick lights go out when I leave the room, and I walk out onto the balcony to whisper to the unfamiliar moons.

Even though they aren't my moons, I feel a pull to them all the same. The gorgeous pink and purple glow bleeds their eerie tone into the water, cascading the light in a lavender haze. The Nocturna Sea spreads out its reach beyond where the eye can see.

As I trace the horizon with my eyes, looking all the way right and left, I notice a planet in the background with rings taking up the entire sky. How I didn't notice before is beyond me.

I whisper delicate wishes to the moons and the planets, asking them both to let me at least see Bash in my dreams tonight to make sure he is safe.

Guilt is climbing through my bones again as I wonder why, on this realm or any other, Dom would be the one to die first. I am here in the gods-forsaken place with the author of Dom's death, eating and drinking and being merry while Dom's body grows cold.

That stitch in my heart that has wound itself around my lungs and woven in and out of each of my ribs nearly makes breathing impossible. I grasp the thorny railing as if to borrow some of its strength. Time feels heavy on my skin, and I wish with all my being to not let it be true.

"Please don't let Dom really be dead. Let that just be a lie Trystan is telling me to make me do things for him."

I don't know who I'm wishing to, but I will take anyone who listens.

Glowing embers of foreign plants dance on the horizon and I'm not sure if it is part of my fever dream or if I'm really seeing it. They look like dancing jellyfish on the air, yet tiny. They come into focus more and more, and just when they are within an arm's-reach, I stretch out my hand as if to offer one of them a place to land.

And land it does.

I am uncertain how I know this, but they are will-o'-the-wisps. The little dancing flower makes my palm glow, and I pull my hand closer to my face to get a better look.

In a breath of air, it evaporates into vapor, and shoots into my nose, forcing me to inhale.

Great. What more fairy drugs and alcohol can I take today?

Drunken melodies evaporate my guilt and my thoughts drift back to Bash again, thinking of his unreal blue eyes and the tether we have that connects me to him.

I don't know what the little dancing fairy thing has done to me, but I feel that I need to close my eyes.

I wander back into the room and climb into the giant bed.

It feels like it is made from clouds—the perfect amount of softness and just the perfect temperature. The sheets are cool, the comforter is fluffy, and the pillows are like giant marshmallows as I snuggle into bed and pull one pillow up to hold, wrapping the fluffy comforter up around my head.

I awake to the will-o'-the-wisp ticking my face and when I sit up, all things in the room have disappeared and I'm sitting in a sea of black, the floor waving and reflective like water, only, it isn't wet when I set my feet down on top of it. A golden tether is the only light besides the will-o'-the-wisp, which cascades feathery silver light over the floor water.

It starts dancing away and I follow it, sure to hold on to the tether.

I don't know where we are going. I look around a few times and it's all just an ocean of black.

I'm kind of scared but something is telling me to keep going, something wonderful is waiting on the other end. I know by the feeling I get from this will-o'-the-wisp.

Up ahead is a red door.

It's blood-red and ominous in the darkness. A gargoyle knocker swirls around the eyehole.

I knock, and instead of someone answering, the door just opens.

Inside is a wide-open apartment, large couches and a loft with a bedroom, a glorious kitchen accented with black appliances and windows that look out to the ocean, an ocean I know is from my home realm because only one moon hangs above the sky.

An entire wall is lined with towering shelves filled with books, stretching so high that a rolling ladder is needed to reach the uppermost volumes. The ladder's track extends all the way to the bedroom balcony, allowing someone to climb over it and step directly into the cozy haven of the bed.

I don't know whose house this is—there are no pictures on the walls with people in them, just artistic rendering of sunrises and other art.

Maybe this is just my brain giving me a sanctuary from the realm of Neverdusk.

Immediately, I am over at the bookshelves, looking through the collections.

Finding a book I haven't read yet, I pluck it from the shelf and find a place to perch on the couch, curling up, the will-o'-the-wisp hovering over my shoulder for light.

Enthralled by the story I've begun to read, I hadn't realized how much time had passed when I hear the handle turning. I stiffen and set the book in my lap, only expecting to see Trystan —this must be an illusion he's created for me to keep whittling my soul down.

But it isn't him who comes through the door.

It's Bash.

I throw my book down and run to him. I collide with him, diminishing my whole soul into his, and meld with his essence. His lips are on mine, and we're kissing. I don't even know if this is real, but it's wonderful and staggering and feels so good, like I've been holding my breath for eighteen years and just let it all out. There is an exquisite ache in my mouth, a burn I know in my soul only one thing can stop.

Tears are wetting my cheeks, and I didn't even realize I was crying; I'm so lost in him and his lips, and I don't even care if he's real or not. He's here in my mind and it's enough for me right now. His strong arms are the only thing holding me up because my bones have melted, and I'd surely fall if it weren't for him. It's as though fate is standing behind me, holding its breath to see if this moment breaks kingdoms and shatters worlds. The intensity of the kiss is tangible; the visceral combustion of atoms explodes outwards as though fireworks were sewn into this patch of the quilt of time.

He stops kissing me, hands on either side of my face and his dark, arresting shade of ocean-blue eyes saw into my life and crack open my soul, stopping my world and energy. Waterfalls freeze, ocean tides pause, the wind halts, and nothing moves for this moment, this tiny moment where he is mine and nothing else exists. The energy pouring off him feels as though he wants to destroy me and make me his queen all at once.

"You're real," he breathes, kissing my nose, and forehead and cheeks, my tears wetting his lips. "This isn't a dream. This is real?"

"I don't know if this is truly real or just our version of real. Seems like we were able to find each other dream-walking again, even in different realms."

A glorious smile picks up one side of his mouth, and a little dimple surfaces on his face. I love that dimple. It's rare, but when it comes out, it means he's content within his skin and the world and life, and it's comforting. It soothes my soul.

"Oh, Sayah." He says my name like someone who's been without water for weeks in a desert and spots a crystal-clear pool of water. Parched and broken and missing parts of their mind, they drink the first drop, and the restorative elixir quenches the brokenness and relieves the thirst instantly. "Gods, I miss you so much. I cannot even explain how much. It's like . . . missing a part of myself. A limb. Only half-breaths and never a fully quenched thirst."

My face folds into a sarcastic half-smile. "Well, that's just because you're addicted to my blood," I tease him, straining my throat in his direction.

"Nooooo, never." He nuzzles into me and feathers kisses down the column of my neck.

Bash's soft lips reach my chin, and he gently places his hand on my throat, pulling my gaze to his.

Heat rises in me from floor-to-ceiling, and I'm overcome with lust for him. I want him—in any capacity, dream or no dream—to rip my clothes off and fuck me like he'll never get to again. Forever greedy for any and every chance to taste each other's skin.

So he does just that.

Before I know it, we're ripping each other's clothes off and getting naked right here in the front sitting room of this strange boathouse.

A few hours later, after multiple orgasms and fucking in every room of this floating palace, we're lying on the bow of the boat, staring up at the stars.

The sky looks like an inkwell bled onto dark purple parchment, and someone threw glitter on the wet ink. The night is breathing, the moons and planets sighing in relief of our unholy reunion.

"Where is this place exactly?" I ask, finally, with the hope he may know the answer.

"This is my place," he says nonchalantly. "In Cali."

Shocked, I prop myself up on my elbow to get a better look at him, clutching a soft brown sheet to my chest. "Your place? You really live on a boat?"

"Yeah," he answers, his brows pulled tight. "Why?"

"I didn't believe you actually lived on a boat! I thought it was just your made-up human story."

He laughs, the moonlight limning his structured face. "You know, pretty much everything I say about myself is true. I just hide the whole 'drinking blood to live' thing from most humans."

"Yeah, but even then, I wouldn't have guessed you lived here."

"Why? Not vampire-y enough for you?" The wrinkles on the side of his eyes crease as he smiles, gazing up into the night sky while tracing lines down my inner thigh. "My coffin is in the lower decks."

This moment doesn't have room for his jokes. "Those books?" I say, gazing inside to the rooms filled with books inside. "They're yours?"

"Yes." His head turns toward me, sending my heartbeat to shatter. "They are mine."

My bookish heart swells. "Bash!"

"What?"

"You read?" I sound shocked by this realization, but I'm just shocked that he loves to read, not that he *can* read.

"I love to read, actually."

He doesn't seem offended. Whew.

"Why didn't I know that about you?"

He snuggles in closer to me. "You were too busy falling in love with my looks instead of falling in love with my brain. I'm more than my dick, Sayah."

I laugh. He picks my hand up, our fingers entangled together, and looks at my nails. I am a picker; I tend to pick at my cuticles when I'm nervous about a situation or things in my life that I cannot control. It's one of those things I don't like people to see, and I tend to try not to draw attention to my nails if at all possible. He sees I've worried away at a few of my cuticles and kisses them. I try to pull my hand away, but he holds it firm.

"I don't care what they look like. I've noticed you do that when you're nervous. Are you okay?"

The question is loaded and catches me off guard. I feel my chin start to quiver, and my eyes begin to fill with tears. "Dom?" I say as a question.

Bash is quiet. He squeezes my hand and turns his head to hide his own tears. His face holds all the agony of a fallen star, broken and beautiful, with eyes so blue it makes everything else look dull.

It's true, then.

Dom is dead.

He purses his lips as if calling all the pain on his face to reenter him, to pull it back and shove it down into his bones.

"Oh, Bash." I let go of our hands to wrap my arm around him and hold him tight. Laying my head on his chest, I feel his breathing go ragged, hitch, quiver; then he exhales exquisite torment. Pain. Anguish. Sorrow. Longing. Ache. All the emotions wrapped into a hurricane, a loaded storm on the

brink of rapture. A funnel cloud about to touch down and deci-
mate and destroy anything in its path.

"I . . ." His voice is thready and uneven. The air turns charged, explosive, combustible sparks have replaced half the oxygen.

"It's okay to fall apart, Bash. You're safe with me. The hardest part of loving someone is the moment you have to say goodbye. The weight of grief is unyielding. It feels crushing and canvassed and fatal. So feel free to fall, my love. I'm here."

And with that, he falls.

He shatters.

He breaks.

Bash is like glass. A hardened glass, but glass, nonetheless. A little crack here and there, over centuries of living and heartache, of pain and sorrow, when a pressure such as this one applies itself to said glass, it shatters. Irrevocably.

This is his shatter.

This pain is raw, angry—like a scream living inside of him that's been threatening to rip him in half if it wasn't let out.

The brother's bond that's been forged, mended, broken, sewn together repeatedly has been severed, never to be mended again, and that breaks something inside of Bash, something deep and hollow and unyielding. Something that will never be repaired.

I let Bash fall completely apart, his chest heaving with sobs, and it. Breaks. Me.

Together, we splinter. Every dark alley and secret corner of ourselves spills out into each other's darkness, and we fall to the bottom of the pit, crying and weeping for the brother and boyfriend we lost to this ancient feud.

Both of our faults that Dom is gone.

Bash drank the blood that could have kept him from the dark, putting him in an envelope of darkness, and I fell for his brother, licking the stamp that sealed that very envelope, delivering him to his ultimate death. We each have our parcels of guilt and slices of shame, each our own amount that wedges its way into our grief.

Once we reach the bottom of our sorrow, beneath our shatter, we grasp for each other again, he the lifeboat in my ravenous storm and me the fractured light in the water.

12

AFTER THE SHATTER

—BASH—

Sayah and I have been lying beside each other for a long time, just listening to each other's breaths. In and out. In. And. Out. Neither of us wants to move. We do not know how much longer we have with each other.

I finally stir, grasping her face—the face that makes me think writing poetry should be my new hobby. My light.

I pull her chin up to kiss her. "Hey, you."

She kisses me back. "Hey, you. You okay?"

"As long as I have you, I will forever be okay."

"I love you, Bash," she mutters. The way she says those three words is like a million little promises, each of which shivering over my flesh and embedding in my bones.

"I love you, my fire queen. I cannot stand being without you. It's killing me. What have you been going through?"

The muscles in her neck tense when she looks up to the sky, her blue eyes catching on the stars. "Oh, Trystan." I bristle at the sound of his name. "He's trying to wear me down or win me over or some shit. I think I fucked up tonight, bad, and now I don't know what to do."

My heart sinks at the weight of another emotion I cannot

quite grasp or name. At just the mention of him, a rolling undercurrent rather than staggering waves—every bit as powerful as a hurricane mixed with an avalanche—builds within me. "What happened?"

She looks back at me. "He moved me from the dungeon to an upstairs room with a view. There's still a boundary spell up there, and I can't use my magick." She holds up her wrists as though looking for a missing bracelet. "He has this gold, shackle thing on my ankle and wrist—they are connected by a chain that stanches my magick." Laying her hand back inside mine, she curls up to my arm. "He had some elf guy bring all this food—"

My mind drifts to what's lingering between her words. "You didn't eat any of it, did you?"

"I did." She let's out a nervous laugh. "I ate all of it, and I never got full. Then I drank this nectar shit, and it was so good—"

"Their glowy shit is so good, right?"

She props herself up on her elbow to look at me again. "So good! Anyway, I had asked Trystan if I could get word to Gauge that I was okay, and he would only agree if I gave him some of my power. I said absolutely not, and he said he could just take it from me, but he wanted to quote-unquote 'win me over.' He moved me upstairs, and I asked again after drinking that nectary stuff. He said he would if I gave him a little bit of my power, and I said okay."

"Oh, no." I practically feel the air curdle. My heart goes out to her. I know she wants to let Gauge know she's okay, but giving Trystan even a fraction of her power is such an undeniably bad decision. I feel it collide with the monsters lurking in every facet of Trystan. "You have to do whatever you can to not give him anything. You should have seen what a drop of my blood made." I shudder at the thought. "We have no idea—on this realm or ours—what a drop of yours would create."

She's looking at me in pure awe and terror, raw and confused. "What do I do? How do I not give him any of my power?"

"Well, if it's the phoenix power he's after, then he'll need to magickally abscond it from you instead of doing something as easy as getting a drop of your blood. When the time comes, and he removes your shackles, give him a different part of your power. Give him the fear one or the floating one. Anything but the one he's after. Bide your time. Tallyn and I are working on a way to get you out of there."

"We're supposed to do the 'procedure' tomorrow morning."

"Okay, just stay strong." I squeeze her knee after she drapes her legs over mine. "I know you can. Try to do anything you can to not let him get that power."

"He also said something else interesting." She says this slowly and lays her head back.

My soul tightens. "What did he say?"

"He said if I were to become his queen of Earth and Never and Luminara, Gauge would no longer have diabetes. He would be able to walk and fly. That he'd give me three worlds for Gauge to become everything he's ever wanted."

Shit.

This isn't good for me. This skitters across my rage, tipping the avalanche in the hurricane's favor.

Of course, Sayah wants to do anything she can for her child. If this dickbag is over here offering her something like that, there's nothing I can do to compete with it.

"I know it sounds nice and pretty and all, but you never know with the fae. It could be something completely different."

"That's what I was thinking. Like Gauge would have to give up his world and never see his dad again, and we'd both have to live in a world of darkness. I don't think either one of us would ever be okay with that."

Okay, so she's weighed her options and really thought this through.

Good. This is good.

"Yes. Definitely never trust the fae. And make sure you keep your power to yourself. Please, Sayah, you have no idea what will happen. The thing that a drop of my blood made . . ." I shudder again.

She shifts her weight to level me with her gaze. "What did a drop of your blood make?"

"A fucking giant flying spider."

"No!"

"Yes!"

"Oh, fuck no. No, no, no, no! No! I can't even . . ." She visibly frays at the thought of this spider.

"Right! Thank you! That's what I've been saying, and everyone's just been making fun of me for it. And. *And* when it bites you, it has a corrosive venom that literally sucks your soul from you and makes your skin gray, so you become one of these abyssal sprites."

"Abyssal sprites?"

I take my time explaining the whole thing to her, about Ember and the blood-stealing. I want Sayah to be on the lookout for her. I also tell her about my seeing ghosts and naming my demon, and Dom's voice helping me with that. She's quiet as I tell her everything that has happened since I last saw her.

"Is he here now?" she asks of Henry.

Then I realize I haven't seen him the entire time I've been in this dream.

"No, maybe he can't follow me to our dreams."

She slams our hands against my chest. "Gods, I wish this wasn't a dream."

"I wish it wasn't either." I pull her in close and she lies her head on my chest.

"What are we going to do?"

"We just have to keep going. Keep doing what we're doing. I will do anything to get you back home to me. And I will talk to Tallyn about getting word to Gauge that you are okay."

"What will you tell him?"

"I haven't thought about that yet. Maybe she'll let me portal to him to explain in person."

"To a ten-year-old? He hasn't met you yet. I don't know if that'll work."

"I'll ask my dad to help. He can mimic people. Maybe he can mimic Dom, talk to Derek, and let him know you are okay."

"I hate to say this, but . . ." She tilts her head to look at me.

"Veilweave him?"

There's a splinter in her eyes as she asks me. The way her brows draw together in tight concern spells how nervous she is to ask this of us. "Yes. Just until I can get back to him. Veilweave him and Derek to think he's going back and forth to both our houses, and everything is fine. Make him think nothing is out of the ordinary, so he doesn't worry. And then when I get back, you can take the veilweaving off him, right?"

"Yes. I can do that."

"Thank you, my love."

"I will never tire of hearing that," I say, feeling my heart settle at the words on her lips. Calling me her love.

"You know, it's funny. Before this dream, I had another one of you. We were in a field, and I was on the hill. I wanted to run to you, but I couldn't, and you said I was being weird. I knew I had to—"

"Bite me."

"Yes. Did you have it, too?"

"I did. And you had vampire fangs. And when you bit me, I—"

"Burned." We say the word at the same time.

"What do you think that's about?" she asks.

"I don't know. I don't know that I want to know."

"Do you think it's something telling us of something to come?"

"I really, really hope not."

Her eyes collide with mine, and my passion for her heats me up to my core. I take her lips in mine and feel her melt underneath me, her bones turning to water at my touch.

Her large breasts come out from under the sheet, and my hands move over them, cupping and pinching hard enough to make her moan. My cock hardens at the sound, and I want to tease more of those sounds out of her, my new favorite noise in this world and any other.

Her back arches as I squeeze her tit, my mouth salivating at the thought. We resemble magnets at how our lips meet. I cover her with a hungry kiss, her writhing making me rock-hard. Her hand slides down my length and I let out a moan. Her legs widen for me as I slither my finger down her slick center.

I love how wet she gets for me.

As I plunge my finger deep into her pussy, she drags her nails across my shoulder blades, her head lulling back into the pillows. She releases a breathy moan.

When I pull her to the very edge of an orgasm, I stop fingering her, and climb over until I am straddling her, her legs draped over my shoulders. In one exquisite roll of my hips, my cock eases into her. Her chest rises and then she holds her breath. I bury my cock into her glorious pussy until my balls are lying flat against her ass.

"Oh, gods," she utters, wiggling her hips, trying to get me to move.

"There are no gods here," I say into the shell of her ear. I pull my cock out to the tip and slam back into her, pushing deep. I want to feel her tastebuds through her pussy. "But I'll gladly accept that title from your sexy mouth." I cover her lips with mine and drive harder into her, swallowing the next gasp that comes from her.

"Harder," she commands. I fuck her like the world is ending, like she is my last gods-damn breath in the middle of a breaking world.

The walls crumble around us. The sky and universe and ocean take pause and watch as I bow to my fucking queen, the bed rocking with us fucking in the middle of the black water.

Her breasts bounce to my pounding. My thrusts grow forceful. I take her legs and pull her to me, sitting up like I'm praying on my knees for her, and she is my ungodsly matron saint.

Her back arches off the mattress. I use her thighs to pull her to me, sinking her down the length of me and raising her back up. Magick holds her body to me, and I grasp her succulent ass and shove her down hard, eliciting the most tantalizing scream.

"Fuck me, Bash. Harder!"

I harden even more for her—the hot, tingly rush of an orgasm shooting down my dick.

Her pussy walls clench around me as I fuck her harder, faster. Water ripples out from under the bed from us rocking the fuck out of it.

The telltale sign of her cumming is the flushing of her cheeks and her muscles tightening around my cock. I pull her chin to look at me as she combusts from within.

She tries to look away, rocking her head back to look at the stars.

"Nope. Look at me," I demand of her, pulling her gaze back to mine by her hair.

"Oh, fuck, Bash! Oh," she pleads, and I wrap my hand around her neck.

The flush of euphoria rocks out from the tip of my dick; I feel the swell of my cock get wider despite holding back until she cums first.

"No." She sinks all the way down on my cock and pushes me

to lie on my back. "Cum for me now," she breathes, straddling me with her feet on either side of me, rocking until I see stars, as if she wants to destroy me and make me her king.

"Gods-damn, Sayah, fuck," I growl, grabbing her breasts.

Before I cum all the way, I use my unnatural speed to flip her over, pinning her with my hands and hips, her face buried in the stars.

"Yes, fuck. Bash, oh gods," she screams when I slam into her, grabbing her hands, and restraining them behind her back. She would let me crush and break her if it meant she never had to let me go.

"Cum for me, fire queen," I demand, and her body lights up like fireworks.

The golden embers of her skin explode, and wings of fire erupt from her back. She screams into the night as she cums, causing the fire in her bones to ignite. The golden cracks of her skin erupt like electric currents, and a vibrating rush of sensations catapults me into the universe.

I cum to the rhythm of her orgasm, us slipping into the ether together. There might need to be a new name for this type of sensation—so much more than euphoria. It's peacefulness and sin, good and dirty, bad and divine.

I ride the wave until a symphony's crescendo hits, the world knitting itself back together. When the sights and sounds of this dream realm return to normal, I collapse onto the bed next to her, pulling her onto my chest.

"You're a-fucking-mazing," she says, breathless.

"Baby, some women cower at the sight of the flames; some women are consumed by them. You, Sayah, are fire incarnate."

She laughs, interlacing her hand in mine.

A cold sensation, like gripping melting ice, divides in our hold, and I raise it. Her still-glowing gold skin gets lighter. "Oh, no," I say, knowing the dream is nearing its end, and I don't ever want to let her go. One dream is not enough; there will never be enough of her.

The intensity with which I feel I don't want to lose her could break kingdoms and build worlds.

She sees it, too. "I guess that means our time together is being cut short."

"I don't want to return to where you aren't."

"I don't either."

I pull her closer to me and smell her hair, her scent—the sweet Sayah scent that envelopes me and usually makes me insane with hunger for her, for her blood.

This makes me think: I've been so close to her for an undisclosed amount of time and have had no cravings for her blood.

The addiction has been quiet.

My craving for her blood is usually restless. There is always a quiet screaming lurking in the branches of my being, bending the wind so her scent follows me everywhere I go. But here I am, calm; her blood is quiet, and everything is right as rain.

Even Henry has yet to be seen.

What does that mean?

"Maybe we can dream of each other every night," she says into my chest. "Can you think of what happened that caused you to dream of me?"

Her hair and arms are fading now. "I was just begging the moon to let me get some sort of word that you are okay, and these weird little jellyfish-looking things—"

"What?" she asks, sitting up, and looking at me.

"Yes," I respond, watching the starlight seep through her ghostly appearance. "Little creatures of Luminara that brought me to the sleep where I would find you."

"It seems like the entire universe is conspiring to keep bringing us to each other," she says before kissing my lips. It feels like wind whooshing through a wheat field, sweet, soft, and fresh.

"I hope they come to see me every night if it brings me you. I have to see you, or I'll lose my mind."

"You won't tire of dreaming with me every night?"

"Sayah," I say, watching her fade. Looking at my hand in hers, it seems I am fading, too. "If I saw your face daily for the rest of time, it still wouldn't be enough."

"I love you," she whispers and wavers even more.

"I love you, my fire queen. I shall see you in our dreams." She kisses me again, and now it feels like air and lips and sun and sky. She is my whole universe wrapped into one beautiful human body, and I can't get enough of her. "I will find a way to get you out of there. And I will get Gauge veilweaved."

"Thank you, my love." Her voice is a whisper in the night. The wind swoops in from the sea and steals her away.

She's gone.

When I open my eyes, I'm back in my room in Feylight Castle. The moon is gone from the balcony view, but it still seems to be night.

Tallyn did say that days and nights are longer here.

I ache from the loss of Sayah; seeing her in my dreams was a replenishment for my soul, and losing her is like a tourniquet, squeezing dry my marrow and blood and life.

I need her.

I touch my lips. I can feel the ghost of hers on them still, as though she were just here, in real life, next to me.

My stomach growls loudly.

Fairy food or human food, or any of this weird liquid shit Tallyn keeps around, cannot quell my hunger.

I need blood.

After splashing some water on my face and bruising my teeth, I meander around the castle, looking for a kitchen.

Eventually I happen upon a room resembling more of a large dining hall than a kitchen.

There's an island made of marble, gilded with gold in the middle, lined with bottles of fairy wine underneath. I grab one of the brown bottles and take a swig, my stomach yowling in protest.

I need blood.

Coming around a corner to a little turret overlooking Feylight's inner ring, Tallyn and Sariana are sitting in a nook-shaped corner with an array of strange-looking food in front of them.

Looks weird, smells good.

"Bash. Good morning," Tallyn greets, her dark lashes curling up toward her black brows.

"Is it morning?" I look at the darkness outside the window. "How do you all keep track of time?"

"We're just used to it," Sariana answers coldly, letting her fork clang onto the plate.

I sit down next to Tallyn and drink more of the brown bottle.

This one is bitter and strange.

I wince. "What is this?"

She takes the bottle from me and smells it. "Emberhart Elixir. Like Tanqueray in your world."

I take another drink and hiss. "Ah, that's gross."

"Why are you still drinking it?" she asks, her eyes scintillating from the candlelight on the table and the spirit lanterns hovering on the walls.

"I need blood. And soon. Here's what I'm thinking," I say, and she glares at me skeptically. I set down the bottle and shove it away from me. "It seems you didn't think the whole 'I'm-bringing-a-vampire-here-to-stay-for-an-undisclosed-amount-of-time-and-I-should-stock-up-on-human-donors' through quite well, so here's what I propose. I need to get word to Sayah's son that she's okay by veilweaving him and his dad. In the process of doing that, we can swipe some human subjugates to bring back for my meal purposes."

Tallyn blinks at me, seemingly lost. She sets her utensils down and wipes her mouth with a black serviette. She delicately folds her hands on the table, almost as though she's offended that I've seemingly made demands of a queen.

"Comprende?" I ask her, folding my hands in mock imitation on the wooden table before me.

Her mouth quirks up. "I'm confused about how you know you need to get word to Sayah's son. And why you think I'll allow you to return to the moral realm to do so."

I shift my arm over the edge of the breakfast nook. "Tallyn. Listen. I am here to help you. But I need to eat. And I made a promise to Sayah. I figured we can kill two birds with one stone."

Tallyn pauses, looking at Sariana, then slides her eyes back to mine. "How did you promise Sayah if she is in Nightshade?"

My eyebrows cinch together. "How do you know she's in Nightshade?"

Suspicious wrinkles wring the side of her eyes. "Trystan sent me a Whispering Leaf when it first happened. Now you."

A knot creases in my stomach, and I push it away. "I have dreams of her. Always have."

"And you two talk in these dreams?" she asks, her expression remaining neutral.

"We can, yes."

I don't want to go into too much detail here because I don't want Tallyn to interfere with my ability to see Sayah in my dreams.

She must sense my apprehension because my subtly arouses

a smirk from her. "No, this is good, Bash. How often do you two dreamwalk to each other?"

"Last night was the first time since she's been gone," I lie. I don't want to mention the whole biting and burning thing.

"Good," she says, sipping from a white teacup. "Maybe she can give us intel on what Trystan is up to, where he is doing his Hunt, when he plans to attack, and things like that."

"I don't know if he tells her anything like that."

The teacup clatters back in its saucer. "Just have her be on the lookout. Tell her to pay attention and try to find out things if she can. Of course, we don't want to put her in any danger, but this could help us."

"I'll tell her as soon as I see her again. In the meantime, what say you about this whole 'get Bash a meal' business?"

"I think it's doable," she says, setting the serviette onto her half-eaten weird food. "Let us meet with your family to see if they have any ideas on how to do this without creating too much of a problem or ruckus."

"Let's," I say, sliding out from the booth and holding my hand out for her to take.

Tallyn obliges, Sariana . . . does not.

13

A STOLEN POWER

—SAYAH—

I wake up to darkness and forget where I am until I sit up and see the Nocturna Sea lapping at the skyscape.

I fall back into bed and cover my head with the blanket, missing Bash, and wishing he was still here with me. I love that we can dreamwalk to each other, but waking up after having seen him and fucking him and then not having him is soul-breaking.

There's a tittering at my door, and I roll to face the sound, shouting, "Come in," from under the covers.

The silence that follows the sound of the door opening has my ears perked.

A few seconds later, "Good morning, my pet," comes from directly outside my blanket. The vibrations penetrate my skin. The voice sends shivers the wrong way down my spine; his voice similar to the slither of a snake.

I have no energy for him yet, so I don't oblige him by leaving the covers over my head. "Yes?" I ask.

"Was just seeing if you wanted some breakfast before we start the procedure you promised me." His voice is silky and menacing, dripping with poison. The sort of tone that makes nice words sound like a million nefarious promises, each of which skitters over my flesh.

"Um, yeah. I'll be right there," I utter.

Suddenly the covers are flown off me and Trystan is standing before me, with a Robbins-egg colored shirt this time, still unbuttoned to show his thorns and chest and muscles. "Now," he demands, and the words pierce holes through me.

I don't want to piss him off, so I swing my legs to sit on the edge of the bed. "Okay."

"I haven't got time for this today. The eclipse is soon to begin, and I have a Hunt to lead."

"Has it started then?" I pass him, making sure not to graze him with my shoulder. He follows my movements as I stroll over to the armoire.

"That is none of your concern," he says, following me to the dresser. "What you should be concerned with is getting dressed and meeting me outside your room in ten minutes."

"How does this work, then?" I ask, setting my hands on the handles.

His wind-colored eyes drink up my whole body. "You just wish for what clothes you want, and they will appear."

"Just clothes?" I ask, hoping I could wish for a way out of here or for Bash to be on the other side or Gauge.

His eyes glitter menacingly. "Just clothes," he confirms and flies over to the door. "Ten minutes."

With that, he shuts the door, and I return my attention to the armoire. "I wish for jean shorts, a tank top, and flip-flops."

A static charge ripples through the air and shoves my breath back into my lungs. When I open the wardrobe, it's filled with brightly colored tank tops, an array of jean shorts, flip-flops in every color, and some necklaces hanging on hooks inside the door. I'm feeling yellow today, so I pluck out a yellow tank top, some light blue-frayed shorts, matching flip-flops, and a choker to go with the shackles on my wrist and arms.

Joking. It doesn't go.

I steal a glance at myself in the mirror.

My hair is nice and tangled, so I throw it in a messy bun and head to the bathroom. After brushing my hair and teeth, I scurry to the doors to meet Trystan before my time is up.

"All right," he says when I join him on the threshold. "Give me your palm."

I hold my palm out for him to slice me open again, my skin separating, and the crimson of my blood spilling on the granite floors.

Pulling me into him, we are again thrust into a vortex of swirling colors as the castle's floors, walls, and scenery rush us.

When we stop, I fight the urge to throw up again.

"You'll get used to it eventually," he tells me, rolling his neck. The popping and cracking echo off the stone walls.

His demeanor is different today. He's indifferent, and his posture is rigid when it's usually languid and easy.

It's like he knows I was in a dream with Bash last night.

Not wanting to bring attention to his salty attitude, I follow him through a set of doors that spill us out into an expansive open room.

Rough-hewn wooden tables line the walls, the rustic dark stone illuminated by orb lanterns and a fireplace. Dozens of Neverdusk soldiers fill each table, some crouching over parchment papers and war plans, others eating from wooden bowls and drinking from rustic metal goblets. The cacophony of chatter fills the air; some languages I recognize, and others I don't.

Trystan walks in front of me, down the aisle of the tables.

Some soldiers stop talking and look at me, others keep on like nothing has changed.

". . . Nixia portal," I hear amongst the chatter. For some reason, this comes in as clear as day. I lean into the voice, though I don't know where it's coming from.

". . . flying fucking spider . . ." Another voice says, ". . . fifteen of my best soldiers before we put it down."

I pretend I hear nothing, but I am certain what Bash was telling me is what they're talking about.

Trystan opens a pair of double black ornate doors and leads me into a room that resembles a void: a black desk, black lamps, candles, windows, and curtains—the entire room is a sea of black.

I quite like it.

He sweeps in and motions for me to sit on a window bench overlooking Nocturna Sea. Following his instructions, I sit, and he remains standing, spreading his wings out for a stretch.

The room has fifteen-foot ceilings, the wainscoting in intricate designs crawls up the walls and decorates the ceiling above us, a dome with a glass roof twinkling with stars.

"So if bloodporting only works to places you've bled before, why didn't we just bloodport into this room? You haven't bled here?" I ask with a smile, looking at the slice on my palm which is all but gone by now.

"Oh, I've done much more than bleed in here," he says, his storm-color eyes wild with menace and seduction. "But for security's sake, I keep a boundary spell on this room. No one enters or exits magickally." After a pause, Trystan shouts "Nyxaria!"

From another room connected to this one, a gorgeous fairy with dusty-rose skin and hair, fire-orange eyes, and a gown made of thorns flits in, her iridescent wings shimmering in the moonlight.

"Yes, my king?" she asks, swooping in next to him with a curtsy.

"Have you prepared the spell?" he questions her with authority, sauntering to sit beside me on the bench.

I feel so underdressed.

Her bright eyes skim mine, and I feel a weird simmer somewhere in my soul about her. "I have. I just need to enter her mind, and I have the device with which we will capture the power."

"Excellent." His face cracks like a cackle is about to emerge, but he bites back down on it, setting his jaw. "Call Sablethorn and Ember in here."

She bows her head, flits off as he stands, and moves over to his desk.

My eyebrows draw together. "Who are they?"

Trystan pours a peculiar concoction into a small crystal goblet. "Ember is my High Councilor and Sablethorn is a soothe-sayer, which is like a shaman in your world. He has a penchant for manipulating crystals and gems and can channel energies. He'll help us get the power we want and keep you from doing anything foolish while those shackles are off. I will have to remove them for your power to become available to us. Ember is here to supervise and make sure everything is done right."

Shit.

This may not help me if I try to give them a different power than my phoenix power.

Nyxaria emerges from the double doors again, and following her in are two interesting looking beings.

A gorgeous fairy with dark red hair and glowing green eyes walks in wearing a corset made of black thorns. Shadows seem to bend to her; every one on the walls twisting as if to say hello. Following her in is a squirly-looking man. He's muscular but wiry, while his silver hair crowns his head so the top of his skull glistens in the light of the orb, the longer part hanging in a silver braid down his back. Muscles jump under his tunic, the visible skin decorated with swirling runes that glow and crawl up the sides of his neck and straight down the left side of his face. His eyes are onyx, not a speck of white within them.

Trystan slams back the blue liquid and loudly sets the goblet back on the table. "Everyone ready?"

"Aye!" Sablethorn says, pulling a long black crystal wand from the inside of his tunic as he strides up to me. Smiling, he shows off crooked and dingy teeth. "When the lass is ready."

"I will take the shackles off," Trystan says, kneeling before me. Ember stands to his right. "Nyx will enter her mind; you make sure when she finds the power to help her guide it to the crystal. Also, make sure she doesn't try to escape or use her powers on us."

"I'm not going to do that, Trystan," I say, offended he's talking about me like I'm not even here. "Even if I was a seasoned witch, I'm in a realm I know nothing about and wouldn't know how to get out of here, even if I was."

The sides of his mouth curl up at this. "Good. Now I will remove the shackles, and Nyxaria will press her fingers on your temples. It may hurt a bit, like a headache, but nothing intolerable."

"And how do I know that you're only taking a little bit, like you stated?"

"You will just have to trust us," Nyxaria says. The words make me feel worse about the situation.

A softness in the depths of her eyes makes me feel fuzzy and confused. I should be scared of her, but I'm really not. I nod, readying her fingers at my temple.

Trystan takes a golden key from his pocket and pushes it into the hole. It clicks, and he removes the shackles from my wrist, the tingling of my power buzzing to life. I never realized how much I missed the electric little currents singeing me beneath my skin, alerting me to my power. Either I never noticed it before, or now that I've been cut off from it, it's coming back with a vengeance. I struggle to keep my poker face, not wanting to draw too much attention to my phoenix power, but it is the most intense and dominating power of them all.

Once the shackles are removed from my ankle, the power rushes back to me in a deluge that nearly knocks me to the ground. Trystan nods at Sablethorn, who readies the crystal wand. Nyx jabs her fingernail into my temples, and my head rocks back.

My vision blurs, turning white-hot, like staring into a blazing sun. It's as if I'm plummeting down the tallest water slide at Elitch Gardens in Denver—the exhilarating drop, the rush of air, and then the world spinning like a tornado that's swept me off the slide entirely. Nyxaria's presence presses in, undeniable, as the tingling of my golden power calls to me, pulling me toward the center of my being.

Nyxaria's essence is a beautiful orange that follows me as I swim through my subconscious. I can sense the phoenix gift is to the left of my heart, so I go right, searching for the bright orange power of making people see their worst fear. I am going toward it when my soul is sucked sideways, and both Nyxaria and I are barreling for the phoenix power. I try swimming away from it, imagining myself paddling against a current, and it's no use; I'm being vacuumed to it by Sablethorn.

The power encompasses my entire vision, and as I tumble toward it, I struggle with snuffing it down and making it smaller so they only get a piece of it. I'm unable to keep us away from it entirely. It doesn't work. We are twisting and turning, tumbling and flying toward it, and when we land beside it, my vision suddenly goes black.

"Hey!" I scream, scared to death that they just robbed me of my entire power.

It doesn't work like that, does it?

My heartbeat races to my ears, my skin prickles even though I am bodyless in this vision, and my muscles melt. I can feel everything about me despite not being able to see myself.

"*Mom!*" I scream into the ether. "Please, Mama, make sure they don't take all my power!"

Nothing but the deepest, darkest black of space.

Silence.

A pinprick of light.

I'm flying toward it.

It gets brighter, and when the light encompasses all I can see, I am ripped back to consciousness. The illusion is broken.

My head slumps forward, and I take in my surroundings. Trystan stands to my right. Nyxaria withdraws her fingers from my temples. Behind her, Ember lingers, while Sablethorn steps back, his crystal wand now glowing faintly. The buzzing in my body has vanished, leaving behind a hollow emptiness. A deep, arctic cold seeps into me, like sinking into the middle of a frozen lake, where the icy air carves out your depths and fills them with bone-chilling frost.

"You didn't take my entire power, did you?" I ask.

A wicked fucking smile almost makes him handsome as he slips the ankle shackle back on my foot and locks it in place.

"Trystan! Answer me!"

Saying nothing, he shackles my wrist, and whatever hope or chance I had at seeing if my power is still there fades with the cool of the metal against my skin.

"*Trystan!*" I scream.

"Oh, relax, my pet. We've left some for you," he goads, walking away from me, and taking the crystal from Sablethorn.

"What does that mean? How am I to know you kept your side of the bargain with these stupid shackles?"

He says nothing, only continuing to walk away.

My blood rushes to my ears, and before I know it, I've sprung to my feet, and Trystan is in my sights.

I know he's way stronger than me, but I don't care.

All I know and love has been stolen from me, and the nonchalant way he's acting about robbing me of the only thing that's genuinely mine makes me want to rip his head off.

But before I can even move two feet, Ember appears in front

of me, holding out her hands to halt me in my tracks. She doesn't even touch me, yet shadows seem to be listening to her, holding me to the floor and keeping me frozen in my tracks.

"Trystan!" I scream over her shoulder. "What about getting word to my son?" I know Bash is doing that for me now, but I want to keep him in here as long as possible to find out if he really took all my power.

"We'll do that after I do something with this." He raises the crystal, indicating what he's speaking of.

I knew what the fuck he was speaking of.

"And what about my power? How can I be sure you didn't take it all?"

"Once you are my queen, Sayah, you won't need it anymore, anyway."

And he walks away.

14

THE WAR BEGINS

—BASH—

"So you just use these orb thingies and it lets you see things?" I ask.

We're in a drafty room of the castle, sitting at a solid oak table with a spirit lantern hovering between us. Thalira focuses on her orb while Tallyn and Halcyon go over battle plans by the roaring fire. My family—minus Laureya— talk amongst themselves in a lounge area off to the side.

Thalira's eyes slide to me seductively. "They're called aether orbs, and yes, one of my gifts is luminkenisis. I communicate with light; it listens to me and shows me things."

I recall the dungeon from earlier—or whenever the fuck that was—and what that Aurora fairy did with the lights. "Is that the same as lum-o-kinesis? That one chick earlier did the thing with the lights—"

"Lumin and lumo are different gifts," Thalira says, waving her hand above the aether orb. "Lumo fairies can control the light. Lumin can use it to communicate."

"Cool," I say, transfixed by how the orb is pulsing, as though listening to her. "So you're using it to communicate with the lightbulbs in the house Gauge is in now?"

She nods. "Yes. By way of light, I can see into people's houses and hear conversations. It seems Gauge and his other family there are getting ready to go to an end-of-summer festival in Windsor, Colorado."

"That's perfect," Tallyn says, coming up behind us. "Windsor happens to be near a portal axis to Luminara."

Tallyn saunters off again. Thalira sends the aether orb back to the wall with a flick of her wrist and stands. "Are we ready, then? The festival is happening now."

"Halcyon," Tallyn orders, and he nods.

I stand as Halcyon's hands glow, pulling magick from the air. He draws his circle, a neon-blue light this time. Once the circle is drawn, the surface becomes liquid light, lightning, and other ominous things normal people—or vampires—would never decide to be like, "Hey, this looks like it'll hurt; I think I'll jump into it."

What's even more strange is that, behind the lightning and sparks and things of pain, an image of a field full of people emerges. The view we have is off in the distance, but from the mirror image of the festival, I can make out a Ferris wheel, kids holding cotton candy, and dads walking around with giant turkey legs—all the makings of good old-fashioned American fair.

"Okay," Halcyon says, backing away from the vortex. "It's ready."

Ollie stands and pulls Claire up by her hand, moving over to the portal.

"Ready?" Halcyon asks.

"Ready," Ollie answers. He steps through, pulling Claire behind him. She scrunches her nose at me as she goes, telling me she loves portal travel as much as I do.

We're all going to hopefully tag team the Turner family. We will each veilweave a member of Gauge's family at once to avoid drawing any attention.

My dad nods at me as he steps through, and my mom holds on to his belt loops to follow. Dad is going to mimic Dom so that we can get close to Derek and Gauge by being someone familiar.

When it's my turn to go, I roll my neck and pop my knuckles, preparing for the destruction portal travel causes my body.

I fucking hate portal traveling.

Stepping through it, I am sucked into the vortex, plummeting through worlds. The upheaval of time and space hurtles me to the brink of madness, waiting for it to be over. The ground bites my ass hard as I land on the bank, taken aback when I realize we ended up in Luminara land.

Standing, I take in the surroundings.

No festival in sight, only a dark and vacant fairy land by a lake. Pelican Lake, if I remember correctly.

"Why'd we portal here?" I ask, dusting off my pants.

Tallyn gives me one of her looks. "Because, Bash, we can't just emerge from a magick portal in the middle of a festival."

"No, but a magickal staircase that appears from the middle of a fucking lake is just fine."

Tallyn side-eyes me and tips her head back in exasperation. "The area around the entrance to Luminara—in any city—has a glamor around it to make it look like nothing is there. Once we cross it, it just looks like we've been there the whole time."

"Ah." I nod and kick a rock, skipping it out onto the water.

Tallyn strides to the lake's edge, her silhouette framed by the fading shimmer of the portal dissolving into the night sky. With a graceful sweep of her hands, the water peels apart, revealing a staircase that somehow descends into the depths while rising toward the heavens at once. Gathering her skirts, she lifts her chin and steps onto the first stair, ascending—and descending— into the unknown. Her outfit is a long halter pickup, with a cape-like black leather skirt in the back, and black leggings. Her thigh-high boots clack on the steps.

Halcyon follows, disappearing down the dark stairwell. I motion for my mom, dad, and sisters to go first.

Ollie and Claire go before me.

And I bring up the rear.

In a mere few minutes, we're mingling with humans again. The scent of blood, sweat, body wash, and hair products wafts to my nostrils, and my stomach immediately growls.

"Okay, we're looking for a little boy in a green wheelchair," I tell the group, scanning the crowd for Gauge and his dad.

"Let's fan out to make it quicker," Tallyn says, ushering us off in different directions.

We weave in and out of crowds. Music plays from a live band somewhere in the festival, and a mixture of foods from food trucks intermingle with all the smells of humans.

"Who should we take back with us?" I ask Tallyn, my eyes scanning the festival-goers.

"Just a few little ones," she says, her head swerving from one human to the next. "We'll feed them some of our nectars, and they won't ever want to leave."

"Beautiful," I say, watching a gaggle of young Gen Z girls pass by in skimpy clothing, brightly colored half-tops and holey jeans, barely paying attention to where they're going because their noses are buried in their phones.

The cloying aroma of perfume floods me in a deluge, snuffing out all smells of blood, which helps clear my mind; otherwise, I'd surely pull one of the oblivious twenty-some-things behind one of the carnival game booths and have dinner right there.

We make a few rounds around the fairgrounds, passing by carnival workers from all walks of life trying to get us to play their games, which are all rigged to never let you win—or the ones rigged to let one person win big to entice other people to try, though they will never win.

I'm rounding the corner past the basketball game booth

again—Tallyn's inhuman gaze roaming over every person—when Ollie comes running up to us.

"We found him," Ollie announces. His face is set in a tight grimace, like it's taking all he has not to bite the humans surrounding him. Gods know how long it's been since he's had a decent meal. His shoulders are tense and rigid as he says, "Let's go."

Tallyn and I follow Ollie to one side of the festival, over by the stage where a band is playing. Gauge's green wheelchair comes into view. He looks bored as shit while his dad and stepmom sway to the music.

"Did you find Dad?" I ask as we stop a few yards from them.

"Yes, he's mimicked himself into Dom. It's a little unnerving." Ollie's voice is hollow. The pain from losing Dom is still very raw, and having Dad mimic him right now wasn't the best idea —but it was the only idea we had.

"All right." I squeeze my eyes shut. When I open them again, I try to block out all the noise and smells. "I'll veilweave the dad, you take the stepmom, and have Mom take the stepbrother. Do we need to do the little sister, too?"

Ollie shakes his head. "Nah, she's young enough, she won't know."

Ollie maneuvers through the crowd, and Tallyn and I follow him. We end up standing right behind Derek and his wife.

Turning to my right, I see Dom emerge from the crowd. My heart still stalls despite knowing it's my dad. My heart stings in a way I'm not ready for, but I swallow it down and borrow strength from the wind. The fake Dom walks up to Gauge while Ollie, Mom, and I go to the family.

As my dad kneels to talk to Gauge, I step around to look Derek in the eyes.

His own eyes narrow, brows drawing together in confusion.

Shh, I say to his mind, my hands on his shoulders, feeling the tension in them abate from my voice spell. *Everything is okay.*

Sayah is just fine. She is at home, and Gauge has seen her and thinks he is going back and forth to her house, even though he won't be there for a while. Nothing is out of the ordinary, and everything is fine—even if you haven't seen or heard from Sayah for a few months. You will still think Gauge is going back and forth. When Sayah is back, things will return to normal, and you will think nothing's amiss. Nod, if you understand me.

Derek nods, his eyes dilating as he receives my silent commands.

That's good. You won't remember seeing or talking to me, and once I leave, you won't think anything weird or out of place happened. Nod, if you understand me.

He bobs his head up and down.

Good. Now, go on with your life and resume normalcy, even though Gauge will not be going to Sayah's house for some time.

He nods one more time.

I release my control on him, remove my hands from his shoulders, and back away.

My mom stands from veilweaving Gauge's younger step-brother, a vacant expression on the young man's face. She waits for Ollie to complete his vocal vexing on the stepmom. Dad as Dom is about done veilweaving Gauge.

"All right, kiddo, I'll see you later, okay?" Dad says in Dom's voice, and I can feel how much it pains us to hear it in all our air.

"Okay, Dom. Bye!" Gauge says as my dad stands, and we disappear into the crowd together.

"Where's Hattie, Scar, and Jasantha?" I ask when we weave around the concertgoers and find our way back into the fair crowd.

"Scar wanted to look at some dresses," my mom answers, slipping her arm through the crook of my dad's elbow. His face morphs back into his own.

"There are shops and other wares over there," Tallyn says,

pointing to a road lined with little booths containing various goods.

Scarlet is standing outside one of the shops displaying Renaissance-style dresses, and Jasantha looks bored as she skims through them as well.

"None of this is anything I'd wear," she says, and Scarlet scoffs.

"That's because you have no taste." Scarlet glances up in time to see us approaching her. "Oh, hey, guys, how'd it go?"

"It went well," I say. Hattie appears, her arm draped around a pretty young blonde woman.

Scarlet turns and smirks. "New plaything, Hattie?" she teases. "What would Amanda say?"

"We have an open relationship," she snipes back at Scarlet. "Besides, this is just a snack." She smiles and nuzzles into the blonde's neck, making the girl giggle. Her eyes are glossy and red—she's stoned and veilweaved.

"Speaking of which"—I look at Tallyn—"I'm gonna grab me a snack to bring back to the LD."

Tallyn's brow crinkles.

"Luminara Domain—the LD."

"Ah," she says, her expression a mixture of amusement and boredom. "Okay. Well, grab the humans you want and meet me back over at the lake."

Don't have to tell me twice. "Got it. See you back over there in like twenty."

I turn and blend in with the throng of walkers advancing down the street.

Two gorgeous women—one with beautiful caramel skin and dark eyes and another, midnight-black with long boho braids—are a few shops down, browsing through spinning displays of earrings and necklaces.

I flash in between them, my eyes landing on the one with braids. "Hey, gorgeous."

A twinge of guilt rides up my neck when my thoughts turn to my beautiful Sayah. I know I'm only veilweaving them to feed; I flirt to get close enough for them to trust me.

"Hi," she says, displaying a blinding white smile.

"I'm Sebastian," I say, looking at her friend as well.

The secret to veilweaving is in the vocal cords, not the eyes, but the piercing color of our irses always helps to lure them in. I let off the magick I keep bound within me, unraveling the tie around it like twine. Mysticism weaves through the inflections in my voice, and when I say the next part, I know they will both be mine: hook, line, and sinker.

"Would you both like to come with me to a magickal place, drink fairy wine, and dance the night away?"

They both smile at me and nod, and I wrap my arms around their shoulders and lead them back to our portal.

Back at the side of the lake, Ollie and Claire have secured their meal—a cute younger man with a pony-tail, and Scarlet and Jasantha are toying with the long hair of a sexy little redhead. My mom and dad have an older couple—a nice looking older chap in a tweed jacket with a mean comb-over and glasses, whose wife definitely looks like a Barbara—and they're talking near the lake's edge.

"So what's this place like?" my girl with light eyes asks me.

"Shh, shh, shh, no talkie," I tell her, pressing a finger to her lips. "No more talking until I say so." I veilweave them, my annoyance from waiting on Tallyn threading through my voice.

"Everyone's got a meal plan?" Ollie asks, coming up to me. Claire and their hippy in-toe.

"Yeah, Hattie has the new fling she's cheating on Amanda with—by the way, whatever happened to Amanda?"

"Don't know; haven't asked," he says as Tallyn finally approaches us with Halcyon.

Her hips sway with her steps. "All right then." She glances at the extra faces. "Everyone ready?"

I nod. She approaches the lake, the surface vibrating as if to greet her. She holds out her hands, and the water twists, rolling off like waves in opposite directions.

"Wow," the woman I've named Barbara says in a gasp, open-mouthed, staring at the magick.

Tallyn smirks with a shake of her head, descending into the dark stairwell.

I usher the girls into the tunnel, the aether orbs light as Tallyn walks passed them. We twist around to the ceiling; gravity following us and keeping us upright.

The bright moons greet us when we spill onto the grass of Luminara, and the empty and ominous cabins on the immediate horizon.

Halcyon comes up behind us, and the sound of the lake sewing itself back up melds with the wind.

Magick sizzles with the opening of the portal. The human subjugates stare blank-faced and wide-eyed like they're all on the craziest acid trip of their lives.

Ducking through the portal, my parents usher Dick and Barb into the vortex first, followed by my sisters, Ollie, then Hattie, and her hot new friend.

"After you," I tell the girls I've chosen. I hold their hand up until each steps through.

I inhale a deep breath and step into the portal after them.

And something goes horribly wrong.

My eyelids are heavy and difficult to open. The sounds of screaming, fire, and war surround me, and the smell of homes, fabric, and flesh burning assaults my senses. I finally pry my eyes open.

There's a throbbing in the back of my head from where I must have slammed it into the stone building I'm leaning on. I stand, rubbing the back of my head. The giant knot on my skull is the size of a lemon, and blood comes away with my investigation.

I rub the blood around on my fingers and thumb as I stumble out onto a cobblestone street, the warmth of the fire in front of me unblurring my eyesight.

Fuck!

A wall of flames knocks me into full consciousness, revealing a world in total destruction.

I back up and look around, searching for any one of my family members. I'm in Luminara, the two moons tell me so, but the city I've crash-landed on is unfamiliar.

Scanning the area and ducking under a fireball barreling at my head, I can't see my family anywhere.

An abyssal sprite lunges for me, and I barely dodge their rows of razor-sharp teeth as I vamp-flash away.

The vision I had when I killed Tallyn's fae people—when they stole my blood—comes rushing back to me. The scene is exactly the same. Pyramids are off in the distance, and a modern city is at war, with fire and destruction everywhere. The beings of Luminara are running and fighting and flying, grimspawn and dark fairies—darkling fae—assaulting them. Large wyverns —with bodies like snakes and one set of taloned legs—fly everywhere, torching everything. Screeches, unlike any creature I've ever heard, accompany the fire they breathe, and it isn't the typical orange and red flames, but green.

Gravel crunches under my boots as I run, holding my breath, and dodging green fireballs. I slide under a broken carriage just in time; a bright yellow and green orb slams into the brick building above, rattling the ground and raining debris. Feeling the demon inside rumble, I bite back on him until I get my bearings.

Up ahead, I spot an alley, and run for it, turning on my supernatural speed to outrun the grimspawn hoarding toward a Luminara fae.

As I enter the alley, I realize it's the exact alley from my vision. This was the alley I saw Sayah in.

I look around for her, a frenzied zap of electricity shooting through my bones. A strange new sensation for caring about someone else's well-being on fire. I zip around a grim that comes out from behind a brick wall and dodge another closely followed by a darkling fae.

If Sayah is here, I must protect her at all costs.

A giant worm-thing with jagged ass teeth and no eyes crawls its way toward me from under a tipped shop sign, leaving a trail of slime in his wake. I use a flash of vamp power to jump over it. He loses the scent of me and slithers after a man fairy and his mate.

An abyssal sprite jumps out of the dark and snatches one of the Luminara fairies from the sky. Blood spatters the walls, ground, and all over me. The path I'm running on is now glistening with fairy guts and bones and wings as I search for somewhere to hide.

Abyssal sprites are fucking everywhere, screeching like banshees, and ripping apart anything that crosses their path.

I'm just about to jump into a hut that isn't on fire when a blast from a giant, golden fireball knocks me on my ass, blowing the stone wall behind me into a thunderstorm of broken cement. Shrapnel of glass, marble, and stone exploding the entire building in one blast.

What the fuck was that?

I scramble back, looking up to the sky to see a muscular fairy with wavy shoulder-length hair riding a flying black panther—or at least that's what it looks like. The being has the head and body of an all-black panther, yet giant black wings scrape through the dark purple sky. The fairy is not wearing a shirt, thorns are coming out of his sternum to crawl up his biceps and back, his blackish-blue wings flap with the beat of the panther's.

His eyes track the movements of someone on the ground. Up ahead, Tallyn is running to duck behind a pile of debris.

Trystan holds his palm out, and with the other, a glowing crystal pours liquid fire into a ball hovering above his hand. It multiplies, doubling until it's the size of a bowling ball in seconds. Trystan winds back and throws it between where I am and where Tallyn was.

Before the bomb can hit the ground, I flash in the other direction, hearing the collision of it explode directly behind where I was just standing.

The smell from the fire is dense, like smog, ash, sulfur, and hay. The entire village I have been thrust into is in flames, streaking the horizon in angry brush strokes of orange, bright yellow, and red. There are also green fires everywhere, mixing the chaos with cool tones of strange emerald and golden fire.

Ash is raining down upon the ground, smog coats the entire purple sky, and even though it's night, the fires make it burn bright.

Where the fuck am I?

What the fuck happened?

I'm struggling to run, to find somewhere to hide from the

crazy thorn fairy and the wyverns, the abyssal sprites, grims, and godsforbid a flying fucking spider.

I spot a slanted set of doors resembling a rain cellar up ahead and push my power to the brink of collapse, flashing over to it. The splintering of wood, crashing of trees, and swoosh of fire spreading echo behind me. I fling the doors open and rush down; the doors slamming shut behind me as I stumble—let's be real, fall—down the set of damp steps.

When I finish my tumble, I look around, and realize I'm a resident of this ruined village's small wine cellar. The space is dark, the only light streaming in through a dusty window revealing the fires outside from the raging war.

This little hut is unscathed so far. It looks like the resident has not been down here or used it in quite some time, as all the racks of bottles are dusty, and spiders' silky webs decorate the space.

I stand up, dust off my pants, and wait quietly to see if anyone has followed me down here.

The noise from the outside war sneaks in through the cracks of the wine cellar doors, but no one has followed me down here —yet.

I don't know what to do.

I don't have the power to take on anything like Trystan was throwing at me. Even in my demon form, the abyssal will rip me to shreds.

I need a way to find Tallyn.

Deciding to make myself comfortable—as I have no idea how long I'll be down here—I grab a bottle of wine and set myself up on a rickety wooden table in the far corner of the room.

My stomach grumbles.

What happened to the humans I brought here for a meal?

Well, Henry says, materializing before me, *I would say that*

Trystan found out you lot were all taking a portal here and intervened.

"You don't fucking say?" I reply. I'm not in the mood for ghostly antics right now. Then I get an idea. "Hey, can you go out and look around? See if you can find Tallyn or my family or those poor subjugates I brought here?"

Henry gives me a pointed look. *I could. But why would I? What's in it for me?*

"Are you fucking kidding me right now? What's in any of this for you?"

I like to torture you. I find it amusing.

"Well, I'll let you torture me anytime you want if you do this one thing for me. I fear there will be no way out of here if you don't. Then I'll be able to haunt the mortals with you because I will be dead, too. Or you will have no one left to torture."

Considering this, Henry cocks his head to the side. *Touché.*

"Well, go on then. Get." Taking a drink of the wine, I watch him smirk and fade away.

I have been sitting here for what seems like hours, drinking as much wine as I can and peeking through the tiny window to see if I can identify anything happening out there.

When I turn back around after my last attempt at using my vamp vision, I jump.

Henry is right behind me.

"Fuuuucking A, Henry." My heart is pounding through my ribs.

Okay. Bad news or worse news, he says, ghosting his way to the table.

"Let's go bad first."

Your humans have been ripped apart and are no longer available for your feeding pleasure.

Not heartbreaking.

"Oh, shit. Did you find any of my family? Or Tallyn?"

I did find her. She, of course, couldn't see me, but Caelum could. I let him know where you were. They were trying to find Halcyon to portal out of here.

"And the worse news?"

He stares at me ominously.

"Well?"

This is the outskirts of Feylight. Trystan has razed the last remaining city of Luminara, besides Feylight Grove.

15

A TRAITOR IN THE MIDST

—SAYAH—

The quiver of madness taking over my body nearly brings me to convulsions. My vision blurs. If the soft sheets beneath me are any indication, I'm lying on the bed in my room, staring at the white haze of the ceiling, focusing on breathing.

I inhale a deep breath and hold it for five seconds, then exhale for five, keeping the racing thoughts and panic from consuming me.

He stole all my power.

I know he did.

The memory of him shackling me and then walking away, leaving me to fall to my knees, mourning the loss of a part of me I never really even got to know.

It can't be all gone, can it?

Ember had held me with her shadows until Trystan returned. He'd been about to let me send word to my son when a giant soldier with beautiful brown skin interrupted, whispering something to Trystan about a portal opening in the newly acquired Luminara Domain.

I wasn't supposed to hear it, but I don't think Trystan real-izes my sensitive hearing is still working.

"Sorry, my pet," he said, staring at me from the threshold as the soldier caught eyes with me and left. "Duty calls. I must tend to something right now. We'll send word to your son when we get back. Come." He motioned for me to stand. "I'll bloodport you back to your room."

Before I got up to join him, I sliced my finger open behind my back and bled onto the stone floor I kneeled upon. I'm not sure why, but it felt like the right idea.

Now, lying on this bed, worrying holes into the ceiling over my powers, the portal they mentioned opening up, I hope it's not Bash and the others in Trystan's destructive path.

I have a sinking feeling it is.

I hope to see Bash in my dreams tonight and discover what is happening.

I can't tell if Trystan took my power in its entirety because of these gods-damn shackles, but every time I even try to sink into my soul and listen for its whisper, I cannot hear it, no matter how quiet I get my head and heart to be.

My bones jump out of my skin when there's a knock at the door. Not wanting to acknowledge anyone or anything in this gods-forsaken realm anymore, I stay quiet.

Knock. Knock. Knock. It comes again.

"What?" I finally yell toward the door.

"It's me, Dreadwynd," comes his muffled voice from outside the door. "I have lunch for you."

"Just leave it outside, Dreadwynd. I'll get it later."

I hear him grumbling something as he leaves. I let the food outside my door grow cold.

I must have fallen asleep because the next thing I know, I'm awoken by another banging on my door, sending shock-waves through my skin.

"Ms. Thorne?" comes Dreadwynd's muffled voice again.

"Yes, Dreadwynd?" My voice is coated in vinegar. I'm not happy he woke me up, and I can tell he's probably annoyed I let my lunch go to waste.

"You didn't eat your lunch. I've brought your dinner."

"Just leave it! I'll get it when I'm ready."

"Please don't let this food go to waste, too, Ms. Thorne, or I'll stop bringing you food altogether."

I don't say anything in response.

I honestly don't care if he stops bringing me food right now.

My anger is keeping me company. And warm. And fed. Obviously.

I didn't have much time to get to know my phoenix power, but it nonetheless became part of me. It felt like a new dress that was too small for me, but I loved it anyway and was excited to workout to fit into it.

That's how I felt about my power.

It was too big for me, but I was working it out, getting to know it, discovering the way it breathed and snapped and stretched and yawned. It was mine, and it belonged to me. Now it's gone—it was stolen, and it deserves my grief.

It deserves my sorrow.

Gods only know what Trystan is doing with it.

Dreadwynd pushes the door open, and the wheels of his squeaky cart ease up to my bedside. He wears a snarl, and his eyes are that beady black onyx. I nearly recoil at the sight of him.

"Yes?" I ask him.

"Eat. Or I shall force it down your throat."

There's more funny-looking food on the cart, more glowing liquid in the pitcher, more strange frothy desert, and odd-looking plants intermingled with the rest.

"You can just set it over there." I wave a dismissive hand.

"I have been instructed not to leave your side until you eat your food. Now. Eat."

I sit up from the bed and take the utensil, poking a bit of the food on the tray. "You gonna explain what it all is, or will I just have to trust that it's not gross?"

"I have no patience for you today, miss. Just eat."

I take my time and finish each one of the strange things on the cart. It all tastes lovely, albeit a little weird in texture. Dreadwynd stands off to the side while I eat, watching me every once in a while. He looks to the door as if someone is watching him to ensure he's making me eat. Once all the food is gone, I drink the glowing nectars and place my empty goblet on the cart with a bang when I'm done.

"There. Happy?"

He emits a low growl from the base of his neck and pushes the cart back out the door.

I'm not full, but my stomach is no longer growling, so there's that.

My eyes get heavy again, so I lay back down, my head falling harshly to the pillows.

I'm shaken awake by a loud explosion.

I scramble to my feet and topple out of the bed, getting tangled in the blankets and sheets I passed out on top of. I run to the open doors leading out to the balcony, and scan the horizon looking for the cause of the loud noise.

When my eyes find nothing, I turn, and run directly into Trystan.

"Fuck!" I gasp, retreating back a few steps. "You gotta stop doing that!"

"Did you have anything to do with the fact that there are now darkling fae swarming my dominion?"

Bash flashes into my mind. I don't know the extent of Trystan's power, and I don't want him to take Bash away from me, too.

"What?" I ask, truly lost as to what he's speaking of.

He grabs me by the arm and drags me through the bedroom toward the exit. "You will go back to that dungeon if you don't start talking. Now!"

"Ouch, Trystan! You're hurting me! What the fuck? Stop, dude, I don't know what the fuck you're talking about."

He stops yanking me, but is suddenly inches away from my face. He has blood and dirt and slimy shit all over his face and his hair is in disarray. "Funny. Because they would have had no idea where we were going to go next if you didn't overhear something downstairs."

"Overhear what? I honestly have no idea what you're talking about."

Although he is angry with me, he still is very sexy; all riled up and sweaty, his shirtless chest heaving with angst. I want to run my fingers along the thorns growing out of him and touch his body everywhere, wondering what is lurking below his waistline.

Wait! What the fuck is happening to me?

I pull my arm from his grip and back up.

It's like he senses I'm experiencing weird feelings for him because his lips, which were once in a tight line across his face, turn up in a smirk. "How was your dinner?"

Is that what's happening to me? The food?

"It was good, thank you."

"Come with me; I want to show you something."

He holds his hand out for me, and I slip my hand into his. Then, we are bloodporting sideways through the castle, like an elevator going horizontally instead of vertically. After a few seconds, we go up, and toward the other end of the castle, the side that doesn't face the Nocturna Sea.

We stop when we are at the tallest point in the northern corner of the castle, and first, I have to bend over with my hands on my knees to stop from hurling my entire weird dinner all over the dark stones of the turret.

When the feeling subsides, I stand, and look at the landscape he brought me to see.

A vast metropolitan cityscape sprawls out into the distance. Modern buildings that resemble New York City conquer the focal point, scraping the sky with their dizzying heights. The entire landscape is a cement jungle, beginning just outside the expansive front lawn of the castle. The stone walls, moat, and drawbridge separate the city from the castle grounds.

It's massive, spreading out across the horizon like an ocean.

But things are amiss.

Little fires are everywhere, smoke billowing into the air, creating angry brushstrokes of black over the once midnight-dark-blue sky. Both moons are out but touching each other. It's not quite a complete eclipse, but it's close.

A crater the size of a sports arena has been blasted into the middle of the city, smoking, fresh, and hot. Whatever building was there is not anymore. Hundreds of beings are flocking around it, trying to put out the fire while more attacks happen across the horizon.

"What's going on?" I ask, walking to the ledge, and laying my hands on the cold stone of the turret.

"The Luminara fairies are attacking my realms," Trystan replies tersely, joining me at the edge. His gray eyes scan the horizon, his expression dark, cold, and hard. "They knew I wouldn't be here. My spies in Feylight informed me they would portal back into Feylight, which means they had a ward down and now was our chance to attack. Once I began my attack there, some darkling fae and other gods-awful creatures only Bash's blood creates got in here and started this assault, forcing me to pull my soldiers back here." He pauses and directs his gaze at me. My heart falls. "Now, the only way they would have known is either you have a way of communicating something you overheard . . ."

"Or," I say for him.

"Or I have a traitor in my midst, and they are conveying sensitive information to Tallyn about our plans of attack."

"Well, it has to be the latter because I cannot communicate anything to anyone." I hold up my shackled arm, the golden manacle glimmering in the twilight. "Maybe the spy you have in Luminara is setting you up so you will not be here at a specific time."

His eyes narrow. A whisper resembling a hiss wraps around my mind, warping my thoughts. He seems to be trying to delve deep into my psyche, his snake-like thorns twisting around my mind, searching for any lies.

I don't think it was me . . .

I think back on the conversation I'd had with Bash in his houseboat, and the only time I ever overheard anything was after my encounter with him in our dreams.

"Well," Trystan goes on, placing his hands on the railing surrounding our entire widow's walk, "if it is the latter, they will be sorry they crossed me. And if it is the former . . ." His eyes turn deadly, and I have no doubt whatsoever that he would yeet me right off this tower.

"It isn't me, Trystan," I say, touching his shoulder.

He looks at my hand, but I don't move it.

Maybe the way into his good graces is getting into bed with him. I mean, I wouldn't mind fucking a fairy.

Sayah!

I wince my eyes closed and try to get the passionate thoughts to leave my mind, but I find myself getting ever more curious about him; his mind, his body . . . his cock.

He turns, and I feel he may still fling me, but surprisingly, he feathers his knuckles down the side of my face. "That's good, my pet. Because if it was you, I would tie you up and burn you at the stake like the witch that you are."

Ouch.

"I know," is all I say. I don't really know what else to say to that.

I remove my hand from his shoulder and look out at his crumbling world.

"Excuse me, my king," says a voice from behind us. Ember is waiting by the door, the thorn corset exaggerating her breasts to the point that they heave with her breath. "I'm sorry to interrupt, but I have news." She looks at me skeptically, as if she doesn't want to say what she has to say in front of me.

"Can it wait, Ember?"

"I'm afraid not. It is dire."

He grumbles something inaudible, and looks at me. "Wait right here."

I nod. As if there's anywhere else for me to go.

He follows her into the room attached to this one. It looks like a bedroom; I can see night-black furnishings on all the furniture. One of his bedrooms, I'd bet.

I act like I'm looking out to the city, but hone my hearing on what they say.

Because of these damn shackles, it's not as clear as it would be, but I do hear her say "portal," "Melodias Cove," and "now's the time to strike."

His deep voice says something I cannot make out, but she follows by saying, "I'll get them ready." Then Trystan moves back toward me.

He's in my peripheral, stepping up next to me. I scan his expression. It looks rigid and focused, a pinch of determination with a sprinkle of desperation.

"Everything okay?" I ask him.

He nods, watching the horizon; the city he seems so fond of burning before his eyes. "It will be." He faces me. "I've got to take you back to your room. The Hunt must continue."

Before grabbing my hand to whisk me back, I stop him. "Did you really take all my power?"

"Can you not feel any of it inside of you?"

Again, I hold up the shackles. "I cannot. Not even a faint buzzing like I could before. Please tell me you didn't take the one thing that was given to me and me alone."

The pearly white of his teeth glistens in the moonlight. Then another explosion draws our attention to the landscape.

This one was closer to us.

"I've got to go," he says, grasping my hand, and bloodporting me to my room.

He was right; this one didn't nearly have the effect the first bloodport did.

We're back in my room in the blink of an eye, the swirling of rooms, colors, and lights stilling as I wobble where we stand.

"I've got to go," he announces, and before I can protest, he bloodports away.

16

A GHOST AFTER MY OWN HEART

—BASH—

The sounds of battle seem to be lessening. Booms echo every few minutes now instead of as a cacophony of blasts.

It feels like hours have passed since Henry left to find Tallyn.

"I don't think you told them the right location," I tell Henry, who is sitting in the chair across from me, picking at his ghostly fingernails. His face wrinkles in consternation.

I didn't see you going out there and try to find them, he snipes sarcastically. A ghost after my own heart.

"Dude, you're already dead. I still have my whole immortal life to live. I don't feel like dying for real today."

It sounds like the battle is dying down. You could try to make your way up to the castle now. Dom's voice comes from directly behind me.

I turn to see if he's there, like Henry.

Nothing. The only thing behind me is a dusty wine rack.

"Did you hear that?"

Henry only crinkles his nose at me.

"Can you see other dead people?"

He shakes his head. *Not in here.*

"Well, not just in here but, like, in general. Do you have ghost parties and get-togethers and ghost gossip?"

Henry rolls his eyes at me and is about to say something when an explosion causes the entire front of the house to blow; wood splinters and windows shatter, sending shrapnel throughout the cellar.

Instinctively, I rush to the back of the dark basement as the ceiling collapses in on us. Bottles shatter from the wine racks tipping over onto each other, and the building falls in on itself. I cover the back of my neck with my hands, fully believing this is how I die: stuck under a pile of rubble in a fae realm with no food or water.

Will I just turn to stone?

Sayah's beautiful face steals all thoughts. A peaceful calm sweeps over me as I accept my death with her memory on my lips.

When the seismic booms similar to an earthquake subside, and nothing but darkness and rubble remain, I find I'm pinned under the remnants of the house I was under.

"Sebastian?"

"Tallyn?" I call back, trying to move a shoulder.

You better make more noise, Henry tells me, though I don't see him in my darkness.

"Dude, c'mon. Go get her for me," I plea with him.

Even my vampire strength won't budge the huge pile of destruction weighing me down.

Using everything in me, I push up, up, up, ignoring the way my back, leg, and arm muscles scream in protest. A bright light lances through the cracks in the rubble, and I scream. I give in to the weight and raise my arms over my head, pushing against the pile.

Either I'm getting stronger, or someone is helping from the outside. As a hole opens up, I see hands peeling back layers of bricks, boards, and furniture until Tallyn's face comes into view.

"Well, hello there, Sebastian," she says contritely. "Care to join us?"

I give her a dirty look and the finger. She grabs my right arm, Caelum my left, and pulls me free of the wreckage.

The entire road outside the house lies decimated, a steaming pile of destruction. "Thanks," I say to both of them, looking around for signs of any Never fae.

"Be thankful for your ghost, Bash," Tallyn says, turning to go. "Without him, you'd have been left here to rot."

Yeah, thank me, I'm amazing, Henry adds, materializing behind Tallyn.

Another finger at Henry has Caelum laughing.

"All right, children, let's move." Tallyn quickens her steps down the broken road. "Halcyon has the portal ready."

Caelum and I follow her around the bend, where Halcyon waits with the open green portal.

"Go on," Tallyn directs, waving her hand for me to go first.

"Did my family make it back?" I ask, before stepping through.

"Yes, Bash, you're the last one. Now, please hurry. We don't know when or if Trystan will continue his attack."

"Got it." I step through the portal.

Fuck how I hate portal travel.

The contents of my entire world upend and go topsy-turvy, flying through nothing, and everything all at once.

I. Will. Never. Get. Used. To. It.

I am deposited into a room with a fire—shocking—and bookshelves and bars and paintings and the like, and honestly, I have no idea if it's one we've never been in before or the same fucking one each time.

It could be the same room that just changes after we leave.

This time, I land on my feet—at least I'm improving.

"Bash!" my mom calls, jumping up from lying beside my dad on a brown couch to rush to me. She holds me by the shoulders and checks me for injuries. "Are you hurt? You're bleeding."

I put my hand to the pain in my head and pull away blood. "Yeah, I'm fine. Just a scratch." Glancing around at all the faces, making sure everyone I care about is accounted for. No one seems to be missing. "Are there any casualties?"

"Just the humans we all brought with us," Mom answers, looking at her family with wide, loving eyes. "Some injuries on our end, but nothing fatal, thank the gods."

"What happened?" I go to ask Tallyn, who seems distraught while talking closely with Caelum and Halcyon.

Her orange eyes catch mine, her face dirty and bruised. "Trystan learned we were not in Feylight and that the wards were down for us to portal in and out. He took that to his advantage and attacked."

"How much of Feylight is destroyed?"

Her disheveled clothes swoosh as she moves from her comrades to the fire. "I don't know," she says, her eyes mimicking the orange-licking flames. "We have to act fast. The war rages on. I had been prepared for something like this, though, so as soon as he attacked Feylight, it triggered a curse that sent abyssal and more spells to his castle in Nightshade to raze it back. It wasn't much, but it was all I had to work with."

Bash! That's Sayah's voice.

The sound throws me for a loop so much that I jump, and everyone who's near me looks at me strangely.

"Side effects," I lie.

That couldn't have been Sayah's voice.

I know she's not dead. I'd feel it.

"So what are you going to do now?" I ask, trying to ignore the nagging feeling telling me to go somewhere quiet to see if it was her voice.

Sebastian!

That *is* Sayah's voice.

"Well, we need to—"

"Hold on just one second, will you?" I stop her by putting my hand on her shoulder. "Where's the nearest restroom?"

The bridge of her nose wrinkles. "Down that hall, to the right."

Once I'm alone in the restroom, I ask, "Sayah?"

Oh, Bash! You can hear me!

"Yes, but how—how are you doing this?"

That doesn't matter right now. I'll tell you in our dreams. I don't know how much time I have. I just wanted you to tell Tallyn "Melodias Cove." I don't know what it means, but I'm sure she'll know.

"Melodias Cove?"

Yes!

"Okay. Are you okay?"

I'm fine. I'll meet you tonight, okay?

"Okay. I love you."

I love you, too, Bash.

Sayah may not be here in person, but the hairs still lift along my spine as though she were a ghost in the room, exhaling on my skin.

I actually do have to pee, so I do so quickly, wash my hands in the posh black porcelain washbasin, and then flash back out to Tallyn and her soldiers.

"Tallyn, does the name 'Melodias Cove' mean anything to you?"

Tallyn's eyebrows perk up, and there's a glint in her eye. "Yeah, why?"

"Hard to explain how I know, but I was just told to tell you that from someone who is in Never."

"Tallyn, that means—" Caelum says.

"I know what it means. Let's go!"

She moves to rush off, and I flash up to her, holding her by the crook of the elbow. "Whoa, wait a sec. what does that mean? Where are we going?"

"No time to explain it. Just get your family ready and let's go. Meet me in the greenhouse in twenty." She scurries away again, her boot heels clicking on the white marble floors.

"Greenhouse?" I call after her, my voice echoing in the large room.

"You'll find it, Bash, just ask around," she says, leaving through a heavy and decorated door.

How the fuck will I find that room and get my family there in twenty minutes?

My mom has returned to sit next to my dad, and the rest of the family is sauntering around, lounging on the couches, and hanging out by the bar, drinking glowing things.

"Hey, guys? We have to go. Is everyone ready?"

Hattie looks up from a book she's reading. "Where are we going?"

"Melodias Cove, I guess," I reply.

Jasantha is suddenly next to me, a blur of purple in her wake. "Where did you say?"

"Melodias Cove. Why, you know it?"

"Uh, yeah, it's like the Mecca for sirens. A lot of my people are there. Why? Why are we going there?"

"Sayah told me—"

"Sayah? Is she here?" Mom asks.

"No, she and I have . . . ways to talk to each other, apparently." My brows wrinkle as I try to understand this newest development of ours. "She's still in Never. She just telepathically told me to tell Tallyn the name. So I did. And apparently, that's where we're going now."

"*No!* No, no, no, no," Jasantha says. "That means that Trystan is bringing his Hunt there. There hasn't been war in Melodias Cove in a millennium. Fuck. I have to warn them."

"That's where we're going. Let's go."

"I have an idea," Ollie announces, approaching us, with Claire trailing behind him. She looks shocked and worried. Her hair is matted and dried blood is spattered over her and Ollie's faces.

"What's your idea?" Dad asks, joining our congregation in the middle of the room.

"When we get there. Let's word each other."

"I don't know," Mom says. "How will you know not to kill Luminara fairies or sirens?"

"We're not completely gone when you word us," I confirm, scratching my head where the wound used to be. "We still have our faculties. We just don't give a fuck."

"Okay, okay. We can word you guys when we get there and see what we're up against. If Jasantha wants to warn her people, we may only get there in time to do so. We have no idea what we're facing if it's anything like what's going on out there."

"Yeah, how are they not infiltrating the castle by now?" I ask as we all begin to round up.

"Tallyn has stronger wards around the inter rings of the castle than she did around the surrounding villages," Scarlet answers.

"Ah. All right, anyone know where this greenhouse is?" I ask.

"I can show you to it," Sariana offers, and my mom's expression is one of sadness and intrigue.

Apparently, they haven't spent much time together yet while being here.

I can see the yearning in her eyes; the torture it must be for her to be so near her firstborn daughter and not be able to talk to her or get close to her. She seems to want to say something to Sariana, but my estranged sister only turns on her heel and bids us to follow her.

We're quiet as we follow her into the hallway, and our footsteps collectively echo. We pile into a small alcove that's shrouded in shadow.

"Okay, I need silence for this next part," Sariana says, her eyes snapping to life in the dark. A kaleidoscope of colors swirls in her retinas and she murmurs something to the darkness, melding with them until only those glowing eyes remain.

From the darkness, her arms emerge, draped in shadow, and she pulls us into her one at a time. Each one of us gets pulled into the shadow and disappears.

When it's my turn, the grip on my arm is ice cold, yanking me into the dark. The wind whips my hair around as a shadow turns me in a circle. When the world is done spinning, someone shoves my back. I lunge forward, tripping on rocks and grass when I emerge from behind a giant tree.

Sariana's eyes come out of the shadow, her body re-materializing.

"What the fuck was that?" I ask her.

"Shadowport. I'm a shadow weaver," she says, her eyes melting into one color. I wrinkle my brows in confusion, but she shakes her head. "No time to explain how my powers work. They're gathering."

She rushes off in the other direction, and I follow her, my family, and the others who are doing the same.

We duck under branches and around trees until we come into a clearing.

Calling it "greenhouse" is really an understatement.

Looking more like a castle or Gothic cathedral, with tall towers and spires, copulas and widow's walks, the entire thing is made of glass and looks to house copious amounts of tall trees, some spurting out of the very top of it.

When we get to the entrance, the doors are ten feet high and made of stained glass. Brass handles line the length of both.

Sariana opens the doors, and I'm greeted with warm air—the smell of damp earth, moss, flowers, and trees cloying the entrance.

Inside, hundreds of thousands of Luminara fairies are facing the back wall. Essentially, we walked into a church—their church. Rows and rows of fairies are facing forward, their backs to us, as Tallyn stands on the dais in the front, addressing them all.

"Now is the time to *fight!*" Tallyn's voice rises above the murmurs, rallying the crowd into an eruption of cheers. "Trystan has invaded our home and is about to take over the last piece remaining of Luminara. If he succeeds, the world will be brought to ruin. The Riftstorm Conflict began the minute he stepped foot in Feylight. He knows that gaining dominance over it will grant him the immense power he seeks over multiple worlds. My friends, this is the beginning of the end if we don't intervene."

A heavy, ominous silence falls over the people of Luminara as Tallyn's words settle in, and a palpable sense of determination replaces the fear in the room. "He is said to be heading to Melodias Cove next, the last stronghold of the Luminara Domain besides Feylight. If he captures it, he will open the Shadow Gate portal, which will bring destruction and death to the people of Earth. For thousands of years, the sirens of Melodias Cove have protected that portal. Should he breach it, the Shadow Gate will tear apart the fabric of existence, causing violent clashes. Entities from countless realms will be drawn into the chaos. You've trained your entire lives for this moment, and I need you now more than ever."

The warriors erupt in cheers, their voices fierce and unified. Clad in their battle regalia, beings of all colors—blues, yellows, reds, purples, greens, and more—begin to sing the songs of their ancestors, the restless nature of the fairies and their thirst for vengeance electrifying the room.

Tallyn raises her arms to quiet them. "Grab your weapons, hone your magic, kiss your babies, and go through the portal when you're ready to fight. I cannot guarantee you will return. I have no idea what to expect. All I know is that we must act now if we are to save our home. I am going, as are my most trusted soldiers, advisers, generals, lieutenants, and corporals.

Come with us and fight for Feylight, for Luminara, for our world!"

Thunderous cheers echo through the chamber, spilling out into the vast night. Above them, the two moons eclipse each other, their combined light bathing the room in an eerie brilliance, signaling that the Dread Harvest is in full effect.

Tallyn steps down from the dais and approaches Halcyon as the crowd begins to shift. Some say tearful goodbyes to loved ones; others quietly steel themselves, fastening armor, and readying weapons.

Then the energy in the room sharpens when a group of warriors form a circle at the center of the hall. They begin a rhythmic chant, their feet stomping in unison, their hands slapping their thighs and chests in a primal rhythm. The air hums with their ritual of power and unity.

I lean closer to Sariana, confused as to what's happening.

"The fuck are they doing?"

Sariana watches the warriors with reverence, her voice low and awed as she explains. "It's the Vaelstrai—the Dance of Light and Shadow. It's an ancient ritual performed before battle, a call to the spirits of Luminara for strength and guidance. It binds them together, soul to soul, and reminds them of what they're fighting for. Watch closely, Bash. You'll never see anything like it."

The warriors' movements grow more intense, their voices rising in unison. The ground beneath them seems to tremble. The Vaelstrai reaches a crescendo, their chant a war cry that reverberates through the hall, igniting the hearts of all who hear it.

The sizzle of magick permeates the air, and Halcyon unzippers a portal on the other side of the dais, ushering in people who are ready to leave. The spinning vortex of blue, green, and silver swirls in an intricate design, and the people of Feylight begin to step into it one by one.

I look at my mom, dad, Ollie, Claire, and sisters.

Expressions of determination and destruction paint their villainous faces. The monsters living within them comfortably out to play with the emerging of their fangs.

The frightening facade of my family makes me proud.

Even though this didn't begin as our fight . . . it will end with us.

17

A NEW POWER

—SAYAH—

It doesn't feel like much time has passed before Trystan returns.

Dreadwynd had just dropped off my evening meal to me—at least, I think it's evening. It's hard to tell in the dreary space. He sat here and forced me to eat again, and I'm starting to feel better about my situation.

At least, I think I am.

There seems to be two people living within me now and it's getting confusing to pinpoint where one of me ends and the other me begins. The serrated edges of the person I was when I got here are crumbling, my resolve weakening, and I fear that whatever I have been consuming is actually starting to consume me.

It's not a subtle change of mind or a simple frame of adjusting; the whispering darkness of this place is maddening and muddling the sinister waters I've stumbled upon. No, this is like an entire person budding up from the murky soil of my being— a seed Trystan planted in me somehow. Every time I eat or drink the food and nectar here, it sows the seed he's planted into another being entirely that's taking over not only my mind but also my body and my soul.

I have no idea how much longer I will be myself, and I need to figure out a way to at least tell Bash what I know.

I fear the next meal I eat here will end me.

My resolve is dimming, leaving shattered embers in my bones in its wake.

The softness of Bash's memory feels like a caress in my sad existence in this gilded cage, and yet his memory is getting fuzzy around the edges—like Trystan is taking flame to the picture of him in my mind. As Bash's picture curls with heat, so too does the memory of Dom and my grief for him and the other's—Ollie, Claire, Adaline, Everett. Even Scarlet, Hattie, and Jasantha.

The other person growing within finds Trystan more alluring every time I see him. Little butterflies crawl up the center of me and coil in my middle whenever he walks in.

The butterflies feel rotten, though—beauty paired with decay, or decadence paired with nausea.

I'm sitting at the table when Dreadwynd closes the double doors behind him, his squeaky cart that really needs some oil screeching into the hall. Trystan appears out of the blue and I know now it's because he bloodported here.

He is dressed in black armor, looking like he's getting ready for battle.

The other me wants to rip the armor off him and explore his ripples with my tongue.

"Yes, Trystan?" I say, blushing at the thought I'm no longer chastising myself for.

Besides, Bash and I aren't a couple. At least, I don't think we are. We haven't established we are, anyway.

"I am traveling tonight," he shares, his armor clanking on the marble floor as he approaches me. "I don't know when I'll be back. I need you to do something for me."

I sit up straighter, letting the heave of my breasts entice his eyes. "Yes?"

"I need a little more of your power. It seems the last batch had a limit."

Interesting. I thought he took all my power from me.

"Did you hold up your end of the bargain?" I ask him, scooting to the edge of my seat and letting my white gown show off my right leg.

"I have. I sent a Whispering Leaf to my brigadiers in Windsor to get word to your son. They are doing so as I speak."

Even though I normally would want proof of this, I somehow don't really care to see proof at this moment. Besides, I trust Bash was able to do what he said he would, and I don't want to let Trystan know I have the ability to see Bash in my dreams.

I don't ever want him to find that out.

"If you promise not to take it all." I'm tired and losing my will to fight. Really, I just want to sleep.

"I promise." The words are metallic, steely—hollow. There is no meaning in them whatsoever.

The thud of his boots echo across the tile as he approaches me, the breeze from the open balcony doors sneaking in and stirring his hair. He kneels before me, his blue eyes sparkling with malice in the dim light of the moons and orb lights floating within grooves in the walls. With a tepid gentleness, he takes my hand in his. I don't flinch.

The temperature in the room drops, so much so that I can see my breath in a puff of smoke in front of me.

"What's happening?"

"I'm taking some of your power." He says so softly that the wind could have stolen his words.

"I thought you needed Nyxaria, Ember, and the other guy to do that."

"Nyx and Ember were there for one thing. Sablethorn

another. I need you to remain quiet and calm and show me to your power."

He removes the key from his pocket and unshackles my wrist, the hard metal clanking to the floor. The buzz of my power is faint this time, but I'm relieved it's still there.

I steel myself, protecting the golden light within me as I feel his electric-blue essence enter my mind. I'm falling through the vortex again, desperately trying to protect all the golden power, secretly beckoning just a sliver of it to unlatch itself from my soul and enter my ribs, to only allow him take the tiniest bit.

As he follows me to my power, I see a spark, like an arrow that's been loosed, and it flies at me, piercing me in what would be my forehead.

Then I'm falling.

Falling.

Blackness—a void—and cold greet me as I fall into what can only be Trystan's mind.

It's vast—wide-open, like the universe—but also small and decaying. He seems to be at war with himself. It is a cavernous hideaway with bookshelves reaching to the heavens, with big planets and moons shining through the open roof, limning everything in a creepy evanescence. The part of him that is power hungry and devoid of emotions is engulfed by thorns, devouring everything in this space. Thorns cover the entire ground and most of the shelves.

Up ahead, a glowing burnt orange light seeps out of cabinets lining one wall. There is a single row of drawers in this space that haven't been succumbed to by the thorns. It is beckoning me in, and I draw up to it, fearing he will soon know I'm in his mind.

Maybe he's still looking for me in mine.

As I get closer, there's a scene playing out in a crystal ball on a table held up by thorns.

Gazing within it, I see Trystan standing there, arms

outstretched, while a being—maybe it's Tallyn, but she's veiled, so it's hard to tell—sucking all the power from him into her.

All his powers—the blue, orange, green, red, and white—are flooding from him and entering her repeatedly like a GIF.

His worst fear is having no power.

Of this, I am certain.

I reach the power seeping out of the drawer and inhale it—that's the only way I can describe it, as I have no body. I absorb the power into myself, and suddenly, I'm falling again.

Falling.

Back in my mind, Trystan's blue energy still flows around. Though it does feel like he lost me for a bit and cannot find me or the power.

The golden arrow of power is nailed to a rib, and I glide up to it, awaiting him to absorb the golden power into his blue waves.

When he does, I rise in a breathless rush, gasping for air.

Trystan is still kneeling before me, his eyes closed, and I don't yet know if he knows I trespassed into his mind.

That I know his deepest fear. His darkest secret.

He fears being mortal. Being powerless.

But what power of his did I gather?

I search my soul for the buzzing and feel it tickling my spine.

Good girl.

She hid.

When he opens his eyes, the blue of them looks like glass, ready to shatter me. His lips are plush and pink, and his face lacks any and all wrinkles—though he has to be at least a thousand years old. Something in the air settles between us, and my breath hitches, waiting for him to speak.

It feels like hours—years—before he finally inhales and says, "Good girl."

The words strike me in a weird way. It's almost sensuous.

He must have secured the power then, and so far, no inkling tells me he knows I've been inside his mind.

"You got some of it, then?" I ask, slipping my hand out of his.

He grabs my hand back, and my heart stops. "I know what you did."

Oh, gods. He's going to send me to the dungeon again. Or tie me up and force me to give all my power to him.

"What do you mean?" I play dumb.

"You didn't let me get close to the source. You only gave me a sliver."

Blood rushes back to my limbs. "You said you only wanted a little."

His head tilts sideways, and I don't know what he's thinking. "Sayah. You'll have to learn to trust me if you are to be my queen."

I nod slightly. "It's going to take some time, Trystan. My power is all I have left of who I was before I came here. I won't let you have all of it."

He tuts. "I thought you knew by now. Mercy has no place in a live wire. I take what I want. If I wanted all your power, I would have it." I look away, and he pulls my chin back to look at me. "It's in your best interest to stop resisting me and submit to me. I promise you, you won't be disappointed. Have you thought any more about what I said? How Gauge will be able to walk and fly and not have diabetes?"

"Yes, I have. But what you're asking is huge. It's asking him and me to give up our world and for him to never see his dad again. You're asking us to live in Neverdusk, and for Gauge to give up seeing the sun again. It's a huge ask. I can't just say yes to that right now."

There's a knock at the door, and a small dark fairy that looks like the universe curled up and soaked into her skin enters. Even her eyes resemble stars.

"Sir," she says, the tone of her voice soft and steady, like water flowing over stones. "The portal is ready. We have to move fast."

"Thank you, Ebonshade. I'll be right there." I shiver as he stands. The air in the room is still so cold. "I must go. I don't know how long I'll be gone. Be a good girl and do as you're told —eat your meals, sleep, and I'll be back before you know it."

"Where are you going?"

He gives me an inscrutable smile and says, "Now, now, my pet. We're both learning to trust each other. Just because I gave you a room doesn't mean I'll trust you with my war efforts."

"I understand."

"The more you let me in and trust me, the more I'll let you in and trust you. But for now"—he takes the shackles and places them back on my wrist and ankle—"you still belong to me. You are mine. And. You. Will. Behave."

"When will you let me see my son?"

He tuts again. "You'll just have to wait and see, my little witch."

He breezes off in the direction of Ebonshade and looks back as he tarries on the threshold. "I shall return soon. Be good."

And he's gone.

Something is stirring in my soul—the new power I stole and have no idea what it is.

I quickly run to the balcony and look up at the moons—as if any moon can soothe my soul.

Closing my eyes and picturing what my mind would look like were it just a room, I fall deep into my own soul to find my powers. Down that tall height I go, steeling myself against the feeling of falling. When I collide with the bottom, I find I'm in a castle tower with a room facing the sea. The ocean waves are a lullaby to my soul. Glancing around, walls of books soar up one side all the way to the sky and cabinets for my memories, thoughts, and dreams on the other wall. The walls are filled with pictures of people I love—Mama, Daddy, Gauge, Bash, Dom, Claire—and they're all moving like captured memories.

I can feel my phoenix power in one of the drawers, and it's sealed with the same padlock that seals my shackles. Running up to it, I try to pry it free, pulling, pushing, and cursing as if my life depended on it, but it won't budge.

I fall on my ass. "Fuck," I say through my teeth.

Where did that new power go?

A purple mist emerges from an ornate jewelry box resting on a table with a beautiful wooden lamp.

As I scramble to my feet, approaching it, I see the words Bash spoke to me about my smiles, swirling words around a memory of him and me.

The words are golden and smoke-like. I want to touch them, but I leave them be and say, "Bash," while fingering them.

Their smoke flits like wind to a candle, but the words remain undisturbed.

Side effects. That's Bash's voice!

Looking around, I hope to find him or see where his voice comes from when I hear more of it wafting.

So what are you going to do now? His voice is as clear as day.

"Sebastian!" I yell, my voice echoing in the tower of my mind.

Hold on just one second, will you? Where's the nearest restroom?

Oh, my gods, can he hear me? Who's he talking to?

A few seconds later, he says, *Sayah?*

"Oh, Bash! You can hear me!" I cannot help the desperation or joy in my voice.

Yes, but how are you doing this?

"That doesn't matter right now. I'll tell you in our dreams. I don't know how much time I have. I just wanted you to tell Tallyn 'Melodias Cove.' I don't know what it means, but I'm sure she'll know."

Melodias Cove?

"Yes!"

Okay. Are you okay?

"I'm fine. I'll meet you tonight, okay?"

Okay. I love you.

"I love you, too, Bash."

The air turns cold, yet I remain warm from the softness of his voice settling into me like a warm fire after being in the freezing cold for hours.

Is this my new power, then? If so, what does it mean?

I walk away from the words and sit on a settee, looking out at the dark ocean, the waves churning below.

It's funny that in my dreams and in here, safe in my mind, I don't feel the effects of Neverdusk Dominion.

Here, I am my own self, and my love for Bash and that world and my son thrives. I don't ever want to return to Never.

Ever.

18

CROOKED WHISPERS

—BASH—

I fucking hate portal travel.

Have I said that before?

I'm thrust into a new realm the moment I step out of the portal, and I can't even look up to see it yet. My stomach is trying to hurl the empty contents onto the silver rocks I'm kneeling on.

I need blood.

Soon.

I'm feeling the effects of not eating starting to take hold. It starts with being out of breath and having little energy to do anything. It then morphs into being unable to utilize my powers, and things as simple as veilweaving and vamp-flashing become things that feel like over-exertion. The longest I've been without blood is only two weeks, and that was because I had been held captive by a pirate hooker once.

Long story.

Vampires don't have to consume blood every day. When we kill to feed, we can go about five to seven days between feeds. But when we don't kill to feed or consume enough to sustain the hunger, we need to feed more frequently. Since I've only snacked on Tallyn in the last day or so, and since she was feeding me dead blood before that—blood that didn't come straight from the vein—I'm feeling it.

When we don't feed for more than two weeks, we start to desiccate. Our skin turns gray like stone, our blood turns brownish-black, and we basically become zombies, feeding on anything that moves if it comes near us. Our state of mind is slumbering in the desiccation phase.

We can't afford for any of us to get to that point.

Maybe some sirens will lend me some of their blood.

Coughing and spitting a gross white ball of sticky spit, I brush my hair back and reel in the salty, cool air of Melodias Cove.

I've never been here, but I have heard of it.

It's a hidden enclave between towering cliffs cradled by the tumultuous Reverie Sea. Phosphorescent moss adorns the ancient rocks, concealing the cave's entrance with a curtain of cascading waterfalls.

The rest of the Feylight army is assembling on the beaches of Reverie as I meander toward my family.

We all seem to be here. All except Sayah.

There are no sounds of war yet, and I look to Jasantha, who's eyeing the entrance with reverence.

"We need to go in first, without this army, to avoid frightening the people of the cove," she says, mainly to Tallyn, who nods approvingly.

"Lead the way, sister," I say, and she flashes her purple eyes at me, the medallion on her neck glowing.

Falling in line behind Ollie, Jasantha leads us to the entrance.

Only the vampires follow her, as we are not about to let her go in there unguarded.

She stops before the waterfall and looks up.

The cliff's face is about two to three hundred feet high. The crashing of the water into the pond below is loud and soothing at the same time. Once the water hits the pool below, it rushes out to join the Reverie Sea.

Jasantha opens her mouth.

The screeching song emanates from her and travels in visible sound waves toward the cascading water. The blue velvet streaks of sound penetrate the water, causing it to part, revealing the cove inside.

We bow under the spray of water; the air becoming thick with the haunting melody of the sirens, their ethereal voices blending with the rhythmic crash of the waves against the jagged rocks.

The cove itself is a breathtaking tapestry of bioluminescent flora, casting an otherworldly glow dancing across the dark waters. Shimmering shells and luminescent coral rest along the shore, creating an enchanted pathway toward the cove's heart.

A massive arch of crystalline material stands tall at the center of Melodias Cove—the entrance to the Shadow Gate Portal. The doorway to the abyss it guards hums with an eerie energy. It pulsates in tandem with the heartbeat of the sirens who stand vigil. Ancient symbols are etched into the surrounding cliffs, marking the boundary between our world and the unseen realms beyond.

Sirens, with iridescent scales and flowing, pearlescent hair, perch on rocky outcrops. Their hauntingly beautiful voices weave a protective spell around the Shadow Gate Portal. The waters respond to their singing, creating a magickal barrier shielding the portal.

"Melodias Cove is a place of mystic beauty and imminent danger," Jasantha says to us as we advance further into the cove. "It's where the sirens maintain an eternal watch, ensuring that the shadowy realms remain confined and the delicate balance between dimensions is preserved."

As we merge into the cove, the singing stops suddenly, and I feel all the eyes within the cove landing on us.

"Halt!" a voice from an alcove etched high up in the rocks yells. "What colony are you from?"

"My name is Jasantha." Her voice echoes. "I'm originally from the Thalassara clan."

"The Thalassara clan?" The siren's voice softens, and there's an audible gasp among the others, as though they all knew Jasantha's family.

The siren, whose face I cannot make out, suddenly does a swan dive into the water. The water splashes up from where she dove, considering the height from which she jumped. Her face emerges from the water, a glittering midnight color. She has raven-colored hair, yellow eyes, and many sharp teeth that make up the front when she grins at us.

She looks like Jasantha when she's entirely in her mermaid form.

"Aaralyn?" Jasantha gasps, her eyes widening in disbelief.

Aaralyn's eyes glisten. "Sister?"

Jasantha runs to the water and splashes in. Her feet begin to morph into a shimmering, metallically purple tale when she steps into the salty liquid. The scales are reminiscent of a pearl —when the light hits it at different angles, it becomes a different color. As she submerges herself in the water, her clothes transform into her fin, her shirt merely rearranging to become the color of a pearly bra that matches her fin.

It's pretty fucking cool.

When Jasantha reaches her sister, Aaralyn embraces her in a hug.

It takes a lot for a monster like us to be astoundingly touched by something. Because we've been alive for a long time, chances are we've seen it. But something like this—a reunion of old families anew—has my own eyes welling with tears.

Maybe it's the thought of my brother and that I'll never be able to have this sort of reunion with him chasing my battle-hardened mood away. When looking at my sister Scarlet, I see the same expression I know is planted on mine.

Lovingly and painfully happy for our adopted sister, but missing our own with every ounce of the hug.

Hattie has a more bored look, as if she couldn't care less about who this being is, but my mom also has the same expression as Scarlet.

My dad and Ollie, too.

"We never knew what happened to you," Jasantha says, pulling out of her sister's embrace and wiping tear-stained water from her eyes. "We went to the isle a few times to see if you were there, but you never came. I assumed you met a man and moved on, a landwalker or a sea one."

"I found a man," Aaralyn confirms, her eyes brightening with joy. "His name is Seraph, and we had three children—Seraphina, Calypso, and Naiara. They're down below, in our home. And you have made peace with your found family?"

She looks back at us with a soft smile. "I have."

"Good to see you, Adaline." Aaralyn bows her head at my mom.

My mom returns the gesture. "Good to see you as well, Aaralyn."

"Gods, I'm so happy to see you!" Jasantha interjects. "I just wish it was on better terms."

"What brings you here, sister?"

More and more of the sirens gather around. Some are pale peach; some are dark, like night, and others are different colors, like blue, pink, and orange. They seem to pop up from nowhere, the abyss with which this cove leads to.

I only wonder what their colony looks like underneath this water.

"War," Jasantha says ominously. "We have received word that Trystan, King of the Nightshades and the Neverdusk Dominion, will attack the cove today. We do not know when or how many he has with him."

As they continue talking in the water, mermaids seem to be slithering beneath the surface, more up on the walls of the cliffs, in the notches of the rocks, and all over the beaches like watchful sentinels. Even though it is night, a deep cloud that's seemingly unnatural falls over the moon, blotting out the light, and even though not many others notice, an imagined chill laps at the nape of my neck.

Something isn't right.

I stagger my hearing to listen to the things in between the voices here, hovering my hearing outside the flowing waterfall where Tallyn and the rest of the Luminara fairies are waiting.

There is a subtle vibrating on the ground, reverberating a sinister air. I feel cold, and knots erupt in my stomach, causing the air in my lungs to constrict. Kneeling to feel the soil, the voices begin to fade into the ether. Clearing my mind of everything around me, I shield my body to connect with my power. The vibrations send little currents of electricity to my fingertips, and a flash of light enters my mind.

My mom comes over to me, resting her hand on my shoulder. "What is it, Bash?"

Scanning the water, my mom casts a wayward glance toward the sirens who linger there, their haunting melodies disrupted by the sudden disturbance.

The water in the cove takes on a sinister stillness, but slowly, ripples cascade outward, like a pounding reverberating through the land.

Before I can answer her, a sound resembling banshees of the night rend the air.

The entire cove goes deathly silent.

Crackle-sounds resembling a live wire slither along the ground—flood even through the sound of the waterfall, and with it, echoes of a battle begin outside it. Luckily, the cove is protected by magick and can only be entered by—

An explosion.

The entire front of the cave comes at us in a fiery deluge, blowing bits of the mountain inward and hitting multiple sirens on the way down. The sirens hurl through the air, breaking bones, skin, and scales on the sharp rocks of the cove.

Before anyone can fathom anything, the beating of a thousand wings cuts through me, sounding like a million bees are flooding the place. The cove sits between two mountains, and the entire valley blacks out from the number of beings flying overhead.

Inside, dark fairies fly in on their own wings or on beasts as black as night, creatures with slithering bodies and filmy eyes. They dip into the water and pluck the sirens out one by one, rising back up to the sky with them.

The cove's tranquility shatters further. Fairies from the Neverdusk descend, their wings flickering with an otherworldly glow. They slant the light from the moons as it shimmers in through the cracks in the valley above.

Sirens, who were once guardians of the portal, steely and stoic and full of warrior auras, are stilled, as though a silent net of coercion has covered them. There is no blood from the creatures plucking them from the water, only to shoot back into the sky. The siren's eyes are almost lifeless, murky, while their limbs lie limp at their sides.

My heart is pounding with the echoes of the explosion reverberating through the cove. Sirens that haven't been magicked with coercion have begun to try and flee below the water, and yet the fairies, and other nightmares of Neverdusk bring with them the chaos of other realms. Beings I've never seen before swoop into the water seamlessly before dragging them out by their hair.

Hattie's leaps over one grimspawn coming after her, the teal of her power unleashing to send a shockwave over a group of Neverdusk soldiers. I go after the grimspawn she leapt over, twisting its head off.

Hattie's power drapes over them, forcing them to freeze, only for them to thrash about seconds later, fighting things only Hattie lets them see. They turn on each other, each one thinking their comrades are the enemy. The silver of the swords clash against each other, while others are loping heads off. Bloody necks lie exposed as its body sink to its knees before collapsing to the dirt floor. Abdomens are grotesquely sliced open and guts fall to the ground.

Tallyn rushes through the exploded opening of the cove, jumping over boulders. A rumbling crashes from where her feet land. She scoops up the vibrations with her gloved hand, shoving the shockwave into more of Trystan's soldiers, sending abyssal sprites flying through the air.

Her white eyes piercing the dark of the cove, Scarlet grabs one of the soldiers by the collar, whispering something seductively in his ear. Her magick is the color of pearls, like breath on a cold winter morning. When it hits his eardrums like a vice, he immediately grabs a Neverdusk fae from the air, pulling her down, and shoving a knife through her eye. When he turns to find more flying enemies, she does this to each man she can get close to.

A swarm of abyssal creatures swoop in from the blackened hole. They move like wraiths on a battlefield, lithe and fast, making no sound as their serrated entrance enhances over the exploded wall. Twelve of Trystan's soldiers and a handful of Tallyn's transform to dust on just their wind.

One is heading for my father, using its obscenely large arms like an ape to disjointedly advance on him. My dad morphs into one of the nastiest looking abyssal, his face darkening to gray, his eyes melting into his head, and his face elongating into a snout with dozens of shiny, sharp shark teeth. He tries to trick them by steering them away from my mom, and four or five of them invert their path to her and follow him. But two of them don't—the largest two, of course.

As they quicken their steps toward her, my mom pulls out her orange power and shoves it at them, but they're unfazed, relentless in their quest for corrosion. Next thing I know, I am running—no flashing—to her, and just as one is about to rip her in half, I remember the way they stopped at the cabin.

My heart falters.

"Stop!"

Every single abyssal sprite that was made from my blood halts their path of destruction at my yell.

When Ollie beckons the water with a motion of his hand, drops, waves, and tornadoes of ocean rise, turning into predatory birds of prey that immediately rip the frozen abyssal to pieces. The sounds of tearing flesh and ripping tendons echo with the cries of war.

After the abyssal creatures within our direct line of sight are grimspawn food, my mom—ever the Viking warrior—makes a motion like she's pulling a rope, and there's a flash of lightning and a rumble of thunder. The thunder is so loud that one of Neverdusk's soldiers looks up, and Laureya, seeing an opportunity, weaves into a large raven, her body vacuuming into itself. She lunges for the soldier, pecking at his eyes while my mom's storm funnels toward her, wind, rain, and lightning encompassing the expansive cove.

I take the vibrations from the thunder and shove the blast at more grimspawns flowing in. They fall back onto each other, some landing on sharp rocks. A severed torso tumbles to the banks of the cove. Jasantha's eyes narrow as she surveys the turbulent sea, rushing to exit the water as her iridescent fins evaporate back to her legs, tugging her sister with her. Scarlet and Hattie rush to her, the blurring color of their movements matching the swirling blood now darkening the water.

Kaston, Draelle, Laith, and Ryan savagely rip into more soldiers, using their vampire strength to pull limbs and heads and hearts from anything moving near them.

My mom has summed the lightning and is using it as a whip, lassoing it around her head and whipping it out, electrifying anything in its path.

Wyverns, ridden by these demented and darkened beings, circle above, casting shadows over the water and blowing flames in warning. The valley top seems too narrow for them to enter. My mom's lightning hits one, causing it to plummet from the sky, landing on top of the narrow entrance at the top, blocking access from above.

Go get Trystan! Dom's voice yells, his voice surrounding me.

I immediately flash toward the entrance, yanking a Neverdusk soldier to me on my way out. I twist his head until I feel bones, tendons, and muscles crack and pop unnaturally. His body falls to the ground with a thud, the sound mixing with the turbulent storm inside the cove.

Stumbling over rubble, bodies, blood, and water, I make my way out to the silver beaches of Melodias Cove and . . .

It. Is. Pandemonium.

Luminara fairies are doing what they can to battle the Neverdusk, but we seem to be grossly outnumbered. One douche runs at me, and I punch into his chest and rip out his heart.

A few more approach.

This one, I bite and rip.

The next one, I snap and pop.

I don't see Sayah anywhere.

There are flying things everywhere, and the entire sky is filled with black blots, flying fae, wyverns, and mayhem.

Another explosion has my eyes tracking that way, and there I see it—the thing I didn't want to see.

Trystan, riding on his black panther with wings, his body glowing like Sayah.

Like fucking Sayah.

His bluish-black wings stretch out ten feet each way. They hover him and his panther above a crowd of Luminara fairies, blowing phoenix bombs at them. He is no longer peach, but sort of dusky gray. His skin is fissured with golden cracks, and his eyes are glowing gold—like living lightning rests under his skin.

Call him out, Bash, says Dom's voice. *Get that motherfucker.*

Not having to ask twice, I lock it down, steeling myself.

Another dumb-ass fairy runs at me. But before he's about to get me, I say, "Agares," and go cold.

I don't black out this time, but I definitely am not in control.

Strength, unlike anything I've ever experienced, takes over me.

The fucking little fleas that come at me now are like paper—easy to rip in two. Tearing them apart is easy and satisfying. One by one, I pluck them out and shred them bit by bit.

Covered in fairy guts and blood, my stomach reminds me I need to eat. So, the next one that falls at my feet, I pick up, and dig my fangs into their neck, sucking them dry in two long gulps.

Tossing them aside, I scan the sky for Trystan, though it's easy to spot him since he's fucking glowing.

What does that mean for Sayah? Did he steal her power?

A tumultuous cloud funnels on the ocean's surface, falling from billowing black clouds speckled with fire. As the funnel spins madness into a vicious updraft, five more of these monsters sprout up from the angry sea.

A row of Neverdusk fae stands on the shore of the Reverie Sea, dark hooded beings wearing robes of black and gold, with arms outstretched to the sky, like they are stirring the storms.

I flex my power to rush up to them when *"Bash!"* interrupts my charge, Sayah's voice mixing with the winds whipping off the ocean.

I whirl around in search of her.

She's not behind me, so I invert my path, heading for the fae when "*Bash!*" swirls up around me again.

This time, the whispers cover me from head to toe, and when I whip around again, she is nowhere.

Yet her voice is everywhere.

The madness tickles my mind, making it bend in the wrong direction. I scratch at my ears with my taloned fingers, trying to get the voices to stop.

Bash, this is Dom's voice; *don't listen to them. They're shadow whisperers, trying to trick you.*

Fuck!

Cursed flames have now begun to dance with the sea as well as cascading down in rain on the beach. It's green fire, and it doesn't burn. Not right away.

But when it hits my skin, the pain begins to set in, inwardly.

Bone harrowing, marrow chilling, freezing your blood kind of pain.

Fighting through it, I find Trystan again.

"*Trystan!*" I bellow, my voice erupting louder. The ground rumbles in response.

The sounds of war and terror and death are too loud; he doesn't hear me over the clang of metal.

The night is warm, there is a cackle in the sky, and I can taste the magick in the air. So many of these fairies have magick. My head is starting to feel fuzzy.

Battles rage around me.

Soldiers are going toe to toe with swords, axes, and shields, but psychological warfare is also afoot. Magick flits about in waves, hovering over us, water coloring the black clouds with blues, teals, and metallic greens.

Among the massive Neverdusk army, generals loom in the

background, waiting, but for what, I do not know. They sit atop a hilltop on horses of rotting flesh, terrifyingly large and unhinged, like they galloped right out of Hell. Their bones, showing through their blackened and rotting flesh, glisten pearly in the silvery moons' light.

I know if I take one of those fuckers out, a whole slew of grimspawns and darkling fae will fall.

The crackle of a vortex opening draws my attention back to the shore.

A bright orange portal has unzipped, and Neverdusk fae, along with more creatures from other realms, leap through in droves.

The dwindling Luminara army is losing its stronghold and sinking even further into loss when psychological warfare weaves strange magick on some of them. They stop fighting the Neverdusk soldiers and turn on themselves, multiple Luminara soldiers slicing and stabbing their brothers and sisters in arms.

This is not good.

A flash of golden lightning streaks across the black clouds above the sea, stealing my attention back.

Trystan.

I track his movements as he zips across the entire shoreline. He ducks and bobs, weaving in and out of flying soldiers, wyverns, and other creatures of Hell, heading straight for the entrance to the cove.

Dodging a spear that appears out of nowhere, I put the same coordinates into my sights and torpedo myself to the entrance before he gets there.

I rush over the boulders and collapsed wall, then race under the out-of-control waterfall that was serene just minutes ago, and quickly analyze the situation inside.

My family—as far as I can tell—are all still standing and fighting.

The sirens are also dwindling; the ones that remain are on

the beach of the inner cove, fighting with silvery weapons of war.

"Don't let him take that portal!" Aaralyn screams, waving her own swords around, fighting the Never fae.

"He's too strong," another siren says. "There are too many, Aaralyn. We have to flee."

"I got the portal open; let's move!" Halcyon screams into the fray, his black and forest green portal he's opened swallow the rocks behind him.

Tallyn is behind him, her black hair blowing wildly as she creates chaotic balls of thunderclouds between her palms, thrashing it at the fae closing in on them, Never and Luminara alike. They fall like bowling pins, being electrocuted by lightning within it.

The Luminara fae that aren't entranced run for the portal.

"We can't let him have the Shadow Gate!" Aaralyn screams as a Never fae pulls her hair from behind, whispering magicked words to switch her to their side.

Her eyes go milky white, and she turns her assault on another siren, a red being fighting for her life. Aaralyn slices across her neck with one swoop, crimson painting her sword and ground bright red.

I frantically look around for my mom and spot her, shoving balls of flames at flying beings, back-to-back with Ollie, who is assisting my dad with the advancing army.

"Mom!" I yell after she hits a swarm of abyssal creatures. The clicking of their teeth severs the night with nightmares. "Dad! Ollie! We gotta go!"

Dad has a sword of the fae, the strange blueish steel of it glinting in the firelight of Mom's magick, decapitating one Never fae. Meanwhile, Ollie helps amplify Mom's fire, using it like firehose caught flame.

"Head for the portal!" Dad shouts. The headless soldier falls at his feet; he steps over it and protects my mom.

Jasantha is using her siren sunder on soldiers she can, screeching in their direction as they fall to their knees. Claire, Kaston, and Draelle rip their limbs apart.

Aaralyn makes a run for Jasantha and I rush to her aide to closeline her into the ground. The sound of the heavy sword swooshes above us.

"Run!" I order her, shoving her into Scarlet's awaiting hand.

Her eyes strike mine with a plea not to kill her sister before she's ushered off, Scarlet running with Hattie and my mom to the portal.

I jump up and am about to end her life when I see Tallyn being vexed by one of the shadow whisperers.

Ignoring the feral Aaralyn, I advance on Tallyn, eyeing my family entering the portal once I reach her.

Her magick has fallen, her arms limp at her sides. She mindlessly follows Neverdusk fae, lumbering up to the Shadow Gate Portal.

Trystan stands atop the once vibrant and protected arch across the cove, helping his soldiers dismantle the portal by using his stolen phoenix power to saw into the heavy stone like a welder. When one brick is magicked loose, it's being handed down to another vortex of blackness and smoke, where it's tossed in to the portal to Never.

Before he can spot his sister making her way to him, I rush to yank her behind a pillar.

Refusing me initially but not being aggressive, I hold her face, and force her eyes with mine. Her muscles are rigid, as if she's fighting the hypnotization.

Her fire eyes are glazed over; her red lips parted as though she wants to scream.

Tallyn, I need you to hear me. You are not listening to the shadow whisperers; you are Tallyn, Luminara Queen.

Her head tilts, understanding flickering in the depths of her milky eyes. I continue to veilweave her out of her silent compulsion. The orange of her irises melts the white, and recognition strengthens her gaze.

The spell is strong; I have to fight it with every ounce of my being, like trying to force a tsunami back away from the shore.

But Agares is stronger.

Together, the two of us make the veilweaving stronger.

You are not going with them. You have an army to run. We have to go back to Feylight and figure out a way to protect it. Now move!

As the last of the white melts away, she shakes off the spell, the warrior within her sealing over her like armor.

"Bash?" she questions, sounding like she just woke from a nap. "What happened?"

"No time," I say, pulling her toward the portal.

Ducking under magick blasts and fire spreading everywhere, the entire cove floor electrified and chaotic, she screams, "Everyone! To the portal! Now!"

We rush by them, grimspawns and darkling fae encroaching on the portal we're heading for. I get one last look at the cove before plummeting into the wormhole.

Trystan's glowing eyes catch mine, and he smiles.

19

DEADLY WICKED WAVE

—SAYAH—

The cold metal shackle on my wrist is digging into my cheek, pulling me from sleep.

I open my eyes to the bathroom on the right of the bed.

I am still determining how much time has passed, and what time of day it is. Everything is blending together.

How can they live their lives not knowing time?

I sit up, yanking the dumb fucking shackle on my right wrist, the steel of it breaking off what little nails I had left, breaking one down past the quick on my left hand.

"Ouch!" I yell, shaking my finger, and immediately putting the bleeding finger into my mouth, sucking the pain away.

I slam the shackled wrist down onto the bed in a tantrum I can't help. The hopelessness with a side of molten rage scrapes down my body, thinking of what the shackles represent and what they are suppressing.

I miss my powers.

I miss the way it feels to have them humming through my body.

There's a ringing in my ear that's growing louder, a high-pitched squealing sound similar to a static TV being turned on in my head—the big box kind from the eighties that has an antennae on top.

It's only in my right ear, and though I stick my pinkie in and wiggle it around to stop the ringing, it only gets more intense.

The jangling of the chains directly in my ear somehow resembles voices, and when I stop gyrating my finger in my ear, they get louder.

Those are voices!

It sounds like they're coming from the room next door—if there were a room next door to mine. But there isn't one. The voices come from somewhere in the castle, but are projected into my mind.

Then fucking assemble it, Trystan's voice says, an icy rage laced into the inflections.

We need more power, Your Highness. We can assemble it, but we need more power to activate it.

I straighten my back, straining my ears to hear more.

Then gather every magick wielder in the realm. Fucking do it. We don't have much time before the Dread Harvest Eclipse is over. This is our time. The Shadow Gate Portal will only work to unlock Desoloth during this eclipse. Any others and it will open the fucking realms we've already been to—

Knock. Knock. Knock.

For fuck's sake.

"Yes?" I yell .

"I've brought you your lunch, miss," Dreadwynd's voice calls through the door.

Taylor fucking Swift, does he ever stop cooking?

"Come in," I utter, situating myself on the bed.

In walks Dreadwynd with his horribly squeaky cart. I almost groan because I don't want to eat more of the food, but my stomach disagrees and lets out a huge rumble when I smell the delicious meal.

I get up from the bed to move over to the table, where he starts to set everything out on it.

"What do we have this time?"

His beady black eyes scan mine, and it seems as though he's tired of being my food-bringer. "Radiant fruit, edible flowers, and ethereal nectars. The main course is ambrosial soup. Pastries for dessert. Moonshadow Nectar and twilight tea."

"Thank you." I will not question what exactly a "radiant fruit" is.

"I'll be back to get the dishes." He leaves me and closes the doors to my room.

My ear still rings, but I can no longer hear those voices.

I wonder what Trystan meant by Desoloth. Is that a realm? Is it a bad one?

I make quick work of eating everything in front of me and finish with the Moonshadow Nectar.

After lunch or dinner or breakfast—whatever-the-fuck meal it is—I go out to the balcony once again.

The moons completely overlap each other now, and the purple and pink mix to create the loveliest shade of lavender. The light spills out from both of them in radiant waves, and the stars and everything the light touches become a soft, dusty-rose.

Even though the sight of the moons eclipsing each other is beautiful, it is one of the deadliest form of stunning.

Trystan needs this celestial event to unlock whatever horrendous door he's unlocking.

Whatever it is—it can't be good.

As I'm looking out to the ocean, thinking of Bash and missing my kid, I feel and hear a rumbling from within the castle.

Looking down the mile-high drop, the rocks of the cliff the castle sits upon lose a few. They fall from the rocky face of the cliff and plummet downward, splashing into the chaotic waters below.

Following the falling rocks, a blast that sounds like a bomb shakes the entire tower. With my heart stuttering, I hold on to the thorny balustrade, my feet quaking so hard I have to spread them to keep my balance.

My nerves are set aflame as a ripple ricochets outward from the castle, creating a reverse tidal wave in the Nocturna Sea. The giant ripple becomes a hundred-foot wave going the other way, colliding with another massive wave in the distance, inverting its path, coming directly at me.

The now two-hundred-foot wave is barreling toward me, swallowing all other sounds and emotions and time. I swear this is something out of one of my nightmares.

I've always dreamt of turbulent tsunamis coming for me, crashing into my world, and ruining everything in its path.

And now it's happening.

It's not tall enough to reach me way up here, right?

In horror, I watch as the deadly wicked wave comes right at this tower.

DROPPING A BOMBSHELL

—BASH—

Tumbling back to the greenhouse we'd left from, I hit the ground running without falling on my face this time. The swirling in my stomach is still roiling from the bending of time and space, and the fae we'd left behind are a blur of swirling faces at first, but at least I'm getting better.

It takes a minute to gain my composure, reuniting with the real world. Well, as real as this crazy fucked-up world is. I am looking down at the earthen ground below me, raking my hands through my hair and focusing on my breaths to keep from throwing up. When my focus returns, the rest of my group is morphing in through the portal in my peripheral, Dad and Ollie, Mom, Scarlet, Jasantha, Claire—everyone unused to portal travel collapsing to the ground. Meanwhile, the fae simply walk through it like it ain't no thang.

Show-offs.

I dust off the dirt from my pants and shirt and see Tallyn being escorted by some of her troops. Having arrived a few minutes before me, she is unbothered and accustomed to upheavals of normalcy.

Apparently, portal travel is an art you have to learn to do gracefully, or some shit Tallyn spewed at me.

On an exhale, I head toward her.

The moonlight illuminates her face, making her hardened warrior look almost softened. She looks formidable as she converses with Caelum, who, when he sees me, his eyes soften, and he hastens over to me. Tallyn's face is painted with annoyance.

"Sebastian," he says, reaching me, "how are you? Are you hurt?"

"I'm fine," I snap. "I just need to talk to Tallyn."

She hears her name and holds up a finger to Eirian and Gwylan before swooping over to me.

Many of the soldiers are dirty and have blood spattered on their faces; some have torn clothes, and others are in complete disarray. There are even a few over on the far wall who are missing limbs, most looking worse for wear.

"What the fuck is going to happen now that Trystan has the Shadow Gate Portal?" I ask.

The entire greenhouse is loud and chaotic. There are screams and shouting, loud voices, crying, sobbing, and loud chatter. I almost have to shout at her.

"The worst-case scenario is that he'll open the door to Desoloth. And that . . . well, that would be catastrophic."

"What is Desoloth?"

Tallyn takes me by the arm and walks me away from prying ears. She doesn't say anything as we make our way down the long aisle and out of the doors of the greenhouse. The night air feels fresh and crisp, dousing the perspiration I'd earned from the battle and the dank and humid greenhouse. I tilt my head back, walk toward a large tree, and lean against it.

Tallyn follows me, digging in her cleavage. "I didn't want some of my people to hear," she says, producing what looks to be a joint from her bodice.

"Feylight is on a crossroad of ley lines," she says, holding the joint in her teeth while she strikes her fingernail across the tree's bark. The bright flame lends her face a mysterious glow, the smoke emitting from the joint plumes upward into the starlit night. She takes a puff and, on the exhale, resumes her tale. "It's like the epicenter of them for the supernatural world. These ley lines lead to different realms: good, bad, terrible, and wonderful. They each have different magickal properties with different beings. Desoloth is one of the worst. The gate can only be opened by the Shadow Gate portal, and only during this"—she points to the two moons now converged into one super moon—"the Dread Harvest Eclipse. Not only does it open the doors to Desoloth, but it is also the gatekeeper of other doors. Once he opens that one, he can enter Desoloth, open another, go into that one, open another, and so on."

"So, what? We're talking about some minor inconveniences on Earth, right?"

She shakes her head, taking another puff, and handing it to me.

It doesn't smell like marijuana, but it does at the same time, like a mystical sort of Mary Jane. I eye the joint skeptically, and she coughs, shoving it further at me. I shrug and indulge.

Why the fuck not?

"No," she says after her coughing subsides. "Not a minor inconvenience, Bash. A catastrophic event that will change Earth forever. Not only that, but each and every door he opens weakens the ley lines here in Feylight. Each one is a key to unlocking a boundary, and once he's opened the seventh and final door, he'll have access to the Aetherian Circle."

I crinkle my nose and cough through the smoke, passing her the joint. "The All-what-ee-an circle?"

She takes the joint, inhales more smoke, and leans her head against the tree. "Feylight is on a series of rings, as you saw. Those are only the top half of the boundary spell, protecting the innermost circle buried deep beneath my castle. There are also inner rings beneath the ground that serve as layers of protection, opened only by myself and my soul, or those portals he will open with the Shadow Gate."

"And what's in the innermost circle?"

She taps on the joint's tip, releasing the ash, and making the smoke dance. "The Soul Stone and Covenant of Feylight, assigned to my soul."

"So that's good then, right?" I hold up my hand to refuse more of the strange weed when she goes to hand it to me. "Even if he gets down there, he has to, what? Rewrite the Covenant or assign his soul to the Soul Stone?"

She shakes her head. "It's more than that. Since he can't get to the Aetherian through his portals or with his fae, he'll open all the portals needed to break those boundaries. Every portal he unlocks weakens the veil between our world, the mortal realm, and the demon realms he's unlocking. It won't matter if the Covenant and Soul Stone are assigned to me by the time he makes it through the fourteen boundaries. Feylight will fall with the collapse of the mortal realm."

Fuck.

This isn't good. Not good at all.

Fuck it, if the world is gonna end, I might as well be high.

I take the joint from her now, inhaling a deep pull of the mystic herb. "What happens when the veil falls?"

"If he opens those doors and those beings start to enter the mortal realm, he'll take over Earth. If he figures out a way to rewrite the Covenant or reassign his soul to the Soul Stone, nothing will be able to stop him. He will own this world and all others connected to it. The sun will fall, and the entire planet will succumb to darkness. A void will begin to eat Earth, and everything that void touches he will control."

"He realizes Earth cannot sustain darkness, right? He knows if the sun goes out, the planet will die, right?"

She takes one last pull from the joint, then stubs it out on the tree, red sparks flying through the air. "He has a crazy idea that even if the sun dies, he can use magick from the other realms to keep the planet alive in darkness."

I laugh at the absurdity. "You're serious?"

Nodding, she says, "Deadly."

"What do we do?"

"We can't let him take Feylight. It's the only way to save Earth."

"And how do you suggest we do that?"

Her eyes shimmer in the shadows. "We need your girlfriend back."

I take Tallyn's words with me and tuck them into the dark corners of my being for the rest of the day—or night.

When I get back to my room, I make myself a drink and wander out to the balcony, watching the giant moons twinkle in the velvet sky.

After Tallyn had calmed everyone down and informed the families of those who didn't make it back, she and her troops retired to the war room to go over battle plans and the next steps.

She said she'd come get us when she had a plan and let us know what we're supposed to do.

Darkness tickles my insides as Agares rumbles deep in my bones, restlessly tugging at the embers of me, begging me to let him out to play.

The fluffy pillows of clouds and the smells of florals and spices embrace me as I sip on the nectar, which is starting to taste good.

All is eerily quiet, allowing my mind to wander to Sayah. I can't help but wonder how the fuck I will ever get her back. The sky has melted to the darkness; the stars blistering the foreign sky, and the two moons connected, making the supermoon lend the atmosphere an unsettling, dusty-rose ambiance.

The last time I spoke to her was through our minds, when she did her own sort of lumokinesis. She told me she'd explain things in our dreams.

How does that work?

Do I need to see those will-o'-the-wisps again, or can I just control my mind and find her whenever I want to?

Every muscle in my body is sore, and all I want to do is lie down and pass out, but something sits uneasily on my skin. It's crooked and heavy, looming over the fragments of each piece of this weird puzzle.

Emotions I'm still getting familiar with gurgle inside my body. It's a panicky sort of bubble I don't really fucking like or appreciate but am coming to understand—these are the repercussions of loving someone. The cost of loving someone with such ferocity, the longevity of it spanning multiple lives and realms and dimensions, and the cost of that love are these awful senses of worry. Knowing the worst day of loving someone is the day one of you has to say goodbye. I don't know how to protect her here. And seeing what I saw today terrifies me to the center of me, and I don't know how to navigate this fear.

My lungs feel hot, and my heart is beating too fast. I down the rest of the nectar, pleading to the moon with my eyes to let it take some of this unease from me. It's too heavy, and I need to think clearly if I am to get her back.

I need to save her.

No.

I *must* save her.

Nothing else makes sense.

The world—any world—makes no sense if she's not in it with me.

Like the wind hears me and understands my desperation, it picks up and rustles through my hair, swirling down my arms, and picking the glass out of my grasp. As I watch it float away into the ether, a soft rustling interrupts my wind.

The amber, red, and orange maple leaf unfolds from the air and lands at my feet, morphing into a scroll.

I carefully retrieve it from the ground and pull the red ribbon loose, unraveling the parchment. Words in elegant cursive glow brightly in gold as they unspool, settling to black ink gilded in the moonlight.

Sebastian,

I fear I am under some sort of spell and don't know how much longer I'll stay myself.

Please meet me in our dreams in twenty minutes.

Love,

Sayah

When the words are read, the parchment becomes edged in flame; the orange licking the paper to ash that blows up in a gust of wind.

Softly, I inhale the ash, finding it smells of roses, willows, and hydrangea blossoms.

I'm not exactly tired, but the ash was definitely part of a spell, and suddenly, the need to sleep creeps up and tugs at the back of my neck. I have to shower before I get into bed, so I head back inside, stripping off my shirt, and unbuckling my belt as I make my way to the wash room.

After rinsing myself off, I feel a million times better. I rub my hair messily with a towel before wrapping it around my waist. I brush my teeth and gargle with a bottle of the fae wine I'd left in here earlier and slip out of the towel to climb into bed, naked.

"Lights out!" I command, and the spirit lanterns—I don't care what they're called, I'm still calling them that—within the room blink out.

Turning to my side, I fluff my pillow, and close my eyes, exhaling a heavy breath as I settle into sleep.

I feel a rush of cold on my face, and my eyes shoot open.

Henry's directly in front of me.

"Ah!" I release the shock in a yell, sitting up so fast the bed moves. "What. The. Fuck, Henry?"

The smirk that splits his face is menacing. He is not even transparent anymore, but a solid-looking human boy. "Hehe!" He stands with a laugh. "You're fun to scare."

"Listen here, little dude, I'm not in the mood for your shit right now," I say, laying back down, and pulling the sheet up over me. "I need to dreamwalk to Sayah and check in with her."

"I know something you don't know," he says in a sing-song voice.

"I don't care. Go on, get!"

You'll want to hear this, brother, says Dom's voice from the wall directly above my head.

Again, I jump up, looking for him. "Dom?"

"He's not dead," Henry says, flickering like a candle in the wind.

"What?" I ask, swinging my legs to hang from the edge of the bed.

"Dom's not dead," Henry repeats, glitching off for a solid second.

"Henry! Wait!" He flicks back on again. "What do you mean, my brother's not dead?"

The gap in his teeth shines when he smiles a wicked smile. "Tallyn has him under a spell to keep him alive. He did die, but now he lingers between life and death in The Gloaming. It's the flora and fauna of Feylight that brought him back."

"What?" I exclaim, standing.

Henry covers his eyes with his hand as he flickers. "Madonna Mia! For heaven's sake, put some pants on!"

I pull the white sheet from the bed and wrap it around my shoulders. "Why wouldn't Tallyn tell me—*us*—that Dom is still alive?"

"I don't know." He glitches away again.

"Henry!"

"Just don't trust her. She's not who she says she is," Henry's voice says from the air.

And he doesn't flicker back in.

21

KNOTTI BASH

—SAYAH—

As the black, monstrous wave barrels toward me, I know I should flee from the watery death coming straight for me. Still, something within me keeps my feet planted. I brace myself against the railing, holding on for dear life. The force of the wind that hits me first is almost enough to knock me over, but I stand my ground and face my death—once again.

The entire horizon becomes that wave, and my heart races in my chest. The sound of the water drowns out the beat in my eardrums.

If there were a time I needed those fire wings, it would be now. But with the shackles keeping my power subdued, there is nothing left for me to do other than accept my aquiline death.

The tsunami shakes the realm. It crashes into the mountainside before reaching up to the very tower I stand on. When it hits the cliff, it rumbles the entire floor but splashes away as though a glass partition separates me from the water. I still flinch, frozen by fear to even run despite how close I am to drowning.

It reminds me of going through an automated car wash, and

how the deluge of water reflecting off the windshield creates the eerie feeling of being underwater.

I realize I've been holding my arm over my face—like that would've done anything against the mountain of water. I drop my arm in time to watch the wave hit the shield at full force and subside.

As the wave recedes back to the sea, only to gather another giant wave, I realize this could go on for hours.

And I have a dream date with Bash.

Even though I'm inquisitive about what's causing the tsunamis and want to find Trystan to find out what he knows, something is braided into my psyche that I need to see Bash.

Aside from the short whispers, I haven't spoken to him since the night in our dreams. Because of the fucked-up time here, I have no idea how long ago that was.

My mind grows hazy, like something is off.

I stare at my hands as I walk into the room. I feel like they aren't mine. Like my hands belong to someone else.

I know that is fucked-up and makes no sense, but it's how this place is fogging my brain, pulling me under some sort of weird and heavy cloud.

The tsunami that's still raging outside on repeat has nothing on how tangled my soul feels.

I topple onto the bed and unravel the comforter and sheets, foregoing even taking off my clothes before collapsing onto the mattress. The cold of the pillow greets me as I pull the blankets over my head and cascade downward into my mind.

***

A seagull caws off to my left, and when I open my eyes, I'm looking out to the Mediterranean Sea. The white stucco balcony I'm standing on overlooks a sea of white buildings, the structures speckling the mountainside with hints of blue accents to match the ocean.

Bash's black hair stands out among the landscape. He is

sitting in a turquoise pool of moonlight, the bright silver stars accenting his eyes.

The tension I felt a few moments ago melts the second I see him.

He's looking out toward the water, but when he senses me, he turns around, and his gaze collides with mine.

I pretty much run to him, and jump into the pool, my white nightgown melding to my skin.

He stands and wraps me in his arms.

"Sayah," he rasps, wrapping one hand around my neck. "Gods, you are a sight for sore eyes."

Tangling my fingers in his hair, I pull him to me like he is my air, and send my lips colliding with his, sucking his tongue and gripping his bicep.

The way Bash kisses me is incomparable to any kiss I have experienced before. It's not just our mouths moving in perfect unison together, the exact same moments at the exact same time, but our hearts tangle together while our emotions blend. The very essence of who we are morphs together, exchanging little bits of our being and even relinquishing parts of us to each other to forever hold on to.

I can feel the chinks in his armor reshape at my touch, the broken bits of him sewing themselves back together with gold lightning.

Heated breath enters my lungs as he sweeps his hand across my breast, eliciting a moan that makes him hard instantly.

Feeling his cock on my thigh, my clit tingles at the thought of him. I slide my other hand down his pants—he's wearing black gym shorts that cling to him in wetness and no shirt. His hard cock's ridges welcome my fingertips; a small drop of pre-cum provides just enough lubricant for my hand. I slide my palm down his dick. The sound I influence out of him hardens my nipples, and, like he senses the pebbled rock under my nightgown, he rips it off my shoulder and takes a tit into his mouth. My head rocks back when he rolls my nipple between his teeth.

The exquisite torment numbs my body to my toes.

The water we're standing in is warm, and as he lifts me up by my ass to have me straddle him, he sits down on a bench, submerging us to our waists.

I rub my clit over his dick, using his mouth as my dirty little promise, saying I'm going to fuck the shit out of him right here and now, and I don't care who's watching.

He lifts the cotton gown over my head and gathers both my breasts to his face, taking turns nibbling, sucking, biting, and licking each one until the moons above us melt and separate into two again.

My pussy is so wet, even in this water. I can't stand to not have him inside me, so I sweep my right hand behind me and guide his dick to my entrance. He is so massive I stretch every time he enters me, but it is the most glorious pain I'll sustain any time.

Sinking down so our bodies are flush, the mountain sky in his eyes implode me, asphyxiating all thoughts and feelings and worlds save him.

"Fuuuuuckkk," Bash breathes, his head falling back. He slides his hands down the center of my body, his fingers stopping at my clit. He stills, hilt deep, our gazes caught in a collision of time and space. All I see is molten adoration. It's fierce and untamable. Our love is so fiercely tangible it stomps me breathless.

He begins to wiggle the swollen jewel. I rock slowly on top of him, riding his cock and his hand ever so slightly.

The bench provides excellent leverage, paired with the water; I slide my body up and down, feeling his large fucking cock pierce me deep within, rubbing up against the magnificent live wires of my G-spot.

As he massages my clit back and forth—the hot tingles

piercing my every nerve on its way down to the tips of my toes —his other hand is pinching my nipple, cupping and biting and pinching some more.

"Oh, fuck!" I yell out as he bucks his hips to match my thrusts, matching my vigor and plunging into me, drilling himself deep into my core.

Spreading his legs wide, he moves both his hands to my back and uses me for his own leverage to slam me onto him. When he's seated within me as deep as he can go, he lifts me up and walks me to the other edge of the pool, sitting my ass up on the ledge, his dick still buried inside me.

He slings my legs over his shoulders and locks his gaze with mine, perfectly piercing my body with his massive cock over and over again while holding my eyes. Pulsing with such ferocity, my mind melts, stars and galaxies flash across my vision. He massages my clit with his thumb, his drunken blue eyes turn white as he savors me, his fangs elongating.

I don't know what it is about Bash's monster that turns me the fuck on, but my orgasm slowly takes hold of every morsel of my soul. I clench around his giant cock, trying to stop it to keep enjoying the euphoria this man brings me. But he pauses for a brief second.

A groan slips from his throat and his smile turns predatory, as if listening to something internal dialogue.

"Agares wants to meet you," he says, kissing me with his luscious lips. He has not stopped fucking me.

I nod as his eyes turn golden-red, retracting into a horizontal pupil. Membranous red wings extend from his back, and his skin congeals into a red hue. The pressure inside my pussy walls has us both pausing, the orgasm simmering as we try to figure out what's happening with our bodies. His cock seems to grow wider, so wide it almost hurts. But when he pulls his cock out to investigate, the wide part is only at the base, while the rest of his dick remains the same—aside from the color, which is a dark red.

"What is *that?*" I ask breathlessly as he rocks his hips back and forth.

Instead of answering me, he seems to get inside his head, having that silent conversation with his demon.

Then his eyes change.

Not the color or shape, but what's inside.

"It's a knot," he says, and while it is his voice, it's somehow not at the same time.

"A knot?"

"Yes. Usually found in the werewolf community. It's for alphas. When they find . . ."

He thrusts his dick all the way inside me, the knot embedding deep. He pulls his cock out slowly, my body curving around the knot and the rest of his ridges until just the tip remains. Within a breath of ruthless sex, he slams into me, using the back of my arms as leverage, causing the deepest moan I've ever emitted to surge from me.

I take a deep breath. "When they find?" I urge him to continue by clenching my pussy around him again.

"When they find their mate."

Mate.

"Like soulmate?"

He slides out to just the knot. It's grown so wide, it'll be impossible for him to pull out of me now. Which makes me hotter.

He kisses me and shoves back inside me. "Mm-hmm."

In between kisses, I ask, "What does that mean?"

Another shove, and he is gliding against me from all sides. "It means"—he moans, biting my lip, rocking his dick in a sensuous and maddening circle—"you are mine for eternity."

In a lustrous fury, he swallows my moans and pulls out to the knot, slamming back into me with such force I see stars.

Eternity.

I like the sound of that.

There's a slicing of his taloned finger down my right arm and I gasp, but the indescribable feeling of his knot inside me muffles the pain of the cut.

He covers the gash with the palm of his hand, and instead of becoming frenzied for my blood, he pulls my chin up toward him with the bloodied, taloned finger, and then shoves it into my mouth.

My arm burns where he cut me, but it's a gentle burn—like part of his magick unhinged itself from him to nestle into me. Small electric currents run the length of me, and as he slices into me with his gaze, part of my magick mingles within him, too.

Whatever happened to his addiction to my blood is beyond me; maybe it was the whole "him dying by werewolf bite" and succumbing to his madness. But instead of becoming frenzied for my blood, he merely continues to rock his cock in and out of me, chasing his own orgasm.

"Fuck, Sayah, I'm gonna cum," he growls, removing his finger from my mouth and trailing it down my body. His thrusts get deeper and harder.

A sound between a whimper and a moan escapes my lips, and he swallows the sound with his mouth.

"Why didn't you let me have this knot before?" I lean back on the pool's edge, scooting my ass as close to him as possible.

"I didn't know about it 'til now," he answers into the shell of my ear, his distorted baritone eliciting chills down my body. He growls again and pulls my ass into the glorious collision of one last thrust, the knot swelling as he erupts into ecstasy.

He rocks his dick sideways inside me, leaning into me, scraping across the live wires within me.

"Oh, my gods," I exclaim as he coaxes my release, cata-pulting me into a feverish rush. I'm hyperventilating, and my breaths cannot keep up with the implosion. He kisses me fiercely while he upends my life into cataclysmic, bone-shattering pleasure.

My orgasm splits the universe, him following me to our doom and riding out the end of us on a blinding explosion of madness.

It's been a while since we both finished, but Bash's knot still hasn't come down, so we're stuck together, and it's kinda hot.

I'm straddling him in the pool in the moonlight, and we've been talking about all that has happened since we last saw each other.

Every now and then, I'll slide up a few centimeters to see if I can get us unstuck, but it only makes him harder and me wetter, which derails our conversation, which leads us to falling back into fucking. None of it helps the knot situation.

"He's making my brain bend in weird ways," I am able to tell Bash in between our bouts of fucking. "Like I'm losing myself inside myself. It's hard to explain."

"Yeah, that's what you said in your Whispering Leaf," he says into the column of my neck, twisting his hips to drive deeper into me.

"My what?" I say, and he stops his movement.

"The Whispering Leaf you sent me to meet you here . . ."

I pull my face away and look into his eyes. "Bash, I never sent you a leaf. I wouldn't even know how to do that."

It seems that's the perfect information to deflate him, for the pressure inside me lessens, and he can finally pull out of me. "If it wasn't you, then who the fuck was it?" The red of his skin has begun to fade back to the peach color—the red of it evaporating like mist on a hot road.

"What did it say?" I ask as I climb off his lap to sit beside him in the pool.

"It just said something like, 'you fear you're under a spell and don't know how long you'll be you for and to meet in our dreams in twenty minutes.'" His eyes are back to their normal glorious blue.

I'm baffled.

Could this be Trystan?

"Fuck, that's not good," I say, pulling my sopping wet night-gown back over my head to cover my breasts.

"No." He helps me get my arms through the holes. "No, not at all."

"Who the fuck would send you a false leaf telling you to meet me?"

His dark brows draw together in a tight line. He scratches the stubble on his face that is entirely his own once again. "I doubt Tallyn would pretend to be you; it just doesn't seem like her style."

"So, Trystan then?" I say, curling up to him, my skin pricking with chills.

He rubs the side of my arms to get friction, helping to chase the chill away. "I'd almost bet money on it."

"So if Trystan sent it, pretending to be me, then he wants me out of my normal mind and in this one for some reason. But for what?"

"I have no idea, but if I were a betting man, I'd wager it has something to do with your power. You should have seen him on that battlefield, Say. He looked like the male counterpart to your phoenix form."

A dread unlike anything I've never known settles into my bones, and I fear what he's doing to my unconscious body as we speak. "I have to get back," I say. The water in the pool splashes when I stand.

Bash follows me up the steps and onto the landing, looking out to the Mediterranean Sea. "I don't want this to end," he says, pulling me into him.

"Me neither, Bash. I wish I could pull you from my dreams into my prison cell back at Nightshade Castle."

"I hate that for you," he murmurs, tugging my head to lie on his chest and stroking my wet hair. "I hate this. I will figure out how to save you from him, my darling. This, I promise you."

"I hope you can, soon. I have no idea what that tsunami meant, but judging by what you told me about how he was dismantling the Shadow Gate Portal, I imagine the wave has something to do with him putting it together and opening new doors to realms."

"Tallyn told me if he gets that portal open, it means the destruction of Earth as we know it," he says, pushing me forward to look into my eyes.

"Holy shit," I breathe, choking back the terror in my voice.

"All I know is that if Trystan is going to bring the world to ruin, I want to make sure you and I will be together 'til the last star burns out in the sky."

"'til the last star burns," I say back to him, taking his lips in mine one last time before I'm awoken by a blood-curdling scream.

22

HATCHING A PLAN

—BASH—

The bright ass sun flooding through the window is enough to make me rise, my heart in my throat.

Climbing out of bed, I find clean clothes are neatly folded at the foot of the bed.

I dress quickly, clamoring into my boots. I am out the door while I button the shirt up most of the way.

I need to find Tallyn.

The dream with Sayah still blankets my mind, and thinking about how Agares and I fucked her, and—that knot, which makes my pants tighten at the erection it incites.

I have heard of knots before, but never knew them to happen in the demon community. I have never once experience something like that in all my 200 years.

It's because you've never fucked your mate before her, Agares grumbles, almost annoyingly.

I come to a dead end and whirl around to see the hall has changed. *Yes, but why then did it happen now and not the first time she and I fucked?* I ask as I flash down and around another bend.

Because you weren't in your demon form.

So I have to be in my demon form for that knot to come back?

No, he answers. I wind down another long corridor. *Now that it's appeared, you can use it whenever you want.*

And just like that, I'm hard again, thinking about everything we can do with the new aspect of me now.

I can't think about that right now.

Getting my mind on different things, I situate myself so my boner is tucked in my waist.

I wind around the long corridors and hallways until voices echo down the halls. In another room similar to all the others, I find Tallyn and her generals at a table, hovering over a map of a world I've never seen.

"Tallyn," I say as I enter.

Everyone stops and looks up.

"Yes, Sebastian?" she asks, straightening her spine to a standing position.

"I need to speak with you privately, please."

Her orange eyes collide with mine in a questioning glare, yet she picks up on something because she excuses herself and leads me down another dark hallway toward an office.

"What is it, Bash?" She closes the heavy, black iron doors. The clanging of its shutting reverberates throughout the room.

"Dom isn't dead." I say it as a statement instead of a question.

Again, those odd eyes are on me as she walks behind her large, intricately carved oak desk. "Who told you that?" she questions in a worried yet authoritative tone, sliding the chair out to sit. Though she points to the one across from it, I remain standing, merely leaning on the chair.

"That's of no importance. What I want to know is why have you kept this secret from us? What are you planning to do with a reanimated corpse of my brother?"

She tuts her tongue. She pulls out another joint from her bra, biting it between her teeth before striking a match from her desk. The crackle of strange herb smoke flits vibrantly in the spirit lantern light. "What did Henry see?" she asks, taking a puff from the joint and leaning back.

I let out a heavy exhale. "He didn't tell me. He just said Dom isn't dead and that he lingers between life and death. Something about the flawna and florna or some shit."

A wicked smile curves her lips. "Flora and fauna," she corrects. "Another reason I don't want Feylight to fall into the wrong hands."

I finally take a seat in the chair, crossing my leg and holding my ankle, imploring her to continue with a seething glare.

"I was able to bring him back from death," she states, tapping the ash off the joint into a bowl on her desk. "But I fear he was too far gone in the Uunderworld when I brought him back. That's why I've kept him subdued in The Gloaming until we can be certain."

"The Gloaming?"

"Kinda like an in-between. Limbo is another word, but entirely different. Hard to explain in a sitting."

"What happens if he was too far gone?"

"A fae in this world can only be brought back from death three times in their chosen body for the lifetime they're in. Each time they are brought back, a little of their soul becomes shadowmarked. On their third ascension back to the living, they will be completely shadowmarked. Something we don't want to be unleashed in any world. Shadowmarked are similar to the abyssal sprites, yet the vampire in him would mean complete destruction to the world—a destruction we would never come back from. They'd be gone from their old selves for good. We don't know if he's ever risen in this world. The swirling marks under his skin tell us that he has."

The meaning of this information settles into my mind in a crooked way. I've never heard the term "shadowmarked" . . . but it does not sound good.

I crook my neck sideways. "So you have him, what, just in a coma?"

She takes another long inhale. "Similar to that, yes."

"And what are you waiting for to bring him back?"

The look she gives me is one of knowing. "Bash, c'mon. Think about that."

"Sayah," I say, fidgeting with my boot string.

"Yes, another reason why we need her back."

"I agree with this. And we need to figure out how to get her soon. I fear Trystan is starting to steal her power."

Her features fall, and a chill spreads over the room. "You know this for a fact?"

"I saw him in the cove. He was glowing like she does, like there's lightning living under his skin. We also believe he sent me a Whispering Leaf posing as her to get us to dreamwalk to each other."

"Why would he want you to dreamwalk to each other?"

"So she'd be unconscious. She's also afraid he's poisoning her, putting her under some sort of spell through her food."

"What has she said?" Tallyn asks, stubbing the joint out in the bowl.

"She just said her mind bends in weird ways, and she feels like she's losing herself. The fucked-up part about it is that's exactly what Trystan put in the leaf."

She nods and looks at the wall, contemplating something. "We need to get her out of there as soon as possible. I'm just not sure how. We don't want Trystan to gain complete control over a phoenix and take Feylight. The consequences would be catastrophic."

"I know I can save her from him. I just need to get to her—see her in person. I know more than anything I can bring her back from his clutches."

Suddenly, her face lights up.

"What? What is it?" I ask, leaning forward.

"I think I know how to get your girlfriend back."

23

SPILLING MY FIRE

—SAYAH—

The scream is enough to pierce through my skin and slither around my ribs, ripping into my lungs, and constricting the very breath in my chest.

It's not a fae scream.

It's my child.

"*Gauge?*" I shriek, rising in a breathless rush.

My room is empty, cold, and dark. The only light spills in from the two moons still eclipsing each other, and the purple orb lights flicker in sconces on the walls.

A coarse breath that isn't mine makes me scatter off the bed, and when I turn back around, Trystan is lying in my bed with his arm over the headboard, like he was laying there with his arm over me as I slept.

"What the fuck?"

His ridiculously luscious lips curl up at one end. "Your naivety suits you, human. Your vulnerability in this realm is almost charming."

Luckily, I didn't sleep naked last night, but I still feel so gross. "You were just watching me sleep? Is that what gets your jollies off?"

He situates himself on the bed, crossing his legs. Again, he's shirtless, and his luxurious wings rest gracefully behind his back. "Jollies?" he questions, his brows furrowing in confusion. "Is that what you humans call when a man ejaculates these days?"

I shudder. "Gross, Trystan." I walk to the armoire to grab new clothes. "What do you want?"

Before I even have time to process, Trystan grabs my arm, admiring a new swirling tattoo moving like a thunderstorm trapped beneath my skin.

"What is this?" he seethes, his grip biting.

"I've always had it," I lie. I can't look at it to draw more attention to it, but it seems that where Bash cut me, and his magick entered me, a new live tattoo lives across my right arm. I have no idea what it means, but I feel Bash there, his soul and presence lividly swimming through my bones.

Trystan emits a low growl and throws me down to the ground. His body weight is then on top of me, crushing me into the cold, hard stone of the floor. His breath is hot and sweet-smelling. I turn my face and try to wiggle out of his grip.

"You took something from me," he says wickedly into my ear.

Panic sets my cells on fire. I try to thrash out of his grip, but his firm, calloused hands are grasping my wrists, pinning me to the floor. If I wasn't so terrified, I'd be a little turned on by this.

"I don't know what you're talking about."

His face stubble scratches my cheek; he stops when he's nose to nose with me.

"Don't mock me, phoenix," he whispers, nudging my nose with his. "You seem to forget, I am a creature forged from stars that died long ago. I was tempered in battles beyond your puny imagination. Bones infused with galaxies and skin, burnt by stars. My eyes contain moonlight, and my nails are formed by comments. The blood that runs through my veins, dust depleted of stars, and my heart beats from the energy of black holes in the universe. My hair is strands of fate, my voice the echoes of time, my teeth are made of nebulas, and my lungs were created by cataclysmic vibrations of planets moving through space."

What do I even say to that?

His lips press into a dry smirk.

Is he kidding? I don't know if he knows anything or is just trying to scare me into confessing something.

My breath's coming and going so fast, and my heart is racing. I've never seen this side of him. "I'm not mocking you. What's gotten into you? You've not been like this to me."

I feel his chest rumble with laughter. "It's amusing how you think I've been anything but pacifying to you." He slides his hand down my arms and caresses my cheek. "I may have let you out of your dungeon, but you are still my prisoner. You'd do well to remember that."

His sternum thorns are poking me. "I thought you wanted me to be your queen."

A wicked laugh. "It's not about wanting anything, princess. It's about *making* you my queen. And you've been getting too comfortable with your freedom up here. Using the Shrouded Dream season to give information to the enemy. What you've failed to realize is, everyone who experiences these lucid dreams projects them into a viewing chamber so those who want to watch can see. I . . . saw . . . *everything.*"

Every muscle in my body tightens. The blood in my veins heats to a boil, and I try to force myself to steady my breathing. I'm about to hyperventilate.

How many people in this realm saw me fucking Bash?

His lips curl up into a wickedly nefarious grin. "Until the last star burns out. Your ass looked so succulent, bouncing up and down on Sebastian's cock. I have to say, when you're my wife, I'll be okay watching you fuck other males in front of me."

Vomit crawls up my insides and threatens to spill out of me. My whole body is flushed, and it feels hot, as if I may faint.

He watched us fucking.

Fucking *watched* us.

I wrench the shackled hand free and slap him, hard. The cold metal hits him harder than I intended. "You're a disgusting creature," I spit at him, my voice scathing, yet mortified.

The slap doesn't even make him flinch.

In fact, it does nothing. He doesn't even move.

The silence stretches on for eternity and covers the entire black world in a blanket of quiet.

"Do it again. I liked it," he nearly purrs, his voice so deep that it settles into my bones.

Part of me recoils against his perverse ideations; part of me is entrapped by the allurement of him. His firm body is pressed so tightly against mine I can feel the length of him harden against my inner thigh. The tingles spread from the bundle of nerves between my legs to my toes, but I try to bite back the desire I suddenly feel for him.

It slightly turns me on that he watched me fuck Bash and felt enticed by it.

No!

Sayah, you are in love with Bash!

It's like a fading part of me is still clinging to the walls of myself, hanging on for dear life and screaming at me to not fall for this spell, this trick, this poisonous web of lies Trystan is spinning for me.

"Get off me," I growl, collecting all the strength and remaining pieces of the real me, and hurling it at him with all the power I don't have.

He remains still, his grip tightening around my wrist, his free hand ghosting his fingers up the side of my stomach, getting dangerously close to my side boob.

"Sayah," he intones subtly, the coarseness of his voice softening like time softens the mountains. "You know you are fighting against those feelings you are starting to feel for me. Part of you hates me, and the other part is weakening to the idea of me."

"I will never weaken to the idea of you," I say as viciously as I can, but it's untrustworthy. Even I doubt myself. The inflections in the words are unstable and jagged.

His laugh—his wicked laugh sends evil little pricks of luscious torment all over my body.

His deep voice, laughing at my attempt at viciousness, scalds me, weakens even the sturdiest depths of me, and cracks something inside, spilling my fire into his darkness.

The darkness of this realm.

His free hand finishes its ascent over the left side of my boob, coming to rest firmly over my throat. He applies just enough pressure for me to feel his strength, but not so hard that I can't breathe. "I could kill you where you lay." A lethal calm forms the words on his lips.

I shake my head, resolute. "You can't kill me. You need my power too much."

"That's twice now that you've tested me. There will not be a third."

This time, it's my turn to laugh. "If you believe that to be true, then you are as naïve as me."

I can't translate the expression on his face.

It's either he's turned on and a little intrigued that I'm testing him again, or he's fucking pissed that I just tested him again.

"You will either be the death of yourself"—he leans in so close to my face, our noses almost touch—"or the queen of the fucking world. I cannot tell which at this moment. But what I can promise you is this." His moves his face to the side of mine and takes the soft skin of my earlobe between his teeth, biting down enough to cause a little pain. "You will bow to me. And after you show me how a queen conquers her king in breaking worlds and colliding realms, I am most certain I will bow to you if it's anything like what I saw tonight."

"I will never bow to you," I snap at him.

He pulls himself up to level his eyes with mine. "You will. I promise you. You will." He gets up and leaves me lying on the cold ground. "It's almost kismet that your last name is Thorne. Now get up. It's time to get ready for our wedding."

24

LIGHT GATE PORTAL

—BASH—

"So, what is your brilliant idea?" I ask Tallyn as we walk the grounds of the inner ring.

Her idea was to get some fresh air and enjoy the calm before the storm.

The inner ring around the castle is acres and acres of trees and rivers acting as a moat that wraps around the entire estate, which is impressive in and of itself.

It baffles me how massive Feylight Grove is.

We are in another dimension, so that makes sense.

"Caelum has been able to decipher some of the language the abyssal sprites use to communicate telepathically with each other. Some of them in Nightshade in fact." Tallyn says, sweeping a hand through her tangled black locks to right what the wind has tossed around. "We also have an informant in Never, and they have let us know that Trystan is unable to open the Shadow Gate Portal to Desoloth because, luckily for us, the merpeople, along with a coven of witches called the Sorenyas, put a protective spell over the portal, ensuring only someone with pure intentions can open it."

"Pure intentions, huh?" I say. We duck under the brambles

and swinging vines of the trees resembling weeping willows, but are purple and glow. "Does anyone have pure intentions when opening a portal to demon realms?"

"Exactly." Tallyn stops walking on a stone bridge arching over a stream. "Like all things in this universe, there are two sides to every coin. The Gemini Covenant. For the Shadow Gate Portal to exist, it needed a balance. A portal to angel realms. Therefore, the creator made the Light Gate Portal, which can be opened to Wyndhallow."

Stopping beside her, I lean over and watch the rushing water cascading down the stream's path. Henry appears on a grassy knoll beside the stream and picks up a stone, making it skip down the water.

"I have so many questions," I state, watching Henry pick up objects as an inanimate object himself—though he isn't see-through anymore.

"And your questions would be?" Tallyn asks, seemingly looking right at Henry.

I crane my neck in confusion. "Can you see him now?" I ask her first before getting into the whole "Wyndhallow-y" thing.

"I have been able to see him for a while."

"What?" I feel my eyes blow wide in shock. "You've always been able to see him?"

"No, not always. Just more recently, when he actually took a human form." Her orange eyes track his movements. After throwing his next rock, he looks up at us and waves.

Fucking. Waves.

Shaking my head, I turn to lean on the stone wall and face the other way. "Okay, what the fuck is an angel realm?"

"Well, like the demon realms, there are realms filled with light beings. Pure and good and innocent. It is dangerous for any mortal on earth to go there because looking into some of these beings' eyes will burn them up from the inside out. Even a sliver of morally gray and they will perish."

"Okay, so none of us can enter it," I reply tersely. "What's the fucking point? Why do we need it?"

"Because we won't be using it to go to Wyndhallow. At least, not yet. We will use it to portal to the Shadow Gate."

"Ooooh. They're connected to each other?"

"Essentially, yes." Her nose scrunches up, and I realize the subtlety with which Tallyn expresses her face. She rarely even raises her eyebrows, so it's much more noticeable when she moves it

She faces the water once again. "They were forged out of the same glass and brass and stone. Therefore, if you walk into one thinking of the other, it portals you to where the other is. No one knows about the Light Gate because no one has ever successfully returned from Wyndhallow. And since it can't be used, it's been long forgotten."

I roll my eyes. I'm tired of her riddles. "Where, pray tell, is this Light Gate located?"

Tallyn pauses, her gaze drifting to the other side of the forest. "It's hidden deep within the Celestial Gardens, a place where the light never dims. The gardens are said to be guarded by sentinels of light, and the gate itself is at the heart of a maze of radiant flora and crystal pathways. It's not easily found, but we might have a chance with the right guide."

"The Celestial Gardens," I repeat, trying to wrap my head around the idea. "I thought there was just Luminara and Neverdusk?"

A small laugh escapes her lips. "There are infinite dimensions and realms, Bash. Just like there are infinite worlds and galaxies. The Celestial Gardens are one of those worlds between worlds."

"Still makes no sense in my head."

She smirks. "I wouldn't expect you to understand in a sentence."

"How do we get there?"

Tallyn smiles, a glint of determination in her eyes. "We'll need to journey through the Valley of Echoes and cross the Luminous Fields. The garden entrance is said to be marked by an ancient, glowing tree that stands taller than any other. Once we find it, we'll know we're close."

I nod, feeling the weight of everything coming together like waves against cliffs in a storm. "Sounds fun."

"If you think that sounds fun, wait until I tell you this next part."

An emotion similar to dread—if I could feel dread—crawls up my legs and rests in the bowels of my being. "Oh, no. What?"

"It would seem"—Tallyn begins walking again. I reluctantly follow—"that Trystan is planning to wed Sayah in a hand-fasting ceremony—"

"I'm sorry, a what fasting ceremony?"

"It's where 'tie the knot' was coined from, as the mortals say, I've heard. A couple's hands are bound together with rope as they say their vows. However," she rambles, ducking under more branches, "in fae, it's used with living vines that tattoo themselves onto the married couple while the vows are spoken, a Whispering Leaf carries off the promises to the wind. Usually officiated by an elder fae, but some have the High Councilor do it."

"Yeah, cool, sweet, awesome," I state with a yawn, kicking the rocks under my feet. The anger is starting to scathe me. "I fucking hate your brother. I will rip him to shreds."

"You have no idea how nefarious Trystan is, how willing he is to use any means to get what he wants . . ." Her aura turns sorrowful.

It insults me that she doubts my nefariousness. "I can take him."

"One day, I will tell you the tale of just how wicked he is, but just know for now, he is the reason I have not, nor ever will, be able to conceive my own children."

I immediately think of her stealing Sariana and begin to ask, but she cuts me off.

"He will use the end of the Dread Harvest and Wild Hunt to finish putting the veil on her," she continues, marching onward like she's trying to stomp out Trystan's memory. "Once her hands are bound with the living vines, he'll capture whatever remains of her mind into his with the final kiss and use it to his advantage. Trystan is a cunning man. Whatever he is planning, he's doing so with conquering the world in mind. If he has Sayah's, he will most likely be able to trick the portal to open for him. I'm not sure how, but that's what our informant tells us."

"We need to stop this fucking wedding before it even happens."

"Yes, but realistically, we won't be able to stop it completely. If we go to the Light Gate Portal, we may get there in time to stop the final part of the ceremony."

"Which is?"

"The kiss." She stops walking to face me again. "Sealed with a kiss. Like in all the fairy tales."

I want to vomit. "And just how will we stop it once we get there?"

Her eyes light up, the flames in them crackling like a live forest fire living in her irises. Paired with the nefarious grin, they resurrect her ferocity. "We're going to blow the fucking place to smithereens."

"I like your style," I say, nudging her shoulder with mine. "But how?"

"Well, we have the second phoenix."

"We *do* have the second phoenix. What will the second phoenix do?"

"Why, make us the most potent phoenix bombs, of course."

"See, now you are speaking my language." I link arms with her as we continue our journey to gods-knows-where, Henry running to catch up behind us.

25

ANTECHAMBER OF WARLOCKS

—SAYAH—

I'm still reeling from the bombshell Trystan dropped and left while I screamed at him to come back and tell me what the fuck he just said again.

All I heard as he traipsed down the hall was, "I didn't stutter."

The stones under my feet are warm from my pacing back and forth from the bathroom to the balcony and back again. I haven't dressed or drank or eaten or anything since he told me the awful fucking news, and I don't know what to do.

I cannot marry him.

I have shouted to the moons for Bash to come and save me, to get me out of this gods-forsaken place.

Shit, I even thought about throwing myself from the balcony, but remembered what he said about the boundary when I first arrived.

That's why he said what he said.

Leaning over the edge and watching my tears fall to the ground below, I think of nothing but getting Gauge and myself out of this mess to see him grow up. This is the second time in my life I have fought a battle for him, to live for him, to stay alive—all to see my son grow up.

The first time was when he was three, and I had cancer.

I must remember that fight in me, that will to live, and use it now to get through this and back to him.

As I think of my little boy's face, sweet brown eyes, and infectious laughter, a rumbling deep beneath the earth shakes the very mountain I stand upon.

I look out again and wait for another tsunami to come for me, to come crashing into the rocks and my life, and think maybe if it comes again, it will sweep me away from here.

But none come.

The moons have begun to separate, and this makes me wonder if Trystan got what he wanted from the Dread Harvest.

Fuck that fairy bitch.

Gods, I'm so mad at him I could scream.

I turn to head back inside, storming past the table with food on it that wasn't there twenty seconds ago.

The fuck?

I look around the room for any sign of who brought the meal, but see none.

My stomach rumbles, and the smells of spiced meat and citrusy fruit call to my senses. Before I know it, I've eaten most of the spread on the table and drank all the nectar.

This time, it tasted similar to boba with glowing balls of something that tasted like Juicy Fruit.

When I stand, my head feels spiny and light, and I feel like I'm walking through a dream fog. The world seems off-kilter.

I teeter to the bed on unsure feet, thinking I'm just going to collapse on top of the comforter and pass the fuck out, when a shadow slithers out from under the bed and shoots for the door, gliding under the crack of it.

I run to the door and throw it open, looking around for whatever-the-fuck it was.

A short woman with long, dark red hair, and glowing green eyes traipses closer. Though her hair is swept into a high pony on top of her head, the blood-red locks go beyond her ass. She is wearing a shiny green corset with her full breasts spilling out of it, tight black leather pants, and thigh-high vinyl boots. As she draws closer, I see she is wielding daggers in both arms; they shoot out of her fingerless elbow-length gloves.

I recognize her from when Trystan stole my power the first time and also when she came to tell him about Melodias Cove.

"Who the fuck are you?" I ask, straining to get my vision back to seeing single.

"Name's Ember. Nice to meet you, phoenix."

Her gorgeous, full red lips are shiny and glittery, and her perfect nose complements her high cheekbones. She has a black onyx pendant hanging from her neck. I still see two of them, but I close one eye to help.

Her face turns mock sympathetic. "Oh, you poor thing. Did you drink that cocktail on the table?"

My heart falls. "What . . . what was in it?"

"Fae wine, of course."

Shit.

The castle feels tilted, as though it's sliding down a mountainside in a mudslide, gaining momentum as it heads straight for a cliff.

All those years of sobriety down the drain.

I fall to my knees, unable to sustain the shaking any longer.

"Oh, you poor thing," Ember says, crouching before me. "Did you not know alcohol is in all the drinks here?"

My eyes sting, but I shed no tears. I'm more pissed than I am sad. "I did not," I whisper, rubbing my brow to banish the pain.

She takes her long, pointed fingernail, and lifts my chin to look into my eyes. "This will make it better."

Opening the pendant on her neck, she blows blue powder into my face.

I wince, rocking my head back with my eyes closed. The blue substance covers the air all around me. It smells like cotton candy and funnel cake, and I immediately want to go to a carnival on a summer night and get on a Ferris wheel with Trystan.

Trystan.

Where is that sexy motherfucker?

I lean my head back and open my eyes. Ember is no longer here with me.

Peeling myself off the floor, I stand, and look around the room.

It feels different. I feel different.

I no longer feel drunk, and the agony I felt at being tricked into losing my sobriety doesn't faze me—which I absolutely think it should.

Something is wrong.

But I really don't care.

I really just want to find Trystan and . . .

And . . .

Lick his thorns?

That's what something deep inside my subconscious wants me to do.

How ridiculous is that?

My mind is racing over all the ways I want to seduce Trystan when I realize I've been walking down this long hallway, noticing all the shut doors and pretty orb lights on the walls and—

Oh, my fucking gods.

I turn around to see my room at the far end of the hallway. I didn't even realize the magick barrier to keep me in was broken.

What is happening?

I continue my journey along the long halls of the castle. I don't know where to go, but I follow my intuition.

A left here, a right there, down the stairs, around a turret, through that gate, up this ramp, down and around the next hallway. Before I know it, I've come to a strange circular room, an antechamber of sorts. A set of old wooden doors is ajar at the end, and voices spill out.

I tiptoe to the door and peek in.

A room similar to one I've seen in movies lies beyond, where stadium seating stretches up and up. In the middle of the floor, surrounded by the stadium seating, sits Trystan on a throne akin to those found in fairy tales.

He sits on a throne of thorns.

In the stands, taking up every wall, are warlocks of all shapes, sizes, and colors. Their eyes are as black as the deepest night, and their skin tones range from pastel pink to ebony black to ghostly white. My heart contracts at how the warlocks remind me of Mederio and Matrasia. Even though I know they are dead, the unsettling air surrounding them is precisely the same as theirs. The sulfur smell swirling around the room plunges me back to the cabin on the lake the night I killed Matrasia.

I should be terrified.

Here I am, ducking in a hallway outside a room filled with the most nefarious creatures imaginable, while I have no powers to fight them.

The old me clinging to the last remaining bits of myself screams at me to run from this room, to act like I never escaped my cell. But the new me is collecting those particles of the old me and sweeping them up, snubbing out that girl, and everything she stands for.

The moons' light is seeping in through the long, stained glass windows in this peculiar room, coloring it in ominous pale blue and red tones.

"But how many have you opened so far, my king?" asks one warlock with skin resembling rubies and wings to match, similar to Bash's wings when he was Agares.

"We've successfully opened every one I intended, save one,"

Trystan replies, one hand playing with his lips, like he's nervous about something.

"Except Desoloth," says another warlock, this one purple and large, resembling an ogre.

"Which will happen as soon as I'm married," Trystan responds. The crowd grumbles, mocking the rumbling I feel in my bones. "We have an army of demons at my disposal," Trystan answers, his voice sturdy and reliable. "I am not worried about being able to open it once the phoenix is my wife."

"We're running out of time for the Desoloth portal to open," the red warlock says. "The Dread Harvest is almost over, and we need that realm to take Feylight."

"The wedding is taking place this evening." Trystan leans forward to stretch his wings. "The preparations are being readied as we speak. I only took time away from that to address and reassure you all that everything is going according to plan."

"You promised us that realm, Your Majesty," a green warlock says. "We only mean to collect on what is owed to us."

"And you will," Trystan answers, his face reddening with fury. "I never make promises I can't keep."

"We overran the world with your grimspawns to be ready for this moment," an orange demon says. "The millions of grimspawns we made for you are ready to take over the mortal realms."

"They've already begun to swarm Earth," Trystan confirms. "They've begun to take over small cities in the states and some in Europe. They, along with the demons, are preparing for the opening of Desoloth. Once that portal is open, the world is ours. Along with the final ring to take Feylight."

"And you're sure the wedding will be the catalyst for opening that door?" a blue warlock asks.

"Absolutely certain," Trystan replies resolutely. "The merpeople put a spell on it that ensures only someone with pure intentions can open the door to Desoloth. With me taking her phoenix power completely, it will override that spell."

Vomit.

Bile.

My blood.

Bones melting.

Boiling.

I should be feeling these things, but all I feel is hollow.

I run from the room, away from that awful smell, and end up lost in a maze of walls, doors, and stone.

I lean against one wall and fall to my ass, struggling to catch my breath.

Everything I've ever known screams at me to be furious.

I should be devastated that he stole my power from me.

But all I feel right now is excitement to be the Queen of Neverdusk, Earth, and Feylight.

And to give my child legs and wings and free him of his diabetes.

I am ecstatic to be Trystan's bride.

26

BATTLE WITH GHOSTS

—BASH—

What Tallyn failed to tell me, in her whimsical, "Oh, it's just a radiant maze of flora and fauna and the Valley of Echoes, and Luminous Fields" blah, blah, blah, (yeah fucking right) is it's up a steep ass mountain, with jagged rocky ledges we have to trudge up, and the side we are to summit is barren of all walks of life. No trees, or birds, or water.

Nope. Just one big fucking rocky mountainside.

At least it's not night here.

It feels good to feel the sun again.

Even more so, since I spent centuries in the dark and have only recently reacquainted with sunlight, I'd forgotten how it feels to have the sun lick your skin, to cover you with warmth and radiance. Being warm is akin to how I feel when I'm around Sayah.

Perfect, peaceful—happy.

Tallyn has portaled us to the base of said mountain, where we begin to climb. The path we walk is a zigzagged trail littered with ancient dried-up tree roots, boulders, and decrepit trees.

This mountain range is the barrier between the Valley of

Echoes and the rest of this dimension. A barrier prohibiting portal travel, forcing any who enter through the trials of the valley.

There's a line of us traipsing up the mountainside; Tallyn and her soldiers take up the front while me and my family bring up the rear.

"Where the fuck are we?" Scarlet demands from in front of me, taking in the desolate landscape. She fails to see an embedded tree root, and it catches the tip of her boot, toppling her forward. Caelum, who's been a few paces behind her instead up with his fellow fae, runs to her aid, kneeling to help her up.

Obliging him with a scoff, she shoots him a disgusted glare as he pulls her to her feet, brushing him off when she's right with the ground again.

I don't know when she'll ever notice that Caelum has found his soul mate.

Whether he is hers remains to be seen.

"Where we are is an in-between," Tallyn shouts from the head of the pack, her black leather cape swaying in the wind.

"Right. Well, that clears that up," I say sarcastically to Ollie, who's a little to my left and behind me. I haven't told my family that Dom is in his own in-between.

Figure I'll let Tallyn take that one on as soon as she deems it pertinent.

"The in-between is the dimensions between the relevant worlds," my dad offers, walking a couple of steps ahead of Ollie and Claire.

It baffles me he knows this sort of thing. He usually strays far away from folklore, even if he is part of it.

"So this world isn't relevant?" asks Draelle, one of Laureya's cronies. I glance over my shoulder to see her at the back of our line.

"It's relevant," grumbles Dad. "Maybe relevant was the wrong word to use."

"How about 'heavily populated'?" Mom offers, hanging on to my dad's hand as she climbs up a little incline.

"The in-between are the dimensions between the worlds that have established life systems," Sariana offers. She glides up the hillside behind Halcyon, who separates us from them. "They are worlds that are not yet worlds. They exist for souls traveling to their next life, serving as a place of respite or to allow one to decide which direction they want to go."

"So, kind of like Heaven?" Ryan asks. Laureya's boot catches on a large rock in her path. She loses her footing, cussing as she falls to her knees. Instead of helping her up, Ryan side-steps her.

"No, you dense mortal," Thalira says, offering Laureya a hand to help her up. I definitely would have just walked over her, too, but Thalira is ahead of me. "It's a world before a world. It's too complex for your puny human minds to understand. Just think of it as a place souls come to rest, reflect, and decide if they want to move on to the next life or if they'd like to roam the dimensions and soul surf."

"Soul surf?" I ask, yet I'm unsure I want to know the answer.

"Watch over your loved ones," Thalira answers.

Yeah, that's what I was afraid of. "So, like Henry."

"What about me?" Henry asks, suddenly walking beside me.

I jump, startled. "Fucking A," I exclaim, and Thalira looks back at me skeptically.

"Who's Henry?" Laith questions, taking the mountain in long strides, barely exulting a stressed breath.

"He's not important." No one else seems to be able to see him except Tallyn and Caelum. "If this is where souls come to decide where to go next, why is it where the Light Gate Portal is kept?"

I survey the distance we've traveled, looking down over the edge to measure

We've summited a whole mountainside in the short time

we've walked. The ground below is so far down that even vampires wouldn't survive the jump.

"I don't know why the creator decided to keep it here," Tallyn answers from the road zigzagging above us, going in the opposite direction.

"Well, how did you know it's kept here?" I ask her, lugging my ass up a heavy incline.

"Being the Queen of the Luminara Domain for thousands of years has afforded me plenty of knowledge of the worlds I deal with, Sebastian," she responds tersely. "It'd be wise of you to not pry too hard."

"Is there going to be anything or anyone to eat once we get to where we're going?" Kaston asks, helping his girlfriend Draelle up a steep rock. The rest of us vampires rumble in agreement.

"If you tide yourselves over with small bites from the fae, you should have plenty to eat once we portal to the Shadow Gate," Tallyn answers.

"Yeah, are we actually prepared for that, by the by?" I ask, stopping to strain my neck and looking at the rest of the mountain we have to climb. I wish I could use my gift of speed to get me up the rest of the gods-forsaken mountain, but Tallyn warned us our powers would be useless in most places here.

Tallyn stops and looks down the incline at me. "Of course we are, Sebastian. Do you think I'd lead you all to a portal to then port to a hostile land and not be prepared for war?"

I scratch my chin. "I mean, you've done some pretty nefarious shit, Tal. I wouldn't put it past you."

"We're going to have Laureya make the phoenix bombs once we're next to the Light Gate," she answers and continues to climb. "We need them as fresh as they can be when we go in to steal Sayah."

After climbing for what feels like hours, we've been traipsing flat grounds for some time now until an outline appears on the horizon.

A jagged line of towering cliffs looms ahead, their sheer faces marked with crumbling stone. Gnarled trees cling to the edges like skeletal hands. The air grows still, unnervingly quiet, as if the Valley of Echoes is holding its breath.

I am holding my breath, as if not to disturb the ghosts of this place.

As we draw nearer, a subtle vibration hums through the ground beneath my feet. It feels as though the land itself remembers the footsteps of all who came before.

The entrance is flanked by immense rock formations, carved by time into distorted shapes that seem almost alive—watchful. The path narrows, funneled between the cliffs, and the faintest whispers begin to coil around us, soft and indistinct, like voices carried on the wind.

Beyond, the valley stretches wide and vast, covered in mist rising like spectral hands from the cracked earth. The cliff walls seem impossibly high, and every sound we make bounces back tenfold—our footsteps, our breath, even the rustling of our clothes.

Tallyn stops us before we emerge ourselves entirely into the valley.

"Be wary of the echoes," she warns, propping her booted foot up on a boulder and tightening her weapons' belt. Her long skirt has a slit up the middle with a garter buckle, which houses more weapons. "They will whisper anything and everything you can think of."

"Like what?" Hattie asks, eyeing the valley skeptically.

"You will likely hear voices of people you've lost, dead and alive," Tallyn replies, fixing the other side. "Whatever you do, do not listen to them."

"What else will we hear?" my mom asks, her dark brows furrowing with concern.

"You will probably hear Dom's voice," Tallyn answers, straightening to glare fiercely into my mother's eyes. I still my breaths, thinking she's about to tell her. But she doesn't. "The echoes will feed off anything you emit in your subconscious. Your wildest dreams, your deepest fears, your regrets. Your lost loves and hopes and dreams. People you miss or people who've died."

My mom withers under her words. "Can everyone hear what they say?"

"Yes, so you all best have your wits about you. This place isn't for the faint of heart. The creator set up these tests to only allow the purest of intentions to make it to the Light Gate."

"And you think that a whole-ass army of misfits is gonna make it through there?" I say, glaring beyond Tallyn into the ominous valley. The place feels like somewhere trapped in time, the shadows thick and restless, hiding whatever might still dwell here. "A group of vampires and fae aren't going to make it through here with that shit."

Tallyn crosses the small distance between us to stare me down. "You all have the willpower of steel to get you through this. Use it. Lean on each other. Don't listen to the voices. Most of you have lived long enough to make it through a silly little telephone game."

"She's right," Ollie says, holding Claire's hand. His unflinching ability to remain calm when angry waters churn will forever baffle me. "Whatever lurks for us in there, we've fought worse things than. Every one of us has tasted death at least once. Let us not forget the cunning and lethal predators we all are."

Claire nods imperceptibly, her face holding a diluted fierceness. Almost like the human in her fears the unknown, and the vampire is learning to fasten to the idea that she's not the prey anymore.

I crack my neck, resolve setting my bones to steel. "We got this."

Agares, if you could just be at the ready, I'd appreciate it.

There's a quake deep within the depths of me, the rumble of a darkened lullaby, keeping Agares pacified.

Tallyn nods and whisks around, her black hair swaying with the movement.

The group moves in unison, but a quiet hush falls over us. We are all anticipating the worst.

The transition is apparent when I pass by the barrier separating the Valley of Echoes from the rest of this strange place. Not only does the temperature change, but the feeling of the air is different, too. It's heavier, almost tangible—like I could reach out and grab a fistful of it and throw it at someone.

"You will lose her," says the first voice.

Oh, okay. Like the voices in the wall. This ain't nothing. I can handle this.

My spine is tingly, but I solidify it, trying not to let that thought poison my mind.

"He's twice the man you are," it says. This time, it is Dom's voice. "He can show her a life you can only dream of. He can give her child working legs. You could never do that."

Agares's hackles rise on the back of my neck, and I emit a low growl. My eyes contract, fangs piercing through.

"It's your fault she died," I hear a voice tell Jasantha. I can see the heartbreak on her face, tethered always to the "fuck you forever" present there as well.

The echoes, alive with a life of their own, multiply, overlapping in a haunting chorus. They twist and shift in ways that make it difficult to tell what is real and what is a lingering memory of those long gone.

I hear one voice tell Hattie she's the reason she'll never find love.

Glancing over my shoulder, she double-flips off the air, spinning around to push through more of the valley.

I'm not worried about Hattie.

She'll brat it up and power through.

"You are the reason all your children are monsters," an echo tells my mom. My dad's solid brick arm holds stronger to hers, lending her the strength she needs to get through the heinous accusations. His eyes are affixed to the shadow, and he puffs his chest out like he's going to battle the ghosts.

"You're a terrible father," a whisper says to Dad, the sound spiraling around him.

"He doesn't love you like you think he does."

"You're not good enough."

"You will fail at everything you do."

"They know you fucked her husband."

"You will be a terrible mother."

"You will never be a mother."

"No one will ever love you."

"Alone is where you will be forever."

"Art is not your forte."

"You stole two of your brother's loves."

"Music is for talented people, not you."

The closer we press to the heart of the Valley of Echoes, the more oppressive the feeling becomes, as though they are more than sound—they're watching us . . . waiting.

I clench my jaw, feeling my muscles lock up. "Don't listen to them!"

I latch eyes with Halcyon, who pushes forward, blocking the voices like he's on the ship's bow in a great storm.

Luminara guards surround Tallyn to protect her, yet they, themselves, have forlorn looks plastered on their faces.

No one is immune to the extemporaneous words.

I jog up to Tallyn, darting the voice telling me everything Trystan will do to my woman. "Question for you, T. If this place is so full of light and casts out those of us who have darkened souls, why aren't they saying good things?"

"Does that question even make sense, Sebastian?" Tallyn snipes, her black hair catching a gust of a shadow, murmuring how she's lied about not having children. "They are meant to find your deepest fears to weed you out." She seems unfazed by the accusation, forcing her eyes forward to the far end of the valley.

"You have a small penis," Henry says to me.

"Really, dude?" I scoff, swatting at him like he's solid.

He merely morphs into the air and rematerializes a few feet from where he was. "What?" he asks, walking backward in front of me. "I'm just joining in the fun."

"If you've ever seen my dick, you would know that it is not small," I retort.

Thalira gives me a sidelong look, and something similar to lust enters her eyes.

"It's huge," I tell her, showing her with my hands how big we're talking.

She smiles and looks away.

"Bash! Stop it," my mom scolds me as she's pulled by my dad, who is pressing on.

"Sebastian is not your husband's son," says a voice coming from above my mom.

"He already knows that, you twat!" she shouts up at it.

"Don't engage with the voices," Tallyn says, uncapping a canteen, and drinking whatever is in it. "The more you acknowledge it, the more power you give them."

"Shut. The. Fuck. Up!"

The yell comes from Draelle, who is several paces back. She's stopped walking and is covering her ears, screaming at the air. Tears streak her dirt-stained face.

Kaston, who's run back to help her, holds her shoulders, trying to get her focus back on him.

The ground starts to tremble beneath our feet.

"Draelle, babe, stop," Kaston pleads, shaking her shoulders to stop Draelle's screaming.

Cautiously, I look around. The high cliffs of the valley soar above our heads a thousand feet on either side. The desolate ground beneath us is soft red sand; no trees or vegetation are in sight. The sun is scorching in the soft purple sky, and clouds of yellow and orange speckle the expanse.

Tallyn, seemingly ignoring the tremble activating rocks to fall from the high cliffs, sustains her efforts to move us through the canyon. The expanse of the valley goes farther than the eye can see, the mist distorting the depth of field that throws off even the supernatural sight.

There seems to be no end.

A scream slices through the valley, causing us all to stop and look back.

Draelle's interactions with the demented whispers have fed and morphed them into flying sparrows of death. They are pecking at her hair and skin, screaming her secrets into existence.

"Stuart was a nice fuck for you, Draelle, wasn't he?"

"Does Kaston know you sucked his dick . . ."

"And liked it?" the voices shout at her, distorted and deafened, high-pitched and relentless. They are picking apart her insecurities and fears, as well as her skin, hair, and tendons.

Kaston is trying to fight them off by swatting at them, but their razor-sharp beaks also pierce his skin.

"You'll never be good enough for her," the voices aim at Kaston.

Fury paints his face a darker shade of mocha. He puffs his chest out and squares up with the invisible assailant.

I turn to tell Thalira that I have a bad feeling about this. She's been hovering closer to me since she learned my dick size.

The air splits with another of Draelle's agonized screams, and she's bolting back into the direction we came from.

"*No!*" Tallyn shouts at her. "You'll just feed them!" But her voice doesn't reach Draelle. Every other sound, save for the now screaming voices, is snubbed out by the intensification of the quaking ground.

Draelle kicks up dust in her flee from the voices. It combines with the plume of debris the collapsing earth had set forth. Churning violently with the winds picking up, the shadows, smoke, and fog morph together, blotting out the sun. The red sand beneath our feet swirls up in people-shaped dust beings, lunging for anything moving in the valley.

The earth drops into a chasm between Draelle Kaston and the rest of us, the ground rising into a shadow army instead of falling deep into the void the falling valley floor is creating.

Draelle stops running and turns around to see us on the other side of this canyon. Her eyes bulge in fear, and she turns to run in the opposite direction toward where we entered. The ground escalates in its collapse, chasing her.

The ground and chasm swallow her whole. Her screams echo in the fissure of the valley, now a dark and bottomless line separating north and south.

Another wail cleaves through me with familiarity, and I spin to see Scarlet trapped in a nightmarish illusion, her form flickering as if being torn between this world and another. Shadows surround her, whispering the darkest truths of her past, and future failures. In an attempt to save her, Caelum rushes forward, but the ground gives way; he barely manages to hold on to the rocky ledge.

A shadow with Sayah's shape takes form before me, and just

as she's extending her arm toward me, I lunge through her, shifting the shadow to dust particles exploding into the wind. The loose sand in the catastrophic winds pierces my face. I force the speed to the brinks, getting to Caelum a second before the ledge gives. I pull him up with a grunt, and he jumps up when I do, rushing to Scarlet.

The shadows have thickened around her ankles, another gathering of beings at her arms, pulling her in all directions, ready to draw, and quarter her.

Caelum retrieves the sword sheathed across his back. With it, he tears into one of the shadows at her arms, the being bursting apart, and coming together again at her back.

Bash! Call on Agares! Dom's voice echoes in the wind.

I don't even have to say the words before my skin expands outside me. I rise in height with movements I can't decipher and gather strength I've only known in my most nightmarish forms.

Caelum frees Scarlet from the shadows, and they run in the other direction.

Amidst the chaos, Tallyn is ensnared by her own manifested fears: a monstrous, twisted version of what could only be Trystan. The enormous, nightmarish version of him rises into the darkening sky, the twenty-foot wind-hewn living sculpture sucking in a breath, inhaling not only dirt and dust but also Tallyn's soul.

Tallyn falls to her ass, futilely trying to scamper away, but the wind is stronger than she is. It rips her sideways, lifting her off the ground by her leg.

Halcyon and another soldier try to pull her back, but they are being haunted by their own demons.

"Don't let Tallyn get sucked into that fog!" Sariana yells to the fae helping Tallyn. As the monsters come for her, too, I fear the fog is pulling Tallyn into the void, to her own personal hell.

I am about to rush to her when "Bash!" interrupts my pursuit.

I spin around to see Thalira sliding toward the chasm. Shadows are dragging her toward the infinite void opening up. I'm there in movements I don't understand, new muscles pushing me forward from my back.

I reach her in time and yank her forward onto solid ground.

"We have to get out of this valley," she gasps, scrambling from her knees, and running into a wall of wind and dirt.

Following her lead, I rush into the chaos, listening for sounds that might be human.

"Get off me!" I hear from the right and push toward it, running into a little fae I know as Elowen. She is on her knees on the ground, covering her ears with her hands—shadows swarm her.

"Hey!" I shout, hearing my voice come out with Agares's agreement, and it throws even me.

Elowen's head snaps up. She looks ready to crawl away from me and into the shadows.

I rush to the other side of her. "It's okay, I'm real. It's me, Bash."

"Bash?" She looks at me questioningly. In my demon form, my arms are red, and my fingers end in talons.

"I shapeshift now. No time to explain, c'mon!" I yell, offering my hand to her. She hesitantly takes it, and I lift her, swinging her over my right shoulder.

"Sylvan is over there," she says into my ear, pointing off to the left.

I shield my eyes from the whipping winds and find Sylvan, a silver fairy who is furiously swiping at the air like she is being attacked.

"*Sylvan!*" Elowen yells.

Sylvan looks up and makes to run, but I grab her by her uniform and gather her up by her waist.

Time to test out these wings.

I snap them out as I bend to the wind, climbing into the air with a not-so-graceful stumble. We ascend through the hurricane-force winds, the calculated beats of my wings pushing us through with precision toward the other end of the valley. Agares pilots us above the maelstrom of nightmares, the whirling dark clouds covering the ground so thickly I can see nothing but them.

Together, Agares and I shove my powers to their absolute max; I'm on the brink of collapse when I feel the barrier between the Valley of Echoes and the other side, the clouds crashing against it like a glass partition.

Even the air is warmer.

I set the two fae women on the ground, and they dismount, their eyes carefully watching me.

"Stay here; I'll be back," I tell them, then take flight to battle the winds again.

It's impossible to hear or see anything from above the bedlam, so I invert back into the darkness, camouflaging myself within the clouds.

A shout that sounds like Ollie causes me to halt.

Standing amidst the air, I concentrate on the sound of my brother's voice, envisioning him fighting for his life. The roaring winds are hesitant to obey my silent command, despite using every ounce of strength to push against them. I am forcing my powers to work in this realm. The barrier spell barring magick is fierce, like a weighted blanket covering the invisible parts of me. My normal powers are severely strained, but to be Agares in this dimension is proving detrimental to our survival. The magick of the demon can sever the mystical chains that bind most magick.

When the yell comes again—directly below me and to my left—I know it's Ollie, and I dive toward the sound. He grunts as we fall to the ground in a collision, and when he sits up and sees me, he's almost surprised.

"No time," I proclaim, jumping to my feet. I tower over him.

"We have to get Claire," he shouts over the wailing winds. "Over there!" He points, and I see a wisp of her white hoodie being swallowed up by the storm.

"Claire!" he calls. "By that rock! She was running from her homicidal ex."

Ollie is on my tail as we plunge into the disarray.

Claire's on the ground, covered in blood, and screaming. A shadow emulating a tall man with a black hoodie is kicking her sides.

I shove through the shadow and pull her up, throwing her onto my back. "Ollie, get on!"

Ollie runs and jumps onto my back as I bound into the air once more. When we're on the other side of the storm, I set them both down. More of the fae have found their way and are lingering by Elowen and Thalira.

"Where's Dad?" I ask Ollie once they climb down to safety.

"I saw him over by where Claire was. He was trying to get Mom. Want me to come with you?"

"No, stay here. I'll be back." I careen back into the storm.

Visibly is inexistent, even when flying close to the ground.

When I spot a black boot sticking out of a mound of red sand, my heart leaps at the possibility of it being my dad. I land next to what would be the head, shoveling the dirt from whose face it is.

But once the dirt and sand are swept away, I see it's one of the fae, their face frozen in a scream. I recognize them but can't remember their name.

That's when I hear my dad yell, "*Adaline!*"

I burst away from the dead fae when I nearly run into my dad, barely stopping before toppling him into the chasm. He's leaning on the edge, holding on, and when I peer over the side, my mom is dangling above the depths of the abyss, her hand slipping down my dad's arm.

I quickly grab onto her other hand and hoist her up.

"Sebastian?" she asks as my dad pulls her to him, his coruscating gaze slicing up me.

"Yes, it's me," I reply. A sharp whisper at my back has me turning to see if it's real or a shadow. "Guys, I'd love to explain, but we have, like, zero time left. Please, just get on my back, and I'll fly you out of here."

My mom moves to oblige, and my dad holds her back.

"Dad, seriously. It's me. I need to get you guys out of here."

"Honey, it's Sebastian," she says.

The murkiness of death and destruction looms behind them.

Dad's expression is hardened and difficult to decipher. His eyes bore into me, then to her, then to me again. "How do I—"

"He looks just like his real father, doesn't he?" a tall shadow says, emerging behind my dad, rising up from the void behind him.

The being's blurry form bends in ways that make it seem he wears a cloak, like a reaper. A bony hand emerges from the wide sleeve, landing on Dad's shoulder. The beige shirt he wears blackens, as though the bony hand is tempered in fire, and before the shadows can embed in his skin, he turns to face it.

"Dad, no, don't engage—"

My dad wears a warrior's mask, hardened and emotionless as he stares down the insipid being, the smell of sulfur thick enough to make my eyes burn. The being's form solidifies further the more my dad interacts with it, morphing into a harbinger of death.

"Everett!" my mom yells, trying to shake him free of the reaper's grip.

My dad tries to fight it, swinging his massive fist, but the monster catches it, squeezing, and the sound of shattering bones clips the rest of the noise. He screams, and my mom moves like she's about to come between him and Death. Before I lose them both in front of me, I rush at Death, knocking my dad free of the grip. The reaper falls backward into the void.

Death becomes shadows and floats away, and I skid to the brink of the toppling earth, almost plummeting into it. My talons scrape the grainy sand as I hoist myself and rush to turn back toward my parents.

My mom is kneeling by my dad, who grips his shattered hand.

I land beside them, eyeing Dad. He looks up at me, gray eyes holding mine in disgust like he cannot even fathom the creature I've become.

There's no time left to argue or try to convince them of anything. Shadows resembling spiders crawl toward us from every direction.

We are surrounded.

"Guys, we have to go," I say, cautiously taking a step closer.

It's when I see my grandfather's face looming over my mother that I know I have to act fast.

My grandfather was one of the worst humans imaginable. He tormented my mother and her sisters. Even their mother. I don't know precisely what happened with my mom, but I know the mere mention of our grandfather's name, Giuseppe, shuts her down.

The tension in my dad's neck reveals that he has spotted him, too, and before my dad can do anything, I run at both of them, grabbing hold of their shirt collars and jumping into the air.

My mom is shouting something, and my dad is swinging at my legs, trying to get me to drop him.

By the time I deposit them in the safety of the grove beyond the valley, I can barely catch my breath.

Magick isn't allowed in the valley, and even though my demon is not made from magick, being in this form in this dimension wreaks havoc on my stamina. Exerting more energy for more mass is beginning to take its toll.

Before they can even thank me—which I doubt my dad was going to do—I swallow my exhaustion and turn to head back.

I spot Caelum and Halcyon emerging from the valley, the swirling dark cloud behind them like a living wall.

Caelum has Scarlet—she's wrapped tightly in his arms as his black wings glide him to the ground methodically. Halcyon clutches Hattie, who looks far less comfortable in his arms, and he drops her uncarefully to the ground.

I catch eyes with Caelum when he gently sets Scarlet down, and we both bound up into the air to head back into the valley.

The fog thickens each time I go back in, and the apparitions become more lifelike. I ignore every single one resembling people I've killed before, ignoring their whispers and promises of retribution.

I can see how easy it is to break in the Valley of Echoes.

I wouldn't survive without Agares.

It's a race against time as everyone in the fog is going toe to toe with their demons, fighting some sort of monster that's become a tangible, destructive monstrosity.

Every being I rescue is tapering toward the sharp end of madness.

The more time they spend inside, the worse off they are.

Caelum, Halcyon, and I run dozens of rescues, going in and out and retrieving as many beings as possible.

On this last run, after I deposit Laureya and one of her friends, Hattie grabs my hand before I can leave again.

"Jasantha's still in there," she tells me, her eyes watery, and face dirty and broken. "Bash, you have to find her."

"I will," I say, steeling myself to enter Hell once more.

One. More. Time.

Each time I go back in, I am that much closer to breaking, too.

Inhaling a deep breath, I'm about to jump into flight again when Caelum catches my shoulder.

"Tallyn is still missing." Caelum's wings snap open behind him. "Whatever has her, it's beyond what I can face."

"Find my sister," I command, and brace myself for another round of psychological torment.

The instruction is no less a command in his eyes. He nods before jumping into the sky.

Following his lead, I barrel into the cloud, focusing on listening past the howling wind to listen for Tallyn's voice. The gusts, gushes, and whistles mix with whispers, screams, and nightmares, and isolating the noise is nearly impossible.

A keening sound overlaps the wind, calling to me somehow, beckoning me to chase it. I invert my path and aim straight for the sound.

Or Agares does; I am still trying to figure out what I'm doing or how to fly.

While zigzagging through the smoke and fog, it begins to thin the closer I get to the chasm in the center. Pools of blood emerge, dark and thick, painting the red sand an even more drastic and angry color. They lead to the ledge of the darkened void that now splits the valley in two.

I land on my feet and follow the blood, coming to a halt and looking down.

Tallyn is dangling from the ledge, her wings a shredded mess. She looks up at me, black tears streaming down her face.

"Sebastian!"

My sister's voice.

I look across the ravine.

Jasantha is on the other side, holding on to a tree root sticking out of the side of the dirt fissure.

"You won't have time to save them both," the voices tell me.

"Bash, help me!" Tallyn yells, reaching out her right hand

while her left clings to the side of the cliff. She tries to crawl up, but she falls another two feet.

I crash to my knees, extending my hand to Tallyn, but she slips, and Jasantha screams, her left hand slipping off the root, her legs flailing wildly to get the grip back.

"Bash, save your sister!" Henry screams, kneeling a few feet away.

"Grab my hand!" I yell to Tallyn, and her boot catches an edge, pushing her up.

Her fingers are right there, and I can just grab them.

I feel her hand grip onto mine. At the same time, I see the root Jasantha clings to come loose from the dirt wall, flinging her backward into the abyss.

27

A WOVEN TAPESTRY OF CLOUDS

—SAYAH—

The evening sky is so beautiful here. I watch it twinkle like magick from where I sit in front of the vanity.

It's my wedding night.

"I can't imagine why I didn't find the nighttime so beautiful when I first got here," I say. Nyxaria takes a curling iron to my hair, twirling a long strand to the hilt.

She had found me sitting in the hallway a ways away from my room and helped me to my feet. I couldn't remember how I had gotten there or what I'd been doing.

It's fits and starts really.

I remember the vampires and Bash, that Dom is dead, and that I was stolen and brought here against my will. But it's like there are two mes living in my body. The one who wants to be the Queen of Never and Earth and Feylight is stronger now, as if she somehow snuffed out the old me living buried inside.

"You were not yourself when you first arrived," Nyx says, the steam from the air sizzling in my ear, swirling up in the dim purple orb light flickering above.

"I guess I wasn't," I say, looking at her in the mirror. "You are so beautiful." She blushes at the compliment.

She really is a gorgeous being. She has long, dark pink hair that's as fine and soft as dusted soot. It spills down her back, adorned with petals, berries, and sprigs of white. Her pointy ears stick out from her dusty-rose locks, decorated with chains piercing her delicate flesh. Eyes the color of pinkish-orange dance like liquid flames, intense and hypnotic. Looking into them makes me feel intoxicated. Her dress is made of thorns, holding up leaves covering her ample breasts. Her skin is the softest shade of soft mauve.

I find myself wanting to touch her, to lick her, to kiss her all over.

Who is this new me?

Fight it, Sayah! screams a voice not belonging to me.

"It's okay, you're you now. Ember, our ShadowMaiden, helped you find your way back to us."

"Back to you?" I question as she rolls another curl over the iron.

"Yes. Your soul belonged to this realm long before you went to Earth," she answers quickly, her campfire eyes bemusing in the somber light. "You decided you wanted a challenge and to do the hardest level a soul can endure. Level Earth."

"I did?" I ask, toying with a strand of ether pearls she had clipped around my neck before we started my hair.

"You did. You and Trystan were married. You were the most benevolent queen the realm had ever seen. But you and the Luminara Queen were at odds."

"We were?"

"Yes. You were."

"Why?"

"Because their mother, Zephyra, favored you over Tallyn. She thought you and Trystan together would bring the most balance to the realms. Tallyn didn't like that and had her poisoned one night, tricking her with Feyfire. It was then

Zephyra wrote her will, leaving Tallyn Feylight. Tallyn had her killed, and then you."

My brows scrunch together in confusion. "If I died, how did I end up here now?"

I'm so confused.

The part of me that's fading knows not to believe anything the fae says, but her tale enthralls the more significant part of me that's taken over.

"Trystan had one of his warlocks sew your soul to the Ember Realm, tying you to this plane. He did this before Tallyn killed you, knowing she was up to no good. When he did this, he tied his soul to yours, sealing your fate as the Celestial Phoenix. Tallyn poisoned you, too, and as you lay dying, you decided to go into a new body on Earth to learn more lessons, to become stronger. Trystan stayed by your bedside and had witches and warlocks conduct spells to ensure you would find your way back to him. You chose Level Earth because it is the worst level a soul can endure. You both thought that once you endured life on Earth, you would be strong enough to beat Tallyn at her own game once you returned home."

I look at her questioningly. "If that's the case, then why all the theatrics? Why not come right out and tell me from the beginning?"

"Would you have believed him if he tried?" Nyxaria asks me, curling a new section. "You have come to believe you are in love with Sebastian Sangravelli."

I think of Bash and his crystal-blue eyes. The thunderstorm on my arm tingles, and a small lightning bolt rolls across the scenic tattoo. Memories of a love so deep that it's consuming wrestle up from the depths of me, but it's like listening for a splash in a hurricane. I cannot hear it any longer, though I remember how it feels surging inside me.

"I'm trying to remember how I felt for him, in real life and in the dreams, but right now, I feel nothing for him. Even if he were to walk through those doors right now, I wouldn't remember loving him. I don't know where it went."

Nyx rolls up a strand of hair and leans in close, staring at my eyes through the mirror. "It's because Ember hit you with that truth serum. The blue powder she blew in your face?"

"Yeah?"

"That was a concoction to try and help you connect to your former life. You have the same soul; it's in there. The powder is just to help you remember it. It'll work slowly, but day by day, you will begin to remember who you once were."

A knot slithers to the back of my throat, but I swallow it before I can get choked up. I shrug, and my strap falls. "Tell me about Trystan," I say, slipping my strap back over my shoulder.

Dreadwynd enters then.

"What would you like to know?" She uncurls my hair, which falls into a beautiful spiral, bounding up and down as she lets it loose next to the others.

"Anything really." I take a champagne flute from Dread-wynd. The liquid within is dark purple and fizzy. It looks thin but it also jiggles. "What's in this?" I ask before Nyx can answer.

"Fruita Berry Juice, non-alcoholic or fae-nectar-y," Dread-wynd answers. "Trystan sends it and says it'll help with your butterflies."

"Trystan can be very selfless when he wants to be," Nyx notes as I sip the dark purple fizz. It bubbles up to the roof of my mouth and tickles my nose. "But he can also be very dangerous. He loves fiercely, and anyone stupid enough to come between him and someone he loves would bring the world to ruin. He protects those he loves with every ounce of who he is, and he hasn't hesitated to murder anyone who crosses him or fucks with anyone he loves."

"Has he had many loves in his—how old is he again?"

Nyx looks to Dreadwynd, nods as he leaves us, and returns

her focus to curling my hair. "He's over a thousand years old. He's had many lovers, but only one love."

"And you're telling me that his one love was me?" I don't know why, but it seems wrong. A sliver of the wound-up part of me says she's lying, but I push it down with the rest of the feelings I'm trying to ignore.

"Yes. In your previous life here, you were his one true love."

I glare at Nyx's reflection in the mirror, trying to dissect her, willing any falsities to show themselves somehow. "And what was my name in this previous life?" I can't help but be sarcastic in my tone.

Her eyes don't falter. "Delaney."

"Delaney? What was my last name?"

"Silverfall," she answers, unraveling the last curl. "Do you want an up-do or a down-do?" she asks, frilling out my hair to separate the curls.

"Ooh, how about down with sprigs and stuff? Like you have in your hair."

"Perfect." She sets the curling rod on the vanity before walking away, and leaving me to stare at her retreating back. "It'll go well with your wedding dress."

I spin around. "What does my wedding gown look like?"

That buzzing feeling is back. It feels like I swallowed a mosquito; it pricks the inside of my skin, telling me there's something off here, something wrong.

Nyxaria reaches the armoire and hovers her hand over it.

Her slender hands don pointy white nails that glisten with jewels, and her bangles have chains connected to rings that jangle at her movement. The wood of the armoire expands outward in light, as though it's desperate to touch her. A glow infuses the room with magick; I have to shield my eyes from the brightness. When it dies down, she rustles the doors open, and one garment hangs inside.

My gown. She pulls it out and holds it up.

It's the most beautiful dress I've ever seen.

The sheer fabric is light like silk but more delicate, resembling a woven tapestry of clouds. Glitter shines in the soft orb of light, peeking out of the fabric. The plunging neckline dips almost to the pelvic bone, and the skirts collide with crocheted lilies, which actually turn into real flowers covering the entire skirt and train. White butterflies flutter their wings but remain part of the dress as well.

"Oh, my gods, that is gorgeous," I say, examining the exquisite fabric.

"The butterflies are real," Nyx says. I reach her, draping the fabric over her arms. "They are spelled to take flight once you seal your bond with the kiss."

"Oh, wow," I whisper. "How magickal." I thumb the fabric carefully to not disturb the butterflies. "This is like something from my dreams. I love butterflies. I have them tattooed on me."

"Yes, I would send you butterflies in your new life just to try and keep my memory alive inside you," Trystan's voice echoes behind us. A few seconds earlier, no one was there.

"Oh," I utter, covering my sheer nightgown with my arms. "Aren't you not supposed to see the bride before the ceremony?"

His laugh is so evil that it would haunt the most unforgiving nightmares. "That is human folklore, bride. No such thing exists here. Put it on. I want to see you in it."

Nyxaria nods, beckoning me to follow her into the bathroom. I oblige, and once inside, with the door closed, she hangs the dress on the back of the door.

It's quiet, save for the sound of our breathing as she stops inches from my face, slipping the strap of my nightgown down to help me undress. The cold air of the room kisses my skin in a shiver, and my nipples harden at the icy draft. The way she looks at me is almost seductive, the glowing amber in her eyes drinking up each and every inch of me.

I'm not self-conscious about being naked in front of her. I actually like the way I look naked.

The dips and spools of my body, the curves and corners, the lightning under my skin where my body stretched to fit my growing baby, the cellulite, the not-so-flat tummy, the ridges and swells under my boobs—they're all mine. I've earned every scar, every mark, every wrinkle, line, and imperfection.

There have been times when I felt uncomfortable in my skin. It took almost dying to truly love every inch of me.

Hmm. The old me's thoughts are intermingling with the new me's mind.

I step out of my nightgown and, as she slips the wedding gown over my head, my thoughts fade.

It smells like daffodils and plumeria, hydrangea, and fresh linen.

The woven clouds mold to my body, the butterflies flutter but remain on the dress, and it looks like it melted to my body or was sewn onto me.

"Beautiful," Nyxaria says, walking me over to the mirror. She stands behind me as she pulls the baby's breath from her hair and tucks little wisps into mine.

I admire my reflection, taking in the way I look like me but don't. I seem the same, yet different somehow.

"All right," Nyx says, standing on her tiptoes to fan in one more white. "Go out there and let your soon-to-be husband see you."

The soft flutters of the butterflies mimic what I suddenly feel in my heart for the man I'm about to marry.

I know he was just a stranger a few days ago—one that kidnapped me—but ever since I had that truth serum blown in my face, he now feels like someone I've known my whole life. I can't wait to marry him.

Nyx brushes past me, leaving a floral scent trail in her wake, and pulls the double doors open. I press forward, spilling out into the room on a gust of magick.

Trystan's eyes, his soft gray eyes, blink, then narrow in seductive slits.

"What?" I say as he circles me in a menacing prowl, caressing the skin of my bare sternum between my breasts when he stops in front of me.

"How can I look at you and not fall in love?" he says sweetly, twirling his finger around one of my curls. "You look exactly like the sword I will die upon."

Whether that's a compliment or a curse, I give him a soft smile. "And you look like night incarnate."

"The darkest night that will bring no sweet dreams and hellish nights," he says, breathing in the scent of my hair. "I will destroy you in the most exquisite way possible. And in the end, you will see why storms are named after people. And you will be queen of night and darkness. It is fitting for you."

"I am fire incarnate," I reply, playing with one of the dress's frills. "I don't know how fitting that is for me."

"Not anymore, dear bride. For I have stolen your fire." He lets go of my hair and walks toward the door, his eyes torpedoing into me, beguiling and disturbing simultaneously. "See you at the other end of the aisle."

IZEKIAL

—BASH—

My mind is eviscerated of all thoughts as I fling myself into the ravine. It's dark, black, and smells of sulfur and rotten eggs. The air is thick and sticky and hot. Beads of sweat drip down my forehead. I flail backward in the air as I fly deeper and deeper into the depths.

I'm not used to the unusual movements of new muscles on my back, controlling the wings, but Agares and I are one and the same now, him blending completely, utterly, and effortlessly into my psyche.

A scream pierces the air, and the speed and pressure in the breeze are making it impossible to breathe. Agares has turned us into hyper-drive light speed; it's hard to determine how fast we're going. If I were to venture into a guess, I would say Mach 10, but I could be generous in that guess.

The scream intensifies, and we follow it, gliding through the ravine, maneuvering around things I cannot fathom or even wish to see.

Abruptly stopping causes my breath to gasp and heave out of me, hovering in mid-air. I look up in time to see Jasantha barreling toward me. She lands in my arms with a thud. I secure her and shoot up, up, up, out of the depths.

"Bash?" Jasantha says. The whooshing of air in both our faces makes it hard to talk or hear.

"Yes, it's me," I say in a not-entirely mine voice.

Jasantha throws her arm around my neck, hanging on for dear life as we careen out of the ravine.

We travel higher and higher, until the air cools, and the smell of sulfur lessens. When I arrive at the surface once again, I fly over where Tallyn had last been seen.

I don't see her, and I must get Jasantha to safety.

"Who else is left?" Ollie asks as I deposit Jasantha off to the rest of the group.

"Did anyone see Tallyn?" I ask, looking around at all the faces.

Pretty much everyone is here.

"Everyone is here except Tallyn," Henry confirms.

I'm about to jump into the air once more to save Tallyn when Halcyon flutters out of the fog with a disheveled and broken-looking Tallyn.

"Is she dead?" Jasantha asks when Halcyon lies her down, her black hair matted. She has bruises and scrapes all over her body, and her arm looks dislocated or broken.

"She's alive," Hal says, brushing her hair behind her ear. "She needs healing, though. And fast."

"I can help," Gwylan offers and kneels next to Tallyn. "I just fixed your dad's hand."

Tallyn's dark eyelashes rest somberly. Gwylan stirs the wind; magick gold dust appears in the air, like watching the purest alchemy, the air particles turning to gold. The golden flecks sparkle in the fae realm's sunlight and hover over Tallyn like a burial shroud. Gwylan, with her long, slender fingers bejeweled with rings, rests atop the gold. Her head tilts back, as though basking in a warm summer breeze. All the crowd around Tallyn is still while watching her bruises and cuts and scrapes pull together and sew themselves up. The pale peach color of her skin returns, the monstrous split in her lip evaporates, and her wings mend together like a collapsed tent reviving. She gasps and sits up.

She devilishly, yet brokenly takes in my demon form. "Better?" I ask.

"Much," she says with a smirk, sitting up. She wipes away the blood from the corners of her mouth. "I just need someone to put my shoulder back into place, and we must continue. We don't have much more time."

"Caelum, put her arm back for her," I command, standing.

Caelum does what I say immediately, and to be completely honest, I only made the command because I love the power I have over him.

Watching him do exactly what I say gets me hard.

"So how is it that we don't have access to any of our powers, yet the fairy lady over here has her healing ability?" Jasantha considers somewhat tersely.

"Because our powers align with this realm's laws of magick more than yours do," Tallyn says, straightening her leathers. "Your magick is severely subdued. Ours is just weaker. You will find that as we venture away from the valley, magick use will be easier."

"This place is fun," I reply, following everyone else to wherever the fuck we're going next.

We've been hiking for hours, down and up mountainsides in a range that seems to have no end. We summit the top of one, only to be given twenty more.

The view from up here is gorgeous, though.

Mountain ranges paint the horizon, and water rings like those in Feylight Grove encircle the floating and stationary mountains. Thick, creamy tendrils of clouds dip and sway, painting the majestic scene unfolding before us with a wispy, serene lull. Wind rocks the trees to and fro, tasting the clouds with their frilly dance, so close to us I could grab a handful and taste them myself.

I look out in the distance, spotting a large land mass that seems to be floating in the middle, only the bottom hanging down, poking out from beneath bloated clouds, like a reverse iceberg in the sky. It looks like something pulled right out of a fairy tale.

"I'm guessing we go that way." My voice now my own since Agares has descended back into my body.

"What would give you that impression?" Laureya says, the snark fierce in her tone.

I snarl and ball my fist to punch her, but Ollie stops me.

Ollie clips his voice. "Not worth it."

"Says you," I retort under my breath,

With a shake of my head, I shove the anger I harbor for Laureya into a jagged box I keep buried deep within me.

"It looks like the land rings around those floating mountains," Claire states, shielding her eyes from the sunlight.

"Maybe if we follow it," Tallyn adds, "it'll loop us to it."

Collective nods and mumbles of agreement echo from our retinue as we begin the journey toward the middle mountain.

It's not until the sun begins to sink down that I realize everything is glowing. The rocks, grass, bugs, water, flowers, trees, the air, even the ground—all of it brighter with our footprints.

It all has a shimmer.

"What is this place?" Hattie questions when a giant glowing bug lands on her finger, illuminating her face.

"We're in the Luminous Fields," Tallyn says, brushing a branch that looks like glowing purple wheat.

"And what are we to keep our eye out for here?" I ask her, admiring how the ground lights up under my boots.

"An ancient and glowing tree that stands taller than any other," she says, looking over her shoulder. "Izekial."

"What is Izekial?" Dad asks, his voice low and icy.

"I don't know. The name of the tree, maybe. It just came to me."

"It's 'cause I told her," Henry says, though no one else seems to see him again.

"Kinda like that one?" my mom says, pointing to the south of us.

Collectively, we turn and follow her line of sight.

Beyond the groves of glowing bushes and brambles painting a psychedelic ambiance, I don't know how we missed it before. Either that or it remained hidden until we mentioned it.

The tree takes up the entire skyline. The sky is the tree.

In fact, we are walking along one of its branches. It seems the entire world morphed into one big, giant tree of life.

"How?" Ollie asks, straining his neck back to see how far up it goes.

A loose breath rattles out of me. "Maybe it was waiting for us to name it," I answer, gazing up with him. "The Celestial Gardens are hidden within that?" When no one answers, I say, "Easy-peasy," and begin my trek onward.

"So, do you think Sayah will be able to overcome whatever Trystan is doing to her?" asks Hattie, her snarky tone still evident. It bites into me in harsh ways I didn't expect.

"She will," I answer tonelessly.

"You don't know her like I do," Claire states, her languid gait sluggish and almost timid. She is not trying to one-up me—she only wants to boast about how badass her friend is. "She'll beat this. She can beat anything. I've seen her."

"You were by her side when she had cancer, weren't you?" I ask. Clouds in the shape of sparrows fly by us, a slight breeze picking up, and the smells of flowers I've never heard of sneak up my nose.

Claire's eyes are timid and sad. "I was. But it's more than that. She's not just a survivor; she's a force of nature. When life knocks her down, she doesn't just rise; she ignites. Her ex-husband left her on her ass with nothing a year after finishing chemo," she boasts as Ollie guides her from the front, holding her hand once we incline up the steep tree branch. "She had a kid and a house and not a dime to her name. Yeah, she may have drunk a lot and done some fucked-up shit to some pretty okay people. But she got sober. Put herself through school. Wrote and self-published a few books. She kept her house the entire time, even when making eleven dollars an hour, and Derek took away her child support. She never brags about it, even though she has every right to do so."

"Was that why she quit drinking?" I ask, stepping over a glowing vine. "The 'pretty okay' people part," I clarify.

"Yeah, she did shit she's not proud of. She slept with a long-time love interest of a friend. She may or may not have had an affair with her ex-husband's brother. He was married, not her. Other things contributed to her quitting, including the fact that all her parents are or were alcoholics, and she wanted to break the cycle. But she would do anything for anyone. She's the type of woman who would rise out of Hell and go back to take water for those still in it. She can't be tempered or tamed; she's here to rewrite the rules and obliterate the game."

I'm supposed to say something snarky and biting here, but I cannot. The thought of Sayah's sweet face constricts my lungs and stings my eyes. I miss her. I miss getting to know her and drinking up each and every expression her face makes. I hadn't realized it until right now, but I've memorized all of them. Every twitch of discomfort, the serene softness that befalls her face when she talks of her son or about anything she loves, how it falls when she is confronted with something she doesn't like or about to embark on something that scares her. I've memorized every line and contour of her, every fierce pocket and emblazoned crevice. The morsels and very fabric of her stitch themselves to my side, embed in my bones, and sing to the demons that haunt me, quieting them.

Knowing where she is at right now and what she is up against haunts me more than any demon ever could.

I just hope that once we get there, I can win her back from him.

"What exactly are we looking for here?" Scarlet queries, interrupting my thoughts.

"Anything that looks like it would lead to a secret portal," Hattie says cynically, holding on to a glowing tendril of the tree as she leaps over part of the stump.

The further up we travel, the further away the tree trunk seems. It doesn't move, no matter how far we climb, but the vast scenery below tells us we've climbed up over a thousand feet.

Hattie spots something in the distance, and quickly skips out onto a branch overlooking our strange world. Using her hand as a visor, she steps on her tiptoes and elongates her neck. "I think I see something."

Tallyn uses her iridescent wings to glide her up to Hattie, gazing where she points.

"What am I looking at?" Tallyn asks Hattie. I climb up to join them.

"See that there?" Hattie explains, her eyes fierce and focused.

Tallyn's wrinkles her nose and squints her eyes. "No."

"It's because you don't have the substantial and excellent

vision we vampire folk have," I say. "Hattie, use your powers to show her."

Hattie's eyes shimmer when she focuses on Tallyn, controlling what Tallyn sees.

We've climbed up above the clouds and the floating mountain's top is now in view. A forest of trees obscures the view, but when honing the supernatural vision, a towering and glowing tree emits an eerie glow to the forest floor. A giant hole is in the middle of the tree, giving Clan of the Cave Bear, which seems to be guarded by two colossal statues with spears.

We still remain a wide valley floor made of ocean water away from it.

"Right," Tallyn says, her wings stretching out as her feet leave the ground, fluttering out to dangle above the tumultuous water below us.

"Yeah, uh, those of us without wings will just hoof it there," I mutter, stepping back down onto the main branch, which is as wide as a road.

"I'll go scout it out first," Tallyn states, searching over my shoulder. "Halcyon, Caelum, Aurelius, Rowan, come with me. You lot wait here or start trucking that way."

The other fae behind me hop to command and rush by, the flap of their wings making glowing leaves and other bits of this realm flutter out into the nothing, adding shimmer to the air.

They fly across the ravine as I start looking around for any sort of bridge or other way to get to the island.

I don't see any, so I climb back down.

"What did you see?" Claire asks as we hike further up the branch.

"Looks to be a spear of a statue," I explain, "like a sentinel keeping watch of something."

"It would make sense as to what we're looking for," my mom says, taking Dad's outstretched hand to balance over a boulder resembling a glowworm splattered on the surface.

A screech from the distance causes us all to stop, followed by a roar, and the unmistakable sound of heavy wings cutting through the air.

"Shit!" I utter, flashing back to the edge of the branch.

In the darkened sky, the unmistakable form of a murder of dragons clots the horizon with a riot of ravenous motion. Dark clouds whirl around their wing beats, the largest of the murder pointing them toward the fae still flying across the ravine like a volley of arrows.

29

SUBTLE, LIKE YELLOW SMOKE

—SAYAH—

The night sky is glittering with more stars than I've ever seen. Planets give off soft light, decorating the realm with the most comforting glow. The air is alive; it buzzes around me as I follow Nyx down a path lined with white flowers, toward a covered bridge over a bright violet river. Marble paths encircle the clusters of greenery in a functionally impractical but artistically beautiful design surrounding the bridge.

Nyx stops and presents a veil. From where it came, I cannot say.

The veil is long and glittering but made from the same fabric of my dress so it looks like wafting clouds, like it will vanish like vapor at the mercy of wind.

As she fixes it atop my head, she stops inches from my face and my breath hitches.

Why do I feel this way about her?

I want to kiss her. To lick her up and down and feel the curve of her breasts under the tip of my tongue. I've never been with a female before, as much as that pains me to admit.

I've always been attracted to females as much as males. I had crushes on girls in middle and high school in the same way I had crushes on boys. I even use visuals of naked females to play with myself at home and sometimes those visuals are the only thing that can bring me to climax.

Saying I've wanted a threesome or just an experience with another female is an understatement.

It is my ultimate fantasy.

Her campfire eyes pierce into me, her luscious full lips parting for a breath I swear that stutters.

Does she feel this, too?

The meadow we're in is silent, save for the river and the wind, no voices carry, and nothing gives me the impression fae are nearby.

"What is this?" she asks, bringing my wrist—with the manacle around it—toward her. The golden rune tattoo peaks out from beneath it and she grazes it softly with her bare fingers, eliciting more than just a subtle touch.

"I don't know," I return, examining it myself. "It appeared a while ago. I don't know what it means."

"It's a Druid symbol. It means 'continuous flow and absorption of energy.'" Her eyes hitch onto mine with a curious sparkle. She seems to know more than she lets on about the mystery on my arm. "What are you thinking?"

"I, uh, I'm . . ." I can't find the words with my heart fluttering so erratically. She's so fucking sexy.

She seems to be experiencing the same feelings as me, for her breaths are quick and uneven. Her giant breasts are heaving beneath the thin fabric of her leaves and I want to grab them and bury my face in them. I want to feel her skin and make her moan and taste every inch of her.

As she settles my veil over my shoulders, her fingers graze my side boob and I gasp, my clit tingling with the idea of her hands on me.

"What is it?" she asks, stepping closer.

Do I tell her I want to fuck her before my wedding?

I've never been with a female before, but I don't care.

She can show me the way.

"I just feel . . ." I release her eye contact and look up at the sky.

"Sayah," she says, pulling my chin down to look at me. "You can tell me. You and I were very close in your last life." She inches closer. "Very, very close."

"How close?" I ask as she grazes my neck with her lips.

"So close that I know what makes you moan," she breathes, her tongue gliding down the column of my neck, erupting pin pricks of goose bumps all over me.

My nipples pebble and I gasp. "Were we lovers?" I ask, straining my neck to the side to let her continue her expedition of me.

"Some people called us a 'throuple,'" she purrs, her hand slipping under my gown to cup my breast.

"A throuple?" I utter, though my voice is thready and uneven now.

"Mm-hmm," she hums, pinching my rock-hard nipple with her long fingernails. The sensation sends shocks of pleasure down to my pussy. I am already wet for her. "So much that I know how much you like the sting of pain roiling through you from your nipple . . ." She trails her fingernail down the outside of my gown, coming to rest on the bundle of nerves resting below my belly button. "To this magick little button right here."

"Do we have time?" My question comes out more of plea as her finger slides my swollen clit back and forth, ricocheting ripples of pleasure all the way down to my toes.

Her soft lips are on mine and my lungs forget how to draw air. I part my mouth for her and feel her soft tongue enter. I cup her enormous breast in my right hand, the weight of it casting feelings similar to starvation and need from the crest of my own being to the tips of my existence.

The delicious curve of her skin, the soft, delicate surface encasing the most glorious set of boobs I've ever seen feels exactly how I imagined it in my head. Soft and plump and gorgeous, I squeeze it ever so gently, tilling a moan from the depths of her. The sound rumbles in my mouth as she kisses me. My other hand napes at the jowls of my hunger for her, cupping the other one under the leaves barely covering the monstrous things.

The leaves fall away, and my mouth is on her nipple faster than I can even fathom, the rush of desire impaling all my thoughts to her. I suck her erect nipple into my mouth, biting, and nipping and grazing, squeezing it into my mouth. I bring both breasts together and lick each one. Her perfect nipples harden further at my grazing while my hunger for her intensifies.

I wish she had a dick to fuck me with.

The breaths sawing in and out of her inflates her chest further. She grapples at my hair while I feast from her churning and violent wave of want.

We tumble back into a tree. The euphoria and stringent depth of my desire blind me to any and all things around me, muffling sounds of the river we've toppled near.

She pulls me free of her breasts and holds my gaze captive in hers, nipping at my lower lip while she cradles my face in her hands.

I've never felt this funny sensation in my gut. My need for release winds me so tight that the mere thought of her all over me undoes me.

Unwinds me.

Unravels me.

Her luscious lips split her face in a seductive smile. She snaps her fingers, and a click reverberates throughout the realm.

A chill laps at my skin, causing me to shiver, and when she takes a step closer, pinning my hands above my head, I realize

I'm naked. Her one hand pins both my wrists while her other dips to play with my wetness.

She teases me, flitting my clit softly, only to dip a finger into me, making me wet and wild and brimming with a noxious craving for her.

"Do you want this?" She nips into my ear, biting the lobe to entice pricks of chill to lap at my nerves.

I nod as she twists her fingertip over the glaze, colliding roughly, then softly, then roughly again. I writhe beneath her hand, trying to ride it where I want her.

As she breaks me, casting stars from my body into the surrounding atmosphere, I'm on the brink of cresting a curling wave when she stops before the crescendo.

Pulling away, she drops to her knees and picks up one of mine, draping it over her shoulder as she licks me from opening to tip.

I cry out in a strangled breath, heart ripping though my ribs enough to shatter the cage it's trapped within.

I.

Want.

Her.

She feasts on me like I'm her last meal, biting and twisting, adding fingers and teeth, stretching my orgasm to mingle with the moons shining in the sky. When a moan reverberates throughout my center, the twitching cataclysmic eruption of euphoria binds me to my ruin. I turn to jelly at her touch.

But just when it becomes too much, she drops me to the ground, still teasing my clit with her fingers.

She straddles me, her thick thighs and perfect ass fluff out around her, her leafy dress having fallen from her top half to sit around her middle with a clear outline of a fully erected and mercilessly large penis.

She.

Is.

Flawless.

She hovers above me, her perfect breasts bouncing as she plays with my tits, leaning to suckle my nipple, biting for sting and collecting her debt.

My moans.

Her long pink hair falls around her shoulders when she leans in to kiss me, creating a lavender curtain around us as she curates more moans from my depths.

My hands find her cock—the most perfect dick I've ever seen. It's so flawless that it must be some sort of fever dream; there's no way something this perfect exists in real life.

I dreamed this up.

My wildest fantasy coming to life.

The thick shaft beneath my hands throbs as I stroke the length of her, becoming fully erect, drizzling pre-cum at the tip. I use it to lather her. It's so large that when she breaks our kiss and leans back, arching her back to the sky with a guttural growl, I get a glimpse of the massive thing.

The explosion of animalistic need hijacks my every thought at the sight of her glorious cock, and wonton desire has me flipping her onto her back and pouncing on her faster than I've ever moved.

I mouth her breasts while stroking her and she moans. The soft ridges of her massive cock feels like the greatest thing I've ever touched. It takes all I have not to climb on that dick and start riding it, but I want to make her scream first.

I bite down on her nipple, licking her entire left breast with my tongue and sliding my hand up and down her shaft. "Fuck. Sayah. Yes, don't stop," she says, aching her back, making me take more of her in my mouth. "I want you."

Like a magnet, my mouth is around her glorious cock, making her squirm and arch and moan. She even scratches her nails down my arms. The pain makes me clinch and wet.

"Stop or I'm gonna cum," she says, pulling me from her cock

and flinging me to the ground, playing with my clit as she mouths my boobs.

The tingly sensations send shockwaves down to my toes. She tongue-kisses my stomach and lands on my clit. I close my eyes and pinch her nipples, continuing to grope her large mountains of pleasure.

Colors start to shimmer in the backs of my eyes as I climb my way to orgasm. First, it's subtle, like yellow smoke. Then she twists her tongue to the right and the yellow shifts to orange. I pull her up before it can switch again, feeling closer to erupting into ecstasy with each flick of her tongue.

She slides her giant dick inside me. I pull her boobs together, mouthing them as she buries herself inside me, seating herself flush with my hips.

"Oh, my gods!" I cry out when the tip of her kisses my G-spot, causing the orange smoke to enter the backs of my eyes again, my head smothered between the mountains.

"That's a good girl," she purrs, rocking herself in and out of me, swirling her hips as she fingers my clit.

The orange switches to bright red and my body lights up with fierce butterflies, the tingly sensation exploding through my body. She takes my mouth in hers, continuing her thrusts; the width and length of her dick stretching the walls of my pussy.

I flip her over and seat myself on top of her, her dark pink hair swirling around her head as she lays in the grass. I grab on to both her boobs and ride her dick like it's my last ride on this plane.

The fire that used to live in my bones erupts and causes me to heat up, the red-hot flame behind my eyes shifting to fire. My orgasm comes with the strength of a freight train, imploding me from within. Once I am leveled by pleasure, I bend down, and take as much of her boob into my mouth as I can, the crescendo not fading but getting stronger.

"Fuck, Sayah, I'm gonna cum," she says as I continue on the most powerful orgasm I've ever felt.

It hasn't even begun to plateau yet, but I feel her cock harden even more, the explosion of cum entering me and mingling with my organs.

The fire behind my eyes turns bright blue. My entire body going numb, her large breasts causing me to climax over and over again.

Just when I think I'm done cumming, she flips me over and takes me from behind, wrapping her hands around my hair and slamming into me again and again, making me scream so loud I'm sure the entire wedding party can hear me.

"Good fucking girl, Sayah," she says as she dives into me to her balls. She stretches my orgasm out and around the universe.

We clash in a snarling beat until I'm cresting on a combustion that might just ruin me, certain I'm about to split into a million jagged pieces.

Fissure.

Split.

Shatter.

I've lost all track of time as we fuck in the woods, not even caring if I'm late for my own wedding.

We fuck for hours, taking turns on top, cumming, riding, biting, scratching.

I could fuck her for the rest of my life.

After my twelfth orgasm, with her boobs in my mouth, she lies on her side as I suckle her. I cannot stop. She's fucking me slowly, her large dick going in and out of me. I pinch her nipples with one hand and teethe the other one.

"We gotta get you going soon," she says, sliding all the way into me before stopping.

I swirl my hips, making her pump into me again. "Mm-hmm."

"Sayah, for real. I've stopped time long enough. I have to resume it soon."

I let go of her breast with my mouth, but continue to grope it with my hand. "You can stop time?"

Her orangish-red eyes glare into mine and she buries her dick in me again. "Mmm," she confirms, taking my lips in hers as she thrusts ever so slowly.

"Don't ever start it again," I plead.

"Cum for me." She lifts my leg, shoving her breasts in my mouth as I climb for the top once more.

"Fuck!" I scream with the explosion of my body, the blue fire in my eyes causing me to black out .

"That's my girl," she purrs. I feel her dick harden with cum.

"I don't ever want to stop fucking you."

We continue pleasuring each other to the point of pain. It's like her dick was always meant to be buried in me and now that it's there, we're just going to have to find a way to go on living while she fucks me for the rest of my life.

"Trystan knows what we were to each other. He won't mind."

She pulls out to the tip and slams back in. "I will want to fuck you every night," I exclaim, sucking her boobs into my mouth again.

"That is okay with me." She dives back in me to the hilt.

I have no idea how long we fuck for, as she has stopped time and I've lost all sense of it. I don't even want to marry Trystan anymore. I want to marry her and fuck her all day every day.

"Sayah," Nyx whispers into my ear. "We really have to go soon."

From how hard her dick is, I can't tell if it will ever go down. "Okay," I say, kissing her, feeling her, rocking onto her cock.

"No, really," she says, finally pulling her cock out of me.

I mourn the loss of her. I will never be the same.

"C'mon." She pulls me to my feet.

Her breasts bounce and my lips are on them again, pulling them into my mouth while she massages my clit. Her head tilts back and I gravitate to her cock, sliding my hand down the completely wet mess I've left on her.

It takes us ten more orgasms standing against a tree to finally tire and get dressed.

With my dress on and her cock hiding behind the leaves of hers, she kisses me once more, and waves her hand to resume time.

"I want to fuck you again," I tell her as she pulls me to the bridge.

"We can fuck after the wedding," she says.

I wrap my hands around her, fondling her breasts once more. I've been admiring them for so long, I will never be able to keep my hands off them now.

"Behave," she says light-heartily. "Save some for Trystan."

"You're everything I've ever wanted," I gasp out as she leans against the railing of the bridge, her nipples still hard, and poking out from the leaves.

"I have both male and female parts, Sayah. I'm everyone's greatest desire."

"You have female parts, too?" I ask, corralling her against the bridge, kissing her lips once more.

She takes my hand and guides it down her leaf skirt. Where there used to be her giant penis is now a beautiful little pussy. I finger her clit and make her rock her head back.

Whatever side of me that has taken over is now in charge. I pick her up by her knees and sit her on the railing. I drape her legs over my shoulders and kiss her pussy, tonguing her clit at first.

After her first moan, I go wild with pleasure and slip a finger inside her, finding the delicate skin of her soft and wet. She grabs me by my hair when a clearing of a throat sounds behind us.

"Trystan!" Nyx slides down off my shoulders and the railing. "I was just bringing her to you."

Trystan is standing at the edge of the bridge, his blonde locks pulled back into a low pony with a leather strap to hold it. Dressed in all black, it doesn't look as good on him as it does that one vampire I used to know, but it still suits him. His eyes, a mysterious and stern color of blue, remind me of a violent storm over the grasslands. The thorns protruding from his sternum wrap around his neck and hide under the loose-fitting button down he has on. Tight leather pants hug his muscular thighs, and heavy boots complete the ensemble. His glorious blue wings glimmer in the moons' light.

"I'm glad to see you two didn't get lost," he deadpans, his face an indiscernible pinch of emotions.

Nyx has climbed off me and fixed her skirts; my own gown is billowing in the soft breeze.

I feel weird things for this moment. I cannot put them into words.

Should I feel bad?

Should I invite him to join us?

His dick is hard and protruding from the tight leather pants. The outline of it is enticing and wicked, and part of me wants to drop to my knees before him and worship his cock, too.

"Don't mind me." The seriousness in his tone tells me I am in trouble, but still. I am not afraid of him.

The clunk of his boots on the bridge mingle with the sound of the rushing water. Fireflies light up the scene, tendrils of a glowing weeping willow stir in the wind.

He approaches me. I back up to the railing and grab the wood from behind. "Sayah," he utters, his breath still peppermint and pinecones. "Did you save some of your cum for daddy?" He slides his hand around my neck and forces me into his face. "Or did you let our nymph take it all?"

This firm, hot-blooded male contains a churn of barely tethered rage.

I feel his hard dick on my thigh and pleasure stirs inside me again, wanting to skip this nonsense of a wedding and go retire to a bedroom to get fucked by these sexy fairies all night long.

"There's plenty left for you, my king," Nyx says, stepping up to him from behind and rubbing her hands down his chest to his erection.

Within a breath of movement, he takes her by the hair and flings her like she weighs nothing. She flies through the air and collides with a large tree, falling to the ground with a thud that reverberates through my bones. His chest puffs out with a barely restrained violence flexing for release. "What did I *fucking* tell you about fucking her before she was my wife, you whore?" he screams at her.

She does nothing to get up, only stays where she landed, looking ashamed. "I'm sorry—"

He waves his hand again and a shockwave flies through the air.

It suddenly feels like I can't breathe, like he's sucked all the air out of the world. I grasp my throat as I struggle to breathe, but it feels like the oxygen is crushing me alive.

"*Silence!*" he shouts at Nyx, his eyes turning a glowing golden color, his presence of scarcely veiled chaos contrasting with his impeccable eyes. "*You thought I wouldn't be able to know you stopped time?*" he booms, his voice reverberating through my bones. "You fucking know what happens when you stop time, you cunt. What was that for this period—twice now?"

She nods.

I grab onto his shirt to get his attention back to me, clawing at my neck, trying to gasp for air.

He laughs. "Sayah, you think you will go unpunished for this act as well?" he asks. My vision blurs. "You both will be held responsible for fornicating before you became my bride."

The last thing I remember before I black out is him taking his cock out and pulling up my dress.

30

THE VOID

—BASH—

We are so high up that the air is thin, as though it is simply being loaned to us. However, it does allow me an inhibited view of the bruised horizon pocked with mountains, cast amongst a bed of distant trees.

It's dizzying.

In my rush to the edge, I knock off a blob of moss attached to my boot, and it plummets into the ether. I watch it disappear into the layer of clouds the giant black dragon slices through, the wind from the beating wing blowing our hair wildly off our shoulders.

The dragon banks left at the last second before colliding with the branch we stand on, the other dragons spreading out to take Tallyn and her soldiers from all sides.

"Uh," Henry says, shielding his eyes from the sun to scope the scene below, "those look like dragons."

I eye him cynically as my dad hooks his fingers in his teeth and whistles. "Tallyn! Look out!" he shouts after his whistle, but it does nothing against the distance, clouds, and flap of their wings.

Another dragon passes above us, this one green and shimmering in the sun.

A sound unlike anything I've ever heard rends the air; a cross between a banshee and a dinosaur—what a dinosaur would sound like, in my opinion.

The black dragon opens his mouth as his wings lower him to level with Tallyn. He swoops his wings to coast; a belt of fire explodes from the front of him, painting the sky in a plume of flame that pours enough heat to turn the trees to ash.

The green dragon lets a wail loose and ducks further, releasing the shock of flames directly at the left flank of flying soldiers. Tallyn halts her flight and torpedoes down, missing the stream of fire in a flash of magick. Three more colorful beasts circle overhead.

One soldier shrieks into the line of fire, it coming too abruptly for him to make a maneuver like Tallyn. All oxygen leaves my lungs at the sight of the fire clot the sky. The soldier is engulfed in flames instantly, his wings a blazing roar of orange and yellow that paints angry strokes across the white fluffy clouds.

Halcyon spreads his black wings and lands on the edge of the floating island, already making circles of magick with his hands when he gains footing. He thrusts the vortex into the air and opens a tunnel, shouting to Tallyn. Her wings extend outward as she twists into a dive, leveraging herself with the winds as she glides into the tunnel.

The crackle of magick zips and zaps behind us. I spin and watch Tallyn fly out, Caelum on her tail, followed by Rowan and Halcyon.

"Are those your dragons, Tallyn?" Laureya asks.

Tallyn snaps a look of vinegar at her. "Yeah, because my dragons would try and kill me." She puts her wings away and walks to the end of the branch, watching the murder of dragons sail down and around, heading back in our direction.

"They must be bound to this realm and enchanted to guard that specific area," Ollie says, stating the obvious but with a note of caution in his voice.

"What are we going to do about them?" I grouse, ignoring the jab opportunity.

"Thistlewynd stayed behind." Tallyn says this as if it should mean something to us. Her scowl is etched so deeply it looks like it's permanently carved into her face.

"Um, and?" I press.

"She's the one who can telepathically communicate with animals." Tallyn walks up to Halcyon, gazing down into the ravine, Caelum and the rest of the fae eyeing the dragons. "I'm so sorry about your friend," she tells Halcyon, lightly pressing her hand to his shoulder. Her whispered words brushed through the leaf-laden branches, coaxing them into a flirtatious dance.

Another roar bellows, and before we can even think, the most enormous dragon of them all, who is a steely gray color, is at eye level with us. He opens his mouth, and the bright embers of fire ignite in the very back of his throat.

A shiver nettles my skin.

"Aromen sanctavidades." Agares speaks in his demonic tongue, his deep, gravelly voice lacing the foreign words with such raw ferocity that each syllable scrapes against my skin.

I, for one, have no idea what the fuck I just said, but as soon as the words have left my mouth, everything freezes.

The wind stops.

Time stops.

My heart skips a beat as I fixate on the swelling orb of fiery-red forming at the base of its ridged throat, bracing for the searing blast to erupt, the heat waves registering like the air above a candle's flame.

I'm at eye level with it.

Half a second, and I would have been dragon s'mores.

I let out the breath I'd been holding and lift my hand out in front of me. My skin is red.

"Good call," I tell Agares. I sidestep out of the direct line of fire. "But now, what do we do?"

I'm establishing a connection to the creature, Agares says in my mind.

"That's fucking handy," I say, running my hand along the shimmering scales of the dragon's side. The prismatic colors of the scales create an metallic shimmer, black shifting to gold, shifting to purple glimmering as teal. The dragon is massive, easily the size of a mountain. Its obsidian scales reflect the light in a metallic sheen, giving an impression of a living, breathing machine. The scales overlap in intricate colors, creating a seamless armor that seems impervious to any weapon.

Its body is massive, comparable in size to the largest dinosaurs, with a serpentine form that undulates with every breath and exudes power and grace. The dragon's wings, frozen and extended in the air, stretch out to cast shadows, blanketing an entire valley. They are ribbed with metal-like bones, webbed and graceful, powerful and deadly.

The terrifying head sports an angular snout that tapers to a point. Its eyes burn molten gold, the very essence of a star residing within them. Its open maw encases rows of razor-sharp teeth, gleaming like polished steel, and capable of tearing through any armor as if it were paper.

On its back, spikes jut out like the ridges of a mountain range, each tipped with a dark, metallic sheen. Its tail—long and whip-like—ends in a barbed spike, glinting ominously in the light.

The dragon moves its head when Agares whispers to it.

It's weird being two people at once.

On the one hand, I can move, control, and think as myself, but then there is this presence—Agares sharing not just one side but all at once.

I hear him speaking to the dragon in another language the beast seems to understand.

The air about this giant being was vicious and deadly before, but something in his amber cat eyes softens at how Agares speaks to him, and a slight movement of his head tells me he agrees with whatever Agares is saying to him.

He is a she, Agares corrects me.

"Oh, sorry, my bad," I utter, a little unnerved that Agares is reading my thoughts.

We're in the same mind, idiot.

"Touché."

She has agreed to help us as long as we help her when we finish our journey.

"And what, pray tell, is it that we will be helping her with?"

Her murder's breeding ground—a sacred and hidden place where their kind lays their eggs and raises their young—is under threat. A flock of wyverns who've taken over most of this land have discovered their sacred breeding ground. They seek to expand their territory and gain control over the land's mystical energies, believed to enhance the power of any being that rules it.

If the wyvern succeeds, they will not only destroy the dragon—

A grumbling that resembles a roar occurs in my head and cuts off Agares' rambling in my mind.

My apologies, if the wyvern succeeds, they will not only destroy Seraphyra's—he annunciates like the dragon is mad he wasn't referring to her by her name—*offspring, but also gain an immense boost in strength, making them nearly unstoppable.*

I make eye contact with Seraphyra. A deep and profound sadness permeates her, and the air about her now is one of mourning.

"Have you lost offspring to these . . . things?"

She has, Agares answers for her.

"And what can we do to help her with this situation?" I move around to face her head-on, the feeling of danger, and dread slipping away.

She says she'll help us with our predicament, letting us have access to the portal of light and even coming with us to defeat Trystan. She only asks that we return once the war between these realms ends to help her defeat the wyverns.

I bite my bottom lip in concentration. "And, how . . . how will this pack of misfits"—I wave my arm around at my frozen family and Tallyn's fae—"defeat these wyverns?"

"You look like a lunatic out here talking to yourself," Henry pipes in, leaning against Halcyon as if he's a fucking leaning post.

"Scat!" I shout at Henry. "Continue," I say to the air.

I really do look like a lunatic.

She says our demonic nature grants us formidable combat abilities, and dark magick can be pivotal in fighting off the wyverns, Agares continues in my mind, although it does echo, so maybe I am saying the words. Who knows? *My knowledge of shadow realms might also help us set traps to ambush them. Your family's experience with ancient magick and Adaline's ability to summon and control darkness could help us bolster Seraphyra's defenses.*

"And the fae?" I say, walking up to Caelum, and looking him right in his piercing blue eyes. "Can they hear us while they're under this . . . time spell thingy?"

No, because I've stopped time, he answers, and even I can hear the bite of annoyance in my nonchalance. *Tallyn's connection to nature and light could provide powerful protective wards around the breeding ground, preventing the rival flock from gaining access. She can also rally the forces of light and nature to aid in the defense, creating barriers using elemental magick to repel the attackers.*

"And you two figured this all out in the span of what? Thirty seconds?"

Time moves differently here; our languages and understanding differ from yours, and we can use thoughts and projections instead of words. The list goes on, Sebastian. Do you want to hear what Sayah can do?

Sayah.

Gods, her name is like a balm to my soul. Like being outside in the cold for so long, and coming inside. The warmth is so good, it hurts.

"What can Sayah do?"

Once we have them cornered, using her phoenix power to obliterate them will ensure that Seraphyra and her family can live in peace.

I take a minute to think about this, scratching my chin. "I don't see a problem," I say finally.

Agares conveys this to Seraphyra.

I'm going to unfreeze time now, Agares says into my mind.

I hold my arm out, seeing if I'm still red. "Well, it seems you are still in control of the body, so why don't you be the one to tell them? And also, let them know how you did that cool, time freez-y thing."

I will. I must also warn you that what I did comes with a price.

My stomach drops. "What kind of price?"

He doesn't say anything; the longer he waits, the colder my blood grows.

"Agares, what kind of price?"

I can only freeze time three times. Each time I do it, I create a crack in the veil that separates our world from the void—a realm of chaos and forgotten nightmares. Every time I freeze time, that veil weakens, and the creatures lurking in the void are drawn closer to our reality.

My heart flips in my chest. "And what happens when the veil shatters?"

Agares's voice is steady in my head, almost too calm. *When the veil shatters, the void will spill into our world, unleashing those creatures. They are beyond anything you've ever faced and will bring destruction that even I may not be able to stop.*

I swallow hard, trying to keep my voice from trembling. "So

you're saying we've got two more chances before everything falls apart?"

Precisely. Use them wisely; each time we freeze the world, we edge closer to oblivion.

"Then we better ensure it's for something truly worth the risk."

Agreed, Agares says, his tone grave. *Now, shall we break the ice?*

I nod, bracing myself for the moment time resumes and the world continues, blissfully unaware of the impending darkness we've just invited a step closer.

31

THE DARK PHOENIX

—SAYAH—

The ground beneath my head is scraping against my scalp as something rocks it back and forth. An ugly grunting sound is coming from above me; but consciousness is a fickle bitch that keeps coming to me and slipping away. I vaguely know I'm being raped by someone, but my mind is swimming in fog, and I cannot determine whether I am dreaming or if this is real.

Since I've been in this wretched place and that bitch blew the stupid blue shit in my face, it feels like someone else is trying to take over my body. This is the first time I've felt my true self fighting back.

Either that, or his raping me has finally broken the last piece of me that was human.

Whatever demon has taken up residence within me, the old me—the phoenix—is roaring and violent against the fog blanketing me.

A strange sort of pleasure surges inside of me like I am being penetrated, but when I remember it's against my will, I inwardly scream, gathering up all the broken pieces of me left and forging them in the fire of my being.

My eyes shoot open and scream the word my mouth struggles to shape.

White-hot rage courses through my body, and a single certainty anchors itself in my heart, as unyielding as the roots of a mountain range—immovable and eternal. Memories of all the times I've been knocked around, pushed down, and made to wrestle demons that don't belong to me flood my consciousness. I unlock the fire in my bones and let it deluge through me, feeling my soul light up and combust.

A scream not belonging to me shakes the delirium from my mind as Trystan fills his chest with a breath I strangle free with magick. The sound is so jarring it saturates the realm with a heavy promise of a fiery violence I know all too well. The guttural sound of agony gouges into Trystan and the tendrils of my shadow and fire rip him off me, flinging him into the air, and slamming him against a large, glowing tree. His hard cock is still out and dripping with what does not belong to him and was never his to take.

There is a stinging on my arm where my swirling cloud tattoo lives, spreading from my bicep down to my fingertips, back up my arms, neck, and stomach, and then wholly covering my legs and the rest of me.

I have become starlight and darkness incarnate.

Whatever power has come over me is twisting around him, tying him to a tree as he goes to shout, but the darkness steals his voice. The fire licks up the tree and feasts on his feet, catching the brush and bushes around it in a strange green fire.

Rising from the ground in a breathless rush, I frantically look around for Nyx.

I see her legs, bloody and broken, poking out from behind a tree.

I hold my hands and let the lightning free in an explosion of power I can hardly contain. It accelerates out of my fingertips and into the nymphs and whatever dark creatures Trystan was allowing to rape her. They explode on impact, disintegrating into ash as my rage buckles their spines and knees in the same swift strike.

Their ashes fall from the sky like clouds weeping snow as I rush up to her. She is unconscious and battered, her pink hair swirling around her head and tangling in the brush and brambles of Never. Her gown is ripped, but I use the tatters of it to cover her lady bits.

"Nyxaria!" I shout as the breaths saw through me, pulling her to me. I slap her face and shake her, trying to rouse her awake.

Sounds of commotion are spurting up from the horizon, but I continue to focus on getting Nyxaria to wake the fuck up.

My boobs are hanging out of my dress, which is ripped and torn, and the breeze passing by my exposed vagina is cold and reminds me of what that fucking bastard just took from me.

It's like the alien that had taken up residence inside me is cowering at the magick thought stolen from me, magick that was merely locked inside of me. It is now inundating my being. The familiar hue of the angel living inside me decorates my body like a lightning storm with skin. My body is bright and glowing, the cracks of gold spreading across my skin, but now it intermingles with shadows—wild shadows capable of disarranging entire universes. My fire and Bash's thunder have become one vicious maelstrom of power. It's unhinged and wild and volatile, and I don't give a fuck about the casualties it creates.

I bend down and bite Nyx's neck, sucking her blood into me.

When she still doesn't rouse, I bite into my own arm and shove it into her mouth, forcing her to drink my angel blood.

As my blood hits her system, the calvary shows up.

Whatever magick they have, they use it to douse mine and put out the flames threatening to consume Trystan.

His shouts enter my ears as the shadows course back into my veins and relieve him.

But that is not what has my attention.

What has captivated me is what's happening to Nyxaria.

The skin on her arms and face, which normally has a dusty-rose complexion, takes on a faint luminescence. Her wings, normally a translucent black color, shift to show more of a rainbow shimmer, still stilted with darkness but almost like light is warring with it. Half of her wings are black, and half are clear and rainbow. Her eyes flutter open, and instead of being their normal amber color, they are now half pearl and half black.

She lurches forward and convulses, screaming in pain as my divine energy clashes with her dark essence. Her body struggles to contain the overwhelming light of my angelic blood. Her agonizing screams rip into my soul as I watch her darkness being torn apart, the light trying to purify her while her darkness resists.

What have I done?

I watch in horror, faced with the reality that I may have just killed my friend when my hair is flung into my face. Someone with strong arms pulls me away from her, whips me over their shoulder, then flings me onto the back of a horse. The breath is shoved from my lungs as I scrape my hair out of my face.

The breeze is cold on my exposed ass, but I kick my legs wildly, making the horse rear up. I slide roughly into whomever climbed on the horse behind me. My body clenches with fierce violence and wrath at seeing him.

His long, sharp features are severe against the burnt terrain, his cold gray eyes scraping across me, his raised brow inching up his head. The sight of him makes me want to vomit. I thrash my legs to try and wriggle my body free from the animal—and the horse—but Trystan leans forward, his face lost amongst the rebellious locks as he blows more fucking powder in my face.

It smells like the blueberry marker I'd had as a kid.

A slithering darkness encompasses me, wrapping me up, and

locking within my bones. The sting of emotion that just gripped me feels like a disease, returning with tenfold intensity compared to when I cast it aside.

I feel it subtly at first.

As soon as he blows the glittering black smoke in my face, the strangest thing happens. The sparkling mist comes at my face slowly, but as soon as it connects with my breath, the smoke collides with my own magick—the dark magick that came unlocked when the last bit of my old self was taken from me. It's like whatever dark magick Bash infused in me comes to life and is a living, breathing entity, and whatever concoction Trystan blew at me has a reverse effect than what he intended. Instead of subduing me, it awakens a beast.

A strange sort of symphony serenades the tiny atoms inside me, and as the symphony grows to a crescendo, what it does baffles me.

The new magick slithers throughout every morsel, every facet, every bend, break, and tear. It gathers what tiny magick I had left from before and collects it, adds it to the strain, and feeds my light to its darkness as it does.

Dark magick sews my broken pieces together, scavenges for severed bits and tattered tears, and creates a new tapestry that blankets the new me now.

The dark phoenix.

I shake my head, the weight of the realization flooding my throat like a suffocating rush of water.

As it scours through every single memory, every second and minute of my life, every moment that made me break, and every fight that saw me bleed, it makes my light magick fucking bow to it, casting another sweep of sting across me, and it doesn't stop cutting. But this cut—this pain—is the kind of pain that levels you. That disarranges kingdoms and births new eras. The good pain.

What Trystan thought he was doing was breaking me.

But what he's actually doing is unleashing a darkness he, nor anyone else in any realm is ready for.

The new magick feels volatile, like a pack of wild horses has just been unleashed inside my marrow and veins. Once it forms a long tendril of glittering darkness, it scours through me, learning every freckle, every blemish, every scar. The way it moves within me is familiar, like an organ I once had that has finally returned. It washes through me like a cleansing river, as though trying to get to know me again, get reacquainted with me after being severed from me so long ago.

The way the darkness melds with the fire is seamless, creating a cluster of bright orange smoke laced with hellfire.

Equal parts light and dark, equal parts angel and demon—this new power has always lived inside of me but had been stolen long ago, possibly by Trystan himself.

And my darkness wants that man more than I've ever wanted any other.

32

WYNTER

—BASH—

In one final display of Agares's essence, he seizes our footing, and drives it into the earth beneath us. The impact sends ripples cascading outward, stirring the wind to sweep leaves through the trembling trees.

The plume of smoke lingering in the back of Seraphyra's throat sucks back into her lungs, and the entourage of people resume their movements as though no time has passed.

"Quick, Bash, shove this through its eye," Caelum states, tossing me his sword.

I catch it and rest it at my side. "That won't be necessary."

Everyone moves cautiously, their eyes fixed on the fire-breathing dragon hovering steadily in place, its mighty wings beating rhythmically to keep level with the tree's ledge. It watches us intently, prompting hesitant steps backward as dread coils in their minds, bracing for what seems inevitable.

Scarlet, toiling within the fiery idea that's so unhinged it brings a strange sense of calm, looks at me as though I rearranged the world and put myself in backward. "Bash?" she questions, and my eyes narrow, seeking the fissures in her stare. "Why are you red?"

It has to be unsettling. One second, I'm me in my skin, going toe to toe with a giant, fire-breathing dragon; the next, I'm red and in my demon form, and everything is calm, cool, and collected—dragon included.

"Hehe, you look funny," Henry mimics as my talons fade back into my skin. I'm half-demon, half-vampire for the real real right now.

"Agares is my demon," I explain, handing the sword back to Caelum. Scarlet's eyes flash with undiluted shock, kindling something she once doused for me. "He froze time and communicated with Seraphyra here. She agreed to help us as long as we help her once our quest is complete." I lay a steady hand on her snout, and she snorts, smoke billowing out from her nostrils. She closes her eyes as though welcoming the touch.

A stretch of tension-riddled silence ensues.

"So, you've made friends with the dragon?" Hattie asks, finally breaking the silence as I grab hold of one of Seraphyra's scales and hoist myself up, using the other scales as footholds to climb up her monstrous side.

"I have. And the rest of her family is coming to help. Those of us who can't fly on our own will ride them to the portal. They also agreed to help us get Sayah back."

Tallyn eyes me and the dragon with contempt. "What have you promised in return for their help?" she asks, sidling up to Caelum.

"Her murder's breeding ground is under threat from the wyverns, and she wants our help to defeat them." I have nestled myself between a few of the spikes on her spine, my legs spread wide over her back. Her wings flutter behind me, and the spikes become a perfect saddle for me to ride on her without falling off.

"Oh, is that all?" Tallyn says sarcastically. "Like we aren't already invested in our own war."

"Tallyn, hush," I tell her, her eyes lit with a soul-crushing gaze. "Her and her murder will help us defeat your wretched brother and get Sayah back. The least we can do is obliterate some of those wyvern thingys for her."

"What is our plan of attack for that?" my mom asks as three more dragons appear from the cliffside and land with thundering booms on the cliff's edge.

"Tallyn, can you show La La how to make those phoenix bombs?" I ask as Seraphyra shakes her head and snorts.

It's almost like she wants to tell me something.

"I can," Tallyn says, stretching her wings out, ready to take flight.

"All right, everyone without wings will get on the dragons. Those of you with wings, follow us to the tree over there. The Light Gate Portal is indeed held within that tree." Seraphyra whinnies again.

I try projecting my thoughts into her mind. *Is there something you need to say?*

This human is a phoenix, yes? She shifts her enormous head to point at Laureya.

Yes, she is not born as one, though. She merely inherited it from her sister.

But she has the phoenix power, along with being able to shapeshift, correct?

She is a formweaver, yes. But how do you know that?

She sorts again. *We have some abilities to see what beings are in this world. Usually, a band of misfits with morally gray and even black intentions wouldn't have made it through the Valley of Echoes. But we knew you were coming. We saw salvation in your auras.*

I laugh out loud. "Salvation, in our auras? Wow, that's one I've never heard before."

Collective gazes eye me like I'm crazy.

I ignore the stares. I know I am.

There is a balance to everything, Sebastian. Dark and light. While rumor has it that anything possessing even the littlest of gray doesn't make it out of here alive, we keep it that way because, usually, we don't want to be bothered. But we saw an opportunity when we got wind of the Riftstorm Conflict and knew it could lead someone to the Light Gate Portal. So we let the echoes go easy on you.

That was easy? I scoff, thinking how close to madness I'd become in that storm.

You have no idea how much worse it could have been.

And you lot are the guardians of this place?

Her chest puffs with pride. *We are.*

And what are you proposing to do with Laureya?

Have her form into one of us. She could use her phoenix power to heighten her dragon fire. It would prove to be devastating for anyone in her path.

That is interesting. How can she form into a dragon?

"What are you two chatterboxes going on about?" Scarlet asks, stepping closer to Seraphyra, and admiring her scales.

"Can you hear us?" I ponder, seeing a look in her eye that tells me she can.

"Not words, but whispers. I know you're communicating telepathically."

"Seraphyra thinks La La here can form into a dragon and use her phoenix power to create a devastating dragon fire."

I push back against Seraphyra as a nod passes over the group, feeling the rumble of her breath beneath me. Such a ferociously beautiful being. She saunters forward to rest her feet on land and give her wings rest.

Another dragon of metallic green lands on the branch, lowering her head to Scarlet.

"Awe, hello there," she says, caressing the beast like one would a dog, a gentleness dressing her expression up fancier than I'd ever seen it on Scarlet.

The corner of Caelum's lips kick up again, and he advances to the side of the beast, where he kneels and offers her his hands as a stirrup.

A derisive snarl flits its way through her teeth, though I saw her face soften a fraction of a second at his gesture. As she uses him to climb up the dragon, he looks at her like he's staring at the eye of a storm, so hauntingly beautiful he forgets he's in danger.

"What does Laureya have to do to form into one of these?" Halcyon asks as his eyes track the murder of three more dragons landing on the giant tree's branch.

"Since we don't have Mom's spell room available to us, we'll have to get creative," Ollie responds as a gorgeous black dragon with pearl-white eyes nuzzles into his chest.

"I think she can do anything she can put her mind to," Ryan answers. This is the first nice thing I've heard him say about her.

"Awe, thanks, babe," Laureya says, nudging him with her hip.

"I think you need to lay your hands on one of the dragons, Laureya, and connect with it telepathically," Mom answers as she approaches a blue dragon. "Use the same technique you do when shifting to a raven or owl, even the wolf, and manifest it."

Demonstrating, my mom lays her hands on the sides of the beast and bows her head, silently speaking with the creature. My dad protectively steps between her and the beast's long neck. In response, the dragon lowers its beastly neck to allow my mother to climb atop it, my dad assisting by lifting her from the bottom. She gets situated and pats the place behind her, my dad's eagerness showing in the way he effortlessly bounds to land behind her.

Laureya wears a dubious expression as she looks to her friends and boyfriend for comfort. I gag at her naivety. Petting Seraphyra on the side, she makes a purring sound. "You can do this, La La. I have full faith in you."

Her green eyes catch mine, and she grimaces like I've mocked her, but she still walks toward a small white baby dragon. The little creature has to be one of the cutest beasts I've ever seen. About the size of a hippopotamus, she has pearl-white scales that gleam rainbow in the sun. Her scales are smaller, her wings span about twelve feet wide, and her short tail is barbed at the end. Large doe eyes the color of a blizzard in the Rocky Mountains, the dragon almost smiles as Laureya reaches her.

Laureya holds out a trembling hand, hovering it cautiously toward the dragon's side as though asking for permission to touch her.

"What is your name?" Laureya queries as she tamps down one of her scales.

Wynter, the dragon responds.

The gentleness of her voice is like soft wind skittering across a cold ocean, like a spill of cold roiling rocks. It is somehow loud enough for me to hear, though no one else seems to be experiencing it.

I wonder what that's about.

"Pretty name," Laureya responds. This is the nicest—albeit scared and trepidatious—I've ever seen her with anyone or anything. "My name is Laureya. I hope you don't mind if I use you to try to form into one flockling."

We prefer the term "murderlings," but go ahead. I won't bite. Hard.

Wynter! Seraphyra scolds her. *They will help save our lands so that you may one day be a mother. Be nice!*

I like Wynter. She seems like my people.

Same, brother. Dom's voice is in the wind, and it catches me sideways.

We still need to tell Mom about him being alive.

"Not now," Henry says, nodding over to Laureya.

Laureya trepidatiously places her hand on Wynter's side. Silence reigns over us, threading through the group as Laureya attempts a form into something mythical.

I wonder if she'll be able to accomplish this.

Laureya's eyes close, and she bows her head. Her lips move

as though reciting a prayer. Glittering waves of what looks like enchanted sawdust filter up through the air, and the wind takes on a teal tint. The air thickens, the grass itself bends to listen, and even the strange bugs that make this place home still to observe. Wynter closes her eyes and lowers her head, seemingly permitting Laureya to take something of hers within herself.

A small scale comes loose from Wynter, and Laureya takes it and places it on her arm, clasping her hand over it. She murmurs as the scale congeals with her skin and duplicates, a pearly armor slathering up her arms. A shudder takes over her as she morphs in size, falling to her knees as her clothes seep into the scales. Her arms and legs elongate into new appendages the color of a Caribbean sunset—fire.

Echoes of new life ricochet off the mountains as her bones break and rearrange, but she doesn't scream. Wynter puts her claw on Laureya's shoulder as she elongates, morphing to the size of Wynter and then larger still until she reaches the stature of her mother, Seraphyra.

When the transformation is complete, Laureya stands before us as a creature of breathtaking majesty—a fusion of dragon and griffin, exuding both power and grace. Her face, snout, and flowing mane mirror that of a lion, while her body is that of a formidable dragon. Her scales shimmer in a molten blend of oranges and reds, with embers and living flames flickering beneath the surface, sending waves of heat rippling around her like the haze over sunbaked asphalt.

Her talons are long and obsidian-black, her wings an extraordinary blend of sinewy membranes and fire-tipped feathers. When she opens her eyes, flames crackle and dance within her vertical irises, alive with untamed energy. At the end of her tail, crystalline and metallic barbs glint like a fusion of dragon glass and hardened scale, deadly and beautiful in equal measure.

Did it work? she asks us, swiveling her neck to examine her new body.

"Either that or you are on some pretty wicked acid," I answer, and her cynically disapproving glare tells me she's still the same ol' La La.

"Try breathing fire," Jasantha encourages from atop the purple dragon she chose.

Thundering booms of Laureya's footfalls echo as she pads over to the edge of the world. Opening her mouth, she lets out a pretty comical roar, yet nothing comes out of her mouth.

You must will the fire within your bones to want to come out and do your bidding, Wynter tells her. *It needs a good word, like "Incendiary."*

Nivera! Laureya voices the command. A plume of an icy updraft shoots outward, destroying rocks, mountains, and trees and leaving an icy frost in its wake. Ice-mimicking fire festoons out of her, jutting out into the ravine and weeping flakes of snow. Turning her head, she creates a mountain of snow and ice, freezing the glowing trees.

The plume of ice and snow dissipates from her maw, and Laureya takes a deep, shuddering breath.

Ignitas! she commands next, and this time, when she releases the breath, the fire is the color of mossy mountains, with heat enough not only melt the snow she brought to life but also the terrain.

"Interesting," Tallyn utters, fluttering at eye level with me.

"What does it mean?" I ask.

"Well, since Wynter is an ice dragon and Laureya comes from fire, it looks like she can use both in this form," Tallyn answers, fluttering away from the ledge and hovering above the ravine.

"Interesting," I echo.

Everyone who doesn't own a pair of wings has adopted a dragon, the fae awaiting the command to take to the skies.

"Is everyone ready?" Tallyn asks.

"Yeah, do we have a plan here, T, or are we just going to show up and start burning shit to the ground?"

"Honestly, Bash, sometimes your stupidity baffles me." I scoff as she shakes her head. "We'll go down there and let the dragons help us enter the portal. Then, once it's open, we'll all enter. We have to catch them before they seal their union with a kiss. Burn everyone else you can aside from them."

"What happens if we're too late and they've already sealed the deal?" I shift my weight to ease the pinch between my legs.

"If they kiss, the seventh, and final portal, Desoloth, will open with the union between the Celestial Phoenix and the King of the Night Shades on the Dread Harvest Eclipse creating a rift and opening a void."

"Another void?" I ask as Seraphyra begins to get restless, her wings flexing outward, and snapping back in again.

"The worst one, Bash," she confirms, tightening the sword strap that wraps around the back side of her. "This one wipes out all wards that Feylight protects, all ley lines will vanish, each and every portal will open up, and the world as we know it will fall to any and every creature that is ready to cross it."

I swallow the dread I feel creeping up my esophagus. "So basically . . . if they kiss, the entire world is fucked?"

"Up the ass without lube," Caelum answers for her.

Tallyn glares at him in warning. "Yes, what he said. If they seal their bond with a kiss, all protection spells that have ever been placed will be broken. We will be more than fucked. We will basically start human extinction,"

To avoid the severity of the statement, I say, "Well, let's get a move on, then, people. C'mon, we have a wedding to crash."

Even entraining the idea that some douchebag fairy thinks my girl would marry him flushes violence to the tips of me. My skin is still slightly red, so I know Agares is not far from the surface of me.

But the thought of Sayah marrying some trash takes my violence to a whole new level.

I would crack open new worlds, rip ours in two and fling them into space, burn it down and leave everything in ruin, and let Agares take over forever if it meant saving her from that fate.

33

THE WEDDING

—ESTREAYA—

A soft gust of floral air brushes against me as I rise from plush pillows, the room before me unrecognizable. My skin feels different. Fog clings to my mind like honey, but one thought crashes through: Today is my wedding day. I am to take my vows and become Queen of Neverdusk, Earth, and Luminara. My son will walk, fly, and live free of sickness.

Where is Trystan?

Standing on unsteady legs, the wild magick within me thrums, restless. I am adorned in a wedding gown woven of clouds and starlight. Soft music drifts in from the window. My ballet slippers whisper across the floor as I approach it. Below, people no bigger than ants gather around an aisle made of shimmering clouds.

The mirrors reveal a stranger.

Yet, I know her.

Galaxies etch themselves into my bones, my skin kissed by stars. Moonlight gleams in my eyes. Comets have forged my nails, and my blood carries the dust of ancient, extinguished suns. My wings, once pure fire, now blend feathers, webs, flame, and ash—a paradox of destruction and creation. Darkness hums beneath my skin, deeper than ever, swirling like a storm, lightning flickering in its wake.

I am darkness.

I am the night incarnate.

The ninth circle of Hell's realm lives in my flesh, in my soul. My hair, woven from the void, devours the light. My skin, midnight incarnate, harbors the whispers of forgotten monsters. My voice, soft yet edged with ruin, carries the wails of avalanches and hurricanes. Darkness and death murmur secrets only my soul understands. I feel the demise of every being, the collapse of realms, the sorrow of widows, mistresses, and the forsaken. The void calls to me—not as an absence, but as the birthplace of all things.

We all begin in darkness.

What right does light have to claim superiority?

Darkness does not merely contrast light—it owns it. Swallows it whole.

Trystan's powder was meant to sever my connection to Sayah, to mold me into what he desired. He was wrong. The magick had the opposite effect—it severed the last tether to my past self. Compassion, morality, empathy—all burned away. Only my love for my son remains. He alone keeps me from unraveling completely.

I glance at my reflection.

The wedding dress must change. White is an insult.

At my touch, the fabric darkens, shifting into a tapestry of storm clouds, constellations flickering within its folds. My slippers sharpen into six-inch stilettos, wicked and spiked. A black veil cascades over my hair, dark magick curling around me like living smoke. My lips turn the shade of midnight; my eyes become fathomless voids speckled with dying stars. A crown of black jewels glints from the dresser.

A sound from the adjoining room stops me.

The sharp click of my heels against the flagstone echoes the magick surging through me.

A storm waiting to be unleashed.

Nyxaria is lying on a bed of black satin, her body still frail and lethargic looking. A black satin sheet is wrapped around her naked body. Bruises cover her body, even some gashes that don't seem to be healing.

She stirs when I sit on her bed.

She is now the opposite of me. Where I used to be light and now dark, she is light instead of dark. But only half of her. Half of her hair is the color of snow on a mountain; the other is the color of a living shadow, a hungry darkness that pulls everything into its depths. One side of her body is pale and ivory, and the other is as dark as midnight. Each of her wings starts as iridescent and white at the tips, the tops of which resemble fairy wings. The bottom half is black and feathery.

When she opens her eyes, one eye is pearl, and one is black opal.

"Sayah?" she asks, her voice harsh and raspy, and it sounds like she spent the night screaming at the top of her lungs.

"Estreaya," I correct her. I know who Sayah is, but she doesn't live here anymore.

"Es-stray-uh?" she phonetically sounds out my name, tasting how it sounds on her tongue.

I nod. "Are you all right?" I touch her forehead to brush a strand of hair out of her eyes. My touch shocks her, sending bolts of electricity through me.

My scar that Bash caused stirs like little spiders trying to break free of my skin and fight this darkness that now consumes me.

"I'm not okay, Say—Estreaya. I've known Trystan a long time, and what he was this morning—who he is now is not someone I know. He never would have done . . . that . . . to you . . . to let his guards do what they did to me. Something awful has happened, and I don't think you should mar—" She's cut off by the sounds of trumpets blaring.

Our gazes shoot to the window, and I stand again. The wild magick makes me feel blurry and drunk.

We're on a crescendo of something wicked.

I feel it.

Gazing out to the wedding below, Trystan is walking with a shaman down the side of dark clouds marred by starlight. Candles in towering sconces line the walkway, and even more tapered candles float above the guests.

The guests—a plethora of dark beings—take up the seats: vampires, elves, goblins, trolls, giants, warlocks, grimspawn, and death.

It's a scene I never thought I'd ever see.

A wedding for the wicked.

Attended by all things that frighten little children in storybooks.

The shaman—a giant at least ten feet tall—wears royal blue robes and a hood large enough to cover most of his face. He leads Trystan to the front of the altar. Bridesmaids I didn't choose march with royal guards of Trystan, two by two, waltzing down the aisle to music fit for a sorrowful death scene.

The Shadow Gate Portal is behind the altar at the end of the aisle.

The portal stands behind him, an ancient, towering archway carved from black obsidian with intricate runes etched deep into its surface. The runes glow a faint gold with a silver hue. The arch seems to drink in the moonlight, with no solid surface on the front. Tendrils of shadowy mist curl and stretch like they're reaching out into every word. The mist is not merely dark; it contains depths of pitch-black voids that shimmer with distant stars, as if a fragment of the cosmos has been trapped within. Occasionally, flashes of violet and deep indigo pulse through the shadows, giving the impression of potent energy.

I turn to face Nyx. "What do I do?"

She rises from the bed with the sheet wrapped around her and gazes down. When she turns to me, her different-colored eyes are a wild panic. "Can we run?"

"No, I want this. I was wondering how I get down there. Do I fly?"

Confusion paints her beautiful face. "You . . . want this?"

"I do," I say earnestly. "To be the Queen of Never and Earth and Luminara would mean my son can walk and fly and not have diabetes anymore." I take her hands in mine to try and convince her that I am the best choice to be queen. "I will be a benevolent queen. You can be my hand. We can make the world see that darkness isn't bad. That dark is where the best things are created. Nyx, we can make the world a better place."

"Sayah—" She shakes her head. "Estreaya, what has come over you?" Putting her hand to my forehead. "Are you feeling all right?"

I swipe her hand away, and the movement stirs the magick again. "Nyx, I'm fine! This is my destiny. This is what I've always been meant to be. Just . . . trust me, okay? I'll never let anyone hurt you." My hand touches her cheek, and fresh mountain snow buzzes against the inside of my storm, the clouds yearning to be free from the prison that shackle keeps them in. "You will be more to me than just my hand. You will be my girlfriend. My lover. My love. I will protect you always, okay?"

A trusting emotion passes over her face as she agrees. "Okay."

"Let's get you dressed. I've got a king to marry."

Branches laden with leaves, tilling them into a flirty dance with the handsy wind wave above us as Nyx walks me down the aisle toward Trystan.

We dressed her in the deepest blue dresses infused with moonlight and stars; her train extends behind her but not as long as my black one. Little fairies hold up the train, and shooting stars dart across the fabric. The moons glow their brilliance onto the wedding party as every being stands to watch my entrance. Nyx holds Calla lilies—the same blue as her dress—and my bouquet is made of black roses and dark purple stargazers.

Trystan looks every bit the image of a handsome prince, his black suit perfectly tailored to his muscular frame, with dark thorns curling up from the collar and winding down his arms. His hair is slicked back, and his piercing blue eyes lock onto mine. As I approach, his dazzling smile reveals gleaming white teeth. His groomsmen, dressed sharply in royal guard uniforms, stand tall and composed, while my bridesmaids, draped in deep shades of black and blue, watch me with admiration as I approach him, arm in arm with Nyx.

The women—all fae of different shades of night—admire me as though they know the well-meaning I have for my new kingdom. I desire to do good for others, have generosity and compassion, and an altruistic nature, uplifting others without expecting anything in return to show them that darkness has a place among us and the world.

When I reach my king, the shaman silences the crowd gracefully, guiding them to their seats. A warrior angel stands nearby, their radiant blue wings stretching wide, gray eyes gleaming like storm clouds, and golden hair catching the light. The fae are so captivating, they stir the urge to write poetry in my soul once more.

Faint whispers escape from the portal—an unintelligible chorus of voices speaking in tongues lost to time. A cold wind emanates from the gate, carrying a sense of foreboding and the unmistakable feeling it's watching—waiting. An eerie pull beckons me to touch the vortex, a compulsion to step through. Though the feeling is mixed with a deep-rooted fear of what lies beyond.

Trystan's eyes sparkle as he takes in my new appearance. He flicks the veil over my head, so my face is exposed and takes both hands in his. This man I used to be afraid of, with his wild eyes and dire warnings. Now, I only want to bring the old world to ruin with him by my side.

My strange magick stirs at his touch, and even stranger still, the scar where Bash left his mark and his magick intertwined with mine screams in pain, making me wince.

Are you okay? Trystan asks as the shaman begins the ceremony. The tender motion seems so at odds with him.

I nod, accepting the dangerous, thorny question as if it were a freshly sharpened weapon—delicate to handle, requiring gentle precision, and measured care.

"In the beginning," the shaman begins, his voice resonating with the weight of countless ages, "there was darkness, vast and infinite. It cradled the stars, gave birth to the first whispers of light, and set the stage for all that is and will be. Light is not a conqueror of darkness, but its child, its partner, in the eternal cycle."

The shaman gestures toward us. I stand before him, my fissures glowing with my inner fire. An aura of twilight shrouds the Neverdusk King.

"Tonight," he carries on, his voice heavy with age and strange in an accent I cannot place, "we witness a union that echoes through the heart of creation. The Neverdusk King, ruler of twilight and keeper of shadows, is the guardian of secrets and nightmares. Together, they embody the harmony of opposites, the essential unity of all things."

He pauses, allowing his words to settle over the gathered

guests. "Understand this: without darkness, there can be no light. Without the twilight of the king, there would be no dawn from which the phoenix could rise. Their joining is not just a celebration of love but a reaffirmation of the sacred balance that binds all worlds, even this one. It is a reminder that there is a spark in every shadow and in every light, a hint of a dark. Their bond strengthens the ties between realms, ensuring that harmony prevails, and that the dance of creation continues."

As he concludes, the shaman's gaze sweeps over the crowd, a silent plea for them to carry this understanding in their hearts. "And now for their vows."

"Lasayah Thorne—" Trystan begins, and I shake my head.

"Estreaya Wyndstorm," I correct him.

His left eye squints while he tilts his head to comprehend my new name, but he nods. "Estreaya Wyndstorm." He stretches the syllables across his tongue to savor how my new identity sits on his tastebuds. "My beloved phoenix, the flame of the cosmos, you are the dawn to my twilight, the fire that ignites my shadows."

"Faebian, the ring, please," the shaman instructs.

Faebian digs in his pocket and produces the most luminous and giant black diamond I have ever seen. I hold out my hand, and as he places it on my finger, that strange magick itches and screams, burns, and resists. I push against it as he continues to slide the ring down my finger.

Vines crawl up both our legs and wrap around my arm, interlacing with the finger on which he is placing the ring.

"In you, I see the radiance that brings life to the darkness," he mutters, his lips the palest of pinks, matching his cheeks, "the light that dances in the spaces between stars; I vow to stand with you through every cycle, through every rise and fall. As the night welcomes the day, so shall I welcome you, my queen, into the depths of my eternal dusk. Together, we will weave the threads of creation, binding realms with our love, keeping the balance as it was meant to be. In your light, I find my purpose, and I shall protect you with my shadows. As long as the stars burn and the darkness embraces them, I am yours."

Once the ring is all the way flush with my hand, the magick turns to a screaming throb, a spasm I find hard to ignore. The vines are turning into ink on my left arm, and the shadowy clouds beneath my skin are fighting it.

"Lady Midnight, your turn," the shaman instructs.

Words that don't belong to me begin to exit my throat, from whence I do not know they come.

"My king, sovereign of the night. You are the twilight that cradles my fire, the stillness that tempers my flame. I find the strength in you to rise again and again, knowing that your embrace is my sanctuary."

"Lady Oaken, the ring, please."

One of my bridesmaids I vaguely remember pulls a ring off the chain around her neck. When she hands it to me, it is heavy and twisted, made of glass from stars. Trystan holds his hand out and I slide it on his finger.

The shaman nods for me to continue, and the vines wrap around his arm, intermingling with his thorns. "I vow to burn for you, to bring warmth and light to your shadows, to honor the balance and sustain them. As the dawn brings hope, so shall I bring my love to you, rekindling the stars in your night. Together, we shall guide the realms, our bond a beacon in the darkness and a promise in the light. In your twilight, I find my strength, and I shall renew you with my flames. For as long as the cosmos turns, I am yours."

There is that inhuman sharpness about him again as he smiles at me, the ring sitting firmly at the bottom of his finger. The vines embed themselves in his skin like ink, and the thorns seemingly embrace them.

The shaman resumes. "These vows declare their love and reaffirm their cosmic duties. Their union symbolizing the eternal interplay of light and dark, creation and mystery, ensuring that all realms, including Earth, continue in harmony."

As the shaman speaks of the sacred balance, an attendant approaches with two ornate vessels, each filled with shimmering dust. One vessel holds fiery embers, gleaming with the soft, ethereal light of a thousand suns, captured from the very fabric of the cosmos. The other contains moon dust, a silvery, glowing powder that seems to hold within it the mystery of magick of countless lunar cycles.

A rumbling in the realm subtly begins beneath our feet as the vessels are set upon the table, like the power they hold is the key to unlocking the portal that Trystan needs opened. The Shadow Gate behind us glows, the shadows churning more violently, blurring together in a siphon of wind.

"At this moment," the shaman continues, "as light meets shadow, as fire joins with twilight, you will share a part of yourselves with each other, blending the essence of the sun and the moon. Just as embers of sundust and moondust are scattered across the heavens, so too shall your love and unity spread across all realms, blinding them together in harmony."

Faebian hands Trystan the moondust and Oaken the sundust to me.

The shaman holds an empty vessel that looks fit to house a king's ashes. "Now you each will pour your dust into the others' hands a bit at a time, and they will add your dust to this vessel, alternating until both your vases are empty."

I take my vase holding the embers of sundust and pour it into the king's hands, the tiny grains catching the light of the moons and glowing as they pass from me to him. They look like tiny coals, but they are not hot. As the sundust touches the king, it seems to merge with his very being, enhancing the aura of twilight surrounding him. He smiles at me as he fists my sundust, gently funneling it into the urn the shaman holds.

Trystan, in turn, takes the moondust, and pours it into my

hands. The dust shimmers with a soft, lunar glow, and as it settles in my palms, it enhances the fire within me, causing the fissures to glow even more brightly, a radiant beacon in the twilight. The dust is soft and fine and seems cool, but my fire rages against it, the scar on my arm now almost blistering in pain.

I add his dust to the jar, and we continue to do this back and forth until all our dust is gone. Once we both have exchanged the dust, we raise our hands, letting the remaining dust scatter into the air, where it swirls together, creating a brief but beautiful display of light and shadow mingling in the space between us. The dust spreads out over the crowd, and a collective ease passes over the attendees. The dust symbolizes our unity, the blending of our essences, and our eternal bond. The shadows that make up my being seem to settle the raging and volatile magick within me, but something is about to burst.

The scar on my arm scorches enough for me to look down. Where Bash's shadows mixed with my fire is an infinity symbol, burning, blistering, and bleeding.

Trystan doesn't notice; he's too busy enjoying the applause from the wedding guests as our dust spreads over them.

"By the stars above and the moons that guide us," the shaman concludes, drawing attention back to him, "you are now bound not just in this realm but all realms. Your love is a force of nature, as enduring as the stars, as constant as the moon. Let this exchange of sundust and moondust remind you of your vow, your balance, and the infinite connection you share."

Trystan faces me again, his calm demeanor and flagrant smile pacifying the burning magick on my arm.

"Remember, dark ones, that darkness is not to be feared, for it is the womb of creation. It is the reason light exists, and tonight, we honor both in the union of the Celestial Phoenix and the Neverdusk King. By the ancient pacts sealed in shadow and flame—" The rumble in the Earth worsens and causes some of the candles to tip over. Beings rush to pick them up before anything catches fire. The winds whip the trees around, and birds scatter from the trees, but the shaman presses on. The clouds and storm in the vortex of the Shadow Gate Portal have dissolved and are now an undulating orb of blue.

"By the forces that govern the unseen and the untamed, I now bind you, King of the Nightshades, Lord of Nightmares, and you, Phoenix of the Celestial Abyss, Sovereign of Eternal Fire. From this moment forward—" An explosion off in the distance has Trystan's guards worriedly looking around, but Trystan gestures for the shaman to hurry and conclude the ceremony.

Though the hood hides the shaman's eyes, his posture is rigid and tense, "Um, f-from this moment forward, let your reign of darkness and dominion be united as one force, a power unmatched across all realms—" The screeching of a beast rends the air. Guests are now standing and gazing at the sky. The wind knocks over chairs, rain falls in a downpour from the sky, and lightning flashes against the now dark and ominous horizon.

"*Finish it!*" Trystan demands, even as the Earth's rumble has become a tremor and the shaman loses his balance, righting himself on the altar to finish the ceremony.

"Uh, um, th-the cosmos shall tremble at your command, and the very f-fabric of reality shall bend to your will."

"*Finish* the *fucking union you sniveling worm!*" Trystan roars, his voice crackling with dark energy as the ground beneath us quakes with his fury and whatever force rejecting our union. The shaman—now pale and trembling—grips the altar with white-knuckled hands, forcing the final words out with desperate haste, knowing that any further delay, his own or the universe, would surely mean his end.

"Rise as the Dread King and Queen of the Endless Night,

bound in darkness, crowned in flame, and let your rule be as eternal as the stars, only and forever sealed with a kiss."

As Trystan leans in, his hand firm on my neck, his lips barely brush mine before chaos ignites.

A dozen murderous dragons descend from every angle, their fiery breath consuming the wedding party and guests in a relentless, monstrous inferno. Dark fae hurl their magick, guards leap into action, and the Shadow Gate's glass shatters with a deafening crash. Shards erupt outward, slashing, piercing, and embedding themselves in everything and everyone caught in their deadly trajectory.

Power floods me, cascading from the shattered gate into my soul, warming me with such heat and fire and cold and powerful physical feelings mixing together, not making any sense. The fissures in my skin heat up like they are about to explode. I am losing control of my power.

I feel it as it detonates.

The last thing I see as my body ignites is a colossal dragon, the embodiment of fire, launching fire and ice into the crowd. Other dragons unleash their fury, and the explosions detonate with the force of an atom bomb, sending earth, wood, flowers, flames, and shattered bodies hurtling through the air—everything but me, untouched amidst the carnage.

34

WORLD ON FIRE

The sleepy town of Honolulu stirs as night surrenders to the creeping embrace of dawn, the sky painted in the bruised hues of its final battle. People emerge from their homes, bleary-eyed, and unsuspecting, as they go to shuffle through the rituals of a new day—morning jogs along sunlit beaches, the hiss of coffee machines in bustling cafés, and the low hum of cars queuing at gas stations. It's an ordinary day until the fabric of reality itself tears apart.

A fiery seam unzips the heart of downtown Honolulu, spilling an infernal glow that spreads like wildfire. From the gaping Shadow Gate, monstrosities of unimaginable horror crawl forth. Towering beasts—larger than dinosaurs—lurch into the city. Their decaying flesh dangles in grotesque strips, revealing glistening bones beneath. Milky, lifeless eyes scan the terrified masses, unseeing yet aware. They leave devastation in their wake.

Screams rip through the streets. Humans flee in chaotic waves, but escape is futile. Wyverns pour out of the portal, their leathery wings blotting out the rising sun. They spew streams of green fire, incinerating buildings, melting steel, and reducing palm-lined avenues to charred skeletons. The air fills with the acrid stench of burning flesh and molten concrete.

A swarm of dark fae surges from the portal, their sharp, serrated teeth glinting in the eerie glow. Like a storm of ravenous locusts, they descend on the fleeing population, tearing through flesh. The Earth itself quakes beneath the force of the portal's seismic eruption. Lava gushes from awakened volcanoes across the island chain, vomiting columns of fire and ash into the sky. The ground cracks open, swallowing cars, and splintering buildings like fragile toys.

Tsunamis, conjured by the chaos, crash against the shore, sweeping debris and bodies into the ocean. In mere minutes, the vibrant city of Honolulu is reduced to smoldering ash and fractured rubble.

But the destruction doesn't end there. Across the globe, new portals yawn open, unleashing the same cataclysmic terror. One tears into the bustling heart of Madrid, casting shadows over its ancient streets. Another splits the neon-lit skyline of Tokyo. In the United States, Shadow Gates erupt in New Orleans, New York, California, and Florida, their infernal legions spilling into the chaos of urban life. Rifts riddle through Mexico and South America, while Canada faces five of its own. Russia becomes a breeding ground for the abyss, with twenty portals scattering their hellish legions across the frozen tundra. Europe burns under the weight of countless invasions while Africa's skies darken with winged horrors.

Flame and fury engulf the world. Every continent evolves into a battlefield of destruction. Abyssal Sprites, demons from unspeakable dimensions, and a swelling army of Neverdusk fae rampage through the streets. Their ranks grow as they convert humans into dark fae and vampires, spreading their monstrous influence like a plague.

With Earth's defenses crumbling, the veil between Desoloth and this world collapses entirely. Freed from the chains of separation, Trystan unleashes the full might of the fae realm, tearing down the remaining barriers. The darkness of Desoloth spills unbridled into the mortal world, heralding the dawn of a new, monstrous age.

35

THE RESCUE

—BASH—

The flight to the glowing tree is seamless now that the dragons are on our side. Their thunderous landings shake the floating island's surface, reverberating through the air as they touch down before the immense, radiant tree.

Aside from the branch we had been dangling from, this is the largest tree I have ever seen—easily dwarfing the tallest skyscrapers in New York City. Standing at its base, gazing upward, the tree's crown disappears into the clouds, blending seamlessly with the sky. At its center yawns the cave entrance, a cavernous tunnel that leads to the Light Gate.

We'll fly over and meet you at the clearing, Seraphyra says, her voice cutting through the din. *The tunnel's too narrow for us to fit through.*

I nod, and we dismount, following Tallyn as she strides into the tunnel. The passage twists and turns, its dim walls glinting faintly with some unknown energy, before opening into a breathtaking clearing. The Light Gate rests atop a central mound, sunlight cascading down as though the heavens have focused on the magickal vortex.

Its presence is unsettling. The aura of purity radiating from the gate prickles against my skin as an oppressive weight against the shadows within me. The archway is magnificent—crafted from pristine white stone that glows faintly, its surface adorned with intricate gold and silver filigree patterns. These designs shift and swirl like constellations, alive and hypnotic. Within the arch shimmers a liquid light, rippling like molten sunlight. It exudes warmth, but it's the kind that sets my teeth on edge, its purity foreign and uninviting, enveloping Agares in an uncomfortable hug.

Agares stirs within me, grumbling uneasily. *Don't get too close to it*, he warns.

"Nobody look directly within it," Tallyn commands. "We merely want to use our portal to hitch to the energy to find the Shadow Gate."

The music emanating from the gate—soft chimes and distant choirs—tugs at me. It's beautiful, yet it resonates against my shadows like nails on glass.

The dragons herald above us, screeching in tones that warn of death and destruction as they land nearby.

"Halcyon, prepare the portal," Tallyn commands as I take another step closer to the Light Gate. I feel a profound sense of calm and an overwhelming urge to enter the light. Agares growls deep within me like the light is too heavy and weighing down on his darkness.

As Halcyon uses the circle portal instead of the zipper, the burning on my arm causes me to wince and almost scream—a manly scream, of course, but a scream, nonetheless.

I hold my arm out to investigate.

A burning infinity symbol now rests there, a mixture of fire and shadow, and my soul instantly knows her coordinates.

"I got it, Halcyon," I say, running up to him. He gives me a wry, confused look as I shove my arm into his vortex, which siphons her location from me.

The portal Halcyon opened now shows the wedding. Sayah's black hair matches the black dress of swirling clouds she wears. The winds are rustling her hair, and her fire eyes are on Trystan. However, they dart down to her arm, where the same burning symbol is now etched.

She looks like Sayah, but then not like Sayah at all.

She's darker.

A dark phoenix? I am here for it.

My gaze impales her through the vision in the chaotic clouds. "There." I jab my finger into Halcyon's bicep a few times to ensure he's paying attention. He is, but he's not thrilled. I remove it and whistle at Tallyn. "Let's go, c'mon," I command, determined to go get my girl before that bastard can seal her fate with a kiss.

Tallyn rallies the group, but my patience snaps. Without waiting for the others—or the dragon—I plunge into the swirling madness of the portal. The journey is chaos incarnate —a maelstrom of shattered worlds, fragmented timelines, and clashing elements. My breath comes in gasps, sawing through me as though my ribs might splinter.

When the portal spits me out, I land hard on Neverdusk's ground, the grass an unnatural shade of dark green. Pain flares as I roll to my side, my ribs protesting with every breath until my healing kicks in, knitting flesh and bone.

Henry appears beside me, his tone dry.

"Funny thing about portal magick—it mirrors your state of mind. You were frantic, so it was chaotic."

"Noted," I mutter, dusting myself off before flashing to Seraphyra's side.

A deafening explosion draws my attention skyward.

The battle has begun.

Dragons tear through the air, their roars shaking the cliffside. Seraphyra launches us into the fray, her wings slicing through the smoke-laden air. Around us, green fire scorches the ground, and screams of pain echo through the night.

The chaos is overwhelming.

As dragons tear through the air, everyone in attendance to the wretched thing I hate calling a wedding scatter, the dragons chasing them across the cliff side.

I pull Seraphyra around the cliff's edge—like steering my Audi through a parking lot to find a spot—following the tree line to the opening where the altar and portal are placed.

Torrents of green fire mar the landscape. Screams of agony and all things evil lash out into the night. The eerie glow adds a layer of maniacal intrigue and impending fatality, the rush of war cascading down to my bones.

Smoke and ash swirl, choking the battlefield with darkness.

But I can't afford to focus on any of it.

Sayah needs me.

The portal has exploded, and body parts are everywhere. A cold sludge courses through me, and it feels like hundreds of pounds of melted ore are replacing my blood.

Where is she?

I focus solely on the altar, where the portal once stood. The scene is carnage—scorched earth, shattered stone, and bodies strewn. My heart pounds, my gaze locks on Sayah. She's crumpled near the ruins. Volatile energy radiates from her. Trystan looms over her, his hand clamped around her arm, his face alight with triumph as he leans in to finish their kiss.

Her golden eyes catch mine as Agares rips through my skin, his wings taking to the sky, plummeting off the dragon, and into the wind itself.

"She's mine now," Trystan snarls at me as I land with a quake, his guttural growl cutting through the chaos. "This power will make me unstoppable."

Sayah thrashes weakly in his grasp, her body shuddering with uncontrollable bursts of energy. Her eyes flicker open for a moment, filled with despair, and her lips part as though to cry out, but no sound escapes. The sight sends a surge of fury and panic roaring through me.

Before I can move, the air grows deathly cold. Frost creeps over the battlefield like a living thing. A deafening roar echoes through the chaos as Laureya descends from the heavens. Her kaleidoscopic scales shimmer with icy fire, and her wings—tipped with blazing feathers—scorch the smoke-filled sky.

"Nivera!" she bellows, her voice booming like thunder.

From her maw, a hurricane of ice and snow explodes outward. The ground trembles with the eruption of jagged spires, encasing rocks, trees, and even mountains in crystalline ice. The icy blast engulfs the altar in seconds. Trystan freezes mid-lunge, his hand still gripping Sayah's arm, his entire form encased in a shimmering layer of frost.

Sayah collapses, the volatile energy dissipating as Laureya's freezing storm envelops her. Steam rises from her body, the ice extinguishing the glow threatening to consume her, but she doesn't freeze the way Trystan did.

"Ignitas!" Laureya commands, her fiery eyes snapping to the remaining dark fae nearby. A torrent of green fire roars from her throat, obliterating the icy remnants of her previous attack and melting the ground beneath the remaining foes. The shockwave sends wyverns scattering and dark fae fleeing in terror.

Seraphyra swoops low, her obsidian wings cutting through the swirling ash. She releases her fire to protect me as I make my way to Sayah. My heart pounds when I finally scoop her into my arms, her body limp but alive. She looks as though a hundred lightning streaks blasted right through her, the energy humming faintly against my skin. Something inside her is fighting to reignite.

I glance at Trystan, frozen in a jagged tomb of ice, his face locked in a twisted expression of rage.

Laureya lets out another roar, her fiery breath streaking

across the battlefield as Wynter joins the fray, her pearly white scales glinting like snow under moonlight. The smaller dragon darts through the chaos, freezing a wyvern mid-dive with a plume of icy breath before shattering it with a whip of her barbed tail.

The wings of Agares burst from my back, lifting us into the air just as Laureya lands with a ground-shaking thud. Seraphyra crouches low, and Laureya's lion-like snout twists into a snarl. She unleashes another icy blast, clearing my path to the dragon. We lower to her back, securing Sayah against my chest. Then Seraphyra bursts into the air.

Sayah shifts in my arms, and for a fleeting moment, I think she might turn to kiss me. But instead, her entire body stiffens, and her tension is a clear sign that she finds no solace in being rescued by me.

"Sayah?"

Her head thrusts in my direction, her gaze sweeping across me like an angrily bristled brush, impaling me with her torrid yet glacial stare.

"Get. Me. The fuck. Down." she demands, squirming to get out of my grip. She spreads her own membranous wings made of smoke and fire and webbing and weird shit, and tries to fly away from me, but I catch her and hold her on the back of the dragon.

I crumble in the desperation of a hot, hurting, and heavy reality. "Sayah, what's wrong? It's me, Bash."

Her face contorts in a shadowy fury, watching me with a haunting intensity that threatens to peel me open.

The sort of look that buckles spines, heartstrings—entire existences—in one quick stroke.

Really turning me on this dark Sayah.

"I know!" she yells, and her magick swirls violently. A vicious aura of orange energy buzzes around her like she'll combust at any moment, bound only by a thin thread—the shackle—_barely holding her together. "I don't want to go back with you. This is my destiny, Bash. To be the Queen of Never and Feylight and Earth, give my son legs and wings, and take away his diabetes."

The fierceness in her pull is enough to make Seraphyra bank left, nearly knocking Sayah and me off. Sayah slams into my chest, and I use all my strength to keep us on the dragon. As Seraphyra straightens her path back toward the fray, the air between us hollows, her words slamming into me like the weight of a meteor. As much as I want Gauge to have all those things, it still hurts in a way that I welcome the fall. I beckon the ground to shatter me into pieces the way her indifference is destroying me now.

I wrap my hand around Sayah's waist and tug her tightly, some of the black butterflies on her dress scattering. "Sayah, you're just poisoned. You'll remember the real you when we get his fucking poison out of you."

"I. Don't. Want. To. Go. With. You!" she screams, sucking and shoving deep breaths. The darkness in her eyes unleashes horrific shocks down to my soul. "Let me down now, Bash, or so help me, Odin, I'll burn this whole fucking world down!"

I manage to get her to face me, pinning her arms to her sides. I am twice the size as normal me in Agares form, and my demon strength is a match for her angel strength. Or her dark phoenix strength. Or the whatever-the-fuck-Sayah-is-now strength.

I cling to my resolve like it's my last breath before sinking under a dark ocean. "*No!* I will not lose you, Sayah. I know you're in there. I need you to come back to me."

The look in her eye is enough to make me think all I needed to get her back was my voice and eyes.

Then she slaps me.

"My name is Estreaya. Quit calling me Sayah. And let me the fuck down."

An angry retort scuttles up the back of my throat, but I snap my mouth around the thought's sharp point. I clench my jaw and square my shoulders as a waft of steam from Seraphyra's disapproving snout congeals the air before us. My desperation to get my Sayah back winds me so tight I'm certain one tap will surely shatter me.

As I search her eyes for any glimmer, something surges through my veins that makes me nauseous and cold. Before I have the chance to do anything at all, that rush of boiling blood ignites the swirling golden tattoo, shocking my nervous system. My breaths come short, sharp, and fast; the terrible tremble that shook me before re-surges with a vengeance.

She must feel it, too, for her eyes dart to the tattoo on her arm, the symbols lighting up our dark before exploding outward, somehow knocking her unconscious. She goes limp in my arms, and her eyes close. The dark, way-too-fucking-long lashes cover her cheeks like a dark curtain of mystery. Her lips —painted black—slacken and turn into a frown, and her head lulls to the side. I turn her around and tug her close to me.

What the fuck was that?

Above the chaos, Tallyn appears beside me, her voice cutting through the roar of dragons and fire. "To Nightshade Castle!" she shouts, urgency in every word.

"What? Why?"

"It's Hattie!" she yells back. "She's there—she got caught in the spell line. If we don't get to her now, she's as good as dead!"

Tallyn zooms off, and Seraphyra pivots sharply, her wings slicing through the air as we follow her toward Nightshade Castle.

Laureya rears back, her crystalline tail smashing into the frozen remains of a dark fae warrior as she turns to defend the retreat. Behind her, Wynter darts upward, her snowy form a blur of white against the destruction.

The wind tears at my face as Seraphyra beats her massive

wings, carrying us higher into the smoke-filled sky. Sayah is still in my arms, her body limp, her breaths shallow but steady. Not only was she about to explode when Laureya's ice storm had stopped her and the volatile new power tearing through her, but she was drained, and fragile from whatever-the-fuck just happened between her and me and these marks on our arms.

Not fragile like a flower.

Fragile like a bomb.

I push Seraphyra harder until we approach the jagged stone ledge jutting out from the side of Nightshade Castle. And that's when I see her—my mom, stepping out of a darkened archway with something cradled in her arms.

My stomach drops as I realize it's Hattie, but she's barely recognizable. Her once short, dark, and spikey hair is now long and white, her skin thin and sagging, and her frail frame looks like it could crumble under the weight of a breeze.

Mom's expression is grim, her sharp features etched with worry. She strides toward the balcony's edge, her massive blue dragon crouching low with its wings spread wide, waiting.

I pull Seraphyra alongside the ledge and leap down, careful not to jostle Sayah.

"Mom!" I shout over the wind, my voice urgently tight. "What happened to her?"

She keeps moving, her voice tight and urgent. "She was thrown into a room full of mirrors—looks like Sayah's old quarters. The spell line must have misfired and dumped her here, and those cursed mirrors aged her. Bash, she's over two hundred years old. She's barely hanging on."

I glance toward the open windows from which my mom emerged. The scent of Sayah wafts from that room, so intense it nearly crumples me. Even from here, the mirrors glint wildly, covering every inch of the large room.

It's almost like Trystan programmed this to happen. He knew, at some point, vampires would come to get Sayah. So he filled her room with mirrors, knowing damn well we wouldn't have ours with us in this realm, let alone be able to send Hattie here to spell any.

My mom reaches her dragon, and carefully hands Hattie to my dad's awaiting arms. He sets her in front of him and then holds it out for my mom. Grabbing hold, she hoists herself up behind him. Their dragon lets out a low rumble before unfurling her massive wings. With a powerful leap, she launches into the air.

I turn back to Tallyn, hovering in the wind, her gaze fixed on me.

"Sayah?" she asks, her voice softer now.

"She's alive," I mutter, looking at her draped over the massive back of my dragon. "But whatever happened today nearly killed her. All of it."

Tallyn's eyes flick toward the horizon, where the chaos of battle still rages. "We don't have much time. Laureya's ice won't hold forever, and neither will she."

I nod, and Seraphyra lets out a huff of smoke as I climb back on.

Tallyn speeds off into the sky.

Seraphyra shifts beneath me, her wings spreading wide. I glance down at Sayah, her face pale, her body too still.

"Hold on, Sayah," I whisper. "We're almost there."

With a powerful beat of her wings, Seraphyra carries us away from this wretched place.

"Where do we go now?" I ask Tallyn when we catch up to her.

"The Shadow Gate was destroyed, but we can portal into the gardens," Tallyn answers. "We just need to get far enough out, as I don't want the Never fae to have access to the gardens."

Silence ebbs as we cruise, the sounds of battle fading among the wingbeats.

In my peripheral, I spot Henry gliding on the clouds next to my dragon like a seagull in the wind. He laughs, pointing. "Look at Hattie."

"Stop," I tell him, my stomach sinking, which is weird for me. But watching her silver hair blow in the wind while she lays unconscious on my parents' dragon has me feeling a certain type of way for her.

Sayah is slumped on my chest. I'm securing her with my arms, which are still not quite mine, making sure to keep Agares's strength not only to hold her on me, but also to ensure that if she wakes up, I can keep her on my dragon.

I have no idea what to do with her.

She's completely lost her mind.

A ripple in the boundary line lets us know we are far enough away from the Nightshade perimeter, and Tallyn lands us all in a field where Halcyon opens the portal for us to enter.

When we return to the Light Gate Portal, Tallyn flutters to the ground.

"We need to be able to portal back to Feylight," she tells Seraphyra. "I know there is no portal magick aside from what we just did and to Wyndhallow, but I need to get us back to my castle and get Sayah secured with boundaries. Trystan, now married to her, will stop at nothing to get her back."

"Wai-wai-wai-wait a minute," I say, holding Sayah closer. "They didn't complete the ceremony, right? I mean, the damn portal shattered for Odin's sake."

"They are still married in the eyes of the fae," Tallyn says, taking her wings to the air to flutter up next to me. She pulls Sayah's left arm up and shows me the green vine tattoos that now mar her skin. "They pretty much completed it. It wasn't a full kiss, so the Shadow Gate Portal exploded, but still opened something. A sliver of Desoloth. And he needs to consummate the marriage to her to get the rest of the way open. That is the loophole in opening Desoloth. His marriage to her and their consummation negates the entire 'purity' stipulation because they just married light and dark. But not completely. Their souls are on the surface level, not the soul level."

Hackles on the back of me raise up. "So he needs to fuck my woman in order to open Desoloth all the way? And you're *just now fucking telling me this?*"

A rage unlike any other—worse than all the other times Agares has taken over—makes me want to rip her to shreds.

"Sebastian, this is why I didn't tell you. I needed you calm. Chill." She flutters back down to the ground, and she's fucking lucky because I'm fucking ready to rip—

Bash. Chill, says Seraphyra, like she's my fucking mommy, too, now.

I am not your mommy, she answers.

"We can fix this," Tallyn reassures, walking back toward the mound the Light Gate sits upon. "But we need to get Feylight. Now."

You have my permission to use your portal to get us to Feylight, Seraphyra tells her, though I can hear it, too.

Tallyn bows her head. "Thank you. Halcyon, prepare the portal."

Halcyon does his thing, and just like fucking that, I'm whirling through space and time again.

36

METRONOME OF FATALITY

—DOM—

Beams of light begin to register behind my eyes. A piercing headache beyond anything I've ever known racks my brain. I feel as though my actual skull is breaking apart and brain matter is spilling through the cracks.

I try to open an eye, but the light is so blinding it makes the headache worse.

I'm vaguely aware I've been in this cold room for some time, but my daydreams of my life with normal Sayah and normal me have kept the madness from taking over.

A haunting melody of wind sweeps through this cold chamber I lie in, a place where the silence speaks.

A burial chamber.

I know I'm in a burial chamber because I can hear the whispers of the ghosts through the cracks in the walls. The whispers split my mind, caress me like a wraith coming to taste my death, while the spirits play spoons on my bones.

Living between life and death is the most mind-bending awareness I've ever experienced.

I know I died.

I felt my death.

On the balcony with Sayah, while still under Tallyn's spell, I felt her warlock control my sentences, move my tongue to intrigue Sayah, and make her believe I wasn't in love with her anymore, and I wanted to be with Tallyn.

I was in a cage inside my own mind, and I couldn't stop it.

Mederio first held me hostage in a rundown shack in Never, draining my blood over and over again to it send to Trystan for his creation of the dark fae. Mederio didn't just take my blood—he plunged deep into my soul, piercing every hidden corner, and shattering me completely.

The experience broke me in ways no man should ever be broken.

Or woman.

Or anyone.

That's what made me snap.

I snapped and turned into the monster they needed me to be, slaughtering innocent people, rotting my soul, and corrupting Mederio's to the point where he was able to open even the most corrosive and demonic portals that one could ever imagine.

On this murder spree, I was instructed—no, no, commanded —to murder a witch named Celestina; my body moved of not my own accord.

I arrived at her hut in the woods and found her sitting in front of a stone fireplace. There was some sort of weird altar around her, but I didn't care. I was out for blood.

In a rapid gust of wind, I careened up to her neck, high from the last victim I'd killed.

But instead of finding Celestina, what I found was Tallyn.

The mirage of Celestina sitting in a chair before the stone fireplace evaporated and Tallyn materialized, blowing a bright yellow powder directly into my face.

The high from the last kill faltered; the potency of the powder knocked me to my knees.

The demonic wraith that'd taken over my body bowed to the newly injected magick and blended with it, allowing it to remain inside of me, and I arose anew.

Tallyn had put me in the cage the moment I went dark for Mederio after Bash consumed all the blood I had needed to keep me from that dark—from that ravine I knew I would eventually plummet into.

I thought nothing of the witch I'd come to kill, nor the powder, and went onto my killing spree. Tallyn would summon me to Luminara here and there, and I'd oblige, following the Whispering Leaves, and letting her drain my blood over and over again.

Tallyn had control over me, but she let Mederio think he still did, giving her intel and coordinates and saving conversations I'd overheard between Mederio and Trystan. She saved them in a jar, a bottle of memories and whispers she could pull out and play in a swirling word tornado at any time.

She was also the one who had control of my body when I went to break up with Sayah.

Mederio had sent me on a mission to kill a family of three in the same area, so he didn't even notice the little detour I took when Tallyn had the portal send me into Sayah's room.

This continued, on and on and on . . .

Until the night the bond with Mederio had broken.

I felt it snap like a twig.

But instead of coming back to the real me, the Dom I've always been, I was panicked, knowing I had to get to Feylight to see Tallyn. Anxiety riddled my bones and hitched my breath. I was lost in the unfamiliar forest, looking for a door I knew not how to find.

When a waterfall in the distance sang to me.

I could feel the vibrations of the plants, each one singing its own melody, guiding me to the waterfall at the edge of spring.

Once I stepped onto the rocks before the waterfall, a stairway opened, leading me down to Luminara.

Tallyn greeted me at the end of the tunnel, and seeing her brought me all the joy in my heart. Seeing her made me feel how I would feel now if Sayah had walked into the room.

I felt the version of myself she had trapped within me, caged by her yellow powder, imprisoning the real me inside my own body.

She took me to her castle in Feylight, riding on the pegasus to get there; I had followed her along blithely, knowing nothing of the horror and torture she was about to impose on me.

Once in her castle, she took me to her dungeon, where she marked me with a magick golden rune that imprinted me to one of her warlocks.

This warlock was a dusty blue, a small nymph with black eyes, trees, and flowers growing out of her hair. She was ordered to drain me, to bleed me dry, to fuck with my mind, and psychologically torture me until I broke.

And again, the vampire was broken.

The warlock twisted my mind, convincing me I loved Tallyn —that I wanted to be with her instead of Sayah. She would invade my thoughts with her torturous black fingernail, dragging it through fire and stabbing it into my brain, embedding false emotions deep into the neurons where feelings are born. The part of me still caged within wept and bled as they reshaped me into this new monster. Tallyn infused her own blood into me, a cruel lifeline to keep me tethered to her will. All to stop the ravine from fully consuming my soul and driving me to madness.

They didn't let me go until I actually believed I was not in love with Sayah.

The night I saw her again, I felt a flicker of a memory, a fluttering wave. But Tallyn snuffed it out, and she and her warlock controlled everything I did.

Until the spear of thorns pierced my heart and gave me the gift of an epic death.

I remember seeing thorns crawling up the balcony behind Sayah and me inside the cage, communicating with my eyes as they went wide, trying to get Sayah to see me inside and run.

And then came the pain.

In the centuries I've been alive, I've experienced pain a mortal could never imagine. Transitioning alone was one of the worst, and I've died a thousand different times in a million different ways, but none a true death of a vampire.

The true death of a vampire is when our darkness bleeds out.

The spear of thorns Trystan had run me through was magicked with the worst spell. The kind of spell that prevents a supernatural from healing and dies for real.

But that wasn't the painful part.

Feeling my immortality crack open the ravine of centuries of memories, filling my empty, dark madness with peril and poison, hearing my heart slow and my breathing thin . . .

Still wasn't the painful part.

The painful part was when the yellow poison keeping me ensconced in my own body and brain lassoed to the flora and fauna that held me aloft in a simmering shadow, tying my body to the soil of Feylight, not letting my soul detach from my body.

I had been in a limbo called The Gloaming, a darkness between life and death, where no one is really alive, but no one is close to death either, and every second feels like an eternity. My body had been frozen in death, soul sizzling while tied to immortality and mortality, the tether a fabric made from the souls of beings trapped in The Gloaming forever, whispering and deteriorating and eviscerating my mind.

That was the pain.

I have no idea how long I've been in The Gloaming for, as, like I said, time is rapidly slow. Living one second here is like living a thousand seconds on Earth.

Forever ticks by like a metronome of fatality.

I've been aware of Tallyn's presence with me when she comes to feed me blood.

I heard my mother's sobs along with my sisters' as they cried at my pyre.

I felt the hardened armor of my father crack when he saw me, gray and frozen, unmoving on my tomb.

I watched from the air, walls, and sky, as I am air right now, tethered to my body.

It has let me wander; that is how I've been speaking to Bash. But I am always tied to my frozen body, never allowed to enter the gates into the next lifetime I may live or back to the one I had before.

But cracking my eye open and being able to feel light—to feel the numbness of death release its icy grip for a minuscule second, if only to feel the brain-racking headache—is a welcome change from the black-and-white life I've been living thus far.

I don't know what any of it means.

But I feel her.

I felt her since her dark presence entered Feylight.

Sayah.

Her aura speaks a language to my shadows, and they smile at her presence here. Only, she's darker now; shadows overwhelm her light and sends shivers along my reviving limbs.

Right now is the first time I've been back in my body since I died and been able to feel it.

I have no breath yet, though.

No heartbeat.

I cannot move anything at all.

I'm still frozen in this in-between.

All I know is that Sayah's presence here in Feylight broke

whatever spell Tallyn had me under and pulled me back to my body.

And this moment right now is the first time since I went dark that I actually want to live.

To live and see her.

37

A DARK DECISION

—BASH—

"And you think locking her up in a cell is the best fucking solution?" I ask Tallyn as we regroup in one of her oversized sitting rooms, the air thick with tension.

"As volatile and possessed as she is right now? Yes, I do," Tallyn replies, pouring herself a silver-tinted drink with her usual detached calm.

"The shackles?" I press, stepping closer, and swiping the glass from her hand before she can take a sip. Her stank face barely fazes me. "Those were Trystan's doing, right? To keep her from using her powers?"

Tallyn narrows her eyes, the irritation at losing her drink settling on her face as she pours another. "Yes, and I think we should leave them on for now. At least until we figure out how to free her from the spell he's cast and sever the bond he managed to trap her with."

"My queen." Thalira sidles up to Tallyn and makes a point to graze her oversized chest against my arm in another one of her unsubtle attempts at seduction. "It seems there is some . . . trouble."

Tallyn's expression darkens. "Trouble with what?"

Thalira hesitates, her gaze flicking to me and sweeping it over the others in the room as though calculating what she can reveal. "It appears that, despite the Shadow Gate exploding, the wedding ceremony partially succeeded. I've received telepathic reports of absolute chaos erupting in the mortal realm."

Tallyn grabs Thalira's glittery pink arm, her composure slipping. "What sort of chaos?"

"Shit's real fucked-up," Henry chimes in, startling me so badly I nearly choke on my drink. I spit the liquid out—straight into his face—but it passes through him like mist as he is incorporeal once again.

"Like how fucked-up?" I manage, glaring at him while wiping my chin. The ones who can't see him shoot me puzzled looks.

Tallyn glances over her shoulder at me with a raised brow.

"Real bad, Sebastian," she answers grimly, her voice low and ominous.

Thalira and Tallyn deliver grim updates on the gates ripping through Earth and the destruction unfolding in real time.

"That's not all," Thalira says after detailing the apocalyptic events. Her gaze shifts to Tallyn. "Your subject in the tomb below . . ."

A heavy silence spreads through the room as my mom stiffens. She doesn't know about The Gloaming—or that Dom has been kept there.

Yet.

"What about it?" Tallyn's voice is sharp, her wary gaze flicking between my mom and dad.

Thalira hesitates, the weight of her words palpable. "When the dark phoenix crossed the boundary, it seems to have . . ."

"It what?" Tallyn snaps.

Thalira takes a breath, her tone grim. "It pulled his soul back into his body."

The room erupts.

"What?" my mom's furious voice slices through the air as she flashes forward, stopping mere inches from Tallyn. "Are you talking about my son?"

I step back, shaking my head at the explosion of emotions. "You better tell her," I mutter, retreating to a chair by the fire.

While Tallyn struggles to explain Dominic's imprisonment, I lose myself in the flames, their flicker a mirror of the chaos in my head. The heat doesn't reach me, but the question burns: How the hell am I going to break Trystan's spell and get Sayah back?

"Hey, you."

"Odin's ghost!" I flinch, clutching the chair at Hattie's sudden appearance in a Henry-style sneak attack. She's still got her speed, strength, and all that supernatural flair, but the centuries have made her look ancient.

"Am I really that hideous?" she asks, lowering herself onto the arm of my chair. Her withered claws—long, white, and sharp—pick at imaginary dirt as her gaze shifts to me.

"No," I lie. "Hey, is there any way to reverse your mirror spell?"

Her face falls, sadness etched into every line. "I don't know if there is. I'll have to dig into it once this war is over."

"*And you're just now fucking telling me?*" My mom's enraged scream cuts through our conversation, making us both jump.

I see her flashing out of the room, with Tallyn chasing her.

"What's going on?" Henry asks, suddenly beside Hattie, sitting as if he belongs.

"Oh, hey, little dude. Where'd you come from?"

I nearly gasp. "You can see him?"

"Why wouldn't I?" Hattie shrugs, her ancient claws gleaming as she waves him off.

Henry smirks and winks at her, clearly enjoying himself.

Everyone else bolts after my mom. With a sigh, I stand to follow, winding toward the tomb I know we're headed for.

"Dom's still alive," I mutter, addressing no one and everyone.

"What?" Hattie's shocked tone slows me momentarily as Scarlet blurs past us, her desperation visible in her speed. The world's winds seem to carry her forward, driving her toward her twin.

"Tallyn's been keeping him in The Gloaming with her cursed fairy magick. She's just now spilling the truth."

"Dom's alive?" Hattie echoes.

"Apparently." I push my power forward, accelerating to catch up with the others.

When we reach the tomb chambers, I see my brother for the first time since that fateful night he died.

He's lying on a slab of cold, polished marble, in the center of a vast, echoing chamber, dedicated to the royal dead. Soil fills the cracks between the stone ground, allowing for glowing flowers to sprout from every crevice of dirt. Their intoxicating scent resembles night-blooming jasmine and fresh rain.

Shadows flicker and dance across the walls, cast by the myriads of tall, narrow candles surrounding the marble slab. Their flames waver and bend as a cold wind slips through the room, stirred by our arrival.

Alcoves line the walls, each holding a tomb of a long-dead fae king, queen, or princess—someone of importance enough to be entombed here. The tombs are carved from dark stone and adorned with intricate bas-reliefs of their deeds and reigns, some chipped and weathered by time. Between the alcoves, faded murals stretch high up to the arched ceiling, depicting battles, coronations, and mythic beasts intertwined with creeping vines, as if nature itself had encroached upon this sacred ground.

The ceiling, far above, is lost in shadows. Still, faint glimpses reveal an ancient mosaic depicting a constellation of stars that seem to shift and change when the candlelight flickers, as if telling the stories of the rulers entombed below. The atmosphere is heavy, filled with a palpable silence, broken only by the distant water drip echoing somewhere in the tomb's depths, like the steady heartbeat of the forgotten.

Like the rest of the castle and Feylight, a giant looming tree trunk occupies the far end of the room. The branches, leaves, and vines hang, almost long enough to touch the floor in places.

Glowing moths shimmer as they flutter throughout the chamber, glimmering with twilight colors. Like butterflies, they feed on the flora surrounding the place, thousands of them milling about.

Large black ravens with feathers tipped in silver and indigo mimic the sounds of the dead's voices, drinking from the pools of moonlit water interspersed throughout the place.

Dominic lies motionless, his skin a cold, cement gray that contrasts starkly with the black clothing he's wearing. His hands are neatly folded over his stomach, and magickal artifacts surround him like a sacred ritual. His dark, spiked hair looks perfect—almost unnervingly so, as if someone had just prepared him for burial.

My mom races to his side, collapsing next to him, and cradling his face with trembling hands. "He doesn't look alive to me, Tallyn," she says, her voice breaking.

My dad kneels beside her, pressing his ear to Dominic's chest, straining to hear even the faintest heartbeat or catch the subtlest breath.

Tallyn, ever composed, folds her arms. "He's in The Gloaming," she explains once more. "Neither alive nor dead. His soul was tethered to his body through magick that braided him to Feylight. But when Sayah entered Feylight's boundary, her presence pulled his soul back into his body."

"What the fuck does that even mean?" I demand, dread

twisting my gut. The thought of having to fight my brother again—for the love of my existence—is almost too much.

Tallyn shakes her head, her calm exterior faltering. "I don't know what it means."

"Well, what do we do now? How do we wake him?" Mom pleads, lifting Dominic's arm, and then watching it drop limply like a sleeper's. His sleeve falls back, revealing something startling.

"What's this?" Mom leans closer to inspect the shadowy markings that twist over his hand like spilled ink. It's darker and denser than Sayah's swirling shadows, blanketing his left hand entirely. It looks like a macabre form of reverse vitiligo.

"Shadowmarked," Tallyn answers tersely. "It means he's been kissed by the void and will carry its mark forever."

My dad rises, his eyes narrowing as he steps toward her. "That's not an explanation. What does it actually mean?"

Tallyn exhales sharply, finally elaborating. "The shadowmark binds him to the void's essence. It strengthens him, but it's a tether to darkness. The void will claim him entirely if he dies again in this realm."

Mom's expression hardens as she rolls up Dominic's sleeve further, revealing the shadows snaking up his arm. "So we just keep him alive. That's it?"

Tallyn hesitates—a pause pregnant with unspoken truths. "Essentially, yes."

Fucking fae. I fight the urge to roll my eyes. There's always more to their answers than they're willing to admit.

"But how do we bring him back from this?" Dad asks, glancing uneasily at the eerie chamber around us.

The room hums with unspoken energy. Whispers crawl along my spine, faint voices that seem to echo from nowhere.

He's cute, one says.

They're vampires, Esmella. Shut up, scolds another.

A third voice pipes up, youthful and teasing as it says, *I like the blonde one.*

They're not going to take Dom from us, are they? a childlike whisper asks, the words laced with fear.

I shake off the haunting murmurs and focus on the conversation.

"I've already told you," Tallyn says. "The magick I used to tether him to The Gloaming was powerful. If we bring him back without care, I don't know what it will do to him, especially since he's a vampire."

"What's your suggestion?" Mom asks, replacing Dominic's sleeve to let his arm rest.

Tallyn hesitates again, but I cut in, my patience frayed. "She wants Sayah to use her phoenix power to bring him back," I say, stepping away as a ghostly figure drifts too close for comfort.

Tallyn shoots me a warning look.

"Sayah?" Mom's eyes widen as she rises to her feet. "Do you think she'll even agree, given her current state?"

"So many questions," Tallyn mutters, turning on her heel.

But my mom isn't done. In a blur of motion, she intercepts Tallyn, gripping her throat with unrelenting force. "You've already taken one child from me, Tallyn," she growls, her voice trembling. "You owe me this."

Dad is beside her instantly, his hands on her shoulders, radiating calm. "Let her go," he encourages.

Tallyn wrenches herself free, glaring. "I owe you nothing!" Her tone is cold enough to cut glass.

My mom hisses, her fangs elongating, but Ollie steps in. "Mom, chill."

Tallyn straightens her collar, her voice tight with irritation. "To get Sayah to help, we'd need to sever her connection to Trystan. She can't be the dark phoenix when she resurrects him."

"And how exactly do we do that?" I ask, my interest finally piqued.

Tallyn's face darkens, her usual composure replaced by grim seriousness. "Sayah has to die."

38

WEIGH DOWN MY SKELETON

—BASH—

The force with which I stand and am in Tallyn's face is definitely from Agares to some degree.

"Come again, sparkles?" I say, feeling my eyes whiten, and my talons threaten to explode my fingers. I have a hold of Tallyn's elbow, not even realizing it. "What the fuck do you mean, my girlfriend has to die?"

Scarlet scoffs, still standing over Dominic's lifeless body. "Your girlfriend?"

"Not now, Scarlet," Adaline scolds.

Tallyn shrugs out of my grip. "Sebastian, please. We have so very little time to move. The fact the Desoloth portal is even open means Trystan has six and a half portals he needs to open to get into Feylight. We successfully got our boundary lines working again, but with Desoloth even a fraction of the way open, means he's probably figuring out a way to get in here to get to her." She moves away from me and over to the fireplace, her tattered cape flowing behind her.

"But I thought the whole point of crashing the wedding and stopping the 'consummation'"—gah, even the word makes me gag along with the thought of Sayah fucking Trystan—"would stop the portal from being opened completely."

"Yes," she resumes, tightening the halter on her thigh with her weapons. "He needs to seal the union to get Desoloth all the way open to take over Feylight. But even a fraction of the opening of a portal like Desoloth set off a cataclysmic chain of events, opening every portal imaginable on Earth." She situates herself in a chair and takes a deep breath. "Most likely, his focus will be on getting Sayah back to finish the union, while his lieutenants and generals and highly trained and deadly army will begin to make an army of dark fae on Earth, readying him for the usurpation of myself and Feylight."

"What happens once he has Feylight?" asks Kaston, who has been relatively quiet since Draelle passed away.

"Trystan will then have the power to be the king of this realm and any others he so pleases."

"We really need to get moving," Halcyon says, his black uniform, and armor clanging as he approaches her. "We don't know how much time we have."

"He's burning the world down to get her back," Sariana says, standing by one of the markers of a tomb with a fae king named Lienikar.

The retinue in the room goes quiet.

When no one speaks for a few minutes, I clear my throat, and move closer to Sariana. "And how, pray tell, dear sister, do you know this?"

Sariana eyeballs me, and I swear her eyes flash purple.

The fuck? Again?

"Why do your eyes do that?" I say, walking up to her, and pointing my finger in her face.

"Do what?" she plays dumb.

"That's the second time I saw your eyes flash purple, like Jasantha's."

Jasantha makes a noncommittal noise and continues walking around the tomb chamber, reading the names and dates.

"Sariana," Tallyn interludes, "has shardweaving as a power." My brows stitch together, and I'm about to say the snarkiest comment flooding my mind, but Tallyn holds up her hand to shush me. "Shardweavers hold the power to manipulate, mend, or command things that are broken, whether physical objects, emotions, souls, or even realities. She can sense that everything broken carries a fragment of its original state and potential transformation, so she can harness those fragments, weaving them into something new, beautiful, or dangerous. She can sense when something is broken, and her eyes will turn purple."

"Hoe-lee-fuck," I say, realizing the potential catastrophic leverage we may hold against Trystan now.

"So she can sense that, what, Trystan is breaking the world?" Hattie asks, and her appearance still gets me every time, even though her voice sounds the same.

"Yes," Tallyn says. It's a withered yes, so it's giving "she's not saying the full meaning of the things she's saying" vibe.

"Doesn't this also pose as a priceless asset Trystan may want to fix the Shadow Gate?" Claire asks, leaning against Ollie as he holds her from behind.

"Precisely," Tallyn states.

"Can we please get back to the part where you want to kill my girlfriend?" I say, not giving a fuck about pencil dick Trystan and his stupid fucking shadow portal. He can burn the fucking world down for all I care, as long as I get Sayah and me and my family out of his way first.

"If we sever Sayah's life, we sever the connection Trystan now has on her," Tallyn resumes. "We have another Phoenix who can rise her from the ashes. If we do this, if we kill her and then rise her, she can use her phoenix power to rise Dom, and then we can get back to saving the fucking world." Her voice holds a heave of exasperation.

"This is too much," Laureya breathes, having been quiet in a corner this entire time.

"Too much for who, darling?" Sariana asks, condescension coating her voice like chocolate.

"All of this!" She waves her arms around. "The Shadow Gate exploding, the world breaking, the fucking fact we have to save the fucking world, not to mention kill my sister, hope I can revive her, so she can revive Dom, so we can go to war, and then go help some fucking dragons kill whatever-the-fuck those things are. What if I can't rise her? What then?"

"And why can't we just have Laureya rise, Dom?" Thalira asks.

"Because of the demonic nature of Laureya's blood," Tallyn answers, exasperated. "Look, I know it's a lot. But we're running out of time. Now whoever the fuck thinks they can get Sayah to trust them enough to let her out so we can take her shackles off and kill her, please speak up."

Agares grumbles something fierce in my bones, and I light up.

"Anyone touches her, and they will fucking die," I say in Agares's voice.

I will rip the world in two, crack it open, and dig around for any other alternate than losing her, to find any other answer to this maddening riddle.

"Bash," my mom says, flashing up to me. "We can do this. We won't let her die. We need her to save the world. She's in there somewhere. Do you think you can go down there and talk to her?"

"I want no part in this," I grunt, moving away from my mom's touch.

Desperation weighs my skeleton down to the depths of my monster, and another emotion I am unfamiliar with creeps up its center.

Fear.

What if Laureya cannot rise her?

If I were to lose Sayah, I would not be able to continue living. I cannot live in a world that Sayah doesn't exist in.

"Bash," my mom pleads.

"No. Leave me be," I say and flash off, following the only essence keeping me from becoming and staying Agares.

39

MOTHER TO MOTHER

—ESTREAYA—

I wake with a swallowed gasp, struggling to pull in air, It's wet—thick—and not air at all.

I'm choking.

No matter how I fight, my lungs refuse to fill. It's dark, and the sharp, metallic tang of blood overwhelms me. Swallowing the bitter sweetness pooling in my mouth, a stray thought flickers: Whatever it is, it woke me.

A groan escapes as I roll onto my side, landing heavily on a cold, unforgiving stone floor. I spit, the taste lingering.

When I glance around, the room is empty.

Another fucking dungeon.

What the actual fuck?

The surrounding walls in this dungeon are different from the one in Never.

The orb lights on the walls offer little light; the glowing embers of a strange purple paint the cell in an eerie ambiance.

The light source is mostly coming from me.

Holding out my arms, my dark phoenix skin paints my flesh with swinging shadows and lightning. A storm with skin. The vine tattoo of twirling green vines around my left arm is new, though.

Bright light flashes behind my eyes at the sight of the vines, and everything comes rushing back to me—Nyx, our heated exchange, the rape, becoming the dark phoenix, my rage, the acceptance of my destiny, the new feelings I acquired for Trystan, the excitement about being the Queen of Never and Feylight and Earth, the wedding, the emergence of our fates, almost sealing the deal with a kiss ill-fated and cut short, the explosion of the Shadow Gate.

And Bash.

Fucking Bash has to ruin everything. He swooped me up in his demon form onto a dragon and stole me away from Trystan. From Nyx.

Getting up requires more strength than it should. My mind is heavy, my bones are full of lead, and my muscles are sore and achy from whatever those bloodsuckers did to me to get me to stop fighting.

I hate all of them.

"Hello?" I call out into the darkness, the echo of my voice ricocheting off the walls, bouncing down the empty tunnels, wrapping around, and coming back to me.

My wedding dress still envelops me; the butterflies must have all fled on the journey here, but the clouds still wisp around the train. I feel my hair for my veil, which is also gone.

My beautiful black diamond wedding ring rests on my finger.

"Trystan," I say aloud, hoping he can hear me somehow. Saying his name sends shivers along my spine, and my vines tingle, as though his vines feel my plea and he is responding to me somehow.

I feather my fingertips along the vines and whisper to them. *If you can hear me, I'm alive and safe. I don't know exactly where I'm at, but I imagine it's Feylight Castle.*

Walking up to the bars of the cell, the heels I still have on click-clacking along the flagstone, I grab hold of the bars and try to pull.

Summoning my phoenix power, every ounce of magick I have left in my body, I try to spread my wings of fire, to exude the strength of the dark phoenix—anything that will get me the hell out of here and . . . nothing happens.

I still have the damn shackle on my wrist and ankle.

Why would Trystan have left it on me even on our wedding day? How the fuck do I get it off?

"*Hello!*" I scream again into the dungeon's darkness, knowing someone must be standing guard to make sure I don't try to escape.

"*Sebastian!*" I yell, hoping he'll think I'm back to being me again and come running to rescue me.

But no one comes.

"*Fuck!*"

I yank off a heel and hurl it across the room. Its sharp crack hits the stone wall, echoing in the silence. The other follows suit, flung with all the force I can muster. The act releases a fraction of my fury, but it's nowhere near enough to extinguish the wildfire burning inside me. Everyone is trying to own me. Chain me. Control me. Expecting me to carry the weight of their world and mine. Trying to get me to do everything. Fucking everything for everyone.

A scream claws its way up my throat, and I let it rip free, raw and unrelenting, like the sky's roar during a thunderstorm, reminding everyone that even the sky must scream sometimes. The shadows laced through my bones, the fire coursing through my blood, the vines etched on my skin, and every fractured piece of my armor surge out in that scream, shaking the walls that imprison me.

Tears fall from my eyes as the keening crescendos, and I find my way back to my cot, sinking to my knees before it and burying my face in my hands. The storm within me is finally given its voice.

I don't even know who I am anymore.

I don't know what I want.

My mind is a battlefield—a clash of chaos and calm. I want everything for my son, yet I'm tangled in the memories of falling in love: first with Dom, then Bash, and now, most recently, Trystan. My love for Dom and Bash feels like it's been locked away, sealed in an iron-clad safe, and cast into a bottomless lake. I can sense it, but it's out of reach, suffocating in the depths.

Different versions of me are warring within, each vying for dominance. For so long, I lived for others—a chronic people-pleaser obsessed with meeting expectations and molding myself to fit what others wanted me to be.

I hate that me.

I refuse to be her anymore.

The person I became—when Trystan's cruel, narcissistic grip shattered the last remnants of my softness—is something else entirely. She's fierce, unyielding, and armored against the world. I buried the love I once had for the vampires alongside that softer version of myself, irretrievable and gone for good.

Now, I am a storm-wearing skin, relentless and unstoppable. I will give my son the world I want for myself—the world I've fought for, the world I've earned.

"Trystan, come find me," I whisper to the vines, and they sway in response.

"Sayah," a familiar voice answers.

Turning to face the entrance to my cell, the very woman who stole my best friend from me is standing there. Adaline, looking battle-worn and beaten, glares directly into my eyes, speaking my dead name like I owe her any kind of response.

"The fuck you want?" I grouse.

I like this new me.

The old me would have never spoken to her like this.

Her warrior facade cracks, and her eyes widen. "Sayah?"

"Estreaya," I correct her, standing, and striding over to her. "I'm not who I used to be."

Her gray eyes narrow on me. "Estreaya?" she asks, more like she's trying on the name than accepting that it is.

"Yes." I'm eye to eye with her now, and the darkness blanketing me furrows, like heckles rising, "What *the fuck* do you want?" I ask again.

"Darkness is becoming on you, darling," she says, tilting her head to get a better look at me.

"You killed my parents." The shackle at my wrist burns with my grief, capable of blowing up the world if I let it out.

Her face falls in questioning. "What?"

A laugh escapes my lips. "Act like you don't know, Adaline. I'd love to see your acting skills."

She moves away from the bars, her face in quiet contemplation. "Sayah—"

"Estreaya."

"Estreaya," she replies. "What are you referring to?"

"You know exactly what the fuck I'm referring to," I deadpan, the embers of my skin glowing brighter, the shadows swirling like the volatile storm I am. "You knew there was some fucked-up prophecy to kill my family—the witches with daughters—so you sent Dom to burn down my mom's house; knowing it was *my* family you sent him to kill."

An expression similar to the resurfacing of a memory flashes across her face. "Sayah, I didn't know it was your mom—"

"*Estreaya!*" I shout, the burning shackle on my ankle causing an ache.

"Estreaya. I did not know it was you. Your mom. I only knew of an address and a last name. I made no connection to it until Dom called me the day you found out it was he who burned your family alive. I never would have made that decision if I had known." Sorrowful rage soaks the admission, as if it's taking everything in her to admit she was wrong.

Another laugh escapes my lips. "You know fucking well you would have most definitely made that decision if you had known. I get that you'd stop at nothing to save your children. I'd do the same fucking thing for Gauge. I'd murder you and everyone you loved if you became even the slightest threat to my child. But that doesn't change the fact that you killed my *mom!*" The last word comes out unsteadily. I'm fighting the tears threatening to rip me apart.

Adaline lets out a sigh. "I did. I killed your family in the hopes it'd save mine." Her voice is soft toward me. Unusually so. "But that also doesn't make it okay. I took away your mama, and for that, I am truly sorry, Say—Estreaya. I would do anything to give you your mama back."

There is light in the dark, my mother's voice whispers, calming my storm, easing the fire and shadows back into my bones.

I look at Adaline, still fucking pissed, but relieved it's finally out there. "I can never forgive you for taking her from me. Ever."

"I understand that, Estreaya, I really do. There's nothing I can ever do to change what I've done."

"What do you want, Adaline?"

"The world is burning. Without your help, there will be no home to go back to. The home your child lives in is being threatened, and we need you to help stop it."

Gauge.

His face is enough to peel back my skin and open my ribs to unleash the furious tornado loving a child with your whole soul creates. My powers scratch against that storm, begging me to set them free to save my child's world.

"What do I have to do?"

"Dom's alive," she says, and the cold, hard words pierce me like an arrow, but like an arrow into an ice storm. Something registers that those words should be something I know the shape of, like happiness, relief, or excitement, but instead, they fall flat, scattering on the floor beneath me.

"And?"

Adaline tilts her head, watching me with a deep wariness. "I know you love Bash. And learning that Dom is alive probably creates mixed emotions, but we need him alive to stop Trystan from taking Feylight."

"I don't love Bash," I state dryly. "I'm married to Trystan. I'm loyal only to him. I'll do nothing of the sort that goes against my destiny."

She regards me with a pinch of disdain. "I know right now you think you're in love with Trystan—"

Trickles of deep, clashing emotions flood my calm. "I don't just think I'm in love with him. I am in love with him. As his queen, Gauge can fly and not have diabetes and will have legs that work—" My emotions cut me off, my chest tightens like the guilt of giving him non-working legs is a thread that is wound around each of my ribs, tugging so tight it renders me breathless.

Her gaze goes distant.

I feel a familiar pull, as if she's attempting to veilweave me. It's like trying to describe a hurricane before it makes landfall— you sense the looming devastation deep in your soul, but it's intangible, unreal until the wreckage lies scattered at your feet.

Something changes in the way she regards me.

"I get it, okay. Whatever you want." Her voice curls at the edge of each word with a smoky rasp. "We just need you to rise, Dom, to save Gauge. Then you can do whatever you want."

Coercion thickens the air like flour to a rue.

Am I being tricked here?

"What will you get out of that?"

"My child back." There's a splinter in her voice, sundering the silence, like conflicting emotions are battling for dominance. Saving her children is all she's ever wanted. "From a mother to a mother"—she reaches her hand out for me to take— "I promise you, I will help you save your son if you help me save mine."

There's always an undercurrent of danger in all of Adaline's words.

Her hand remains steady through the bars, urging me to grasp it and accept her deal.

I know I need her to get me out of here. And Gauge needs me out of here to save him.

Taking her hand, the cold of her touch shocks me at first. But it's when her smile turns predatory that I panic. A momentary wave of something I can't decipher—something that almost —*almost*—resembles compassion flits across her face until it's quickly replaced by vengeance, death, and the quest for blood.

Until I feel her shove a knife through my heart to my spine.

40

FIERY LICKS OF DEATH

—BASH—

The visceral reaction from watching my mom walk in with Sayah—head and hair dangling from her arms—is akin to a shock from an electric chair. A hot, brutal current racks me like a poisonous gas, rough and ragged and slicing me from the inside.

Scorching anger ravages me, completely unlike anything I've ever felt. Twisted and morphed and undecipherable, indiscernible from even when Agares takes over me.

Wrath. This must be what wrath feels like.

Every sound in the burial chamber echoes into a hush all at once.

The bond formed between Agares and me—a bond with the wrath of demons—explodes, and two undeniable facts collide so violently that I find myself wavering in the transition from vampire to demon.

Sayah is dead.

My mom killed the love of my existence.

Who fucking cares if Laureya can revive her or not. Who fucking cares that I knew it was what had been decided, even though I refused to be a part of it.

Those two fucking undeniable facts flick a switch, and death itself bonds to my skin, assisting in my full transition to Agares.

"Bash," I hear my dad say, but it's morphed.

"Someone grab him!" another voice shouts, but it means nothing to me.

I'm moving so fast to get to Sayah, and someone tries to pull me back, but they are flung.

Who? Not a clue.

Where? I cannot be sure.

I'm yanking Sayah from my mom's arms and rushing away with her.

"Bash!" my mom calls after me, following me into the winding tunnels of Castle Feylight.

Her voice chases me like a ghost as I let the wind be my guide, blinking through the castle, up and away from the room full of ghosts.

I don't know where I'm going, but moving at these speeds, it's hard to decipher where the walls are. The sconces on the walls become blurs of light.

I would pull her through fire if I had to, haul her from the clutches of war, from falling cities and breaking worlds.

This pain feels raw and angry, like a scream living inside me, threatening to rip me in half if I don't let it out.

I'm holding on to her like the promise I intend to keep.

Until I hit a solid wall of an invisible force and am bounced back so hard that Sayah flies out of my arms. I'm soaring through the air below her, watching her black hair and dress float above me like we're underwater.

Like we're in slow motion.

Landing on the hard stone floor with a thud, straining my neck to look around at what caused this barrier, I see Caelum standing over me, his hand held out to me.

I will rip him to shreds.

"We need to act fast to bring her back, Bash. You need to

trust us," he says, and although he's still bloodlinked to me, he seems to follow his queen's orders.

I shake away from his outstretched arm and rise to my feet, but something is twisting up my legs, bounding them with twine. Before I can do anything, Thalira is in front of me, blowing powdery shit in my face.

This time, it takes a bit longer for me to come to. I hear muffled voices and whispers, and when I open my eyes, my head is pounding so hard I have to massage my temples as I rise from the stone floor.

Sayah lies motionless on the marble slab beside Dominic, her body still and lifeless. My family gathers around them, with Laureya positioned near Sayah, her hands hovering over the fatal wound in Sayah's heart—the wound that ended her life.

"Gwylan is prepared for the healing." Tallyn's voice is instructing, cold. Indifferent. "She has Ephemeral Healing, which helps channel the ethereal energy of Feylight. It should aid Laureya in her attempts to rise Sayah."

I'm over to the group within a blink, my mom eyeing me with contempt.

"I don't know if I can do this," Laureya says, her doe-green eyes sharp with fear.

"What did Sayah do to rise me?" Ollie asks.

"She used a tear," I offer, seemingly finding some calm in the torrential rain of fury, speaking past the noose that's threatening to end me. I outstretch my arm and see it's back to the peach color of my vampire skin. "And her blood."

Laureya looks at me, and Agares growls inside. I taste smoke at the back of my throat. The urge to burn her alive is still fierce, the sweet nectar of corruption lacing my demon thoroughly, coating me in a layer of vengeance and radiant wrath. She hesitates like she's biting back an angry retort and drives her focus back down to her sister, hovering her hands over Sayah's wound and closing her eyes.

Laureya's skin isn't glowing—nothing phoenix-like taking over—and she mumbles useless fucking words.

Candles flicker in the cold tomb as we watch in tepid anticipation, waiting for her phoenix to appear.

"Nothing's happening," Claire says, panic weaving through her voice.

"Hurry the fuck up, La La," I say derisively, the growling rumbling again.

"Stop pressuring me!" Laureya shouts, keeping her eyes closed, her red lips still mumbling incantations.

"Fucking cry about something, La La, you need a tear!" I yell at her.

"She has to become the phoenix first," my mom retorts.

"How can she do that on a whim? Not being the actual phoenix?" Scarlet asks.

"You're not helping anything by pressuring her," my dad snipes at Scarlet.

"Just turn it fucking on!" I yell at Laureya.

"Bash, chill the fuck out," Hattie snaps at me.

"You know what, granny?" I say, squaring up to little ol' ancient Hattie.

"Come at me, bat boy!"

"Children!" my mom scolds us all. "None of this is helping Laureya bring Sayah back."

"Fucking hurry!" Claire yells, rushing over to Laureya, her eyes glowing like her volatile power may combust from the inside out.

I rush over to Laureya. "Need something to cry about?"

Her green eyes catch mine, and she gives me a derisive look, tickling my demon's dark needs.

"Touch her, and your insides will be on your outside," says Ryan.

The soul deficit in my bones instantly tips the scales toward that fiery wrath, and in a blink, I'm upon him, boiling over. His disheveled mop of brown hair and his stupid fucking facial hair that's barely grown in and patchy makes him look more like a teen than a man, and I almost feel bad for what I'm about to do.

I see him tremble, which doesn't help his cause since seeing people scared gets me hard.

"Or what, tough guy?" I say, shoving his chest.

His eyes whiten, and he bares his fangs, hissing at me. "I'll fuck you up, Se-Bas-tain." He draws my name out like some sort of taunt.

I laugh.

His head twists off easily, like pulling the head off a dandelion.

The sickening splintering of bone churns my hunger, and I toss his head to the ground, his body thudding to join it. I bash his head in with my heavy boots, watching his brains squirt like a grape.

"What the fuck, Bash?" Ollie scolds me, although I don't know why he thinks I'd do anything differently.

A tormented scream pierces the night. It's loud enough it could wake the dead.

Instead of focusing on Sayah, she flashes up to me, fangs out and hysterical, ready to fight.

Agares is ready, always ready to take over my body and be in full control. The talons sting as they begin to emerge, and my membranous wings cause my skin to itch where they're trying to break through my skin.

Before I let him all the way out, Ollie's calm face is in front of me, hand on my shoulder, separating me from Laureya.

His elemental power thrums through him as he uses calming, warm air to surround me, trying to ease my demon to back down. "Killing her will not help the situation," he tells me as Tallyn tries to pull an inconsolable Laureya back over to Dom. "We need her to rise, Sayah. She's our only chance to bring her back."

My dad helps Tallyn restrain Laureya, who is screaming and thrashing wildly, desperate to get back to either Ryan or me—or maybe both. She's completely frantic, her movements uncontrollable, until the melodic scream of the siren sunder, carried by Jasantha's voice, pierces the air.

Jasantha's striking purple eyes and medallion glow softly as she sings. Her steps are slow and deliberate as she approaches Laureya. Her gaze sweeps over the room, taking in each of us as her song fills the chamber. The enchanted notes seem almost tangible, shimmering as they drift from her lips and medallion, floating delicately through the air. They weave toward Laureya, entering her body with her next breath, and Laureya calms in an instant.

It might be the first time I've truly heard the siren sunder. The melody—haunting and ethereal—crawls along the cold chamber walls, its notes alive, flickering like fireflies. They drift through the air in a mesmerizing dance that settles over everyone. The song tells a story, each note resonating with love, loss, and heartbreak, weaving a tragic tale of devotion.

It speaks of a man who loved another man so deeply that he would abandon his world to find another where they could be together. In a life where their love was forbidden, he journeyed across the stars, seeking a new home for them. Along the way, he discovered stars unlike any other—rare and luminous, each glowing with a faint purple hue. These stars—scattered millions of light-years apart—were said to be formed from the purest of tears—tears shed for true love. As he gathered them, he charted constellations to guide him back to his lover. Each star he collected glowed brightly in his hand before melting into his skin in a luminous promise of his devotion.

After discovering a world where they could finally be together, he began his journey home, having collected six of the seven special stars. When he presented his lover with a ring, its brilliance was so otherworldly that he gazed into it and saw an entire galaxy contained within the stone.

"I would leave my world to find you another," he told him, and a single tear fell from his lover's eye. He caught it in his palm, and in that moment, the six stars appeared, merging with the tear to form a jewel. This jewel transformed into a portal to their new world.

"And this," he said, presenting his lover with the jewel, "is the distance I traveled to find it."

Laureya's eyes go slack, then ignite with fiery gold as her phoenix aura seeps into her skin. In a trance, she glides toward Sayah, tears streaming down her face. Once she reaches her, she wipes a hand over her tears, her wings unfurling magnificently. Laureya rubs the tear over Sayah's wound—and in an instant, Sayah catches fire.

The scream that leaves my throat is raw and agonized, desperation and pleading and loss and sorrow and anger all swirling together in a feral volcano eruption as I run up to her.

The music notes still haunt the room. The fire is too bright and hot; I cover my face from the scorching torridity, falling to my knees as I watch my love burn.

Again.

Sayah is all but ash when time finally seems to come back to me. When awareness returns to me.

I crawl up to the ash that was the greatest person I've ever known, and lean up to her, sifting my fingers through the soot that was my Sayah.

My fire queen.

The only thing left of her are the golden shackles of magick detainers Trystan had put on her.

A tear falls into the ashes.

The earth rumbles and shakes, the mountains break, and the oceans hold their breath while the stars and moons bleed their silvery tears onto the ashes.

Fire comes anew and almost burns me. I have to back up from what feels like an explosion.

An atom bomb.

Blinding light causes everyone in the room to shield their eyes, and an ear-piercing ringing snubs out all other noise.

When the light dies down, the ashes begin to take form.

To see movement within the fiery licks of death shock my heart back into its normal rhythm.

Sayah, donned in her black wedding dress and raven-black hair, sits up in a swallowed gasp. The vertical-opal white pupils dart right to me when she opens her eyes.

Her fangs—not her phoenix fangs—elongate from her gums, and she hisses, scanning each face around her, her hands at her sides, ready to launch her off the marble slab at any one of us— at any moment.

A collective questioning of expressions passes along the group as they all look from Sayah to me.

Sayah is now a vampire.

And she needs to feed.

41

DISMANTLE HIM FROM THE INSIDE OUT

—SAYAH—

Ravenous hunger permeates my body. A hunger unlike any other rumbles deep in my bones; it latches on to each and every molecule in my body and draws forth every addiction craving I've ever had.

A craving.

That's what this feels like.

A craving mixed with a desire to slice open every vein in this room, to watch the blood burble up like the small geyser pools in Yellowstone, and wrap my entire mouth around the wound, consuming deep, delicious crimson into my body until I feel sated.

My vision is different now, sharper and more precise than it has ever been, as if the world has been stripped of its veil. I can see Bash's guarded yet concerned expression, the tension in his clenched jaw revealing more than his stoic demeanor ever could. Beside him, Adaline's soft features are twisted in confusion, her piercing eyes darting between me and the others, searching for answers no one seems to have. Ollie shifts uneasily, his boyish face taut with unease, while Claire stands rigid beside him, her lips pressed into a thin line. Scarlet's fiery presence commands attention even in her stillness, her auburn curls catching the faintest shimmer of light, while Jasantha's icy calm radiates an eerie sense of detachment.

And then there's the old woman. Deep lines weather her skin, like rivers carved into stone, her eyes a mirror of Hattie's —wise and unrelenting in a way that peels back my layers to expose the raw truth beneath. Tallyn, regal and commanding, stands tall among her fae warriors, each bristling with quiet, lethal energy. Their shimmering armor catches the candlelight, creating a glow around them, but their eyes remain fixed on me, wide with disbelief and something that feels unsettlingly like fear.

But it's not just their faces I see.

I. See. Them.

I see the micro expressions they can't control—the twitch of a lip, the flicker of doubt in a glance, the rapid pulse in a throat. I notice every fine baby hair on their faces and how they tremble ever so slightly from the draft in the room. I see the subtle quiver of eyelashes as they blink, every flutter a heartbeat in this tense, silent standoff. Tiny dust motes swirl lazily in the candlelight, suspended in the cold, heavy air, their slow descent mesmerizing against the backdrop of darkness.

Even the room itself feels more alive than it should. The damp stone walls pulse faintly, seeming to resonate with the collective breath of those gathered within. Shadows stretch long and lean across the uneven floor, twisting and contorting with the flicker of the flame. I can feel the chill draft winding through cracks and crevices, brushing against my skin like ghostly fingers.

Everything feels heightened, exaggerated, and unbearably vivid. The weight of their stares is suffocating and unyielding, as though some unseen force anchors me to the moment. They may see me as something foreign, something changed, but the truth is, I see them more clearly than ever before—and I don't know whether that is a blessing or a curse.

Normal muscle movement is wild; I barely turn my head to look to my right, and it's way too fast. It's like whiplash. My neck pops in response. My vision zooms into the stone on the walls, the swirling colors of granite, and every atom in the atmosphere.

The smells.

I smell skin and nectar, citrus, and fruit, candles and incense, hair molecules and shampoo scents, body odor, and musk. I smell pinecones and earthly scents, like soil, mud, and waterfalls —the fae. I smell the unmistakable smell of flesh rotting away and the delectable scent of blood. I smell the bones of the dead surrounding this chamber, in their tombs for centuries.

I smell Dom.

Looking to my left, I see Dom, gray and ashen, still and unmoving, looking like a human in a casket ready for burial.

I smell Bash.

Midnights and magick and deep, delectable darkness. Demons and secrets, dreams and fire, fury and parcels of madness, pockets of ruin.

My stomach rumbles so loud the entire Earth quakes, and a buzzing on my arm like a lightning storm is crashing beneath my skin, matching the rumble of hunger. I look, seeing the black shadowy storm swirling, with the infinity fire symbol in the middle.

Bash glances at his arm and sees the same thing.

I attempt to flash away from the room, eager to escape everyone's gaze. But instead of smoothly vanishing, I find myself hurtling through the air, moving far too fast. I slam into a wall, and the impact knocks me unconscious.

Shadowy warmth wraps me up into a soft blanket of comfort, the scent of Bash cradling me in the dark. I hear his breath. I smell his charisma. I would recognize his footsteps in any realm, the way he breathes in any timeline, the rhythm of his heartbeat in any dimension, his fingertips on my skin in any life.

Bash.

Opening my eyes, I see the dark angel of death looming over me, his piercing blue eyes cutting through my strange new existence and reeling me back in from the ledge of this odd plane or dream I had just been in.

"Bash?" I ask, and my voice is hoarse, uneven.

His rough, calloused fingers ghost the side of my face, feathering his touch over my cheek, eyes bright like it's the first time he's seen me in thousands of years. "Yes, Sayah, I'm here."

My stomach rumbles again. "What's happening?"

"You need to feed." He says this like it's normal to say to someone who is not a vampire.

"What?" I question, hoping I heard him wrong. My head is pounding, and the fogginess of the former me—the dark phoenix mixed with the old Sayah—paired with this new feeling grumbling deep inside me has me nauseous. A sick sort of vomit crashes against my insides.

He sets his jaw. "Sayah," he begins, and I try to sit up again, but the movement is too fast, and I almost fly out of his arms. He catches me and brings me back down.

We're sitting on the cold stone floor of this drafty chamber, the vampires and fae still surrounding Dom but giving furtive glances my way, almost in anticipation.

Adaline is here in a wink of breath, and the way I can smell her now, the way she moves . . .

Vampires are more lethal and calculated with every single movement, even their blinking, breath, and eye movements. They are predatory in every sense of the word, and for some reason, now I can calculate her movements; I can see her take measured breaths. Lithe and stealthily, she lifts my right arm. In her touch, I can feel her power, the buzz of it electrifying her nervous system. The witch in her surrounds her in an aura so bright it's nearly blinding.

"The vines are gone," she says with a breath of relief.

I see her heart pumping beneath her neck in her jugular, and I salivate.

My mouth widens on its own accord, and I'm lunging for her, needing to drink from her as badly as I've needed to scream sometimes.

Bash's strong grip clamps down, nearly crushing me to death with his arms around me.

The feral powers swirling within me churn violently against my ribs, the shadows of him, the fires of me, a stolen power from Trystan, a new magick I feel swimming around my nerves like it's getting to know me.

It's too much.

I heat up.

I may explode.

"Bash?" I say in question as Adaline backs away.

"We don't have much time," she says, whisking herself back to Everett.

Tallyn's gaze collides with Bash's. "At least her connection to Trystan is severed."

"Not entirely," Sariana says, but her words fade as fury ignites within me, searing through my core. It twists and coils, merging chaotically with the fragmented shards of who I was, who I am, and who I'm becoming—all on the brink of exploding.

"What the fuck is going on?" I ask, squirming in Bash's arms, fearing the next words he will say.

My fear will damn me, but my anger may nearly make me explode. His cerulean eyes embed themselves like slivers into my skin, talking to my shadows, easing my fire. The look in them tells me all I need to know, and my face falls.

"I had to," is all he says, and his expression, his demeanor, his wildness breaks. "I didn't know if Laureya would be able to rise you and so I fed you my blood while you were still knocked out." His sorrow seeps out to dance with the taste of mine.

I didn't want to be a vampire. But how the fuck is it possible that I am?

"I'm so sorry," he says, and my shadows swirl around, escaping from my skin, searching for him, yearning to touch him, and feel him, and make him make me feel better.

I'm stuck in a haze of who I once was and who I'm destined to be. It's coalescing like smoke in my hands. No matter how hard I try to grip one, it slides away slowly through my fingers.

The desire to be Queen of Never, Feylight, and Earth is still a soft echo in my mind, but it seems to be fading the more Bash's voice speaks to my darkness.

The dark phoenix I'd become is still inside me, still with me, and the thought of that is comforting somehow.

I was always meant to be the balance between light and dark.

It's been good getting to know the dark me. It feels wild and reckless and like an extension of me I've always known and yearned to meet and get to know.

But this?

I did not see this coming.

"How is this even possible?"

Bash releases a heavy breath, and I watch how his skin shivers, how the hairs on his arms rise a fraction of an inch, how his muscles twitch, and how his eyes dance. "I spoke with Freya. She, uh, advised against it. But I had Agares. And I trusted him."

So many questions swirl through my mind. "What? How? When?" I cannot comprehend the words.

My hunger bites at me again, and the fire swirls.

"I froze time. Listen," he says as flames start to eat me inside. "You need to feed, then I'll give you answers."

He's right. If I don't get some blood into me soon, I'm afraid the fire will consume us all.

I nod, and he offers his arm.

I cannot help the ravenous way I bite into his flesh and slurp the glorious nectar from his body. The euphoria I feel from drinking from him arouses me in all the ways it did before, but this time, it's heightened. As I suck and drink and guzzle, not only does it quiet the starvation, but it awakens the hunger I have for him and only him.

The cold, shadowy chamber fades into nothingness, leaving us surrounded by stars and planets. I'm cradled in his arms, my gown flowing behind me as I drink from him. Every sensation I feel echoes through him, his arousal evident beneath his dark black jeans. I trail my hand over him, stroking through the fabric as I drink . . . and drink . . . and drink.

I don't care who sees.

I need each and every piece of Sebastian Sangravelli, and I will dismantle him from the inside out if necessary.

42

BONE TO PICK WITH THUNDER

—SAYAH—

"Sayah." An echoing voice comes from the shadows. "Sayah, stop. You'll kill him."

This voice I recognize, but it's not anyone from my family or his.

It's Freya's voice, like a rippling winter-spring. She pulls me from Bash, and she and I are alone in the vast universe, with Bash fading into the blackness, his head lulled to the side, eyes closed, the outline of his erection still evident.

"Freya?" I ask, standing, wiping the blood from my mouth.

She's as beautiful as she always is, regal and composed, her long blonde hair unmoving and still in our empty space. "Yes. I'm here."

"How? What is this place?"

I look around, taking in how the universe melts into a castle. Soft light pilfers through mosaic windows, casting rainbows along the walls and floor of an expansive, royal-esque room. She wears a crown of gold on her head. Paintings of gods and goddesses watch her movements like sentient beings of the castle.

"We are in Wyndhallow," Freya states, moving as though she's floating toward the Dias in the far side of the room.

"I've heard this word before," I admit, though I'm unsure where or when. It just sounds familiar. "The air is kinda burning my arms."

"Typically, beings of darkness are barred from this place, but you are the balance—an equal measure of light and dark. Thus, the light welcomes you here." She sits upon a throne of seaglass, its teal surface smoothed by the relentless caress of the ocean over millennia, cloudy yet luminous.

"How can I be a vampire if I'm the phoenix?" I ask, watching shadows ripple beneath my skin, seeping out like tendrils of smoke, searching for Bash.

She folds her hands in her lap, her composure unshaken. "You survived the transition and live with the demon blood because you've risen once before. Demon blood already runs through your veins." Her eyes meet mine, taking on the same hue as her throne. "Now, you are witch, demon, formweaver, phoenix, angel, and vampire."

"But Bash said he spoke with you, and you advised against it?"

Her gaze pierces me, sharp as wind through a waterfall. It stirs something wild and untamed within, a mix of pleasure and pain, wicked and pure.

A memory surfaces.

Sitting on my living room floor, Bash's voice wraps around me as he spoke of my smiles, of things I couldn't have.

That was the moment I knew.

I was in love with him. And I would walk through hellfire to save his soul.

I'd challenge storms and wrestle mountains. I'd command the oceans, whisper to the clouds, and wage wars with the tides. I'd bend the winds to my will and tame hurricanes, scatter the sands, and push back the waves—whatever it took to bring him into the light.

I'd find him in any lifetime, any realm, any dimension, guided by the rhythm of his breath.

The memory tugs at me like it's being siphoned away. My eyes snap open to see Freya holding a wand, its tip glowing as it draws the thread of the memory from my mind. It doesn't leave entirely but also exists outside of me, shimmering as it trails into a seaglass bottle. The wand guides the strand inside, swirling like captured starlight, painting the bottle's interior with a luminous, firefly glow.

She says nothing as she hands me the bottle.

Confusion and so many questions enter my mind, but I take it.

"Add that to your collection," she says, the ghost of a smile painting her perfect, angelic face. "It will be your secret weapon."

The bottle morphs into air and slides into my skin, entering my magickal maelstrom of already feral and confusing powers. I can feel it seeping into the tower of my mind, watching as a disembodied hand pours the memory next to the floating one I already had there, but this time images projecting with the words.

"You still didn't answer my question," I point out, looking at my hands where the bottle used to be.

"Anytime you want to relive that or any memory, you merely need to pluck the bottle from the tower in your mind and drink it. You can bottle memories. Any memories. And you have the power to do the same to anyone else you choose."

"So, essentially, I have the power to trap someone in a memory?"

She gives a slight nod and moves over to a table by the window, beckoning me to follow her with a flick of her chin. I oblige.

The solid oak table has two chairs, whittled wood by some ancient carpenter. Atop it sits parchment and scrolls with ribbons around them. A bottle of ink in a small jar sits next to the scrolls, a feathered quill resting beside it. The quill is a brilliant gold, the feather white and frilly, like someone plucked it directly from the wings of an angel.

"Write something you want to see happen," she tells me, handing me the quill while sliding into one of the chairs.

Hesitating, I take it, dip it in the deepest ink as though night itself was pooled inside it, and sit down at the table, thinking of something I want more than anything.

I think of everything I've wanted in life, everything I've wanted to have and achieve and undo and redo differently. A hurricane of emotions washes over me as I write the one thing that sits above all else.

Freya watches what I write and nods.

As soon as the night-stained ink is set on the parchment, it turns gilded. It glitters brightly, and the parchment morphs into a bird, fluttering through the open window.

"What did that just do?"

Freya says nothing again and rises from the chair, returning to the dais.

"Am I in some sort of crazed, new vampire fever dream? What is happening?"

"You better get back now, Sayah. They're waiting for you."

A stone falls, like the walls are crumbling, and the sun turns into its golden hour, gilding everything it touches in soft, tranquil light.

"Wait, Freya, you never answered my question."

"Which one?"

"Bash said he talked to you about making me a vampire, and you advised against it," I say, even though I want the answers to all the strange things that just occurred.

"Bash stopped time while you were transitioning to summon me. I advised against it."

I bite my lip. "Why did you advise against it if you knew I could withstand the transition?"

"Ascension," she corrects me. "Your ascension into the darkest part of you." Her stoic face holds a firm line.

Frustration rattles me, causing my shadows to shudder, contrasting against the fire, churning like waves inside me. "You are talking in riddles."

"Bash needed to believe it with his own heart for it to be true. For his own ascension."

Another stone falls as the sun sinks deeper, the sky melting into twilight as the darkness eats the light, falling over the sky like a curse. "What?" I utter, moving closer to her as the ground shakes.

"Bash has his own battles he's waging. You two are mated like moons, but the planets keep you apart, in your own orbit, around your own light and darkness. You needed to succumb to the dark. He had to square up to the light."

Thundering collisions of multiple stones falling cause the ground to shake, and I right myself from the tilt.

"Bash had to believe in something strongly enough to make it happen, even though it was already going to happen?"

As the sky darkens, stars brighter than headlights peek out from the collapsing roof, lending a silver light similar to melted mirrors, lancing down on Freya's aura. "Bash had to love something more than himself to stop time in order to try and save you. In doing so, the strings of power he's stitched in you became stronger, allowing the change to happen without severely damaging your soul."

"Stopped time?" I recall Nyx stopping time. Trystan said something about it being the second time, and she knew what would happen on the third.

"Ah, now you see."

More walls fall away until we're floating in the vastness of space again.

"I really don't think I do," I admit, my body feeling like I'm swimming in water, weightless and weighted and strong and weak, a soul at the mercy of an ocean in a ravaging storm.

"Sebastian's soul has been so morally gray, it's almost been easy for Agares to attach himself to him forever and take over for good."

I think of never seeing my sweet Sebastian's face again and only seeing the face existing behind the huge, red exterior Agares is. While he's still sexy when he's Agares, I don't ever want to lose him to that demon forever.

"What keeps him from attaching completely if it's almost so easy?" I ask, knowing indefinitely what she's going to say.

"You." There seems to be hesitation in the word, as though it's weighted, as fragile as a bomb.

My own body has disappeared, and I am but wind in a canyon now, the eternal nothing of the universe. "But?" It echoes and morphs.

"But you are not enough to stop the shadowmarking. Bash has one more chance to freeze time. Every time he or Agares freezes time, he gets shadowmarked. He's been shadowmarked twice now."

I am floating farther and farther away from Freya. "What happens on the third?"

Her next words seem to come from the stars themselves; Freya's ethereal body has melded with the starlight. "He will forever turn into Agares."

43

LULLABY FOR MY BONES

—BASH—

A passion surges through me in a deluge, taking over entirely as Sayah's mouth seals over the bite on my arm, burning me with exquisite pain.

I'm vaguely aware of the people in the room, but the way Sayah makes me feel as she drinks from me snuffs out all other feelings. I'm engulfed by want for her. Every drop she takes is replaced with parcels of her fire, and the embers feed Agares like rainwater feeds soil.

The addiction and bloodlust collide, and in one swift movement, I sweep her up into my arms and whisk her into the drafty halls of the antechamber. Someone calls my name—probably my mom—but I don't fucking care.

I need to be alone with her, dismantle her body with my shadows, and climb our pyre together like broken fire.

The purple spirit lanterns waiver lavender light in my wind, bending the shadows. I zip around bends and turns, going left at a fork in the tunnels here and a right there, searching for any empty room to throw her down and let her conquer me like the queen she is. Her fucking darkness is bringing me to the brink of unhinged.

I need her; I need to feel her from the inside.

Vigor and ferality stun all other thoughts aside from getting her mouth on mine, and I stop my quest for finding a dark room to taste her skin.

Screeching to a halt in an alcove with some saint-like goddess statue, I slam us against the back wall behind the statue and pull her from my arm, forcing her to look at me.

Her white eyes, stark against her raven-black hair, smolder with yearning, brimming with heat, power, and the collision of darkness and light. They radiate from her as though tangible forces, pulling me under. A pained groan rips from my throat as I crush my mouth against hers, the sharp taste of blood igniting me as I finally plunge over the edge her blood has been calling me to. I pin her arms above her head, licking the darkness from her mouth, its taste mingling with my own blood. It's buckling and I fight to keep my fangs at bay, careful not to graze her gums, but the pressure builds like a volcano ready to erupt. I wrench myself away, feeling Agares and I violently crash against the edges of the ruin unraveling within me.

My fangs emerge and plunge into her neck, enticing the sexiest moan she's ever emitted.

The euphoria morphs into something ethereal. Not just physical want, but every fiber of who I am screams for her, yearning for her as we destroy one another from the outside in.

Something I can't hold on to snaps inside of me. We'll both never be the same. As I drink from her, I no longer feel the way I had before, where it was a drug, and I had to quench some sort of thirst, give in to the burning addiction.

No, this is different.

This time, it feels like I'm getting back a part of myself that I'd lost long ago.

Her shadows and fire, my demons and violence, her angelic darkness, my demonic light—they crash together like waves, everything everywhere all at once. Her magick enters me and runs through every fiber of my being, as though trying to get to know me better.

My dick is hard enough to break stone, and I rip away her wretched wedding dress, exposing her glorious breasts, pausing my drinking from her to suck her tits into my mouth.

"Bash, fuck!" she moans and pulls me into her harder when I bite down on her pebbled nipple. She loves my exquisite torment.

Blood covers my mouth and her tits, my arm and her mouth, the sweet, addictive nectar painting us in the villainous light we belong in.

Then she's shoving me with a fierceness she's never exuded. I slam against the far wall on the other side of the statue. She sinks to her knees, unclasping my belt, and unbuttoning my pants. As my erection springs to life before her, I hear someone yelling my name down the hall, but this moment doesn't have room for reality.

"Sayah." I moan her name in anguished pleasure, desperate to taste her name on my tongue.

I hold her angelically demonic eyes as she circles her tongue around the head of my cock, lapping up my pre-cum like a gods-damn ice cream cone, and it makes me harder, the knot threatening to grow. I grab the back of her head and shove my cock into her throat, soaking up what a glorious sight it is to see such a powerful woman on her knees for me, winding me up, unraveling me. I fuck her face with vitality, like making love to the sun goddess herself, and when she looks up at me as she gags me down her throat, the look of desire mixed with the murderous monster she is right now is enough to make me feel like I'm starving.

The slurping sounds of her guzzling my cock fills the space and robs me of the composure I'm desperately clinging to. Agares is ready to burst from me and fuck her into oblivion, worshipping her like the goddess she is.

"Gods, you are gorgeous," I whisper to her. "Your darkness is breathtaking."

Her wicked smile caresses her face after she pulls her lips off me. She licks my cock down the sensitive back side, following her tongue with her hands. She plunges down on me again, hollowing out her cheeks to suck me all the way down to the back of her throat.

"Fucking hell." I pull her head back with my grip on her hair, slamming back into her until I'm about to explode down her throat.

By my grip on her hair—which she loves—I pull her mouth off me. I want to fill her up with my cum. I want her tight little pussy snug against my cock.

I kiss her roughly in a barely tamed fury, and it's taking every bit of my control not to consume her. I wish to leave no part of her body undiscovered, unclaimed by my shadows, by Arages.

With a growl, I rip her dress all the way off her, pull her up by her knees, and slide her onto my cock.

"Oh, Bash, fuck," she utters, mining a gravelly sound from deep inside my chest.

Her fire cracks open the fissures in her skin, and her wings of fire explode into light.

I lift her to the tip to slam her back down to the hilt. "You fucking undo me every time you say my name like I'm your fucking god."

Her seductive glance collides with mine, her white eyes desperate with yearning. "I'll worship you for the rest of time, Sebastian," she says, and I careen her into the wall, fucking her tight little cunt, my body shaking with pleasure as I take in the way she's watching me plunge into her.

"I like to watch you watch us fuck," I admit in a growl, thrusting harder, faster.

I thumb her clit while I pierce her to her bones, falling to the edge of despair while Agares begs to be set free. "Talk to that pussy," she purrs, the mixture of her phoenix and vampire hardening me still, braiding my heartstrings into a perfect rope she tugs on.

My shadows seep out from me, my skin threatening to creep into red, the demon begging to take over and enlarge every part of me.

As though she senses him, she asks, "Can he come out to play, too?"

I oblige her and let Agares out enough to swell my knot, her tight pussy swallowing up the knot on my cock. Her wings of fire brighten in welcoming the demon into her being.

A strange buzzing rings in my ears, like sirens calling out to sailors in the moonlight. It's something I don't understand at first—the delicate waves and dips of the tones singing to my skin, a lullaby for my bones.

While Sayah writhes on top of me, the shadows seep from her, crawling into my pores, and mixing with the spirit of my demons.

As she bounces up and down on my cock, her breasts are bounding seductively, beckoning my hands to grab them. Agares's darkness overflows from the cage I've unknowingly kept him in, making love to her fire, the embers of salvation intertwining with the shadows.

The buzzing in the room makes the hairs on my arms rise. The sound is coming from us, our souls—the darkness and light, the fire and shadows, the angel and the demon.

Only then do I realize the echoes of us—the alter egos—the dark and light phoenix, and the vampire-demon—speak to each other in frequencies only they can understand.

Now that we've accepted the other parts of us—Sayah, her darkness and me, my light—we can hear the language only they know. The language they've spoken to each other through dreams, through torture and wars, through ruin and ascension, through lifetimes and realms and other versions of us. Through us having to lose ourselves and finding new ones, through prophecies of death and past lives, seeing each other with the wrong person, and falling in love each and every lifetime.

There would never be anyone but her.

As our bodies unite together, as our echoes make love to each other, we enter a level beyond anything we can return from. Her desire for me, and mine for her, just became the most dangerous weapon anyone could ever use against us.

And that scares me more than anything else ever has.

I would bring the realm to ruin for her.

"Bash, I'm gonna cum," she says, grasping for my arms, scratching at my skin, drawing blood, and licking it up while I bite her neck.

The intensity with which I fall off the world nearly brings me to my knees, and they buckle, but she holds us up with her new vampire strength.

"You're not made to bow to anyone," she says as she clenches around me, the twitching from her own orgasm and the flush of her cheeks my sign she's cumming, too.

I stop drinking from her and fall into the luxurious high it brings with the ecstasy of my climax. "I bow to you and you alone. To your wickedness with every inch of my life, my queen." My voice rumbles as I ride out the last wave of my orgasm, our echoes slow to return to us—hesitant to leave one another.

"I'm sorry I fought you," she says, my knot still buried in her while our echoes say goodbye.

The blood on her face and neck and arms and tits, her vampire side, the dark phoenix, her skin glowing in fissures, lighting up our darkened alcove . . . Yeah, it may take a while for the knot to go down.

She's the sexiest fucking thing I have ever laid my eyes upon.

"I would've taken on any realm to bring you back," I tell her honestly, taking her lips in mine, basking in the relief it feels to have her back.

"I don't really know who I am now," she confesses when I release her lips. "I'm scared."

Trailing my fingertips down the side of her face, I caress her while her fire subsides. "I know. I am, too." Leaning my forehead against hers, she takes a withered and stuttered breath, like she'd been holding it in for as long as time. "But whatever it is, whatever is happening, I'll never let him take you from me again. I will die before I let that happen."

A tear slides down her face, and I wipe it away with my thumb. "You don't know what he took from me."

My bones clench at the weight of her words. "What. Did. He. Take. From. You?"

Our echoes finally part from each other, and Sayah slides off my dick, her feet padding on the stone floor. "He . . ." Her breath becomes uneasy. She finds her dress and merely clutches it, sliding down the wall to the floor.

I sit beside her, wrapping my arm around her shoulders as she buries her head into her knees. "You can tell me," I softly tell her. "You can tell me anything."

She lets out a sob that could break an angel's heart. "He broke me, Bash," she admits after sobbing into the echoes of the alcove. "He poisoned me, withered me down, planted lies inside my head, and then he raped me."

Heat and anger and violence surge, and it takes all I have to tamp down the rage. "He will die screaming," I seethe through my teeth. She sobs some more, and I console her, only speaking once she's let her agony out. "I cannot give you back what he took from you, but I promise his death will be tortuous and slow."

She lifts her head and looks at me, her dark ocean-blue eyes drinking the white. "No," whispers, wiping away her tears. "I will make what he took from me into the most dangerous weapon of all and end him myself."

I cock my head to the side, hard again for the vengeance and villain in her voice. "What is the most dangerous weapon of all?"

"Me."

44

TASTE THE WIND

—SAYAH—

It's strange to exist as multiple beings at once, each swimming through my subconscious, poised to seize control. This must be what Bash constantly feels like.

I'm still unsure of the sequence of events—blacking out, waking to feed from Bash, blacking out again, and then waking to find myself locked in a lust-filled encounter with him. The strange moment with Freya felt so vivid, I can't tell if it was a dream. If it was real, what happened between completing my ascension by feeding from Bash and the intense passion that followed?

Did time freeze again?

When I came to after being with Freya, a frenzy consumed me—hunger, desire, arousal, passion, and raw lust. Everything Trystan had stolen from me surged back in an instant. At that moment, I needed Bash more than I needed air.

Freya's words echo through my thoughts, sharp and clear, as I feel the new powers stirring within me. The familiar orange power of fear and the golden power of the phoenix remain, but now there are others. A shimmering blue power—the one I stole from Trystan but have yet to understand. A vibrant purple. And a stunning teal.

I don't know what these new powers do, but I see them clearly, swirling like glittering mist in the tower of my mind every time I close my eyes.

Bash and I are still sitting in the alcove, the silence between us growing its mournful pulse.

His other arm is resting on my knee, and I notice the shadows now—the swirling smoke that's darkened his fingers and climbing up his arm, disappearing beneath his rolled-up black shirt.

He didn't get all the way undressed in our passion; we were so in need of each other that being completely naked was not a necessity.

I lean back from him, noticing the shadows peek up from under the collar of his shirt.

"What?" he asks as I examine him, turning his chin to the side to see the shadows more.

The purple orb lights make it hard to see, but one tendril of shadow swirls up and around his left ear. "Oh, Bash," I say, holding his gaze. A tremble rattles through me, as though I just dislodged a ghost. "I know about the shadowmarking."

His brows fold into checkmarks, confusion marring his beautiful face. "Shadowmarking?"

I pull his arm up to show him the swirling shadows like he hasn't noticed them before. "These. You don't know what these are?"

He examines the swirling shadows more closely. "No. Agares only told me that when I freeze time, it creates a crack in the veil, and we can only do it three times."

"Freya told me every time you freeze time, you become shadowmarked. And on the third, Agares will take over you completely, and you'll forever remain in your demon form."

Bash goes still, his muscles tense. His eyes fall from mine, and he looks to the ground as though he's having a silent conversation with his demon. Color manipulation begins on his skin, the peach warring with the red, his eyes going vertical and golden, then round and blue again. Like glitching on a computer screen, where one freezes, and the other tries to force its way through. He inhales deeply, like retrieving the stale air from the dank dungeon of tunnels we're in will solidify his resolve in letting Agares take over when he wants to.

"Bash?" I ask when he hasn't said anything for some time.

His pale peach color enhances over the red. He shakes as his neck strains, and he sets his jaw. "Yeah?" he asks like nothing passed between him and his echo just now.

"You okay?"

He nods, biting his bottom lip. "Yup. Dandy. Just something Agares conveniently forgot to mention."

Exactly what I suspected.

A distant boom reverberates through the castle, shaking the walls. Frames tremble along the tunnel, and the orb lights flicker in their sconces.

"What was that?" I ask, fumbling to gather my dress and piece it back together.

Bash pulls up his pants, zipping them before offering me a hand. "Not sure. But if I had to guess? Trystan."

Bash helps me dress, and we step out from the goddess statue we fucked behind, entering the dark and echoey hallway. "Which way do we go?" I ask, looking left and right.

Both directions look the same.

"That way." He juts his chin to the right. "Wanna try vamp-flashing, or want me to carry you?"

"Fuck being carried; I wanna try it!" I say, and the little bubble of excitement pales the terror I feel around everything happening, everything I am now, everything coming.

"Okay," he says, grabbing my shoulders and holding me still, looking deeply into my eyes. "Vamp-flashing isn't just about speed; it's about control. Imagine it like driving a car with a very powerful engine. You don't want to floor it, or you'll crash into something. Instead, you need to feel the power under your feet and keep a steady pressure, like tapping a gas pedal.

"First, feel your body wanting to move faster—instinctual now. Focus on a spot ahead of you, like a point on the wall or the ground. Keep your eyes on it and think of yourself being there, not just running to it. Start with short bursts. You'll want to keep your movements tight and quick, like a snap. It's all about pacing. When you feel the rush, don't let it overwhelm you. Think of it like a dance step—smooth and fluid, not a frantic sprint.

"And remember, it's not just about how fast you can go, but also about how quickly you can stop. So, when you're ready to slow down, picture a wall of energy in front of you and ease off the gas. You'll get the hang of it, but take it slow. Or, you know, faster than a human—but not too fast for you."

I nod, feeling the speed and need to taste the wind beckoning me like a bird being beckoned to the sky. "I think I got it," I say, the buzzing in my bones ramping up.

"Okay, just try it to the end of this hallway," he explains, getting ready to take off with me. "Ready?"

I focus on a point down the tunnel, feeling an intense rush building within me—like a coiled spring inside my muscles, ready to explode. My vision narrows, locking onto the target ahead. "Ready."

"Go!" Bash says, and I let my foot off the gas.

I barely have time to think before my body reacts. Suddenly, the world around me blurs into streaks of stone and shadow, and my feet barely seem to touch the ground.

It's like falling forward, except I'm in control—or at least I think I am. The speed is unlike anything I've ever felt—faster than thought, faster than fear. The air whips past my face, cold and sharp, and there's a brief, dizzying moment when I'm not sure if my feet are under me or if I'm flying.

My instincts scream to a stop, and I pull back, my whole body jerking as if I've slammed on invisible brakes. I skid to a halt, my back slamming into the damp stone wall, breathless and windblown. My heart thrums with the rush of the new power, and I realize I'm trembling. I feel both exhilarated and terrified, like I've just tapped into something primal and barely controlled. The energy coursing through me is electric, and every muscle hums with it.

Bash zips up next to me and stops inches from my face.

"That was intense," I breathe out, half wild-eyed, half panicked, already feeling the addictive pull to try it again. "I can see why you choose to move that way any chance you get."

His eyes are gleaming. "Fucking nuts, right?"

"So nuts." I face the next point I wanna zip to. "Let's go again!"

"Race you to the tomb chamber!" he says. He takes off before me, flashing down a bend faster than I can process.

A rush of speed takes over my body, and although I've lost sight of Bash, I can sense him. My magick and bones and shadows and light know him, and I'd be able to find him in the deepest depths of darkness, in any realm or any ocean.

Tapping into my new vampire speed, I talk to it, and tell it to follow Bash.

Before I know it, I come to the antechamber, Bash already there, leaning up against the wall with a wry smile plastered on his face. "Beat ya," he says egotistically.

"Barely," I say, and he pushes open the heavy iron doors to the burial chamber.

45

SOFTENS HER SHARPENED EDGES

—BASH—

The tomb chamber hums with subdued energy. In the back corner, Tallyn and her lieutenants, generals, and other fae huddle around a table, examining a spread of documents. On one side of the expansive room, my mom and dad sit closely on a stone bench, his arm wrapped protectively around her shoulders.

Caelum shadows Scarlet as she drifts from tomb to tomb, her fascination undiminished. Across the chamber, Hattie and Jasantha perch on a bench by the window, staring at the unseen world beyond.

Claire and Ollie hover near Dom, whose ashen, motionless body is a somber reminder of our losses.

Laureya, knees hugged to her chest, sits beside Ryan's lifeless form. Her friends surround her in a quiet show of solidarity, though Jasantha's siren sunder still holds her in its grip, leaving her distant and despondent.

Henry, unnoticed by everyone but me, slides out of one of the tombs on the wall, reminiscent of a ghostly waterfall on stone. He pools at the foot and coagulates together, a smitten expression laced through his lips.

"Oh, good, the lovebirds are back," Tallyn says dryly. Though the room is vast, her voice carries as if she were standing right next to us.

I'm supposed to say some cutting insult here, but I can't.

Tallyn's expression is dire.

"Who's the kid?" Sayah questions with a tilt of her head.

Before I can respond, my mom appears in a blur, her urgency palpable. "Bash. Sayah. Please—we need you now more than ever."

Tallyn and her generals, Halcyon among them, stroll toward us. The weight in my mom's voice contrasts sharply with Tallyn's deliberate, almost casual pace. "Trystan has breached a boundary of Feylight," Tallyn says. "He's getting closer. We need to act before—"

"We need you to rise Dom, Sayah, before it's too late," Adaline cuts in, her words sharp and urgent.

Another deafening explosion shakes the castle walls.

"What's the plan?" I ask Tallyn, but my mom steps between us, grabbing Sayah's arm. "Please, Sayah. Use your phoenix power to rise him before Trystan destroys the castle. We're running out of time."

"You think he'll destroy the castle?" I ask, turning to Tallyn.

"I'll destroy this whole gods-damned realm before I let it fall to him." Her voice is steel; her expression unyielding.

"If he gets any closer," my mom says, tugging Sayah toward the marble slab where Dom lies, "Tallyn will destroy the ley lines to keep him from what he wants."

Sayah's face twists in confusion, and for a moment, I'm lost in the unfamiliarity of her new features. I'd memorized every line, every subtle shift of her old face. It might take a while to learn this one.

"The flora and fauna holding him in The Gloaming," my mom says, as though that explains everything.

"The Gloaming?" Sayah repeats, trailing after her toward Dom.

"There's no time to explain. Just rise him. Please."

"Why didn't you have Laureya do it?" Sayah asks as she ascends the marble steps to where Dom's lifeless body rests.

I glance over at La La, her face void of emotion, her eyes hollow.

I should feel bad for killing Ryan. But I don't.

"Laureya's under a trance right now," I say. "Best to leave her that way for a bit."

Sayah's gaze shifts to Laureya, taking in the headless body of Ryan sprawled beside her, a dark pool of blood encircling him like a grotesque halo.

"Bash, what did you do?" Sayah asks, her tone sharp, already knowing the answer.

I step up beside her, letting a smirk tug at my lips. "I needed her to bring you back. And I'd do it again in a heartbeat if it meant saving you."

The vastness of her soul feels like it could consume me, and the depth of my love for her terrifies me. To love someone this much and fear that love might be your undoing—that it might hold the power to ignite wars and topple empires—is too great an emotion to try and even form into words.

Trystan is coming, waging war on Feylight to take back the queen I stole, like she's Helen of Troy.

But I'll be damned if I let him. I'll burn the world to ash before I give her up.

"Sebastian?" she mutters, her voice questioning, the world around us seeming to dissolve.

It's as though she knows—knows that when she rises Dom, the spells he bore in life will be gone, just as Trystan's hold on her vanished when she died.

"I know," I whisper, brushing a stray strand from her forehead. "We'll deal with it together."

I see the conflict raging within her—the light and dark phoenix battling for dominance, the old Sayah who loved Dom, and the new Sayah who loves me.

"Please, Sayah, hurry," my mom urges, standing on the opposite side of Dom, her voice strained with desperation.

Sayah's gaze collides with my mom's and darkens. "You tricked me and shoved a knife in my heart."

My mom's face falls. "That was only to break your connection to Trystan—"

"Shut the fuck up," Sayah tells my mom, and this new dark Sayah turns me right the fuck on. "First, you killed my mom," Sayah says, stepping around the marble slab, moving closer to her. "My parents. Then, without even so much as an 'I'm sorry for killing your parents, Sayah,' you also tried to have me killed. Multiple. Times." She's closing the distance between her and my mom, and even though my dick hardens as the dark Sayah takes over, I know I should do something. "Then, you give me a false apology, using my son as your leverage to get closer to you so that you could kill me." My mom doesn't back away; she merely stares Sayah down as she inches closer to her. "Now tell me, Adaline Sangravelli, witch, mother of vampires, what would you do to someone like that if they did that to you?"

Fuck me, I'm hard. "Sayah, I—"

"Shut up, Bash," she scolds me, making me want her more.

Another blast in the distance has us all turning our heads toward the far windows.

My mom steps closer to Sayah, unafraid of her or anyone else. There's never been anyone I've seen my mom afraid of.

"You may think you're some tough shit now that you have risen again and are part vampire, little girl, but you know nothing of the things I've seen and done. I am sorry for your parents, Sayah. Truly, I am. But I make no apologies for the things I've done to protect my family. And whether you choose to believe me or not, I killed you to break your connection to Trystan, therefore saving your bloody ass, so . . ." My mom's eyes narrow, flashing white. "You may think you're strong enough to take me on, and that may be so, but I'll still go down swinging on you, Lasayah Thorne. And don't you ever fucking doubt that I won't."

The two women are so close they could lick each other's noses, tension crackling in the air, neither uttering a word.

"Eh-hem," Tallyn interrupts, her voice slicing through the silence as she steps onto the podium where we've all gathered. "Hate to break up this little 'airing of skeletons,' but I've got to leave soon to fetch the dragons. So, you two want to decide whether you're rising Dom or not?"

Before anyone can respond, the ornate iron doors slam open, the sound reverberating through the vast chamber.

Rowan, a small green fairy, flutters in and makes her way to Tallyn. "Apologies, my queen, but the fire boundary is down. That's Earth, Water, and Fire. All that's left is Air. The wyverns and other demons are pouring in faster than I can patch the gaps. I don't know how much longer I can hold the remaining barriers."

Tallyn's face darkens, her expression turning grim. "Thank you, Rowan. Do what you can. We'll join you shortly to prepare for war."

Rowan dips into a bow before zipping away.

"Sayah, please," my mother pleads, her voice raw with urgency. "If not for anyone else, do it for yourself. He deserves a better end than what he got."

Her fierce demeanor softens, desperation bleeding through in a way I've never seen before. It's enough to crack even Sayah's resolve. She steps back, moving toward Dom's still form.

I follow her, standing close as her phoenix power ignites.

Darkness recedes from her aura, replaced by golden fissures that ripple across her skin. Her white vampiric eyes shift to molten gold as her hands hover over Dom's chest, the fatal wound concealed beneath his dark shirt. Fire spreads from her like wings, illuminating the room.

Across from us, Gwylan and Sylvan prepare their parts of the ritual. Gwylan, her mystic black skin shimmering, begins swirling her hands to pull energy from the flora and fauna Sylvan summons. With fiery-red hair and intense brown eyes, Sylvan calls the essence of the plants to the air, her voice whispering to the earth's creatures. Moths, ravens, beetles, and other creatures gather, swirling in a glowing stream of magick that twirls above Dom like a golden tornado.

A single tear escapes Sayah's eye, gold as the surrounding light around her. Her phoenix fangs emerge as she bites into her wrist, mixing her blood with her tears.

I step forward and rip open Dom's shirt, revealing the wound that claimed his life.

Sayah spreads the mixture of blood and tears into the wound, her hands steady as the swirling magick seeps into him. She clasps her palms over his chest, sealing the ritual with Feylight's power.

At first, nothing happens.

Then, a violent explosion rocks the castle, nearly toppling me. I spread my feet to stay upright.

Dom's gray skin begins to flush with color, a brilliant, angelic light bursting from his chest. The intensity forces everyone to shield their eyes.

The energy builds, pulsing like a heartbeat. Dom's chest arches toward the heavens as though struck by lightning, and he takes a deep, gasping breath. His skin shifts fully back to its living apricot hue, the wound gone, his tattoos now swirling with ominous shadows.

Sayah removes her hands, her breath shallow.

We step back, waiting, watching.

Dom's hazel eyes snap open, clear and bright, locking onto Sayah.

And then . . . he smiles.

A EPIC DEATH

—DOM—

Although the sight of Sayah seems like a mirage, my heart smiles as her face registers. The warp and weft of reality finally come crashing to a halt into the craggy cliff's edge of my existence, and the force with which I plummet back to actuality is biting.

The feeling is similar to when a limb falls asleep after lying on it for too long. First, it's completely numb. Moving it around, flexing and un-flexing a hand, to get the natural feeling of skin to come back. Hot tingles that feel like biting ants underneath the muscle follow this, gnawing their way to the surface of the skin.

My whole body feels that way.

Feeling the eyes of a hundred people on me, I try to focus on the vines above my head. The dark ceiling of stars above blinks in and out as the wind swirls the tendrils of plants around.

I clench and unclench my jaw while I ball my hands into fists, trying to get accustomed to the feeling of blood running under my skin.

And suddenly, I'm feeling . . . *everything.*

My muscles ache, my bones are on fire, my tonsils hurt, my

eyelashes are heavy, my mouth is dry, and I can feel my hair growing like it's trying to catch up from being in The Gloaming.

Then comes the deluge of memories.

Flooding, rushing, gushing, drowning me all at once. All the way back from the moment I went dark.

Everything I saw and felt and did.

Everyone I killed.

Emotions slice through me. Some I'm familiar with, some I've never felt, but they cut through me and hollow me, gutting me from the inside out.

I didn't want to come back. I didn't want to live this atrocious life anymore.

I wanted to move on to the next life, be human again, do things differently. Live to a ripe old age and die of natural causes. I wanted to find someone to love the way my mom loves my dad. Give them the world, get married, have children, and watch them grow. Spoil their children and end up on a porch in my 90s with a bottle of bourbon while my great-grandchildren run around the yard. Passing away peacefully in my sleep next to my soulmate.

"Dom!" My mom's voice evaporates my daydream. I turn to see her, my vision still blurry around the edges, my neck popping as I turn my head.

She collapses on top of me, and it creates pressure where the wound that killed me once was, causing me to wince.

"Oh, Odin's ghost, I'm so sorry," she exclaims, rising up, and caressing my face. "Oh, my sweet boy." She kisses my forehead. "I'm so unbelievably happy you're back with us."

Wish I could say the same.

"Me next!" Scarlet announces, shoving my mom to the side to throw her arms around me as best she can since I'm still lying on this cold marble slab.

A distant boom outside seemingly rattles the ground under

us, and Scarlet lifts from me, smiling before turning to look at Tallyn.

Tallyn nods subtly, and Scarlet moves. An ancient lady I don't think I know is stepping up to me next.

"Hi, Dom," says the old woman with Hattie's voice. Her eyes collide with mine, and her expression turns to levity as she shrugs. "Yep. It's me. My own spell bit me in the arse."

Ollie is here next, kneeling to look me in the eye. "Good to see you back, brother. Missed your stupid face."

I laugh, and my ab muscles scream at me. I try moving my hand to put pressure on them, but my arms are still very heavy. "Good to see your stupid face, too," I say, my voice raspy and hoarse.

"I hate to interrupt this glorious family reunion," Tallyn's voice echoes to my left, and I track my eyes to the sound, "but, Gwylan, can you use your healing power to speed up his recovery? We must move quickly now. Rowan had multiple barriers up, but the more Trystan breaks down, the closer he gets to the castle. They're ring barriers, each stronger than the next, but he's broken down the two Earth barriers, two water, and two fire. He only has the one air ring left. Granted it is the most destructive, but he's plowed through the last six, and there are only seven."

As the fairy that must be Gwylan steps back up to the slab I lie on, my eyes land on Bash.

The memory of Sayah and Bash floods into my mind.

We were in one of Tallyn's many sitting rooms. She had me in her trance, so I followed her wherever she wanted me to go. She took me to the far end of the room in an alcove of a turret, where she had a large crystal ball. In the brilliant swirling glass, I saw Sayah and Bash kissing on the banks of Lake George. The glowing rune on his arm allowed Tallyn to see everything he saw.

I saw Sayah's beautiful face as Bash took my woman's lips in his.

She received them like an elixir, and her soft moan was all I needed to show the real me that she liked it.

She was in love with Bash.

This memory submerges me in anger, accelerating the thaw of my bones before Gwylan even approaches me. I surge in a gasp of urgency, my achy muscles protesting opposingly, reminding me of my frailty. I ignore their pleas to return to life gradually and slam into Bash, grabbing him by the collar of his shirt and rushing him into the nearest pillar. Flowers vining around the pillars lose their petals like tears from drunken clouds as I find my vengeance on him once again consuming me.

"Oh, Odin's fucking ghost," my dad's voice echoes as I slam my fist into Bash's face, the connection making the entire world shake.

Or at least that's what it feels like.

Before Bash could retaliate and hit me back, the explosion I assumed was from my punch turned out to be something far worse—a blinding, bright green bomb detonating just outside the castle. The wall behind us erupts, sending debris crashing down as the searing flash of green light blinds us.

"Shit, he's taken the it down to the last barrier ring!" yells Tallyn. "Halcyon, portal us out of here to the dragons."

"Dragons?" I ask Bash, who's unfazed by my assault on him.

His face turns grave. "No time." He yanks himself out of my grip and dashes over to Sayah.

While anger still permeates me—my bones, muscles, and blood still adjusting to being out of The Gloaming and back in my body—I scan the surroundings, trying to register what I should be doing.

I knew there was a war coming when I was alive before Trystan killed me.

Tallyn had told me as much.

I knew she was using my blood to make darkling fae, using

Bash's blood for whatever nefarious reasons she had, but I didn't realize it was already upon us.

It was already here.

I'm still trying to wrap my mind around being back in my body.

Seeing Sayah with a new appearance has me rattled. The way her sable locks lay flat and straight all the way down to her ass, her eyes that'd been golden when she rose me have returned to their ocean-blue, but there's something off about her now—something different.

It's as though she moves with restraint to look and act natural. But still, an unnatural essence sits about her body, her face, and the energy surrounding her.

Everyone in the room runs to the soldier, who must be Halcyon. His cerulean skin adorns his massive muscles and shoulders, and his military uniform declares him a lieutenant or general. Waving his hands around, a dark teal vortex unzips from thin air, a swirling of mass and energy and time and space. One by one, the beings in the room begin to enter the portal, disappearing to wherever the vortex is leading them.

As Sayah and Bash stand next to each other, waiting in line to enter the portal, an explosion on the other end of the room sends a gust of shrapnel into the space, scattering tombs, coffins, and bones. One of the stones hits Claire in the head, knocking her down, and Sayah vamp flashes—*fucking vamp flashes*—over to her.

It takes a moment for me to process what I'm witnessing, but as Sayah gathers up her best friend, Bash is next to her while yet another explosion rattles the chamber.

Sayah's a vampire? I feel my feet moving me toward the throng of fae and vampires going through the vortex. I can feel my own vampire speed beckoning me to blink over to them, but something dark inside me protests.

I don't want this anymore.

This life. This power.

My mom is across the room, scanning the damage and oncoming onslaught, assessing the danger with stiff posture beside Hattie. She and my sisters are on high alert, watching every wall, every crevice, every corner.

Sayah is still trying to rouse Claire awake. Ollie and Bash are zipping up next to them as unnatural shadows slither in through the new holes in the chamber walls.

Another explosion down on the far end of the room has my mom rushing up to me, seemingly to pull me along faster to the vortex.

"Sayah's a vampire?" I ask my mom as she grabs hold of my elbow and tries pulling hastily.

"Long story," she says, tracking the movements of the shadows. They're morphing now; even shadows belonging to the chamber before the assault seem to move differently, as though gathering up twistedly. "It has to do with breaking her marriage connection to Trystan."

Ollie has lifted an unconscious Claire onto his shoulder, and flashes over to the portal.

But something has caught Sayah's eye, and she's not moving in that direction. She's going toward the other end as beings with jagged teeth and slimy monster-like worms enter the holes in the walls.

My heart rate picks up with worry, watching as Bash tries to stop her. Too much is happening in my body and mind at once, the old me who once loved Sayah and still does, the spelled me who thought I was falling for Tallyn, and accepting Sayah and Bash as a thing fading away.

No, that's gone, and what remains is just jealousy and rage, watching him try to coax her into moving toward safety instead of danger.

"Marriage to Trystan?" I hear myself ask, watching as some

of Tallyn's soldiers battle the creatures seeping in, more of her soldiers appearing from the entrance to the chamber.

My mom's demeanor is panicked, and her gray eyes carefully watch everything around her. "The night you died," she starts, while one of the demons rushes at Ollie and Claire, and he shoves it back with his air magick. "Trystan kidnapped her and stole her away to Never. He poisoned her into thinking she loved him and wanted to be Queen of Never and Luminara and Earth."

Jasantha lets out her sunder as another shadow being lunges for Hattie, Scarlet flashing over to a few grimspawn that've fallen through the hole at the top of one wall.

"And making her a vampire was the way to break the connection?" I ask, trying to figure out if this is all a dream, something The Gloaming concocted.

It's all too unreal, too hazy.

Part of me just wants to disappear into the chaos. I had already accepted my death. It wasn't my fault I was tethered to The Gloaming and unable to move on.

The sizzling sound of the vortex, the clicking and unnatural rasping of grimspawns and darkling fae, the explosions, and the nightmarish slithering create a storm within the chamber. A wind picks up, followed by thunder and lightning.

"I knew she needed to die in order to break the connection," my mom answers as my dad skewers a dark shadow monster with a long sword he pulled from a tomb. "We thought Laureya would be able to rise her, but Bash didn't trust her abilities, so he fed her his blood before I killed her."

"Adaline!" my dad shouts at her. "Go now!"

Ollie hands Claire to one of the soldiers, and they enter the portal. Ollie ushers Hattie and Scarlet through next.

Something still has Sayah transfixed by something at the other end of the room. Bash is pulling her arm and trying to get her to let whatever she sees go.

"You killed her?" I look at the woman who gave birth to me, who carries more secrets within her own mind and body; she should be twice the size she is with the weight of them all.

"Dom, I did what I had to do to break her connection to Trystan." Her voice sounds panicked_as her eyes dart over to Bash and Sayah, whom Ollie has flashed over to.

More grimspawn and beings with rows of jagged teeth have swarmed some of the soldiers, the grimspawns feasting on the flesh of one while one of the more nefarious dark shadow beings lifts a soldier twice its size into the air and sucks his soul out of him, desiccating him, a shriveled gray shell with a uniform thudding to the ground.

"Adaline!" my dad yells again, standing near the portal, begging her with his hands and eyes to come.

"Sebastian!" my mom screams, her voice cutting through the chaos like a blade directed at Bash.

He looks over, his expression maddeningly nonchalant, shrugging like a father watching his kid refuse to leave the playground—except we're in the middle of a war, and soul-sucking creatures are wreaking havoc all around us.

Sayah's attention, however, is elsewhere. Her gaze locks onto an eerie blue light emanating from one of the ancient tombs. She moves toward it as if in a trance, her steps deliberate and unyielding.

The light seeps through the tomb's cracks, spilling like a silent call. She grips the rusted handle on the front and yanks, but it refuses to budge.

"Sayah, leave it!" Bash calls out, his tone a mix of exasperation and worry. He's moving now, but not fast enough.

"Come on, we don't have time for this!" Ollie urges, darting toward her, and grabbing her arm. "They're coming. We have to go!"

Sayah doesn't budge, her focus consumed by the blue glow.

Something about it mesmerizes her, as if it holds answers—or doom.

And every second we delay, the enemies close in.

Another explosion sounds on the other side of the chamber from them, and through the smoke, a massive, spider-like form emerges—its eight legs crashing to the ground like thunder. Where its head should be, a fae torso rises, membranous black wings jutting from its back. It fixes its eight beady eyes on us beneath sharp, pointed ears.

What the actual fuck?

"Adaline, we gotta go, now!" my dad shouts, flashing over to her, grasping her arm, and trying to yank her toward the portal.

"You go," she says to my dad, who shakes his head, pulling free of his grasp. "I have to get my children in first."

The shadows, grimspawn, and darkling fae are coming from all corners now. The Luminara soldiers are doing what they can, but there are too many.

"Sayah!" I shout, hoping she'll hear me, and forget about whatever it is she's trying to do.

Sayah doesn't listen; she and Bash open the tomb door, the eerie blue light cascading into the dark chamber.

The giant spider is crawling toward her and Bash.

"Dom, please!" my mom pleads, her face scrunched like she's in pain. "I'll get them; I just need you to go. I'll explain more later."

"Why did you bring me back?" I spit, rage simmering. "So I could watch the love of my life choose him over me?"

I've got so much anger for everything that's happened, so much regret and remorse, and I'm ashamed I let myself get to the depths I did.

I didn't want to come back.

Sayah and Bash pull whatever—or whomever—out of the tomb and Ollie flashes over.

"Dominic!" he shouts to me, standing by my dad, who is

trying to get to my mom. The winds are whipping debris and other detritus around. He ducks as one of the giant pillars falls with the next explosion.

"Ollie, go!" she yells at him; the sounds of war, death, and violence permeate the once-serene burial chamber.

Tallyn shoves one of her soldiers into the portal and yanks Ollie with her as they vanish.

"Dominic!" yells my mom while my dad holds his hand out to her.

"Adaline!" he screams, a dozen of Tallyn's soldiers trying to fend off the flying spider, making its way toward Bash and Sayah.

Sayah, scooping up a fae woman who's half dark and half-light, tries to use her vamp-flash and runs right into a stone wall, dropping the being, and falling to the ground.

Bash is flashing over to her, pulling her up. Shadows build behind him, an army of grimspawns and darkling fae crawling in through the newly blasted hole next to the tomb they were just at, barely missing the spider that came flying for him.

"I'm not leaving her!" Sayah yells at Bash, who's pulled her into his arms, and tries to flash toward the portal.

Sayah manages to get free of his arms and is back at the unconscious fairy, scooping her up.

The spider is upon Bash.

My mom is grabbing for me.

Sayah is flashing to the portal with the fae woman dangling in her arms.

My dad moves for my mom as I let up on my powers and flash to the spider about to spear Bash with one of its long, sword-like legs.

The air thickens with the stench of death. Shadows writhe at the edges of my vision. I step forward, ready to meet the blade meant for Bash. Let this end with me. I'll be set free and leave him to be with Sayah.

"*Stop!*" Bash yells, and the deadly tip of the knife-like leg halts, hovering inches from my chest. Everything in the room with jagged rows of teeth freezes in place except the grimspawn and other demon creatures swarming toward us.

Bash grabs my arm, trying to drag me toward the portal, but I resist.

Sayah flashes past, tossing the unconscious fae through the portal before reversing and racing toward Bash.

"No," I tell him firmly. "I'm not going."

The grimspawn are closing in on us now. I stand firm, wanting to die the death I deserve.

My mom is next to us in a breath, grabbing for my hand. I yank out of her grasp, backing up into the claws of the demons who are to be my true death.

"I have to close the portal," I hear Halcyon say from the other side of it. "Whoever is left, you have five seconds to get through it."

"Adaline! Now!" yells my dad.

"Dominic!" she screams.

"Bash!" Sayah shouts, and I realize then that I gave my heart to a traitor.

I got addicted to a losing game.

I lost her.

I back up, feeling the icy breath of the grimspawns upon me, the darkling fae, and beings I don't even know what to call.

Before I can even comprehend what's happening, my dad blurs into motion faster than thought, his presence a sudden and overwhelming force. In one fluid movement, thick, twisting vines erupt from his hands, snaking around us—binding me, Bash, Mom, and Sayah together. The vines pulse with a faint emerald glow, their surface rough yet unyielding as they coil around our limbs and torsos.

The chamber quakes with every second that ticks by. Shadows and grimspawn swarm closer, their guttural cries a dark symphony of chaos. My dad's expression is a mask of fierce determination, his eyes locked on the portal as if it holds the only salvation left in this crumbling nightmare.

With a raw, guttural shout, he channels his strength. The vines tighten as they jerk us forward with impossible force. My body lurches, feeling weightless for a fraction of a second, the air rushing past my ears as we're propelled through the shimmering vortex. The portal shudders violently, its edges flickering and shrinking. Eerie light cascades in fractured beams. It zippers closed behind us with a deafening crack, sealing us away from the terror we left behind.

The last thing I see is my dad—standing resolute, a lone warrior in the face of annihilation. Trystan's shadow looms behind him, blade gleaming as it arcs toward his neck. His gaze meets mine one final time, unwavering, even as his life is claimed by the dark with the portal's vanishing.

47

SOOTHE MY FIRE

—SAYAH—

daline's scream is the most grueling, harrowing, and sorrowful sound I've ever heard. It clings to me, echoing through the rips, and bends of time and space as we are hurled forward. Her lament is raw and keening, entwining with the fabric of the vortex itself. Her cry stains the portal's walls, its vibrant teal darkened to shades of deep violet, indigo, and black, transforming it into a swirling blackhole.

We are violently flung into a trench carved by Tallyn's soldiers, zigzagging through a pale purple field on the outskirts of Feylight. The impact is jarring. Bash lands on his back, with me sprawled on top of him, Dom to my right, and Adaline to my left—all of us are still bound together.

The moment we hit the compacted dirt, the blackened vortex snaps shut. Adaline thrashes, the vines snapping apart as she tears herself free.

She lunges toward the empty space where the portal had been, Halcyon pulling his magick back into himself.

"*Everett!*" she screams. "Bring it back! Bring the portal back!" Her fangs emerge, her fingernails elongating into razor-sharp claws as she rakes them down Halcyon's arms.

Tallyn rushes forward, shoving Halcyon behind her like a protective mother.

Ollie flashes beside Adaline, grabbing her arm in an attempt to hold her back.

"*Open. It. Back. Up,*" she demands, her furious gaze fixed on Halcyon over Tallyn's shoulder.

"There's nothing left to do, Adaline," Tallyn says in a strained voice, utterly unconvincing in its attempt at compassion. "If he'd kept the portal open even a moment longer, any one of those beings could have breached Rowan and Caelum's barrier, tainting it and letting Trystan's abyssal army in."

"Then we'd be fucked," Briar, one of Tallyn's soldiers, adds bluntly.

"*Fuck you!*" Adaline spits, her voice venomous and soaked in grief. "I need to get back to him!" she wails, slashing Ollie's face, her nails drawing blood.

"Mom," Ollie mutters, his tranquil presence grounding even me. His voice is calm and steady, like a balm for a frayed soul, even one on the verge of breaking. "Mom." Unshed tears sheening his eyes as the bloody gash on his face seals itself. "He's gone."

Adaline's sobs, raw and unrelenting, tear through the trench, mingling with the distant booms of battle, the crackle of magic, and the growling thunder of impending storms.

Two centuries of memories—of love and laughter, of raising children, watching them grow, enduring deaths, rebirths, curses, and prophecies, battling darkness and fate—all of it gone in the blink of an eye.

The longest relationship I ever had was with my ex-husband. Eight years. And even though we divorced, I mourned that bond as though it were a death.

I have nothing to compare to the anguish radiating from Adaline. The sheer, unadulterated agony reverberates around her, echoing through the trenches, and ensnaring everyone within earshot in the same suffocating sorrow.

To watch a vampire unravel like this is like witnessing the fall of a once-stoic cathedral or the collapse of the Roman Empire—something grand, powerful, and timeless brought to ruin. It's like hearing a mournful melody or watching someone lose a battle they've fought desperately to win.

The war rages on behind us, but all I can see is Adaline. I watch as she fractures, her armor cracking and dismantling her from the inside out. Her mouth opens in a silent scream, the horror dawning on her as her mind processes what her heart cannot. She goes limp in Ollie's arms.

I watch Ollie break, his sobs muffled in his mother's hair. His arms wrap around her, desperate and tight, as if he's trying to hold on to every fleeting memory of their shared life. He clings to her as though grasping at smoke, sifting through sand, collecting the stars of his childhood with his father, each one slipping further from reach.

Then I see Hattie. Her long silver hair stirs in the wind, her face etched with wrinkles as deep as canyons, her milky eyes filling with tears. She slides to the ground, her back against the dirt wall, her skeletal hands clasping together as she pulls her knees to her chest. She mourns her father with every ounce of her being, the weight of her grief pressing down like an ancient, unyielding force.

Scarlet—her beautiful face falling as she mimics her mother's shatter—falls to her knees and laments her sorrow into the wind.

Jasantha moves over to Ollie and Adaline, agony and loss coloring her expression. She melts into their embrace as they grasp onto each other—they're the only comfort in a world on fire.

Dom's face still holds anger, but paired with the agony, the expressions meld into new emotions words have not yet been invented to identify. He's still lying on his side, staring at Bash like he wants to murder him, but the death of their father is preventing him from moving at all.

Knowing Dom is awake, alive, and healed takes a bit longer to reach the surface. Unlike when I was fully human—when I was loud and expressive and unapologetic, laying bare any emotion that would enter my mind the moment it did—I keep my expression neutral, clinging to any and all calm I can retrieve from the air.

Bash's endless pools of sapphire are staring up into my eyes. He wriggles out from under me, ducking under the vines, and then unravels them from me and Dom, helping me to my feet. It's an awkward situation if I've ever been in one.

Dom rolls onto his back, looking up at the night sky, which is blanketed in ominous smoke and dark clouds that completely blot out the moon and stars.

Nyx lies unconscious against the dirt wall. I kneel beside her, brushing my fingers along her cheek before standing and wiping the tears from my eyes and nose. Her skin has returned to the normal dusty pink, looking as though the light and darkness of her settled into her bones.

The moment I straighten, Bash pulls me into him, clinging to me as if I'm his lifeline. He never had the same bond with his father that his siblings did, but Everett was still the only father he'd ever known.

His sorrow radiates off him, mixed with a quiet ache of longing—regret for a connection he never fully had and pain for the fleeting chance that will never return, drifting away like a glowing ember carried on the wind.

I inhale a deep breath, realizing I'm savoring something I haven't felt in ages: safety. Bash doesn't shed any tears, but his grief is palpable as he buries his face in my hair, his thumbs tracing gentle circles on my arms. It's as if holding me grounds him and keeps him whole.

Beyond us, Castle Feylight is in chaos. Its once-glorious walls are scarred with smoldering green craters. Twisted, dragon-like creatures—more horrifying than any nightmare—and other hellish beasts circle the castle and its grounds, their eerie blue flames scorching everything that moves, is lush and green, or shows even the faintest sign of life.

"What the fuck are those things?" I say, pulling out of Bash's embrace and watching as the flying serpent-looking thing flies overhead above our bubble barrier again.

Bash looks up, his eyes tracking it. "Tallyn called them wyverns. What's up with her?" he asks, jutting his chin toward the sleeping Nyx.

"Oh, hell no," Tallyn's voice pierces through our conversation; her march to Nyxaria is brutal and determined. "What the fuck is one of these sorry pieces of shit doing here?"

When I flash over to her, she's about to lift Nyx by her hair.

I could get used to this.

"Wait!" I tell her, stepping between her and Nyx. "Please. Don't hurt her. She's not like the rest of them. I promise," I lie, hoping the steel in my voice is believable. "She wanted out; she told me to help get her out, and he must have found out she was a traitor. I didn't know how I would get her when she lumo-kenisis'd me and told me she'd teleport herself to me if I pinpointed where I was. She must have been found out, which is why she was unconscious in the tomb."

Tallyn's orange eyes redden as she steps closer to me. "So, it's your fault Everett is dead, then?"

My stomach hollows out. "What? No, that's not what this is."

"How else do you think Trystan got your location and access into the burial chamber? I have that area spelled so he couldn't get in."

I take a step back. "There's got to be another explanation, Tallyn. Nyx would never do that to me."

Tallyn's fierce eyes pierce into me. "You better hope you're right."

Ravens pass overhead, glowing and otherworldly. Their caw roils through my bones as though my soul understands what they're saying.

It's then that I notice Thistlewynd staring up at the crows, her eyes white and milky and blank, as though seeing through their eyes and communicating in an avionic tongue.

Her eyes return to their chocolate brown, and she faces Tallyn. "Trystan's army has breached the outer perimeter."

Tallyn's boots pad roughly against the compact dirt as she tracks her way back to Thistlewynd. "Fuck. Call the dragons. Sayah, I need you and your sister to prepare phoenix bombs. We must get to them before they get to the Aetherian ring."

"Yes, Your Majesty." Thistlewynd bows, her eyes turning milky again as she summons the dragons.

Tallyn turns to me. "Gather your sister and meet me at the other end of this trench. I'll need as many as you can make. Do you feel comfortable flying on your own wings, or would you rather ride with Bash on Wynter?"

Her words echo in a jumble I don't quite know the meaning of. I look to Bash for solace while I try to hold on to my sanity.

"Sayah?" she says louder, like I'm just supposed to jump up and do what she says the moment she speaks it, even though I don't understand half the shit she said.

"What?" I yell back to her, steeling myself against the parts of me that want to save Trystan, the parts threatening to crumble into dust or to take flight and go be by him, redeeming that dream of being the queen of everything—for my son.

I square up to the Luminara Queen, fleeting recklessness taming the wild, my feral magick surging inside me again. "You fucking spew some shit at me, thinking I just randomly know how to . . . *make phoenix bombs*, not even taking into consideration that this family just lost their patriarch to *your* war, and just expect us to jump up like some fucking puppets—"

She takes a step toward me. "You might want to watch your tone with me, little girl—"

"Little girl?" I laugh, hysteria bubbling inside me, mixing with the already turbulent chaos asphyxiating all rational thought, all the old, people-pleasing me's that usually stop me from doing anything this reckless. "Do you have *any* idea what *your* fucking brother took from me? How he poisoned me— *took my sobriety*—and made me think I was some sort of *Delaney* in a past life, come back to life in a new body but still sewn to his—"

"He fucking what?" Tallyn seethes, her eyes burning.

I return her glare. "Which part? The part where he raped me or the part where he poisoned me?"

"Your Majesty, the—" Thistlewynd tries to cut in.

"Excuse me, what the fuck?" Scarlet cuts in. "What did that motherfucker do to you?"

"Oh, please, Trystan's done way worse than that to me; get the fuck in line," she says to Scarlet, making Adaline's head perk up.

"You act like you're so fucking innocent!" Adaline screams, mascara painting her face in a warrior-esque façade—well, not façade; it actually becomes her and makes her Viking-like nature stand out. "You're the one who stole an innocent baby from my arms! My firstborn baby girl!"

"Because of Trystan!" she snarls, her voice wavering yet set inside a storm. "He forced a hysterectomy on me. While I was unconscious! I was never able to have my own children because of him!" The distant sound of bombs intensifying her fury.

Everyone falls silent.

Bash struts over casually. "What in the in-bred fuck are you yacking on about?"

I don't even feel bad about it. The old me would've shushed

him for being so inconsiderate to a woman who was about to spill her soul to virtual strangers.

"Trystan was mad that Mother chose me to leave the realms to," she answers, staring daggers into Bash. "He was determined to get the realm back and didn't want there to be any chance for me to have an heir. He tried killing me. Multiple times. But like Sayah's mother, our mother, Zephyra, put a mirror spell on us so we wouldn't be able to kill each other. So, the next best thing was for him to force a hysterectomy on me, so in the event that I did die, I wouldn't have an heir."

Dom's face softens toward Tallyn. Bash's only intensifies. "Wouldn't that have castrated himself, then?"

Tallyn shrugs. "Guess he didn't care."

"So you thought you'd just steal *my* baby?" Adaline says. "Now you and your brother's stupid feud has also taken my husband."

"Excuse me, my queen, but it's urgent," Thistlewynd interjects again.

"Oh, what is it, Thistlewynd?"

The fae is small in stature as it is, but she visibly shrinks, cowering away from the queen's gaze. "I have a message for Sayah," she says, my heart dropping as her soft pink eyes graze mine.

"From?" Bash says, standing straighter to block me.

"Trystan."

"How in the fuck would you have a message from him?" Bash's voice is filled with rage; I can almost see Agares bursting at the seams inside him.

The little pink fairy timidly glances at Bash. "He interrupted my communication with the dragons. He said to go to the middle of the field. He said he won't hurt you; he just has something to show you."

"Odin's balls, he does," Bash states.

"What would he possibly have to show me?" I ask, coming

around from behind Bash. The powers are burning me up from the inside; I may explode at any moment. "I'm not putting anyone in danger for him. He can go fuck himself."

"Sayah, maybe you should see what he wants," Tallyn urges, fear lancing through the dancing flames in her eyes.

"Fuck that," Bash says. "She's not leaving this trench."

"H-he thought you may not be so willing to go," Thistlewynd sputters hesitantly, "so he wanted me to tell you 'Gauge.' I don't know what this word means, but he said it would hold weight with you."

The fire becomes too much. I cannot hold it back anymore. It's like a dam breaking inside me.

It feels like my skin is detaching from me; pieces of soul shooting like shrapnel, piercing anyone close to me. The fire explodes in a furious rush, burning brighter than the sun, and I cannot see anything; I just know it feels so fucking good, like relieving pressure or popping a zit that was so big it was hurting.

"Sayah," I hear Bash's voice through the ferociously burning veil. "Sayah, listen to my voice."

The shadows within me love his voice; they shiver toward it like it's their master. They calm the fire as they search for him in the burning inferno my body has become.

"Sayah." The shadows purr, growing at the sound of his, coaxing the fire into the shadows. "That's a good girl, Sayah. Follow my voice."

"Bash?" I call out, feeling as though I'm behind a waterfall. I can't see him, but I can hear him through the flames—except the flames aren't burning me.

"C'mon, Sayah, you're almost back. Listen to my voice."

The shadows grow again, taming more of the fire.

Like the flames, the shadows breathe, flicker, and dance as though the echoes of us are having their own silent conversation.

"That's good, baby, almost there."

Yes, sir, Mr. Shadow man. My skin awakens to him, the chill of the shadows dousing the intensity of my fire. The amalgamation of our two facets is like aloe to a burn, refreshing, calming me, summoning the fire back into my being.

The angry flames simmer to a flicker of a candle on the tip of my finger, and one of my shadows reaches out from the depths of me and licks it away.

Bash's blue eyes are in front of me, and my shadow caresses the sides of his face before retreating back into my soul.

"What just happened?"

I feel everyone staring at me, the war waging on in the background, but all I see is Bash.

He is all I see.

His fingertips—now black—graze the side of my face, his stare adoringly colliding with mine. "Some women cower at the sight of the flames. Some women are consumed by them. You, Sayah, are fire incarnate."

Someone clears their throat and knocks our trance off-kilter.

"Sayah," Tallyn says, her face coming into focus behind Bash's shoulders. She's holding a piece of parchment.

I step out of Bash's grasp and walk up to her, grabbing the parchment.

I have your son.

Return to me immediately, and no harm will come to him.

Meet me at the west tower, and come alone.

–Trystan

48

ANTITHESIS OF NORMAL

—SAYAH—

The fire threatens to engulf me again, the parchment still clenched in my trembling hand.

Nothing will break me faster than the mention of my son

Bash's calm demeanor and shadows speak to mine, our echoes seemingly leveling us, cementing his calm to me.

"We'll get him back," he reassures, but it's far away and echoey.

It's taking every last bit of strength I have to keep the fire contained, to clench down on every power I now have—new ones I can't grasp the purpose of, and old ones that are morphing, and it feels like my skin is going to burst apart again.

I don't know how to translate this storm inside me.

"Just keep your eyes on me," Bash says, his voice sounding like he's veilweaving me, but he isn't.

Or he can't now that I'm a vampire.

But was he able to even when I was just Sayah, the phoenix?

My eyes track to Dom, whose hazel ones had been on me, and he sheepishly looks away.

A tiny flicker of guilt knocks against the rest of the turbulent emotions flooding through me, but it becomes a dewdrop in the ocean of things overwhelming me. My fangs are begging to be let out, someone's jugular is screaming to be sliced open and drained, the ascension or transition into vampire still fresh on my skin.

"Breathe," Bash tells me, the soft burning of the infinity symbol nestling against the inside of my skin. "Everything is overweening when you first become a vampire. Emotions are heightened even for someone in a normal-ish situation, and this is like the antithesis of normal. You have every valid reason to feel like your skin is coming undone, but pull it all back. Imagine it like a dark cloud you can wrangle with your phoenix power." His hands are on my shoulders; he holds my eyes and takes a deep breath. "Go on, close your eyes for me."

Inhaling, I take the same breath he just released, pulling him into me, and close my eyes.

I'm standing on the same cliff I always visit in my subconscious. Behind me is my tower. I keep all my memories, wants, dreams, and wishes looming atop the craggy cliff.

In front of me, the turbulent ocean; dark, ominous, wild, and reckless. It's being controlled by the dark cumulonimbus cloud, growing in width and strength as it stirs the wind and water.

Now look at your hands. See it? Bash's voice echoes like a soft flutter, winding around me, and flitting into the sky.

Looking down, I find myself clutching a golden lasso. Its strands glimmer so brilliantly that they seem to pierce through the surrounding darkness, making the ominous cloud overhead feel even heavier and more oppressive. The golden light pulses faintly, alive in my hands.

That's your phoenix power, Bash says, his steady voice grounding me. *I want you to lasso that cloud of emotions in. Pull it to you.*

I don't know how to lasso, Bash. I'm not a cowgirl, I argue, my grip tightening on the glowing rope, its warmth radiating into my palms.

You'll just know. Trust me.

I close my eyes briefly, breathing in his certainty, letting it bolster me. When I open them, I twirl the lasso overhead, the movement seeming instinctive. My right arm swings with precision, the golden rope spinning faster and faster, a perfect arc of light against the shadowy gloom. My left hand stretches outward, steadying me, and guiding my aim toward the churning cumulonimbus cloud.

With a deep breath, I release the rope. It streaks forward like a comet, glowing brighter as it extends into the vast, stormy expanse. The lasso strikes its target with unerring accuracy, wrapping itself around the writhing cloud. The rope coils tightly, the cloud buckling under the pressure as the golden light seals it in, binding the chaos.

I dig my heels in and pull, the weight of the cloud resisting me. It feels like dragging an entire storm—rage, despair, fear— all compressed into one stubborn mass. But with every inch I draw closer, it shrinks. The thunder inside it softens, and the lightning flickers less violently.

When the cloud finally reaches me, it's no longer a monstrous force of nature but a tiny, fragile raincloud cradled in the palm of my hand. A single droplet falls from its silvery surface, sliding down my fingers. The storm that had loomed is now just a whisper.

Good. Now put it up there in your tower and lock it safely away.

I close my eyes tighter and imagine the tiny raincloud sitting atop the same table where Bash's words and memories live.

Taking a deep breath, the waves return to calm waters, and I open my eyes again.

"Better?" His voice is louder now, and the storm is quiet.

I nod, imagining any jostling will wake the giant wave and end me.

"How can we even be sure he has him?" Scarlet asks Tallyn, her eyes tracking a flaming green thornbolt hitting the translucent boundary high up in the air.

The cloud inside me rumbles, and I tighten the lasso on it, ensuring it remains where it should be.

"Either way," Tallyn says, her eyes raking across her soldiers in the trench, then up to those taking flight to mitigate the assault. "He's getting too close to the Aetherian Circle," she says to Caelum, Halcyon, Thalira, and Thistlewynd, mostly. "We need to go to plan B."

"I'm sorry now. What circle and what's plan B?" Bash asks, letting go of my hands, walking up to Tallyn.

Tallyn lets out an exasperated breath. "The Aetherian ring is the innermost circle where all the ley lines cross. It's where the Feylight Covenant and Stone of Souls are. These are spelled to my soul, keeping me in power. Trystan cannot get near them without me; the magick is too strong."

"But," Bash presses when she doesn't continue.

More meaning to her words than she leads on, as always.

Another green thornbolt flies overhead and crashes into the invisible barrier.

"We need to act soon, my queen," Halcyon says, stepping in front of Bash to address her.

"Ah ah ah," Bash says, butting his way back in front of Tallyn. "We already know he had found some sort of loophole by marrying Sayah and opening Desoloth."

Tallyn watches the sky carefully, glancing at Thistlewynd, and nodding.

"Trystan *thinks* he's found a loophole. If he opens all seven rings, the seven portals, and marries a phoenix—the Celestial Phoenix—he'll be able to enter the Aetherian Circle and destroy the covenant, sew his soul to the stone, and rewrite the document with Sayah's new power of being able to write things into fruition."

"But the ceremony wasn't complete. He only partly managed to open Desoloth," Ollie says.

"And I killed Sayah to break that connection," Adaline says, a bit too proudly for my liking.

"How the fuck do you know about my writing power?" I ask, not hearing any of it but that. I experienced that on my own, in Wyndhallow, with Freya. I didn't know what it meant at the time. But now, hearing Tallyn explain it brings me right back to that moment.

What I had written down.

How the parchment turned into a bird and fluttered away.

How the fuck does Tallyn know about that power?

The wing beat of a massive creature scrapes through the sky, interrupting our conversation. The sound grows louder until the ground shakes upon its heavy landing above the trenches.

"No time to explain. We must destroy the ley lines. Sayah." She marches over to me and grabs my shoulders. "I need you to make those phoenix bombs. We have to move quickly. We cannot have Feylight fall to Trystan. No matter the cost. It cannot fall to him."

"And by destroying the ley lines, you mean?" Bash asks for me.

Tallyn's expression turns grave. "We destroy Feylight. I would rather see it destroyed than for it to fall to my brother."

My shoulders tense. "By no matter the cost, you mean what, exactly?" I ask. My resolve and motherly instinct to protect my child at all costs snuffs out everything.

"Sayah, listen to me," Tallyn says, her face quickly limned by an explosion overhead. "There's a chance that Trystan is just toying with you to get you back to him. He's desperate and would say and do anything to get the power of Feylight."

Anger bubbles inside the cloud on my mind's dresser, the golden lasso straining to keep it secure. Like rubber bands around a watermelon, I don't know how much more I can add before it bursts. "But there's a chance he has my son with him. And because of that chance, no matter how big or small, I will not help you destroy Feylight. Not until I can be certain he doesn't have Gauge."

Tallyn's glare turns murderous, like she's trying to strangle me with her eyes.

But this I will not budge on. This is a hill I will gladly die upon.

"You need me to make you those bombs. I refuse until I know Gauge is safe. So, let me go back to Trystan. I know what I'm doing. I am not afraid of him. Or you."

"Sayah—" Bash starts, but I shake my head.

"No, Bash." I turn to face him. "You neither. I will not bend on this. He says he has my child. I will go to him. I am not afraid of him."

As he wraps me in his arms, a rush in the air surges through me like a chill. My bones freeze, wrapping my ribs in fiery delight, and my shadows blanket me in warmth. I close my eyes. A glitch in time happens, or perhaps a jump. I'm not really sure, but when I open them, a whisper answers.

Did you get what I needed you to get yet, my darling?

I did. I'll see you soon.

49

FAMILIAR ECHOES

—BASH—

The rips and tears on the edges of me, the parchment and scrolls making up my existence, threaten to burn in Agares's fire, in Sayah's flames, at just the thought of Trystan's hands on her.

Like the fables of other worlds, our echoes are so familiar with each other now, tilled from the ashes of our cagey pasts. They reach out to each other outside of dreams now, even when Sayah and I are standing inches apart. I know that if death claims her, my soul will find her again. I just hate the thought of spending a second without her, let alone a lifetime.

Once we are miles apart, our echoes will keep track of one another.

The shadows will let me know she's okay, even if I can't see her.

But I still hate this.

Every. Fucking. Part. Of. It.

This is the worst plan in the world.

"You sure you're okay?" Sayah asks, her voice like a spill of warm, roiling stones.

"Oh, yeah, def," I say, coating my voice with honeyed sarcasm, but all because I'm trying to cover the terror in it. I push back against the trench wall, head full of thoughts I can't tame to push free. "What will he say about taking this one with you when he said to come alone?"

She's carrying Nyx in her arms like she's carrying a bundle of clothes. Vampire strength is becoming on her.

Her eyes widen, as the pupils eat the icy color of her eyes. "Pretty sure he just meant no vampires."

Words are caged in my mouth as I walk her to the end of the trench.

Halcyon is preparing the portal for her.

Her demeanor is softer somehow, even though becoming a vampire usually makes someone harder. The cracks and fissures seem at rest for now, leaving lightning scars almost across every inch of her. But her hair is still raven-colored and beautiful, making her subtly tan skin all the more golden in the moonlight.

"Bash," she says, shifting Nyx to look at me better. "I know what I'm doing. We all came up with a great plan. It's going to work. Trust me?"

Another thornbolt flies above our heads, and we watch it, this time causing a crack in the barriers Caelum and Rowan had placed above us.

"Sebastian, c'mon!" Tallyn shouts over to us. "Wynter's waiting."

I wave my hand at her behind my back.

She can wait.

"Okay," Sayah says to me, the magick of the portal Halcyon unzipped crackling.

"So he's going to portal you to the where now?" I ask. The crack above the barrier sounds like the cracking of a frozen lake in a canyon.

Sayah glances up at the sky, her ocean-blue eyes calm. "To the fields near the west tower. I'll use our echoes to communicate."

"Don't let him get those shackles on you."

"I won't. I promise."

Another blast of a thornbolt hits the barrier like a rock to a windshield, spiderwebbing together with the other one, making it wider and more vulnerable.

"One more of those and the barrier is going to burst!" yells Halcyon, toward us but more at Tallyn. "Wait long enough and you won't even need me to portal you out of here; he'll be able to just waltz right in and get you."

"Shit," Sayah says, looking to me for comfort.

"Go. In order for our plan to work, he can't come get you. You have to have the upper hand. And do what I said when he tries to shackle you, okay?"

"Okay."

"To death beyond," I say, taking her lips in mine, savoring her as though a hundred-foot wave is about to claim us, yet she remains as calm as a flat day at sea.

"Death beyond," she says once we part. "You tame my fire, Sebastian."

Then she glances over her shoulder at the impatient Halcyon.

"And you have deciphered every bit of my soul," I return, grabbing her by the back of her neck. I slam one last kiss onto her mouth and then shove her away.

She runs to the portal as fluid as the ocean incarnate, eyes tracking to me with a final glance.

There's not even a crevice for my heart to hide within. I watch her step through, my whole body mourning the loss of her like a severed limb.

I just got her back.

I want her back now.

What if our plan doesn't work?

What if he gets those shackles on her and I can't get her back?

Easy friend, it will work. Agares's voice rumbles low and raw.

If one hair on her head is harmed, I will devour the world, and harvest every living being on it.

THAT STEADY STILLNESS

—DOM—

Seeing Sayah and Bash embracing the way they are tears into my being in so many different ways.

In a way, I always knew Sayah and I were doomed from the start.

The way I felt about her and how drawn I was to her was almost unnatural—which is strange to even think, being that I am supernatural.

But now I know it was all to bring her to her destiny.

To my brother.

But gods-damn, did I fucking love her.

I mean, really, really love her. There was just something about her that spoke a language only my soul understood.

For the last—however the fuck long I was in The Gloaming —she was what was keeping me from being completely submerged in the ravine of my mind.

Wherever I was, time didn't exist, but for little blips of this strange construct we call time, I would be on a secluded beach with Sayah at sunset, on a blanket, watching the waves. We wouldn't say anything to each other; we'd just sit in this comfortable silence and watch the undulation of the water, the aquatic dance of the waves on the surface of the world.

Sayah and I are like that ocean, in a way.

The water, so desperate to be with the sand, surges up and over time and time again, only to be pulled back by the moon. The moon's refusal to let the water be with the sand makes the water angry, and at certain times of day, when the moon was far away from it, it would creep up further and further just to get a taste, one more time . . . one more time . . . one more time.

The water cannot stay with the sand no matter how long the moon is away. The tide is too turbulent and wild to stay in one place. And the sand—well, she's that steady stillness, the calm and solid that the water needs to taste every once in a while to keep the water stable. And the water keeps the sand wild.

While they can never be together in this life, forever as one, they will always be waiting for each other. They'll always embrace one another like an old friend and take the fleeting kisses, the fluttering touches of memory, to calm the raging waters and to cool the scorching sand.

I used to be the water, and Sayah was the sand. But something happened to her while she was in Never—something that changed that.

She is more wild now. More turbulent.

It's her time to find her wild, and Bash can help her tame it if it becomes too strong.

But in this Gloaming, I knew we were like the water and the sand.

I knew I had lost her long before I was ever gone. Before I even had her.

She never truly belonged to me.

What hurts the most is knowing that my soul doesn't speak to hers the way hers speaks to mine.

It always felt like a one-way street. No matter how passionate we once were for each other, she was still far away and distant, even when we were sitting right next to each other. Pieces of her will always be with him, and no matter how hard I tried to own all her heart, only a particle of it truly belonged to me.

There are certain people in this world with whom we feel a deeper connection. Whatever souls are made of, two had to be of the same material. And then there are those people who are not meant for you, but you'd give everything you had to make it not so.

But those people are only meant to be a chapter in your life, not the whole story.

Without that chapter, your story wouldn't be the same. No matter how long or short they graced your life, they still left it different and rearranged.

Her chapters in my life will forever be dog-eared.

It's just going to take some time for me to get used to the new, rearranged me. It'll take even longer for me to get used to Bash being her person and not me.

Speaking of the devil.

"All right, we ready?" Bash asks. I straighten up, dusting my pants off.

Another thornbolt lands above the other two, cracking like a windshield about to spiderweb across the whole barrier.

Tallyn flutters her wings while strapping a knife garter around her leg. "We have maybe two minutes before he sails another one of his thornbolts into our barrier, and I imagine the next one will blow it wide-open."

"And our plan C is?" Bash says as he follows Tallyn around like a lost puppy while I try to muster up any motivation to participate in this dreadful war.

"Just don't blow up the middle ring," Henry tells Bash.

Henry from our childhood.

Why is Henry from our childhood here?

"La La finished up the bombs?" Bash continues his questions while I maneuver around him to check on my mom.

"She's finishing up the last batch . . ." Tallyn's voice trails off as she and Bash move toward one end of the trench while I find my mom around a bend in the other direction.

She's sitting cross-legged against the dirt wall, a vacant expression plastered on her face. She's staring at nothing, the dirt wall across from her, absently spinning her diamond ring from my dad around and around her finger.

"Mom?" I say, kneeling to be eye to eye with her.

It takes a second for her to register I'm in front of her, her eyes looking into mine but seeing right through me. "Dom?"

"Hey," I answer, moving a piece of Earth stuck in her bangs. "You sure you want to be involved with this?" I ask, her eyes narrowing on me and growing angry.

"What?" she says with such ferocity that it seems she's angry with me.

"Well, with what just happened, you can always have Halcyon portal you back to Lake George. Wait for us there—"

She drops her hands into her lap and balls them in first. "If it wasn't for your driveling, your father would still be her," she snipes at me, her mascara like war paint. "I will burn Trystan's kingdom to the fucking ground for what he took from me."

I'm still burning from her jab. "Mom, I didn't mean—"

"Hey, you guys coming?" Ollie asks, appearing from around the bend, Claire being pulled behind him. "They say we have to get to the dragons, the barrier—"

A loud explosion interrupts Ollie.

The sky is lighting up in the most brilliant orange and green. The hole blasted through the barrier, causing the rest of the globe-like substance above us to crack like lightning across the entirety of it, shards of glass-like material raining down.

A piece of the barrier material falls, landing on one of Tallyn's soldier's heads, splitting him in half. Before we can even think, swarms of demons and wyverns, darkling fae, and Never-dusk soldiers are pilfering in through the hole, followed by a blast of magick.

"C'mon, Mom, we gotta go," I yell, pulling her up.

We race to where Tallyn has gathered, her soldiers taking flight to fend off the onslaught of enemy soldiers.

Bash is bounding into the air with ease, clearing the ten-foot wall of dirt we stand in.

"What's the plan?" I shout to Tallyn, my voice nearly lost in the cacophony of roaring dragons and the crackling chaos around us. Scarlet and Jasantha vault into place behind Bash, their movements sharp and practiced, ready for battle.

"Dom, watch out!" Ollie's voice tears through the din.

He crashes into me, shoving us both to the ground just as a massive shard of the barrier plunges down, obliterating the spot I was standing in, a deafening explosion of debris and light.

"Just get on a dragon and blast whatever you can!" Tallyn commands, her voice a blade cutting through the madness. She's levitating now, feet hovering inches off the ground, her eyes ablaze like molten suns. "When Sayah gives the signal," she says, turning to Bash, her words trailing off as I scramble to join my siblings.

Bash climbs onto a white dragon, its wings stretching wide, catching the fiery glow of the burning horizon. He glares up at the sky, his voice steady and lethal. "He wants war?" He pauses, gripping the reins. "We'll give him war."

Tallyn's gaze sharpens, her fiery eyes meeting Bash's for a moment before shifting to the skies. Her presence is magnetic, the fierce queen of a crumbling battlefield. "Burn. It. Down." Her command is both an order and a promise as she ascends into the air, her soldiers following in formation.

The ground beneath us vibrates as the dragons roar and take flight, a cacophony of screeches and thundering beats of wings filling the air.

"What the fuck am I supposed to do?" I yell over the chaos as Hattie clambers onto the blue dragon beside my mom.

"Get on one, brother," Bash calls down, his white dragon already in the air, flames licking from its mouth. "Or get on with me."

"No thanks," I shout back, frantically scanning the war-torn landscape for a free dragon.

The horizon is alive with destruction—explosions light up the sky, and black shapes dart between streaks of dragon fire. The acrid stench of smoke and sulfur fills my lungs as distant thunder rolls. No, not thunder—something else. A sharp whistle cuts through the air, followed by a fiery arrow slamming into the ground beside me.

I freeze for half a second, my instincts warring with my thoughts. Then I spot it—a small yellow dragon crouched and waiting. I make a break for it, weaving through the carnage, but before I reach it, a scream rips through the battlefield.

It's not just any scream—it's raw, piercing, a cry that cuts through the noise and leaves everything else silent in its wake.

I whirl around, my heart lurching into my throat.

Ollie.

He's on the ground, a green thornbolt buried in his chest. Blood bubbles from his lips in weak, gasping chokes, his body twitching in his fight for air. Claire clutches him, her soot-streaked face twisted in anguish, rocking him back and forth as if she can will him back to life. Her sobs cut through the madness, drowning out the fire, the war, the chaos. But all I see is Ollie—dying in her arms, his breath slipping away with every agonizing second.

51

PLEASURABLE SORT OF PAIN

—SAYAH—

The crackle of the vortex zipping back up mingles with the distant explosions in the direction I just came from.

Halcyon departs, leaving us in the grassy knoll across from the west tower.

Glancing over my shoulder, my heart lurches. The protective bubble capping the trenches where Tallyn, Bash, and the others have taken refuge is under siege. Flames lick its surface, devouring it in an eerie, mesmerizing pattern. It reminds me of when you take a lighter to a stray thread on a sock—how the fire races across the surface, consuming everything in its path with a quiet, relentless whoosh. But this isn't just sock fuzz—it's the barrier holding back annihilation, and the fire isn't racing.

It's crawling.

The flames spread slower, deliberate, as if savoring every inch of their destruction. The barrier sizzles and cracks, melting away piece by piece, each charred section unraveling the hope of safety beneath it. What once felt invincible now seems fragile —each mile of it consumed like an agonizing countdown to disaster.

And I can't stop watching it burn.

Trystan's army fills the air—dark beings with leathery wings, wyverns that spiral through the smoke like living nightmares, and other soldiers seemingly from Hell. Their grotesque forms dive into the opening in the protective bubble. They descend with ruthless precision.

The war within me mirrors the chaos above. I can't tell which side I want to root for.

When I'm with them, this side of me feels fuzzy—the dark phoenix who wants to be with Trystan and save Earth and Never and Feylight to show the world that darkness isn't all bad.

But the light burns inside me, fire interwoven with shadow. It sears my arm, a painful reminder of what I've hidden and couldn't let the vampires or Tallyn see. The dark part of me still clings to Trystan and Nyx.

As if sensing my thoughts, Nyxaria stirs in my arms. Her eyes flutter open, and all the destruction around us fades for a moment.

"Hey, you," I mutter, a smile tugging at my lips despite the turmoil.

"Estreaya?" she asks. Her eyes are still mismatched—one white, one black—fixing on mine as they widen.

"Sort of," I reply, and her lips curve into a lopsided smirk.

"Beautiful either way," she says, and I'm helpless. Drawn to her like gravity, I press my lips to hers. The kiss is electric, a force that cuts through the storm within me. Even now, even after everything, I can't get enough of her. My ascension hasn't dulled the need; if anything, it's intensified it.

I pull back before the fire between us ignites into something I can't control. She groans, her body shifting against mine.

"Are you okay?" I ask, concern breaking through the haze of desire.

Nyx slips from my arms and lands lightly on her feet,

swaying only slightly. "I'm fine. Just . . . teleporting through shadows as far as I did drains my well of power. Pretty much knocked me out." She rolls her neck and stretches, the cracking of her joints somehow grounding in the madness.

"Teleporting through shadows?" I repeat, distracted by her, by everything she is.

"Yes," she answers, stepping closer, her eyes glinting. "I'm a ShadowMaiden. It's part of my power."

"Mmm, shadow mommy," I murmur, pulling her closer with a smirk.

She laughs softly, but a green thornbolt strikes the ground ten yards away before our lips meet again. It explodes on impact, sending green fire and waves of searing heat washing over us.

I snap my head up toward the source. And there he is.

Trystan.

Perched on a balcony jutting from Feylight Castle, his wings spread wide, flames licking the surrounding air. He balances effortlessly on the iron spires of the railing—a king surveying his battlefield.

"Coming?" he bellows down, his voice cutting through the chaos. His face is plastered with a smile carved from impatience.

Nyx tilts her head, studying me. "Want me to fly you up, or you got this?"

I glance at her and then at my wings—wings of fire, my birthright, my power. I've never used them to truly fly before. The thought both excites and terrifies me.

But I trust them.

Like a bird perched on a fragile branch, I don't need to trust the branch not to break. I trust my wings if it does.

"I've got this." With a deep breath, I let the fire carry me.

My skin cracks open as the fissures split, and the fire engulfs me, dousing my shadows. I feel the wings unfurl from my back, tingly and painful, like the most pleasurable sort of pain.

Nyx smiles, her teeth gleaming in the moon's light. Her iridescent wings unfold from her back, two sets, like a dragon-fly's, with the tops wider than the bottoms. They make a beautiful rainbow as she jumps into the air, and I envy her grace.

I put all the strength I can muster into my wings of fire and jump into the air.

Muscle memory expects me to plummet right back to the ground. But this time, I flutter my wings on instinct, and instead of falling, I rise further and further into the sky.

From this angle, I can see up Nyx's skirt, and I almost fall back to the ground, but I focus on rising and flicking my wings, bonding with the wind.

As Trystan's balcony approaches, Nyx rises over the railing, and I follow her lead.

Her majestic balletic flight seamlessly makes her one with the ground again as I try to mimic her. The spire sticking up over the railing catches on my wretched wedding dress, causing me to tip forward and kiss the ground.

Trystan's husky baritone of a laugh permeates the air as Nyx helps me up, his blue wings fluttering him to the ground as he grabs my other hand. "We really need to get you out of that dress, fire queen."

I scoff and dust off the tattered, burned, and dirty dress. "Got anything my size here?" I ask.

"Mmm, come here, baby. I missed you," he growls, pulling me into him. "We never got to seal our union and consummate the vows."

His mouth is on mine. It sends heated tingles to my core, the dark phoenix making herself at home against my skin again. "Yeah, sorry about that. I got kidnapped. Again."

He pulls my left arm up to see that our vines are gone from

my skin, the infinity fire symbol dull but still burning. "Fucking bloodsuckers."

"You know I am one of those bloodsuckers now, right?"

His blue eyes twist in menace. "I do." His voice holds a tinge of resentment. "They thought they could break my connection to you just by killing you and making you one of them. They don't know that you belong to me now." He pulls my left hand up where the black diamond ring still sits and kisses the stone. "This stone kept me tied to you. They erased our vines, though."

Lifting his left arm, he examines it. The vines have all but vanished on his arm as well.

I pull his chin up with my pointy fingernail. "Hey, it doesn't change how I feel about you."

He growls again, dropping my arm, and cupping my breast. "I could start fires with what I feel for you."

Erotic jolts of pleasure bubble up deep in my body, and even with bombs and war and fire, I still want that fantasy. Fucking him and Nyx while the world burns down.

He lowers his mouth onto mine and bites my lip. "So they bought it?"

The sting from his bite courses through me. He pushes back and wipes the blood from my chin. I lean back into him, whispering to the shell of his ear, "Every word. Nice work using Gauge as my way out of there. They didn't question anything."

The flashback of me timbinding jolts through my mind. This new mimic power is hard to control sometimes.

The wicked smile prances across his face again. "Because they know nothing will stand in the way of a mother scorned. Can't fucking wait to plant my seed in you and you be the mother of my children."

He kisses me roughly again, slipping his hand under the thin fabric of my gown and pinching my nipple, sending shockwaves to my clit.

"Guys," Nyx says, seductively leaning against the tower wall, the gray stone making the pink of her skin smokier. "Are we going to go fuck, or are we gonna win this war once and for all?"

Trystan bites my earlobe. "Fuck, I wish I could just fuck you two senseless, having you on your knees pledging your allegiance to me with your mouths and tongues." He grabs me by my neck and kisses me roughly, then throws me backward. "But we gotta get what you stole for me activated so I can get in that gods-damn circle."

"And how are we going to do that?" Nyx asks, toeing her way over to us.

"Well, with what Sayah stole, the barrier around the inner ring should just let us in."

"Can I change first?" I ask, looking down at my tattered black dress. "Really, I just need pants or sweats or anything but this."

Trystan pulls me toward the sliding glass doors, and I realize the balcony we're on looks exactly like the one he kidnapped me from. "We can just rip it off you and have you run around naked," he says, sliding the door open and pushing me through it.

"Mmm, I like that idea," Nyx says, following us in.

"As much as I do, too," I state, waltzing toward the closet I know is Tallyn's, as we are definitely in her bedroom. Or one of them. She brought us to this same room the night Bash was bitten and almost died, the night I first saw Dom again, the night Trystan killed him and stole me. "We should probably get down to the Aetherian Circle. We don't know how long it'll be until Tallyn decides to just light this fucker up."

"You have any more timebinds left?" Trystan asks Nyx.

"Not in this cycle. I'm at two." She holds her hand up, showing the dancing shadows swirling all the way to her neck. How the gray cloud-like swirls look on her pink skin paints a perfect picture of a sunset. "But," she says, strutting up to him, "you know you have your power. You can mimic all three from me. It's time you told Sayah about your power."

The look on his face is a cross between anger and intrigue. "I think she knows about it already."

"I'm confused."

He walks up to me, danger and enchantment dancing along his bones. He grabs me by the neck, and my heart races like he knows something. "I'm a siphon. I can siphon other people's power when they let me into their minds and mimic it."

"So you never needed Nyx, or what was up with that weird wizard dude with the crystal? What was all that for?"

His wicked smile becomes the main focal point of his face, loose strands of his hair falling out of the leather strap framing his gorgeous face. "For show. Well," he says, pulling my gown down from my left shoulder, "Nyx was for show. I mean, look at her. She's fucking sexy as hell, and I knew you liked women. Sablethorn's crystal did make it so the power I siphoned from you was amplified to last longer. Once we wed, your well of power becomes part of mine."

A bolt of realization hits me.

The power I stole from him. I didn't steal it; I only took part of it.

The power to mimic other people's power. That's how I can timebind and portal travel, acquiring new powers as I go. Each ability etches itself onto my skin, a story written in magick.

The thunderstorm spiraling across my arm—a gift from Bash—lets me harness the Earth's vibrations, grounding me in its power. The infinity symbol, another of Bash's gifts, ties us together: shadows from him to me, fire from me to him.

My wrist bears a swirling tattoo, an emblem of continuous flow and absorption—my mimic power. Others have appeared, subtle but significant. A bottle-shaped mark traps someone in a memory, a prison of their own mind. A feather quill dipping into an inkwell writes things into existence, bending reality with a single thought. The time piece with a bind around it—timebinding.

The timebind power is perhaps the most striking—a pocket watch etched on my right arm, intricate and gleaming. I must have taken it from Nyx, her essence woven into the shadows around it.

And now there's a new mark: a shadowy shield. ShadowMaiden?

These tattoos are more than just powers; they're pieces of the journey. Stories of what I've taken, what I've given, and what I've become. On my right arm, they tell my story. On my left, my sleeve binds me to who I was. Together, they make me whole.

"And that's why you're not shackling me? Because you can tap into my well?" I ask as he feathers my shoulder with kisses.

Nyx walks up behind him and unbuttons his shirt from behind.

"Well, not entirely. Not until we consummate."

"And get the vines back," Nyx states, rubbing her hands down his exposed washboard abs, the thorns jutting out from his sternum aching to be licked.

Trystan releases an exasperated sigh. "Yes, yes, the dreaded vines." He turns around and grabs Nyx by her throat. "Let me in."

Her eyes grow wide, and she nods.

Trystan's whole body goes still as he delves deep into Nyx's soul. The entire atmosphere feels as though all the air is being sucked out of it as he siphons her power from her.

When he's done, he lets her go, and stands back from both of us.

Timebinding is wild when you're in control of it and the one doing it, but it's otherworldly when you watch someone else do it.

It's as though a tangible, electrified sensation passes over me, touching everything with a frequency that could make even the ocean still for.

The curtains in the window, waving in the wind, freeze like an ice storm. The dust in the room and the flame from the candle are frozen like a painting. Even sounds cease.

The only things moving in the room now are the rise and fall of our breaths.

Trystan turns to Nyxaria and reaches his hand out behind him to pull me closer. He reaches Nyx and grabs her dress, yanking it off her torso. "You need to change."

"Yes, my king," she says as he mouths her breasts, trailing his hand down the front of me to pause between my legs. He lightly massages through the fabric of my dress.

Nyx releases a steamy exhale, and I reach around Trystan to feel his cock through his tight leather pants, growing, not fully erect.

"Which part would you like?" Nyx asks him as I begin to unbutton his pants.

"Give Sayah your cock. I want to watch her ride you."

She nods and closes her eyes, the outline of her thick member piercing the fabric of her dress.

I'm drenched as I unzip Trystan's pants, his own erection surging to attention as soon as it's freed from the leather.

"Bow to me," he tells Nyx.

She falls to her knees and licks the tip of his dick, the pre-cum now like a beautiful pearl on the tip of her tongue. I move my hand up and down his shaft as he rocks his head back towards me, the back of his head leaning on the top of mine. He's pulling my gown up until my pussy is exposed, and he slides his finger down my center. My hand is following the flow of Nyx's mouth; I move up when she sucks his dick upward, slathering his cock in her saliva, and move my hand down when she takes him to the back of her throat. Trystan moans in pleasure as we both massage his massive dick, Nyx fisting her own cock as she gobbles his down.

The sexy sounds of Nyx's slurping echo in the silent room, and I let out a moan.

Trystan shoves Nyx's mouth to the hilt of his cock and then pulls her head back, forcing her to stand. He pushes her over to the bed, then yanks me in front of him, ripping my dress off.

Nyx lands on her back, her large cock beckoning me to sit on it, and before I can even think, I'm straddling her, seating myself on top of her while cupping her breasts.

Pleasure lights me up as she pierces me. I wriggle my hips back and forth, feeling the luscious torment of her large cock ravaging my insides. Her giant breasts bounce as she bucks her hips to get deeper, and I shove down harder on her, bringing her tit to my mouth.

Trystan steps onto the bed and kneels in front of Nyx, his ten-inch cock slapping her on the face. He hits her other tit as he guides his dick into her mouth.

My pussy is swimming at the sight of Nyx sucking Trystan and I rise to the tip of her, slamming back down again while pulling full of her breast, biting the bud of her nipple.

Trystan pulls my mouth off her breast and kisses me, fisting my tits and hers while I swallow one of his moans.

A colorful swirl of light passes over us and Trystan lets my mouth go, his eyes rolling back into his head.

"Fuck I'm gonna cum. Nyx, stop!"

Nyx only sinks further down on his cock, gagging, the saliva pooling at the base of him. The same light swirl passes over me and the orgasm blooms from nowhere, curling over before I even had the chance to prepare.

Trystan's orgasm spills out of Nyx's mouth and down her cheeks. He shivers in delight, taking his dick out, and jacking himself off, a ribbon of cum shooting all over Nyx's gorgeous tits as he moans with euphoria.

Bright colors swarm my vision as Nyx fingers my clit to finish the wave of pleasure.

After our breathing returns to normal, he sits back, and looks at Nyx. "Did you cum?"

"No, but that's okay," she says; I'm still seated on top of her rock-hard dick. I feel it flinching inside me, like she's trying to tell me something. "I'll cum next time. The timebinding is about to wear off. It was a weak siphon because I had already used two."

Trystan's eyes turn contemplative, almost suspicious. "Then we better get dressed and get on with our war, yeah?"

He stands, his penis softening.

When he turns to go over to the wardrobe, Nyx winks at me.

I don't know what she did, but I'm certain it was to save me from something.

52

HAZARDLY JAGGED

—BASH—

"**S**omebody do something!" Claire yells as I leap off Wynter, flashing over to where she cradles Ollie in her lap.

A green thornbolt is embedded in Ollie's chest, piercing his heart. Blood bubbles from his mouth in agonizing gasps as he chokes for air.

I duck as another thornbolt whizzes past my head, skidding to my knees beside him. His blood soaks the ground beneath Claire, the dirt dark and thick.

The subsequent explosion erupts too close for Wynter's comfort, as she bellows and leaps into the sky, her wings thrumming with power.

"Caelum!" I shout over the chaos as arrows and thornbolts rain around us like deadly confetti.

The air is suffocating—thick with sulfur, smoke, and the iron tang of blood. Visibility is almost nonexistent, and the swirling haze hides our enemies and the incoming projectiles.

"Ollie!" my mother cries, blinking to us in a heartbeat, my sisters behind her.

"Why isn't he healing?" Claire sobs, her voice cracking as she strokes Ollie's dirt-streaked face. Blood pools in her lap, spreading like a crimson stain.

"The thornbolts," Mom murmurs grimly, sitting beside him, and clutching his hand.

Ollie coughs again, spraying more blood.

"*Caelum!*" I roar. Even if he's out of earshot, the bloodlink will bring him.

"Ollie, please, don't leave me," Claire whispers through her tears, her voice trembling as she rocks him.

Caelum materializes from the smoke like a specter, his eyes wild.

"Do your dew-drop-y shield thingy," I bark, trying to keep the crack out of my voice.

Without a word, Caelum bows his head, and raises his arms. Moisture from the surrounding chaos condenses and spirals together, forming a shimmering barrier around us.

Ollie struggles for breath again, his gray-blue eyes staring upward at the fragile dome shielding us—a bubble amidst the inferno.

"Ollie," I whisper, clutching his other hand, my throat tightening.

His breaths grow shallower, rasping like knives. His body spasms before stilling completely. The light leaves his eyes, and his head lolls to the side.

"No!" Claire screams, her wail shattering the relative quiet of our fragile sanctuary.

"My sweet Ollie." Mom sobs, collapsing onto his chest.

"Can't Laureya rise him?" Scarlet asks, panic etching her features as she kneels by his legs.

Another explosion rocks the ground, evaporating parts of Caelum's shield.

"There's no time to find her," Caelum grits out, his arms shaking as he fights to keep the remnants of the shield intact.

The battlefield is chaos incarnate. Arrows, fireballs, and

wyverns rain hell from above. My grief—raw and jagged—churns inside me, but I force it down. Survival is the priority now.

"Mom, move!" Dom shouts, diving toward her as a thornbolt zips toward her. He pushes her aside, catching the brunt of the blow as it grazes his side.

Seraphyra swoops down with an ear-splitting roar, her wings sending shockwaves that rattle the ground, spraying her fiery wrath upon dozens of Neverdusk soldiers. She swoops away again.

"We have to go!" Caelum yells, his broadsword slashing through an advancing Neverdusk soldier in a single, brutal motion.

Claire wraps her arms in a vise-like grip around Ollie's lifeless body.

"We're not leaving him!" she cries, blood dripping from an arrow embedded in her back.

More enemies surge forward. Scarlet moves like a deadly tempest, leaping onto an abyssal sprite and snapping its neck while Jasantha skewers it through the skull with a single swipe of her blade.

"Agares, call Seraphyra!" I shout as Dom pulls Mom to her feet, the thornbolt still lodged in her shoulder.

The heat of another detonation scorches the air. Wynter lands heavily, her massive claws digging into the soil.

"Call the others!" I plead to her.

Dom helps Mom onto Wynter's back, and I launch into the air to grab Claire and Jasantha. As I reach for them, the world blinks out, shrouded in an all-consuming darkness.

My voice cuts through the void. *Bash, I've got him. Light the place up*, Sayah's voice cuts through the void.

When the light returns, I'm face-to-face with the ground, frozen in mid-air. Somehow, I right myself, landing on my feet instead of my face.

Holding Scarlet in his arms, Caelum retreats into the smoke, shielding her from an incoming barrage.

A dragon above them cracks its maw and paints the sky in the flume of flame that pours enough heat into the land surrounding the ditch to turn the mud slushy.

I grab Jasantha, Hattie, and Claire—still clutching Ollie—ignoring the ache in my chest as I sprint toward Wynter.

The chaos of the battlefield fades into the background as survival overtakes grief.

There will be time to mourn, but not now.

I try not to think about it as I gather them in my arms and head back to Seraphyra.

As I'm landing on her back, another murder of dragons land.

"We'll go on one of those," Jasantha says, grabbing hold of Hattie's hand and jumping down.

A black cloud darkens the horizon again, mixed with bright lights of green, blue, and yellow. When I realize it's another army of wyverns, demons, and darkling fae, an immediacy rushes me and mixes with my anger.

The death of my father.

The death of my brother.

Claire lying over the back of Wynter, probably dying.

The infinity symbol burns with rage.

"Light it up," I tell Seraphyra as she huffs, crouching before springing into the air. Her giant wing beats cut the sky with streaks of black.

When we're high enough off the ground, she inhales deeply, then releases a stream of fire so bright and hot, it feels as though every hair on my body will be singed.

A dozen wyvern and flying demons catch fire and fall to the ground, screaming.

She swoops closer to the ground to release her stream of fire on anything moving.

More of our dragons and Luminara soldiers appear the

closer I get to the castle and further away from the part of our trenches that had been covered.

In the distance, I catch sight of Tallyn. She's soaring through the air, lightning bolts cracking from her hands, illuminating the surrounding chaos. Anything daring to fly too close plummets from the sky, charred and lifeless. After a dozen or so foes fall, her focus shifts. She banks hard, her wings slicing through the thick smoke, and makes her way toward the castle.

I don't hesitate to follow her.

From above, the blueprints of Castle Feylight are etched in my mind. The structure resembles a massive target, with each concentric ring being a deadly barrier meant to repel invaders.

The outermost two rings, once formidable mountain ranges, lie in shattered ruins. Jagged peaks have crumbled, their once-mighty forms reduced to smoldering rubble. The towers that once stood defiantly atop the summits now lean at precarious angles, some nothing more than broken husks swallowed by landslides. Fires burn in scattered patches, choking the air with smoke.

The second barrier, once an intricate maze of rivers and cascading waterfalls, has been twisted into something unrecognizable. The water runs black with ash; some rivers now dried to cracked, steaming earth. The once-deafening roar of rushing water is now punctuated by the groans of fractured stone and the hissing of steam where molten rock has spilled into the currents.

The fifth ring—the wall of fire—has been breached, but at a cost. The flames still burn, wild and unrestrained, but their perfect circle is broken, creating a jagged pathway of scorched land where Trystan forced his way through. Charred bones litter the edges, remnants of creatures, and warriors alike who were incinerated before they could escape.

The sixth ring, once a relentless wall of tornadoes, still spins in chaotic fury, but its pattern is disrupted. Gaps have been torn open where Trystan's power ripped through, allowing his forces to slip through the destruction. The air crackles with residual magic, unstable and unpredictable, the wind itself screaming in protest.

Beyond the chaos, the final ring—the heart of Feylight—awaits, its last defenses weakened but still standing. And somewhere within it, Trystan presses forward, leaving devastation in his wake.

I remember when Tallyn and I walked these very grounds, back when the castle was calm and serene. Back when the rivers sparkled under the twin moons' light, the mountain breeze carried the scent of wildflowers. It feels like a lifetime ago, a distant memory of peace before war darkened the horizon.

Now, the valleys are ablaze, the once-still waters churn in violent rapids, and the air howls with the storm's wrath.

The calm before the storm.

I shake off the nostalgia as Tallyn descends toward the castle's inner sanctum. Whatever lies at the center of this chaos, I must reach it before she does.

The seventh ring is the smallest. A circle of stones marks the entrance to the Aetherian Circle.

My infinity symbol burns brighter the closer we get to the center circle.

Sayah's there.

She's down there with him.

"Burn. It. Down," commands Tallyn through lumokenisis.

Laureya and her dragon fly through a fluffy cloud, heading right toward us.

At one choreographed moment, Laureya pulls out an enormous ball of swirling golden fire, drops it, and right before it hits the ground, one of Tallyn's dragons breathes fire on it, causing everything within a ten-mile radius to explode.

53

THE AETHERIAN CIRCLE

—DOM—

A flash of light, as blinding as the sun, engulfs my vision. I stagger, momentarily blinded. The explosion —a phoenix bomb ignited by dragon fire—feels like a star being born, its raw power akin to the atom bomb dropped on Hiroshima.

Time stretches. Seconds feel like hours as I brace myself, waiting for the inevitable. The blast will come for me. It will burn us all to ash, reduce us to shadows etched into stone, and incinerate our bones. Yet, for a heartbeat—a single, impossibly long heartbeat—everything freezes.

Even the wind stills.

The scene before me is surreal, too wild to be real. It's like a dream—one I'd immortalize on canvas if I were a painter.

Laureya sits astride her red dragon, her wild red hair a halo of flames riding the breeze, frozen in time. Her hand is outstretched, fingers splayed, as if reaching for something. But I know the truth: she's just dropped the bomb. A thick and fluffy white cloud swirls around her, glowing with the brilliant golden light of the phoenix bomb's detonation. Against the starry expanse of the sky, it looks otherworldly, like the birth of a celestial body.

Below her, Tallyn rides her massive black dragon. Its neck is arched like a serpent's, muscles coiled with power. The stream of fire pouring from its maw is so intense it almost looks like molten gold. It cascades downward, striking the phoenix bomb with precision, and the collision amplifies the detonation tenfold.

The explosion is breathtaking. The golden brilliance of the phoenix bomb melds with the vivid orange dragon fire, creating a blinding light that burns into my retinas. It spreads outward in slow, rippling waves, illuminating the battlefield like dawn breaking across a shattered world.

In the distance, I catch glimpses of other dragons and fae, their forms suspended mid-flight. They are ghosts within this moment, frozen figures silhouetted against the radiance. But it's Laureya and Tallyn—those two dragons locked in this tableau—who demand attention. Together with the explosion, they are a scene pulled straight from the pages of an epic fantasy novel.

But why isn't anything moving?

The question pulls at my mind like a splinter, sharp and insistent. The world feels suspended, as if trapped in the web of some powerful magick. I strain my ears, waiting for the roar of the explosion, the screeches of dragons, the wind tearing at my clothes—but all I hear is silence.

The stillness is unnerving. It's as if the entire world is holding its breath, waiting for something.

Waiting for me.

A strange, clear bubble forms around me, around all of us, the sound similar to water freezing over. The vortex's unzipping catches my attention then. The swirling green, blue, and black creates a hole through the fluffy white cloud above Tallyn.

Then we're all drifting, dragons and all, toward the vortex—like we're being pulled into a black hole in the universe.

I can't move anything except my eyes to watch Tallyn's dragon move away from its stream of fire like an ice sculpture breaking away from a part of it.

As I drift toward the vortex, the dragon and I spin so fast that I can no longer see the scene behind me.

Once we enter the vortex, time hurls forward, twisting, bending, breaking, and stitching itself together again.

The dragon I'm on begins flapping its giant wings through the complex vortex of time and space, as if familiar with the bends and twists and knowing exactly where it leads.

There is no light at the end of the tunnel; it simply opens to a large, underground circular area made of dark obsidian stone. Floating lights with a soft purple hue are ensconced all around us. Tunnels leading to gods-know-where dot the stone walls with large archway alcoves. The architecture is vast but encased, like an ancient cathedral made for giants.

My dragon lands with a thud, rumbling the stone ground as everyone else plummets through the portal's exit. My mom is sitting behind me, holding on to my waist, the thornbolt still embedded in her shoulder.

Bash's large black dragon follows mine, also landing gracefully in anticipation of the landing as well. His appearance as his demon shocked me when he first picked me up on the battlefield and threw my mom and me on this dragon.

But even though it was odd to take in at first, it almost becomes him.

Like he was always Agares; now he just wears his face.

He still looks disheveled, though, with Claire draped over the dragon's back in front of him, arrows sticking out.

Tallyn and hundreds of her soldiers are already here.

"Tallyn, what the fuck was that?" Bash asks, his eyes fierce and pissed, paired with terror and shock.

"I'm sorry, Sebastian, I just couldn't risk Trystan getting to that stone."

"Well, what the fuck did that do?" he asks, his dragon maneuvering like he's riding on a horse.

"I destroyed Feylight," Tallyn responds, fluttering to the ground.

"Then where the fuck are we?" Bash demands, his skin darkening in red as he seethes. "Where the fuck is Sayah and the Aetherian Circle?"

"We're in it," Tallyn says, marching over to Caelum and her other generals. As she speaks to them in her elder tongue, Hattie, Jasantha, and Scarlet arrive through the portal on their dragons.

"Excuse me, Maleficent, but I still don't know where the fuck Sayah is!"

"Bash." She tuts, walking toward him and his dragon. "We're beneath the ruins of Feylight Castle. This is the Sanctum of the Aetherian Circle. It's an underground labyrinth complex carved from ancient stone and forgotten magick. The maze walls, location of the stone, and covenant are constantly changing. So, while she may be here, the location of the stone and covenant remain hidden, while the exit is sealed off because of the explosion and every one of the soldiers he had placed around it. I want him dead once and for all, and this is how I'm going to kill him."

"Then what the fuck was blowing Feylight up good for if the stone and covenant are still intact?" Bash asks, his black hair wild, and twirling around the horns jutting out from his forehead. "If he gets to it before you do, he'll own all the realms. Feylight."

"I blew up the ley lines," Tallyn replies, as though she didn't just destroy the one thing she's been trying to protect for thousands of years.

A flicker of doubt that she's telling the truth stuns me.

This doesn't sound right. She's lying about something.

"What's the point of the war?" I ask her. "If you blew it up, what would Trystan be after?"

"Because it can always be rebuilt. The ley lines can always be restored. It's the covenant that needs to be rewritten, and the Soul Stone connected to a different soul. Only the person with the power of the Soul Stone can restore the ley lines and control Feylight."

A far-off explosion echoes through one of the tunnel archways, and her gaze flicks to it. "The dragons won't fit through the doors. If you want to find Sayah, Bash, you better dismount Seraphyra and help me find Trystan. Because she'll be with him."

Tallyn and her soldiers hustle toward the archway, where the sound of battles echo. I start to climb down when my mom slumps forward.

"Mom?" I turn around and push her backward to see her face. She's fallen unconscious, but she's still breathing. "Tallyn, wait!" I shout before she disappears into the tunnel. "What about my mom? And Claire?"

She stops and turns around, eyeing me, then Claire. "Leave them. Sylvan, stay behind and get them back to fighting condition, okay?"

A silver fairy with pink hair nods and flutters to Bash and Claire. Bash picks her up and hands her to Sylvan, then jumps down. After Sylvan deposits Claire gently on the ground, she flies over to me. I scoop my mom up and hand her over to Sylvan. Her silver eyes hold no malice, only a gentleness. I let my mom go and jump down, flashing to the tunnel, following the rest of the entourage and army into the darkness.

As we descend further into the tunnel, it opens up in places where the word *"tunnel"* wouldn't suffice to describe it.

Massive pillars, each adorned with glowing runes and overgrown vines of glowing flora, stretch high above the vaulted ceiling. The walls, etched with glyphs I don't recognize, pulse faintly with the energy of the Covenant and Soul Stone sealed here eons ago.

Sounds of a battle weave louder through the labyrinth, and we're heading right toward it.

The air is thick—heavy with the weight of old magick, vibrating with the tension of what is to come. Flickering lights —remnants of long-lost enchantments—cast eerie shadows along the grand hallways.

We bend and weave through many of these wide-open "rooms," before finally entering one with wide platforms of stone bridge gaps over a dark, swirling abyss of unknown depth, their surfaces cracked and worn by time.

The sound of battle, mixed with the crackle of magick, hits full force as we enter.

Luminara soldiers who've already arrived fight the darkling fae, and bolts of magick and the clang of metal echo off the multiple levels and vantage points.

"Open the portal," Tallyn yells to Halcyon, who nods as she takes to the skies and begins fighting anything that comes near. "How the fuck did he gain access to the chamber?" she screams at Thalira and Sariana.

"I don't know, Mom," Sariana shouts back, dodging a fire bolt shooting right at her.

Chaos fills the air as battles rage on bridges, high balconies, and towering pillars, each vying for control of the narrow spaces. Some platforms crumble as dark magicks take hold, pounding unlucky warriors to the void below.

Tallyn's dragons enter from a portal Halcyon opens, their wings beating against the ceiling's arches, while Bash and I look at each other, ready to fight the darklings coming for us.

In the distance, a circular chamber glows—the heart of the Aetherian Circle. There lies the Stone of Souls, protected by an intricate web of shimmering magicks that twist and pulse in the gloom.

Using my supernatural vision, I zoom over to the platform with which the stone and parchment sit and see none other than Sayah, with Trystan, awaiting Tallyn to come for it.

What I don't expect is what comes next.

Another portal opens on one of the ledges, and through it comes an army of something no one ever wants to see, even in the calmest circumstances.

An army of child vampires.

As the portal expands, the first of them steps through. At first glance, it could be a lost child—pale, wide-eyed, and no taller than my waist—but then the shadows catch its face. Hollow, blackened eyes peer out, filled with an unsettling hunger. Fangs glint unnaturally bright against their bloodless skin.

More of them spill through, their ragged, tattered clothing clinging to their small frames—once innocent garments now soaked in dried blood. They're like a nightmare come to life, their movements unnervingly quick and predatory, their soft, childlike giggles echoing in the cavern, twisted into something sinister and wrong.

One of them hisses, exposing their fangs, and the glow of the runes catches the faint outline of bloody handprints smeared across their tiny arms. The smaller ones leap nimbly across the broken platforms, their childish forms belying the ferocity.

And the sound—oh, the sound of their laughter is high-pitched and gleeful, chilling in its purity. But underneath it is a constant, guttural growl, like wolves circling their prey.

A DARKER EVIL

—SAYAH—

"You made child vampires?" My voice is sharp, disbelief lacing every word as I glare at Trystan. He's leaning against the impenetrable stone encasing the Covenant and Soul Stone, his posture infuriatingly nonchalant.

An epic battle rages on in the cavernous labyrinth behind us —dragons roaring, magick crackling through the air, and steel against steel echoing off ancient, rune-etched pillars. Trystan stands unfazed, his cold, calculating eyes fixed on Tallyn, daring her to meet him in combat.

"Yep," he replies with a smug grin. "They're so fierce and small."

The casualness of his admission turns my stomach. I've been a vampire for less than twelve hours, and even I know this is a line that should never be crossed. To create child vampires . . . it's more than cruel. It's monstrous.

To freeze a child forever in a body they'll never grow into, to trap them in eternal adolescence, unable to experience the milestones that define humanity—puberty, adulthood, love—is to rob them of life itself.

It's worse than death.

I glance at Nyx, hoping for a hint of shared outrage, but she shrugs as if this is just another one of Trystan's twisted experiments. Dark phoenix or not, this is not what I signed up for.

"All right," Trystan mutters, his sharp eyes narrowing as Tallyn's forces rally in the distance. "She's bringing the dragons. Get ready."

Nyxaria steps forward, casting an electric bubble of protection around the platform where we stand. The shimmering barrier hums with power, shielding us from the chaos erupting below.

I scan the battlefield, my heart pounding. In the distance, I spot Hattie and Jasantha mounting their dragons. The creatures leap into the sky with a deafening roar. Scarlet and Caelum are locked in brutal combat on the ground, their blades flashing like streaks of lightning. Dom's black one already lighting up the battlefield with bursts of fire.

But where's Adaline? Where's Ollie?

And where's Claire?

A cold dread curls in my gut. I try to reach Bash through my lumokinesis, but it's like slamming into a wall. Something—or someone—is blocking me.

Trying to mask my unease, I glance at Trystan, his gaze like a knife slicing into my soul. He's watching me closely, his lips twitching with suspicion.

"Oh, good," I say, forcing an air of calm as I look out over the battlefield. "That'll help."

But inside, I'm screaming.

Above, Bash's dragon unleashes a torrent of fire, incinerating dozens of the child vampires and abyssal sprites in mid-air. Dom's dragon follows suit, scorching everything in its path. The air fills with the smell of burning flesh and the shrill cries of the undead.

And yet, Trystan's army fights on.

The child vampires are relentless, their small forms darting through the chaos with unnatural speed. Their leathery and black wings, tipped with Neverdusk's signature silver, carry them high above the fray, where they dive-bomb soldiers like predatory birds.

How long has Trystan been planning this?

The question hangs in my mind as I watch the horror unfold. Scarlet and Caelum battle grimspawn on the ground, their movements precise but desperate. Hattie's dragon tears through a cluster of abyssal sprites, while Jasantha uses her sunder to force the enemy into submission.

And then, a strange new sensation washes over me—a raw and unfamiliar tickle of power. It whispers to me, coaxing and urging. I flick my fingers experimentally, and a ripple of energy surges outward.

To my astonishment, the fallen soldiers—on both sides— begin to stir.

Their bodies rise jerkily, like marionettes on invisible strings. The Luminara fairies blink in shock as the undead soldiers turn their weapons against the Neverdusk forces, fighting for Tallyn.

Trystan steps to the platform's edge, his brows furrowing as he watches his army of abyssal sprites, grimspawn, and child vampires falter. The dead are rising—but they are not fighting for him.

He spins around, his gaze locking onto me. "Are you doing this?" he demands in a low growl.

My heart stalls. "Doing what?"

His eyes narrow to slits, and in a flash, he's in my face. "Don't you dare play fucking dumb with me, you whore! Are you doing this?"

His voice reverberates through the cavern, spittle flying from his lips as he grabs me by the throat.

Out of the corner of my eye, I see Tallyn, Dom, and Bash closing in. Nyxaria catches my gaze, and I nod subtly.

She lowers the barrier.

Just as Bash's dragon lets out a deafening roar, preparing to unleash its fury, Trystan yanks me around, pressing a blade to my throat.

"Not so fast," he sneers, his grip tightening.

55

A STORM WITH SKIN

—SAYAH—

Everything is frozen.

Except for Bash and me.

He used his third and final timebind to save my life.

"Bash, no!" I shout, the blade of Trystan's knife biting into my skin. Blood trickles down my neck, sticky and hot, pooling in my cleavage.

"I had to," he chokes out, his demon wings unfurling as he flies toward me. When he lands, the eyes I once loved—crystal-blue and familiar—are now amber, vertically slit like a serpents. He's forever in his demon form. "I would do anything to save you, Sayah. I'd rewrite the stars for you."

He wraps me in his massive, red arms, and for a moment, I feel him. The man I love is still in there.

But not entirely.

"Did our plan fail?" he asks, his thumb brushing away my tears.

I think back to the moment we made the plan . . .

As Bash holds me, a strange rush of energy surges through me, cold and sharp as a blade. My bones freeze to the core, my ribs wrapped in fiery delight, while my shadows blanket me in warmth. Closing my eyes, I feel a tingle on my arm—the timepiece tattooed with a rope around it pulses. I look to Bash, who stares back, his confusion mirroring mine.

"What did you just do?" he asks, his eyes like a dream I know the shape of.

"I don't know," I admit, feeling the tingling intensify. "It started as an itch—a deep, bone-deep itch. When I reached for it, I felt time. My echo asked it to still . . . and it obeyed."

His dark brows knit together. "How?"

"I can steal or borrow others' powers. I'm still learning how it works, but I must have picked up the timebinding along the way."

"I don't fully understand it either," he says, his tone taut. "But we don't have much time. What do we do about Trystan?"

I pull away from him, glancing around at the frozen battlefield. My mind races. "I need him to think I'm double-crossing all of you. He has to believe it."

Bash's expression hardens, suspicion flashing across his face. "Meaning?"

"He's already been communicating with lumokinesis. He believes I'm using this timebind to steal a part of Tallyn's soul and open the Aetherian Circle."

"So he doesn't really have Gauge?"

"No. He used that as a way to get me to separate from you all."

"And what are you actually doing?"

The ink-and-quill tattoo on my right arm tingles with a familiar, cat-scratch sensation.

"I need something to write with." Bash looks at me quizzically and notches his neck. "No time to explain, but it's important."

He shakes his head as he moves to the side, digging in a satchel that belongs to one of the soldiers. Withdrawing a small pad of paper and pencil, he hands it to me.

I write down: Bash has the power to materialize any object.

The ink glows and sets the parchment on fire, the embers glinting in the wind.

"What just happened?"

"I gave you the power to materialize objects," I explain. "I need you to conjure the shackles Trystan used on me—the ones that suppress power."

The secluded darkness where Bash reigns opens and drifts into my mind like fog. I guide him toward his new ability, showing him where it lies, and he seizes it. I watch as he folds it into himself.

Avidity glints in his icy gaze, his hot breath igniting something in me that both excites and terrifies. He holds his hands before him, concentrating until a glowing ember erupts like a geyser. He shapes it, sharpening its edges with the precision of someone who has spent years mastering this craft.

When the manacles take form, their golden gleam catches the frozen light. He holds them up, letting them dangle.

"You did it!"

"Do you take them, or should I?" he asks.

"No, you keep them until the time is right."

He slips the manacles into his pocket and steps closer. Lifting my right hand, he examines the shadows creeping over my fingertips.

"Three times," he murmurs, his baritone voice a fog wrapping around me. "You can only use timebinding three times in a moon cycle. Only use it one more time, Sayah. Promise me." He pulls me closer. "You are closer to me than my skin. I won't lose you to the void."

"I'll only use it if I have to," I promise.

A bright streak of sunlight cuts through the frozen moment, and the world around us begins to stir.

"Tallyn blew up Feylight," Bash announces, still holding me. His voice is part his and part demonic, the dual tones echoing across the frozen battle. "I thought you were dead."

"Something's not right," I reply, a strange tingle unfurling across my back, like ice melting into my skin. "Why would Tallyn destroy the most important piece of Feylight?"

"I don't know," he admits, his amber, slit-pupil eyes scanning the battlefield.

I follow his gaze to Tallyn, frozen atop her dragon. Her eyes are locked on Trystan. But it's not the gaze of a scorned sister about to kill her brother. It's something else—almost like she's seeing a long-lost lover.

I shove the thought away and focus. "I'll unfreeze time. You do what we planned."

"If I have to, I'll freeze it again. I'm stuck like this anyway."

"You don't know what you've done," Agares growls, his voice vibrating through the air rather than Bash's mouth.

"I let you out forever," Bash replies sharply.

"And ripped the veil wide-open in the process," Agares retorts. "You've doomed everything—Earth, Feylight. Everything will fall to darkness."

My stomach hollows at his words. I glance at the void where the child vampire army slipped through. It spills outward, frozen but growing, its tendrils twisting into the Aetherian Circle. The sanctum begins to unravel; glowing runes flicker and fade, pillars crack, and the air thickens with impenetrable darkness. Only the Stone of Souls remains alight, glowing like a beacon in the chaos.

"What does that mean?" I ask, clutching Bash's arm.

"It means we stick to the plan," Bash says, handing me the golden shackles. "Throw these at him. They'll bind to his wrist and ankle."

"And don't let him get the stone," Agares warns, his tone a razor's edge.

I nod, stepping back as Bash prepares to unfreeze time. Facing Trystan, I lock eyes with the evilest being I've ever encountered. His nefarious gaze is sharp with vengeance and greed, his lips curled as if ready to siphon my power before taking my head.

"I don't know if I can do this," I admit, the weight of Estreaya's love for him pressing against my resolve.

"You can," Bash reassures, his voice steady. "You are a storm with skin."

Steeling myself, I extend my hands, pulling every ounce of power from my bones, my ribs, my very core. Shadows churn within me as I prepare my greatest fear spell.

"Go!" I shout, hurling the shackles at Trystan.

Bash and I are like two pieces of chaos colliding. As he snaps his fingers, a shockwave ripples through the air, and time resumes. The shackles glow gold as they streak toward Trystan, his arms jerking inward as they bind him. He looks at me in stunned confusion, just as my fear spell spiderwebs from my fingertips, sinking into his skin like molten threads. His expression twists, terror etched deep as the spell convinces him his greatest fear—mortality—has become reality.

He drops the knife, his gaze frantic.

"Tallyn, now!" I scream.

But instead of unleashing dragon fire, Tallyn hurtles toward me, a phoenix bomb blazing in her hands. Her eyes lock with mine, burning with something I can't name. She throws the bomb—not at Trystan, but at my face.

The explosion of light blinds me.

56

CHAOS FEARS TO HARM HER

—DOM—

I didn't know what else to do aside from using the new power I accumulated.

It has to do with me having been in The Gloaming, which is part of the void.

Timebinding.

The itch began at bone level, winding through the sinews of me. I didn't know what it was at first, but as I saw Tallyn's demeanor change, her eyes locked on Sayah with the golden ball of fire in her hand, I knew what she was about to do. The power nearly took over me on its own accord, scorching me until I could do nothing else but grab hold of time itself.

And everything froze.

I sit rigid atop my dragon, my chest constricting as the frozen battlefield stretches around me. The world is locked in an eerie, unnatural stillness. Tendrils of void energy flicker and dance at the edges of my vision, casting jagged shadows that refuse to move. Every sound is absent, as though the void itself has swallowed the air. My dragon's wings hover mid-beat, the muscles beneath its scales taut. The stillness amplifies the storm inside me—the roiling blend of anger, betrayal, and the unyielding remnants of love.

My gaze lingers on Sayah. She moves through the midst of it all, her glowing form an impossible contrast against the darkness creeping in from every corner. She's a traitor—there's no denying that. Her actions have fractured the fragile trust we once shared. And yet, the sight of her pulls at something deeper within—something I hate myself for still feeling.

My fists tighten on the reins.

Why do I still care? Why can't I let her go?

Sayah's sharp and commanding voice pierces through my spiraling thoughts, arrowing her gaze straight through me. She's standing at the base of the clear casing protecting the covenant and Stone of Souls. Her golden eyes burn with an intensity that matches her molten skin. She seems untouched by the chaos around her, as though the chaos itself fears to harm her.

"What the fuck just happened?" she asks me, the accusatory lilt limning her resonant glare.

"I don't know," I reply, my voice hollow and distant from where I sit atop my stilled dragon. "Just grab that stone and covenant." I look around for Halcyon. His massive wings are arched like a predator about to strike, suspended in the act of diving toward a Neverdusk fairy. The tension in his body is palpable, a coiled spring on the verge of release, but in this frozen moment, he is nothing more than a phantom of action yet to come. Flying like an eagle about to scoop up prey on the other end of the ravine, ready to rip a Neverdusk fairy in two. "Then we can try to get Halcyon to open a portal out of here. All I know is that Tallyn is obviously hiding something."

"I know what to do," she says, her tone resolute.

She turns her attention to Halcyon. Her breaths slow, as if she's communing with the air he moves through. Even amidst the surreal calm, her movements feel deliberate, her determination a beacon against the encroaching void.

The golden ball of fire is hovering directly in front of her, the fire still bright and wavering, the heat emanating all the way out to me. She grabs it like it won't scorch her skin or incinerate her bones, and it doesn't. She doesn't even flinch; she merely walks up to the clear casing around the covenant and stone and sets the ball at the base before turning to face me again.

"When you unfreeze time, aim at that bomb and yell 'Ignitas,'" she tells me, her skin glowing lava in the darkness. Her golden eyes find mine, and even though she's a traitor to me, I still love her. I don't want her to get hurt.

As if she hears my thoughts, she says, "I'll be okay, Dom. Just do what I say, okay?"

Her words are simple, but the conviction behind them sends a pang through me. My fingers tighten on the reins, the leather biting into my skin.

Why do you trust her?

She's the balance. She knows what she's doing.

But what if she's wrong? What if this is another betrayal?

I glance at Tallyn. Her luminous figure seems to mock me, a glowing reminder of everything we've lost and everything she's taken from me.

My heart twists as I find Sayah again.

The memories of our past—her laughter, her fierce determination, the way she once looked at me with something more than hatred—clash with the present reality. Her unwavering confidence still steadies me, even as the doubts scream in protest.

I nod, throat tight. "I'll do it." My voice threads apprehension and anxiety through old, complicated feelings that will not be easily shaken.

The weight of the decision settles heavily on my shoulders. The void is pressing in, the sanctum cracking under its influence. The Stone of Souls glimmers faintly, the only light left in the encroaching darkness.

Inhaling a deep breath, I steady myself. I can't let the turmoil inside dictate my actions, not now. "Unfreezing time is going to unleash hell," I mutter, half to myself and half to the dragon. The beast's eyes remain fixed on the battlefield, its instincts ready for the incoming chaos.

I glance at Sayah one last time. For a fleeting moment, there's something in her eyes—regret? Hope? Love? I shake my head, banishing the thought. Whatever it was, it doesn't matter now.

My dragon's chest heaves as though he's unthawing. The frozen battlefield seems to hold its breath, the stillness before the storm.

"All right," I exclaim, firming my voice, each syllable crisply annunciated. "Let's do this."

FIRE INCARNATE

—BASH—

When time unfreezes, Sayah's silence is thunderous, her calm a warning. She no longer seeks approval. She knows her worth. Her wounds and scars are no longer weaknesses but ramparts she's built around herself—and now, around all of us.

Everyone can either rise to meet her or get out of her way.

She moves, swift and sure, to the covenant and stone. A ball of golden fire, the size of a yoga ball, hovers beside her, its heat palpable even from where I stand.

And then it happens again. Time freezes—but not by my hand. I feel it as a cold glitch, a shiver under my skin. The sensation has grown sharper since permanently becoming Agares. Maybe that's why I understand the void's pull more intimately now.

Tallyn, who was supposed to toss the phoenix bomb at Trystan, had aimed it at Sayah instead.

The betrayal knocks the breath from my lungs. My hands tighten around the reins, the leather biting into my palms. This was never part of the fucking plan. I let out a trembling breath.

"Odin's balls. This is farcical."

Patience, Bash, it's going to be okay, Ollie's voice.

My heart can't take the thought when Dom's dragon stirs.

"Ignitas!" Dom yells, and time itself seems to have decided to die.

The dragon beneath him reacts instantly, its wings curving in a sensuous arc, muscles rippling as it adjusts mid-air. Its dark green scales glisten like algae slicked over a swamp, and its horns curl from its forehead like jagged crowns. Blunt red eyes lock onto Sayah and the phoenix bomb, a fiery orb glowing bright in its throat, climbing like a rocket.

When the dragon opens its maw, fire pours out in a steady, terrifying stream aimed at Sayah. For a split second, fear lances through me. What if Dom is out to kill her?

I'm about to command Seraphyra to charge when Sayah raises her hands, holding the flames at bay with an invisible shield. A rattling breath escapes me as she stands, unyielding, her skin aglow, molten gold in the darkness—the purest alchemy, fire to gold.

A loose breath rattles out of me as she makes me see new colors; my love for this woman knows no bounds. She moves with it—a dance with fire. It's as though she draws the inferno into herself, molding it into a sphere larger than before. The dance lasts only seconds, but in those fleeting moments, my shadows yearn to join her fire.

In one swift motion, she shoves the blazing orb into the hovering flame, igniting it on impact. The explosion blooms like a star being born, light cascading out in brilliant waves. I shield my eyes, but the blast doesn't touch me.

It forms a gibbous shield around her instead, fire raging along its edges, marking her untouchable. She's truly become fire incarnate—a woman who controls everything and fears nothing.

Across the battlefield, Tallyn's wide eyes betray her disbelief. She's unable to reach us, her path blocked by Nyxaria's magick. The realization dawns on her as she watches the world she's built crumble.

Sayah steps to the alcove where the covenant and stone lie encased. With a simple gesture, the fire melts the casing, and it drips away like ice on a summer's day. Retrieving the items, she tucks them under her arm and unzips a portal, shoving the objects through before sealing it shut.

Behind her, Nyxaria shifts into shadows, reappearing behind Trystan with a blade glinting in her hand. The slice across his throat is deep. The scent of his blood fills the air.

"Nooo!" Tallyn's scream rends the silence.

Before Tallyn can reach her, the shadows consume Nyxaria once again, and when a shift in weight and wind beckons behind me, I crane my neck to see her sitting on my dragon with me.

Tallyn leaps into the air, her wings propelling her toward the ledge where Trystan collapses, clutching his neck. But instead of finishing him off, she pulls a glowing blue vial from her pocket and presses it to his lips.

"Get ready to fly," Nyxaria whisper-yells in my ear.

Sayah unzips another portal, wings of fire spreading wide as she soars into the heart of the abyss, dragging the portal with her.

"Go!" Nyxaria yells. "Dom, follow us!"

The dragon beneath me obeys, plunging into the black trench of nothingness as the void seeps over everything. The ledge beneath Tallyn and Trystan cracks, crumbling into the pit below.

"What about my family?" I ask, the words torn from me as we plummet.

"Trust us," Nyxaria says, her tone a grim promise.

"Fuck it. We're all going to die now, anyway."

A vortex of undulating green and blue matter yawns open before us, swallowing us whole. It drags us into its swirling depths, thrusting us once again into the gods-damn ether.

APPEARS LIKE SMOKE

—SAYAH—

I didn't know where the portal was going to lead us, but once we landed in Wyndhallow, I knew everything I'd done to prepare for the worst was worth it.

I stand, dusting my pants off.

The scenery is not one I'm familiar with, but one that's as familiar to me as my own skin.

The once-radiant haven used to be untouched by shadow, where only those pure of heart could tread. It used to be a place of eternal daylight. Its skies shimmered with soft, golden hues, and where the air hummed with the songs of radiant beings. Towering trees of white and silver stretched toward the heavens, their leaves glittering like starlight. The ground was soft, covered in lush grass that sparkled faintly underfoot, and streams of crystal-clear water wound through the landscape, reflecting the brilliance of the sun. The Light Gate Portal—its archway formed from beams of pure light—was the only passage into the sacred realm.

But now that I'm the Celestial Phoenix, the balance of light and dark, Wyndhallow has transformed. No longer solely a sanctuary of purity, the land has adapted, harmonizing both light and shadow. The once-perfect sunlight now casts a dusk-like glow over the landscape. The trees, once pure white, now have darkened trunks veined with gold, their leaves shifting between light and shadow with each breeze. Streams of water still flow, but they sparkle in shades of silver and obsidian, reflecting both the light of the sun and the mysteries of night.

Where once darkness could not enter, shadows now dance across the land, not in malice but in balance. Patches of the ground have turned a deep violet, interwoven with glimmers of silver, as if the earth itself has accepted both the sun and the void. The sky, too, has changed, with stars visible even in the day, their faint light guiding those who walk this twilight realm.

Wyndhallow breathes in rhythm with my presence now, responsive to my will. The once-mighty Light Gate Portal stands as a relic, unnecessary in a realm I command. The very fabric of this place bends to my desires, a reflection of my duality. Others might see discord in its contrasts, but I see harmony—a perfect union that makes Wyndhallow mine in every sense.

I felt it the moment I visited Freya here.

As I gaze across the fields of gold and shadow, figures begin appearing, materializing as though summoned.

Bash.

Dom.

Hattie.

Scarlet.

Adaline—healed and stoic, yet bearing sadness etched into her soul.

Nyx.

Claire—her wounds mended, but Ollie's absence a shadow on her energy.

Jasantha.

Henry—solid now, no longer translucent, fully present.

What I wrote down has truly come to be.

No matter what happens after this, I want everyone I love in one piece, in one place, safe in this same garden of light Freya called Wyndhallow. Everyone on our side—the side who believes darkness and light can co-exist.

More arrive.

Halcyon.

Thalira.

Sariana.

Sylvan.

Kaston.

Laith.

Caelum.

Rowan.

Briar.

Gwylan.

Eirian.

Elowen.

Thistlewynd.

All the dragons.

As the Luminara fae gather, one absence gnaws at me.

Tallyn hasn't appeared.

She should be here. Despite what she did—trying to throw my own bomb back at me—I held onto hope. Hope that there was still good in her, some trace of the fae I believed in.

When my aunts step into view, my heart clenches. Seeing them again feels like a dream, their smiles soft with an air of expectation, as though they've been waiting for this moment.

And then, like smoke forming from the air, Gauge appears.

He's in his little green wheelchair, positioned next to Bash.

My breath catches. My eyes betray me. I must have died in that fire.

"Mama?" he asks, his voice small, his eyes wide as they dart across the unfamiliar faces surrounding him.

I fall to my knees, scooping him into my arms, holding him so tightly I might break him.

"Oh, my baby," I whisper, inhaling the familiar, moon-kissed scent of his hair. "I missed you so much."

"Where are we, Mama?" he asks, his voice uncertain.

Pulling back, I cradle his face, gazing into his doe-brown eyes. "I'll explain everything soon, my love. I promise."

A tap on my shoulder pulls my attention. I look up into Bash's amber-demonic eyes. My heart clenches. He's here—but he'll never again be the Bash I fell in love with. "He's okay. He's been given a potion in his journey here, so as not be frightened by all the fae and . . . well . . . me."

I rise, wrapping him in a hug, relief warring with sadness. When I pull away, I ask the question burning inside me. "What happened?"

Before Bash can answer, Sariana approaches. For a moment, I think she might hit him, but instead, she turns her intense gaze to me.

"Come into the castle," she says. "I'll explain everything."

59

A BOND WITH THE SHIMMER OF SHADOWS

—BASH—

A "comfortable sitting room," my ass. We've gathered in a sprawling open area dotted with trees and jagged rocks, yet somehow scattered with sleek modern furniture. Waterfalls cascade into crystal-clear ponds, their mist catching the light.

Like a sitting room for fairies.

"All right, darling sister," I snap, my voice laced with impatience. The coppery scent of blood still clings to some of the soldiers, making the hunger pang whorl in the pit of me.

What do demons even eat?

People, Agares grumbles.

I ignore him and continue, "You gonna tell us what the hell happened back there?"

Sariana's glare is direct and unwavering, which she seems to deploy masterfully to get her way. Without a word, she strides to a massive boulder and perches on it, her dark leather uniform stark against the glowing brightness of the hallow.

"Okay," she begins, her tone commanding. "What I'm about to tell you will shock most of you. But please, hold your questions until I've explained everything I know."

Around me, everyone shifts, finding their places—some on the ground, some on furniture, others leaning against trees, or sitting on moss-covered rocks. The hallow feels charged, the sound of rushing water fading under the weight of Sariana's words.

"Tallyn and Trystan aren't just brother and sister," she says. "They're also husband and wife."

The silence shatters. Gasps ripple through the group, followed by a cacophony of chattering voices. The revelation drowns out even the waterfalls.

Sariana raises her hand, and the room falls quiet again, though my thoughts are anything but.

My mind races, unraveling everything I thought I knew about Tallyn. Every memory, every interaction, everything I believed—twisting into something incomprehensible.

How could this be?

I'm so baffled, unable to form a single coherent thought, trying to piece together the impossible.

"Zephyra." Sariana cascades her voice over the crowd, a thunderous sound for such a small female. Everyone's murmur turns to a quiet hush. "Zephyra was their mother—an evil queen of the seven realms. She put multiple spells on them, including a mirror spell so they could never hurt each other and a spell for them to fall in love and have children to protect her realms and keep them together, keeping the bloodline intact. But her husband—their father—was quite possibly worse and did some unimaginable things to both his children. This broke Trystan. So damaged by childhood trauma, it broke his brain into three different parts. He has what the people on Earth call DID or dissociative identity disorder.

"One part of him—the part under the spell—was genuinely in love with Tallyn, but the rest of him was not. He married Tallyn while the spelled part, his echo, controlled his actions. However, something inside him shattered, driving him to

492

madness. In his desperation, he waged war against himself, eventually tearing the spelled part of his mind away. This act enraged Zephyra. Later, Trystan married Delaney, a daughter of Lilith, and together, they plotted to kill Tallyn. But every attempt backfired, causing Trystan pain because of the mirror spell.

"Zephyra caught wind of this and left the realms to Tallyn and her heirs, leaving nothing to Trystan. He heard of his mother's betrayal and kidnapped Tallyn, ripping out her ovaries so she'd never be able to have children, avoiding the mirror spell because he didn't have ovaries, giving their mother no other choice but to leave the realm to Trystan.

"Tallyn, being ever the clever witch-fairy she is, figured out a way to spell her own mother into leaving the realm to her before Trystan killed her, creating the Covenant of Feylight and binding her soul and any heir she produces to the land with the Stone of Souls, forever to be kept in the Aetherian Circle.

"Tallyn is smarter than Trystan and actually stored a seed of hers away before he deflowered her. When the time came, she met the right witch." Sariana looks at Adaline. "She knew she'd be able to implant her own seed inside her when she agreed to Tallyn's bargain."

"You're the heir to Feylight?" I ask, putting the weird little pieces of the puzzle together. "You're only our half sister?"

She nods. "That's correct. I'm Tallyn and Everett's biological daughter, who Adaline merely housed."

"That still doesn't answer why Tallyn tried to kill me," Sayah says, squeezing my hand.

"Because she's not Tallyn," Sariana says, and this time, Halcyon grunts with disbelief.

"What?" he breathes, clearly tensing, his neck muscles straining.

"I'm not sure exactly when the exchange happened, but we believe it occurred during Never's attack on Feylight while we were in Melodias," Sariana says, shifting her weight and leaning on her right hand. "It would explain how Tallyn knew about the attack ahead of time. That's likely when Delaney took over Tallyn's life—wearing her face."

"So, you mean, like body-snatched her?" I ask.

"More like they kidnapped Tallyn, and Delaney took over, mimicking her exactly. Every detail. Every nuance that made my mom, my mom. I had no idea until . . ."

"Until when?" Sayah presses.

"Until my mom had no idea that Thalira was also their daughter."

More gasps ring out.

This time, it's Thalira who bursts out with noncommittal scoffs. "Wait, what?" she demands.

"Not only did she produce me with her seed, she produced you with his. And hers."

"What the fuck?" I growl.

"She made Thalira in a lab, using the flora and fauna to bring their baby to fruition, further solidifying her claim to the throne."

As echoes of chatter grow louder, my mom stands. "How do we know you're not just filling our heads with bullshit while the married Tallyn and Trystan take over Feylight and Never and Earth?"

"Yeah, and how did you come to find out about this?" asks Thalira.

"I found out by my power of finding broken things. I found you, Thalira, and knew you were part of Tallyn and Trystan's brokenness. I used Ember to dive deep into the shadows to find out what my mother was up to since she was working for both sides. Once she came into the knowledge, I veilweaved her to forget since I am part vampire. And as far as you believing me about Tallyn not being Tallyn, you really should. Because, right now, Delaney, Trystan, and Laureya are planning a way to get the Shadow Gate Portal back together to find wherever Sayah portaled the covenant and stone."

"Wait, how are you part vampire if you aren't really my biological child?" Mom asks.

"The spell you put on your womb to protect all your babies didn't just have to be of your seed. If we were housed within you, we were cursed by you."

Mom scoffs and sits back down.

I scan everyone here.

Wait a minute.

"Laureya isn't here."

How the fuck did I miss that Laureya wasn't here?

"That's right, dear brother," she says condescendingly. "With Trystan being a siphon and Laureya being the other phoenix, I have no doubt that Trystan will marry her now and become Sayah's exact counterpart."

"I have a question," Henry pipes up. "I may be a ghost and all, but there are some things I don't understand. If Trystan could portal into Feylight and kidnap Sayah but then had to break seven barrier spells to open the Aetherian Circle, what's that about?"

Thalira's face falls in questioning, wondering who the hell Henry is probably.

"Because Sayah was in the tallest point above the Aetherian Circle below—which is where the barrier spells are, beneath the Earth, too. Not just the seven outer rings of physical substance, but seven inner rings protected by ancient magick. To conquer Feylight, or usurp it, you have to break all fourteen barrier spells, rewrite the covenant, and bond with the Stone of Souls."

"So what the fuck do we do?" I ask.

"We find the pieces before they do," she says all the neutrally. She stands, blowing the puffy bit of flower she tore out of the ground into the wind. "Find where they're keeping my mother. In the meantime, rewriting the covenant to say Thalira and my names so it doesn't fall to him and Delaney. We can do that with Sayah's new power."

"And why, pray tell, should we help you?" I ask, standing.

"This whole war has cost us everything," my mom says, her voice breaking.

"Because the void is currently taking over Earth. The veil was shattered by all the timebinding. Too many people abusing the power. The Earth is in darkness right now, being overwhelmed by monsters of Hell."

"And how the hell will we stop that?" Sayah asks.

"A bond with the shimmer of shadows," she says, walking over to a large tree with a pond behind it.

"Whaaat the fuck does that mean?" I ask, following her to wherever the fuck she's walking to. I grab the handles of Gauge's wheelchair, maneuvering it through the grass.

"My mom has the power to shimmer," Sariana continues. "To turn dark things into light. The shimmer is the only way to defeat the darkness taking over Earth right now. It counteracts it."

As we emerge from behind the tree, we see Ollie lying on a bed of flowers. Butterflies surround him, landing on him and beating their wings, then taking flight over and over again.

"Ollie," Claire says, running up to him, collapsing to her knees, and stroking his face.

"He's still dead," Sariana says unsympathetically. "But he's in The Gloaming right now."

"The fuck is The Gloaming?" someone asks.

"The in-between," Dom answers. "I'm familiar with it."

"With him in The Gloaming and Sayah's new power of deathlink, she can communicate with Ollie, who can find my mother, since she's not anywhere I can reach. And using my powers, I can find the pieces of the Shadow Gate."

Sayah pulls up her arm and examines a new tattoo—a marking on a tombstone with a chainlink coming out of it.

I return my gaze to Sariana. "What will putting that thing back together do?"

"When Sayah threw the stone and covenant into the portal, it shattered into seven pieces and went into realms only the Shadow Gate can lead to."

Sayah looks over at me and shrugs. "I didn't know that was going to happen. I was just trying to keep it from Trystan."

"It was spelled to do so," Sariana answers. "Take your time and think about it. We'll rest here and set out for pieces next full moon."

I rock my head back. "Oh, for fuck's sake, what is with you fairies and the waxing and waning of the fucking moon?"

"Bash." Sayah stops me from whining.

"Because, Sebastian. My best chance to find the broken pieces is when the moon is at its fullest. It would work better with a celestial event, so if you want to wait months before bringing Ollie back or saving Earth or—"

"Odin's Ghost, all right!"

"We can also unhook you from Agares, so, you know, you can have your own body back."

This has my attention. "You can do that?"

Sariana nods before walking off in the direction of a door, leading to the castle proper.

I turn to face Sayah, Dom in my peripheral, making this a little awkward.

Gauge is still lost in space, trying to comprehend everything he's seeing.

Dom is going over to him, crouching to talk, and Sayah watches.

"You okay?" I ask her, bringing her attention back to me.

"Bash, I just . . . this is a lot. Trystan and my sister? What if we can't do this? What if—"

"Hey, stop," I say, kissing her on the nose. "You've broken

mountains with your wit. You're fire incarnate. If there's anything in the world you got, it's this."

She gives a small smile. "Are you sure?"

"I'm more than sure."

"We can also get the real you back. As much as I love this part of you," she says, stroking the side of my face, "I miss your real face."

I smile as Bash-like as I can. "I miss my old skin, too."

"Excuse me, Sayah?" Nyx is approaching us. I'm still not sure if I trust her completely.

"Yes, Nyx?" she asks, letting go of my hand to approach her.

"There's something you definitely need to see," she says.

She leads Sayah toward the cascading waterfall, its roaring spray catching the light and breaking into iridescent shards. I follow, my boots crunching against the damp earth. I glance back at Dom, still crouched beside Gauge.

"Go on," he says, with a gesture for me to continue. "I'll stay with him and explain everything."

I nod, quickening my pace to catch up.

As we near the falls, the air grows cooler, droplets misting against my skin. Then, through the shimmering curtain of water, light twists and shapes itself. A faint outline takes form, its edges fluid, like the water itself is molding a figure from its spray.

The hologram solidifies, and there he is: Trystan. His face is sharp and cunning, his eyes glinting with a cold light, the thorns defiant and poking through the water. The illusion is so vivid it almost feels as if I could reach out and touch him—but there's an unnatural translucence to him, the way his image ripples in tandem with the water's flow.

Anger surges through me, sharp and instinctive. My body stiffens, every muscle coiling with the heat of my rage. Being Agares now, this emotion feels like an old friend—an ancient and unyielding resonance deep in my marrow. It doesn't flare wildly but hums steadily, a smoldering ember waiting to ignite.

Still, I force myself to stay rooted, my shadowy aura curling around me like smoke as I stare at the illusion of the man who's caused so much destruction.

Just listen to him, Bash, Ollie's voice coaxes me. *You need this to find out information.*

As much as I detest hearing my brother's corporeal voice, I know he's right. I nod and stand next to Sayah as she squares her shoulders at Trystan.

"Ah, there she is," Trystan says, his watery hologram still an arrogant prick.

"What the fuck do you want?" she seethes, Sariana coming over to stand by her.

"Why, for you to be my queen, of course."

"You have Laureya now, you don't need me."

"Ah, but I still want you." He takes a step toward her.

I move in front of her, but she pushes me aside. "Why, because I didn't break for you, Trystan? Because I didn't shatter?"

He laughs. "That mouth of yours, Sayah. That's what I want. I want you to finish pledging your allegiance to me with that mouth."

Okay, now I'm pissed. "I'm going to fucking gut you, you fairy piece of—"

Bash! Ollie scolds, ever the peacekeeper, even in death.

Trystan laughs again. "Oh, Sebastian. That color is becoming on you. You know, you could join us. I love dick as much as she does."

I lunge into the water and swing on him, but my fist merely punches through the liquid.

His evil laugh booms. "It's rather a pity, Bash. Your woman was a rather fun fuck toy. I bet you'd be just as good."

A deep flush of shame spreads across her face. "Fuck you."

"You did, and you enjoyed it." His smirk vanishes, replaced by a cold, unreadable mask. "Hate me all you want, princess, but you'll never regret me. I'm the reason you became who you are."

"What do you want, Trystan?" she volleys, quick as a blink.

"You think you won? You didn't." His voice is wooden, sharpened like an arrow shot through with anger. He's somehow both beautiful and terrifying, his smile turning predatory. "I own Feylight now. You thought darkness was your ally? It is to be your ruin."

I step back from the hologram and look at Sayah, then Nyx.

The hologram falls, returning to the puddle once again.

The sheen of unshed tears in Sayah's eyes has turned into fire. "What the fuck? What do we do now?"

"Don't let him scare you," Sariana says. Sayah gives her a narrow look, decidedly mistrustful. "His ego is all he has. We'll get my mom back and beat him. He is obviously playing royal flush with a pair of twos. He doesn't have anything. He doesn't know about Thalira. Or me, for that matter."

My lip curls irrepressibly up. "How can you be so sure?"

"Because," Sariana says, walking away, "we're on the winning side. Broken things make the sharpest weapons."

60

SHADOWMARKED

—SAYAH—

I watch as Sariana walks away and looks to Nyx, then to Bash.

They both smile at me, but I need my son right now.

I rush over to him.

Dom is still crouching before him, trying to answer all his questions.

"Hey, baby, are you okay?"

"I'm okay. Are you okay?" he asks. I'm sure I look crazy to him with my marred skin, my black hair, and my vampire appearance sitting uncomfortably on my surface, ready to burst me open at any moment.

"I'm okay."

"Mama, I'm hungry," he says as Bash comes up behind me.

"I can take him to find something to eat," Bash offers, eyeing Dom and me. "Give you two a moment to talk."

I look into Gauge's eyes, and he nods. "That's fine with me. I like Bash, he's red."

Bash grins as he grabs the wheelchair handles, and spins Gauge around.

"I told him Bash's a good dude," Dom says as he stands.

The swirling of his shadows is deeper now, darker.

His eyes find mine, and they hold sorrow, whirling with anger and maybe a little jealousy. "Dom, I—"

"Don't say anything, Sayah. I know you don't belong to me; you were merely borrowed."

He walks off toward the pond Ollie rests in before and sits beside him, stroking his face.

Ollie is still and as gray as cement, his chest unmoving and veins as black as night spiderwebbing across his temples and down his neck. I follow him and sit next to him.

"We'll get him back," I whisper, stroking one of Ollie's hands.

"It's not that I'm afraid of," he mutters, his eyes locking with mine in a way that feels like a blade piercing straight through my chest, cutting all the way to the other side. "It's what he's enduring right now in The Gloaming. It's pure hell. I wish I could save him from it."

"What's it like there?" I ask him.

He looks at me, and the Dom I first met glimmers to the surface. The Dom who sat at my table in a crowded bar and smelled so wonderfully magickal. The Dom who fucked me into oblivion in Vegas and at his parent's house. The Dom who's gentle and loving and who got royally fucked over by being marked and going dark.

But also the Dom, who never takes any accountability for anything he does.

"It's fucking hell," he says, looking away as though the words are too big to wrestle free. His gaze drifts off over Ollie and onto the horizon.

"Dom. I will always love you. You forever changed me."

"You forever changed me, too, Sayah. But you belong with Bash. You were never mine to love. You reminded me of every-thing I could never have. It was all part of this"—he takes a long piece of grass, snaps it, and throws both parts in front of him—"master fucking plan. Who the fuck knows anymore."

"I'm sorry about your dad," I say, even though it was the one thing I hated most when people would say it to me.

He says nothing.

The silence stretches between us. The winds have tangled around the wheat-like grass, unraveling it on a handsy gust.

"Do you miss your mom?" he asks suddenly, deluging my head with thoughts I can't tame.

"Um," I say, holding back the tears at his unabashed question. "It's so much more than 'miss.' I miss the world that had her in it."

"That's what I'm feeling about my dad. Except it's so new and raw and angry. I don't know if I can fight in this fucking war anymore." His brows crush together. "I wish Tallyn had just let me die."

Hearing him say he wishes he were dead makes my heart stutter. Words shatter in my mind, jamming in my throat, sorrowful and wrapped in such guilt I cannot push them free of my mouth.

"Dom," I say, trying to bring him back from that darkness, "you're here for a reason. And we need to rid the world of Trystan. If we don't, there'll be no world to return to."

"Yes, but you don't need me for that. I have no gifts of any purpose, no special talents or traits. Really, my role in this story was to lead you to your destiny. To Bash."

The silence grows prickly and needles me from behind.

When the stretch of silence grows too loud, a loud crash comes from the castle.

We look at each other before I let off the gas and fly toward the sound.

Scanning the crowd for Gauge, I find him eating cookies and milk in a corner away from the commotion.

"Hey, baby, are you okay?"

"Yeah, Mama, I'm fine. Bash gave me cookies and milk and went to get me something to color."

"Okay," I say, stroking his face. "Stay right here. I'll be back shortly."

He nods, and while I try to humanly rush away from him without moving too fast.

The shouts and hoots and hollers are coming from a room around the bend.

When I reach it, I push through the crowd to find Eirian and Bash in a rumble.

"What the fuck is going on?" I ask Kaston.

"Eirian said something about you being unable to save us and said we're all doomed, and Bash lost it on him."

"Bash!" I yell, but he's beating the poor man to a pulp.

As Agares, he's twice the size of Eirian.

I watch as Gwylan grabs a sword off the mantle and runs toward Bash, and all I can think of is to use one of my powers to stop her from running him through with it.

But something stutters time, and when I blink again, Gwylan is across the room, bloodied and broken. Eirian is the one with the sword through his middle, piercing and pinned to a wall, his head limp and lulled against his chest with a puddle of blood beneath him.

Dom is crouching by Bash, holding out his hand to help him up.

His arm is now completely covered with swirling black shadows, his skin the color of a thunderstorm darkening a southern sky.

Bash's concern for his brother is evident on his face. "Dom," he says, and Dominic shakes his head. "I could've handled it. You didn't have to give yourself to the void for me."

I run up to them both, grabbing Dom's hand. "What did you just do?"

"I timebinded three times. Apparently, that's a no-no," he says, looking at Bash.

"What does this mean?"

"He was already shadowmarked because he was brought back to life in a fae realm," Sariana says, stepping through the sarong. "It also comes with the power of timebinding. Because his soul entered the void when he died, again when he saved you from Trystan. This time he binded time; he bound his soul to the void."

I blink rapidly, hopefully showing my confusion.

"It means he's shadowmarked for life. Tied to the void. Forever to walk in the shadows. His soul belongs to the dark."

"My bond with the dark is back, it would seem," he says calmly.

"Yes, but what exactly does this mean for Dom?" Adaline asks, motherly concern coloring her voice.

"We cannot know exactly," Sariana says, looking him up and down. "It usually means, on their third ascension, back to the living or resuming time, they become similar to abyssal sprites, but with a vampire, it would mean complete destruction to the world. A destruction we would never come back from."

"He seems fine to me," Bash says, getting all up in Dom's face. Dom pushes his giant red head away.

"For now," Sari says, making a circle around him like she's looking for a tail or something. "But that doesn't mean he won't go dark."

"Fuck me, there's just no saving me from the fucking madness, is there?" Dom says, pushing everyone away, walking over to the fireplace, and laying his hands on the mantel.

"Maybe you can break him from it like you mentioned breaking Bash of his echo," I tell Sariana.

"We can do what we can for him and *try* to separate each of them from their echoes. But that doesn't guarantee that either of them will . . ." She trails off, looking at Bash, who's going over to comfort Dom.

"Either of them will what?" I press.

"Succumb to their darkness and never be able to return from it."

61

JAGGED AND RAW

—SAYAH—

ire flickers against the stone walls of the alcove where I sit, cradling Gauge against me. Relief crashes over me in waves, so fierce it nearly steals my breath. He's here. Safe. His tiny body pressed into mine, his warmth seeping into the cracks that had formed in his absence.

His small fingers clutch the fabric of my sleeve, his breathing slow but steady. His wheelchair sits empty beside us —abandoned, unnecessary for while he burrows against me. The tunic the fae gave him hangs loosely around his frame, but he doesn't complain. He's exhausted; his trust in me absolute as he lets sleep pull him under.

Hilda and Maggie sit across from me, their gazes sharp despite the softness that age has settled into their faces. They were always forces of nature—formidable women who once filled my childhood with stories, wisdom, and a relentless sense of protection. Now, they are here, in Wyndhallow, because of me.

Because I've pulled them into something bigger, darker than anything we ever imagined.

I swallow hard, my throat thick. "I know this is a lot," I say, my voice quieter than I intend. "But I need you to understand—none of this happened by choice."

Maggie scoffs, crossing her arms. "Choice or not, Sayah, you're knee-deep in something that reeks of old magick and war."

Hilda's gaze softens as she reaches for my hand. "Start from the beginning, sweetheart."

I exhale slowly, pressing my cheek against Gauge's hair. The scent of him grounds me. The words come hesitantly at first, unraveling the chaos that has led us here: Trystan, the war, the power he tried to steal from me, the shift in Wyndhallow's magick. I tell them about my transformation, about Bash, about everything I've lost, and everything I've gained in return.

Hilda listens intently, nodding at times, her fingers absently tracing the rim of her cup. Maggie, ever the skeptic, frowns deeper with every word, but she doesn't interrupt.

They don't look at me like I'm a monster. Not yet. But the weight of their judgment lingers in the space between us.

A whisper of lavender drifts through the air, curling around me like an embrace.

My chest tightens.

Mama.

I don't see her, but I feel her—the way I always do when I need her most. A ghost in the wind, a scent in the dark, reminding me that she's still here. Still watching.

I tighten my grip around Gauge. "I don't know how to fix this," I admit, my voice barely above a whisper. "I don't know how to keep him safe."

Maggie leans forward, her expression softening. "Then we'll figure it out together."

Hilda squeezes my hand. "You're not alone in this, Sayah. We may not understand everything, but we're here."

A shadow moves at the entrance of the alcove, and I glance up as Elowen steps inside, her pale green eyes flickering with quiet resolve. "I need to speak with you all," she says, her voice laced with the weight of something unspoken.

I shift, careful not to wake Gauge. "What is it?"

Her lips press into a thin line. "You're going to have to stay in Wyndhallow." Her gaze moves between me and my aunts. "Earth is in shambles. It's not safe for you there—not anymore."

The words settle over us like dust in the wake of a storm. I process them, the implications sinking in like a stone in deep water. If what she says is true, then Trystan's loss wasn't just a moment of desperation—it was his undoing. And my ascension? It wasn't just survival.

It was power.

Sariana lingers only long enough to lead my aunts down the winding halls of Wyndhallow, their hushed voices fading into the distance. Gauge barely stirs when she carries him away, his small fingers still curled in sleep, his head tucked beneath her chin. The loss of his warmth is immediate, a hollow ache against my chest.

I exhale, rubbing my palms over my face, exhaustion weighing down my limbs. The fire crackles in the alcove, its glow stretching long shadows across the stone walls. Bash is already there, waiting, his presence as steady as the pull of the tide.

The fire licks at the darkness of the small alcove where Bash and I sit, his broad chest like a warm pillow beneath me. My eyes trace the dancing tendrils of flame, their glow consuming the surrounding silence.

Henry approaches with a glass of orange liquid in hand. "Drink this," he says curtly, extending it to Bash.

Bash sits up, his taloned hand curling around the tumbler. "What's in it?" he asks, sniffing at the contents.

"A concoction we developed for vampires," Henry replies, settling on the arm of a nearby chair. "Since Wyndhallow lacks blood sources, this will help keep your hunger in check."

Bash raises a brow. "But I'm a demon now. Agares says I eat people."

I suppress a giggle. "Bash, you might be a big bad monster, but you'd never eat people. I know you better than that."

Sariana steps out from the shadows behind us, another glass in hand. She offers it to me. "The vampire in you hasn't disappeared," she says, her tone measured. "You'll still need this elixir to avoid desiccation and feral urges."

I take the glass, sniffing it cautiously to find it smells of cinnamon and oranges.

Bash downs his shot in one gulp, exhaling sharply as the liquid burns its way down. "Delicious."

I stare at the glass in my hand, my thoughts suddenly heavy. My sobriety. It being taken from me against my will.

I rise, gripping the glass as the heat of the flames mingles with the fire beneath my skin.

"What's wrong, love?" Bash asks, noticing my hesitation. He thrusts his empty glass into Henry's now-solid chest and stands, too, his presence overwhelming as he moves closer.

Bash steps behind me, his chest pressing into my back, his arms winding around me.

"My sobriety," I murmur, the words jagged and raw, slicing through my throat.

He exhales against my neck, pressing a kiss to the sensitive spot beneath my ear. "There's beauty in the ruins, Sayah. You didn't choose this. It's not defeat—it's armor. Use it to destroy him," he growls, his voice a low rasp of feral intent.

"It still hurts." The admission scorches a trail to freedom. "What he took from me."

I turn to face him, and the weight of his gaze steals the air from my lungs. His lopsided grin is sharp and menacing, a promise of both pain and devotion. He tucks a strand of my hair behind my ear. "Every scar has an echo if you're willing to look deep enough."

His eyes glimmer, molten embers trapped in stone, and the air between us tightens, fragile and ready to shatter.

He lifts my arm, studying the intricate tattoos now etched into my skin. As I explain the powers they represent, he leads me back to the couch, settling me as I clutch the glass.

"So, you can write things into existence, trap people in their memories, and gift others new powers. But what does the net symbolize?" he asks, his voice sharp with curiosity.

I glance at the tattoo. "It's the greatest fear power your mother gave me. My first gift."

His expression hardens, and his gaze pierces me like a blade. "Look into my mind."

I hesitate, unsure, but then my vision darkens, and I'm pulled into his memory—a night at the Lake George cabin.

Bash is on the floor, tears streaking his face, his hands soothing the hair of someone unseen. But now, the figure takes shape.

It's me.

The image shifts, my form marred by wounds, burned to a crisp, and then sickly and gaunt, bald from leukemia's cruel touch.

"My greatest fear," Bash says, his voice breaking through the memory, "has always been losing you." His words pull me back to the present, his face a mix of raw emotion. "Even before I knew that ghost had a face, it haunted me. But now . . . it's changed. It's what I saw last. You, taken from me."

The truth cuts through me, jagged and undeniable. The leukemia. It's always been there, lurking in the shadows of my mind. Even as the phoenix, I thought I was safe.

"Hey, what's wrong?" he asks, concern flickering in his tone. "I thought you'd be charmed to know my greatest fear."

Before I can respond, Sariana clears her throat, breaking the tension. I'd forgotten she was still here.

"You should drink that, Sayah. It's not alcoholic," she reminds me.

I force my fear into submission, lifting the glass to my lips. The burn slides down my throat, leaving behind a strange sense of calm.

Sariana takes the empty glass as Nyxaria joins us, her presence settling on the edge of the cushion beside me. Our earlier conversation resumes, and the memory of Bash's vision sinks into the depths of my soul.

But his words linger, woven into my thoughts like an indelible thread.

"It was you in the headshop Laureya and I visited, wasn't it?" Bash says to Nyx, pouring some of the fairy liquor into an empty glass.

She smiles at him flirtingly. "It was."

"Wait," I interrupt, "so you knew me in that first meeting in Trystan's office?"

"I didn't," she admits.

"How did you know what this tattoo meant?" I shove my wrist into her boobs.

She eyes me seductively, and my desire for her surfaces above the reluctant shudder that it was born from an ashen past.

"I have seen that rune before. But I knew when Trystan entered your mind, he was trying to steal your whole power. He didn't want you left with any of it. But you stole some of his instead, which made you into a siphon. Unlike his, where it is finite, you steal a piece of whoever's power you're near. If you're near them, you can absorb it. It's something new, something unheard of. That you can also gift people power and write things into existence."

My heart knots in a savage twist when I think of Trystan. "What does that mean? And how was he going to steal all my power?"

Nyxaria tilts her head, studying me. "Trystan was using an ancient method, something only a handful of beings have ever mastered—soul siphoning. He wasn't just taking your magic; he was unraveling the very essence of your power, pulling it into himself thread by thread. If he had succeeded, you wouldn't have just been left powerless—you would have ceased to exist as you are. But something disrupted the process, and in that chaos, you stole from him instead."

The weight of her words slams into me like a hammer.

"When the home planet of Embervalia was dying, Trystan helped the witches find this plane, this Earth. Because of this, they granted him gifts. Tallyn and Trystan have stood on this planet since the dawn of time. They all worked in peace and harmony at first—the witches and the Druids of Earth. It is why the artifacts came to be and why the witches agreed to help Trystan create the warlocks."

My heart stumbles on the memory of first entering this chaotic world.

"I miss the times we only had to worry about grims and warlocks," I utter, my steady voice betraying none of the violence roiling between my veins.

Something dawns on me. "Wait, so . . ."

Sariana glances at me. "What?"

"Since Bash's dad is Mederio, wouldn't that mean that since Trystan made him, Trystan would actually be Bash's dad?"

It would make sense since he and Sariana both have black hair—like Tallyn and Trystan.

Bash stiffens beside me.

Sariana glances at Bash, who's risen from the couch. "Technically, yes," she says, gazing up at him through a fringe of dark lashes. "Since the witches are the ones who make the warlocks from the requester's DNA, technically, that would make Trystan and Adaline his biological parents."

Trystan is Bash's biological father.

Bash's blue eyes blaze beneath the new amber, his emotions detonating within his skeleton. "That man is not my father."

The words are profound, gut-wrenching like the wail of an avalanche, powering out of him with such savagery they're almost tangible against my skin.

"He will die screaming."

—TRYSTAN—

"What are you doing?" Delaney asks me as I finish my hologram message to Sayah. "Still trying to play house with your fuck toy?"

We've bloodported back to Castle Feylight—specifically, the one tower that survived Delaney's ill-fated attempt to kill Sayah. I'm crouched by a fountain, channeling my water magick to project my hologram. Sayah is in Wyndhallow, but with the Shadow Gate destroyed and my soul black as night, the Light Gate will never admit me.

"You're the fucking one who almost ruined everything we've worked for," I snap, standing and flicking the water from my hands. "What the fuck was that, anyway?"

"You didn't see it either!" she shoots back, stepping closer, her voice rising. "You're the one who didn't see that Nyxaria was your fucking mole!"

My hand moves before I think, striking her hard across the face. Her head whips to the side, blood spilling from the fresh tear in her lip. "Know your fucking place, wife."

Even after all this time, it's hard to see Tallyn's face glaring back at me with Delaney's soul trapped inside. She spits blood at my feet, rushing to the fountain to rinse her wounds.

"Baby, come back," I say, grabbing her arm and pulling her upright. My thumb brushes her chin, smearing the blood. "I'm sorry. You know it's that face you wear—it drives me insane."

Her orange eyes soften. "I know. I'll shift out of it as soon as we get to Nightshade. Sablethorn's the only one who can give me my true body back."

I press a rough kiss to her lips, my hands grasping her greedily. But my body betrays me. No matter what I try, I can't desire her.

Not when she's wearing Tallyn's skin.

She sighs as I pull away, her tone turning sharp again. "You're too focused on the past. We've made progress. I duped them into thinking I was Tallyn; we've captured the other phoenix"—she gestures toward Laureya, tied and hanging in a cage over the fireplace's empty shaft—"we got one of her dragons. You siphoned some of Sayah's writing power, and the covenant is nearly ours. Once we rewrite it, it's game over."

I release a low laugh. "Blind as ever, I see. I didn't need you to achieve any of that."

"What?" Her voice falters just before I shove her.

Her scream knifes through the night, ending with a sickening thud as her body shatters against the ruins below. Blood and entrails paint the crumbled stone like a twisted masterpiece.

"What did you do?" Laureya whispers in a trembling voice from her cage.

I turn, my boots echoing in the hollow chamber. "I'd rather have dangerous freedom than comfortable servitude."

"What the fuck does that even mean?" she snaps as I approach, spinning her cage in lazy circles.

"It means, faux phoenix, that she was a tool. She served her purpose."

Her piercing green eyes lock on mine. "And what purpose was that?"

"She had the timebinding power." I stop the cage to cup her face. "But you . . . you're different. You're hauntingly beautiful. Beautifully broken. And I'm drawn to broken things."

"I'm not broken," she hisses, her defiance flickering like a dying flame.

"You will be when I'm done with you."

"What do you want from me?"

A grin splits my face. "You'll see. But I'll let you in on a little secret. Everyone thought Sayah outmaneuvered me, but I was prepared. Before she took the covenant, I rewrote it. My name —and yours—are etched into its very essence."

"Wha—how?" she asks, her brows furrowing. "What does that mean for me?"

"I siphoned Sayah's writing power and wrote my name with yours, knowing she'd portal the stone and the covenant as far from me as possible."

"That still doesn't answer my question."

"Since my soul is too fractured to bind to the Stone of Souls, I need you. Only by marrying a phoenix can I anchor my claim to Feylight and the seven realms."

"You expect me to believe that? What do I get out of it?"

"You'll be queen," I say, leaning closer. "Not just of Feylight, but of Earth and every realm under the heavens. You'll reign beside me, crowned in fire and glory. Feylight belongs to me now. I own it and everything the void touches. But the only way to prevent the real Tallyn and those filthy bloodsuckers and her army from taking it back is to find the Stone of Souls before they do and bind our souls to Feylight."

"Still Greek, babe. No idea what that means for me."

"It means you will be the Queen of Feylight, Earth, and all seven realms. You will reign with me and be my queen."

Her eyes gleam, the weight of my words sinking into her.

The thought of ultimate power ignites something deep within her. She'll give me everything I need.

And then I'll kill her, too.

Then the world, the realms, and every soul will fall to darkness.

To the shadows.

THE END (ISH)